Aries and the Prince No More

By

Taylor Stephens

© Aries and the Prince No More 2021

Book One of the Usurper Chronicles

2nd book out 11/30/23

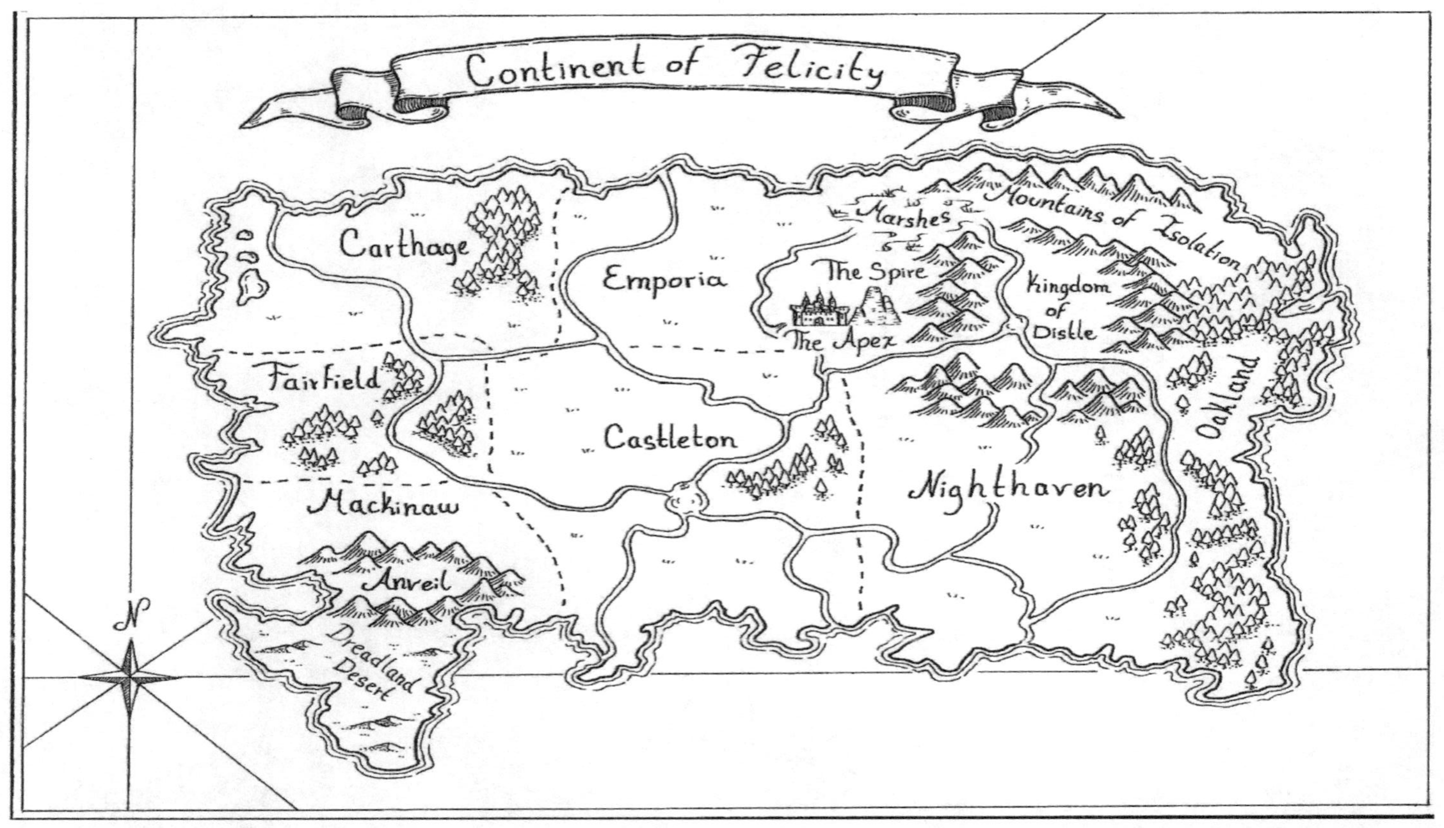

Continent of Felicity
Carthage
Emporia
Marshes
The Spire
The Apex
Mountains of Isolation
Kingdom of Distle
Oakland
Fairfield
Castleton
Nighthaven
Mackinaw
Anveil
Dreadland Desert
N

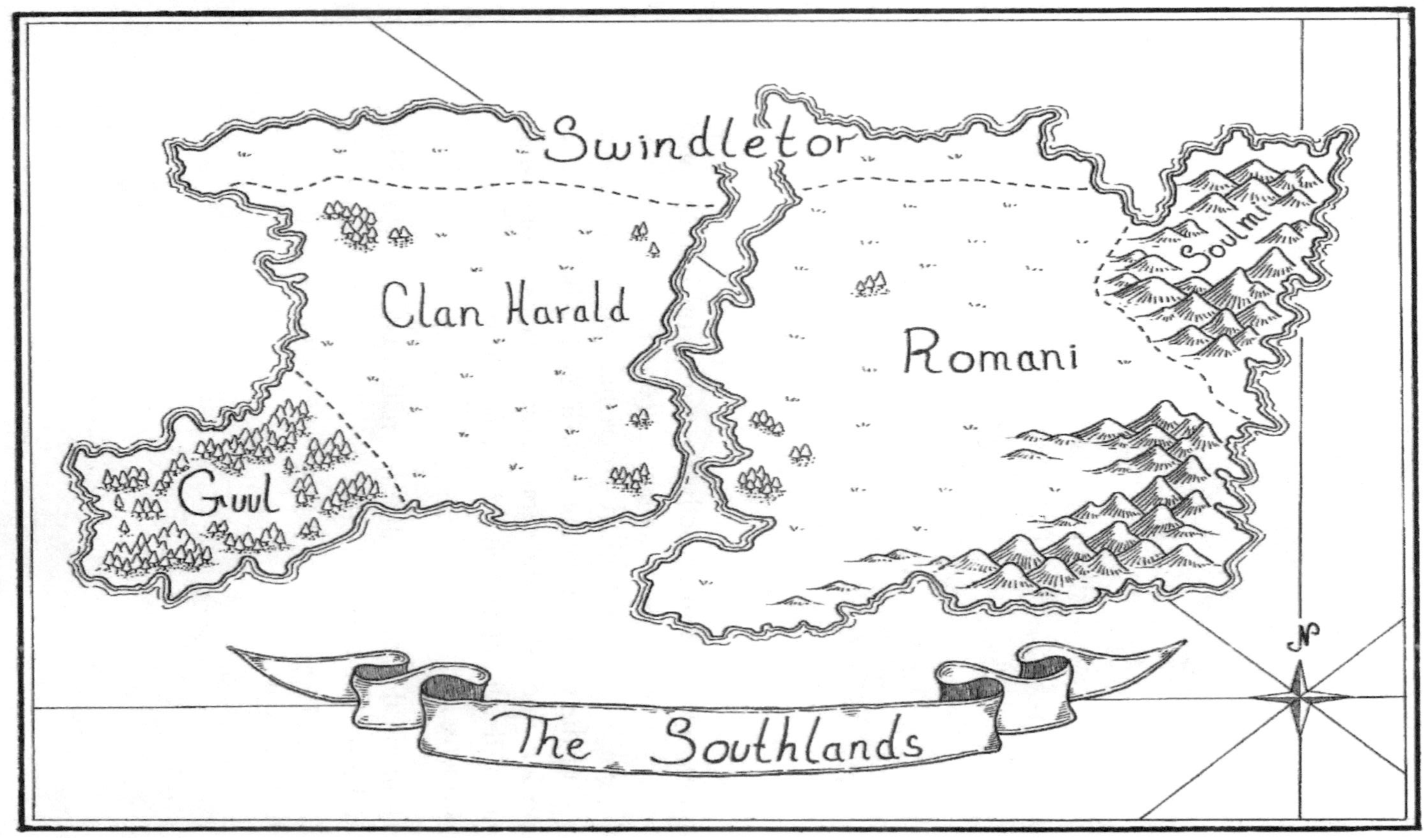

Swindletor
Clan Harald
Romani
Soulmi
Guul
The Southlands
N

About the Author

Hailing from the heart of the Midwest, Taylor Stephens is not only a licensed therapist but also an author with a penchant for crafting tales where fantasy meets suspense. Stephens writes with a down-to-earth style, infusing each narrative with the quiet magic of everyday life and the thrilling anticipation that keeps readers turning pages.

Drawing inspiration from both the professional and natural world, Taylor weaves stories that are accessible, engaging, and subtly reflective of the human experience. Whether through therapy or the written word, he is dedicated to helping others explore and understand the depth of their own emotions, while offering a delightful escape into fantastical realms sprinkled with suspense.

When not in the therapy office or crafting tales, Taylor finds joy in the simple, serene life that the Midwest provides, often using these moments of calm as springboards for new storytelling ideas.

To my daughter Taylin.

Never extinguish your *fire*—no matter
what they tell you.

"Do you trust me?" asks the man in exquisite armor, wrapped in dense fur. Amidst the darkness, snow falls gently surrounding the armored figure with a tranquil glow. He stands above two individuals, kneeling before him. The mysterious figure places an ornate knife into one of the men's outstretched hands. The night feels eerie, as if invisible eyes are watching with unsettling intensity.

"Absolutely, my prince," they reply, in unison.

A satisfied grin appears upon the man's face. "Your commitment will shape our destiny."

"Your Grace, surely there is another way," pleads a voice, hidden amongst the shadows.

"I'm afraid there's no alternative, cousin. Power demands sacrifice. These men understood the risk our mission posed and yet they courageously agreed. For they know something must be done to stop the oppression our people face. None thought it would be possible to traverse the lands I spoke of, and yet still they had faith in me—faith in our cause," the prince explains, placing a comforting hand upon the shoulder of the man kneeling before him. With a slight nod, he steps back. Without hesitation, the man uses the blade to open his own throat. He fights to remain upright, but soon collapses. Fresh blood begins to encompass the nearby snow.

The prince ignores a horrified yell from his cousin, before picking up the knife and handing it to the remaining man. The process is repeated, and a second lifeless body litters the snow-covered ground.

"Their sacrifice will never be forgotten. For without them, our crusade would end here. Lower them into the pit," commands the prince. Soldiers, obscured in large fur coats, obey, casting the corpses into the dark abyss. An ominous purple glow emanates, briefly illuminating the prince's resolute face before fading suddenly into nothingness.

"This cannot be. I've done everything you required," murmurs the prince, with desperation in his voice. "There must be another way," he protests as if something, or someone, is commanding him.

His gaze then shifts to his cousin, who is still restrained by soldiers. The weight of regret evident upon his face. "Cylon, my blood and dearest friend—it requires a third."

"I will not willingly give my life over to such evil. Think of your parents—"

"My father's weakness is the reason we must do this. Unlike him, there is no price too high for my people's safety. Surely you understand," interrupts the prince in a convincing tone.

Cylon responds with conviction, "That's where we differ, cousin. There is no power worth your soul. Without my consent, the ritual cannot proceed. So, find another fool."

The prince's eyes remain cold and unyielding, as they fixate on the blood-stained blade in his hand. "The pursuit of power exacts a heavy toll, yet it pales in comparison to the price of weakness," he murmurs, advancing on his cousin.

"Grandfather would disown you if he could see what you've become."

"I'm sorry," whispers the prince with a grief-stricken face. He stares silently for a few moments before swiftly moving his blade across his cousin's throat. Blood splatters his face, as he watches Cylon fall violently to the ground. He steps away, allowing his soldiers to place another lifeless body into the pit. Vibrant purple light begins to radiate from the depths below, growing more profound by the moment.

"It worked," says the prince as he looks on.

A strange sound rings throughout the cold dark night. The prince and his soldiers step back as they see an ominous looking altar ascend from the pit. Suspended in midair atop the altar, is a brilliant scepter producing purple light from a remarkable jewel, nestled above the dark metal shaft. Cautiously, the prince approaches, studying the sight before confidently reaching out and taking it for his own. He appears to be empowered with a strange energy as his body tenses drastically. Raising his newly claimed weapon high above his head triumphantly, echoes of cheers ring out from his soldiers.

"In my hand, I hold the power to dismantle the oppression that has bound us all for centuries!" He closes his eyes and concentrates intently. "It's as if it can read my mind." Suddenly purple light begins to radiate before sending blasts of energy toward the corpses of his fallen allies that lie at the foot of the altar. An unholy breath of life appears to fill their lungs, as they climb to their feet and walk toward the prince. Despite their resurrection, whatever humanity they had, died with them.

I jolt awake—my heart pounding. The voices from my dream echo through my mind before fading quickly. Nightmares of the prince and Cylon have haunted my sleep frequently, and each morning it becomes harder to separate fantasy from reality. I hear unfamiliar voices coming from downstairs, and I wonder who my father may be speaking to. Their tone sounds serious, which makes me want to eavesdrop.

I quickly don casual tights and a white blouse. My brown hair falls neatly enough for me to avoid having to brush it. Catching a glimpse in the mirror, my breath hitches – for a split second, I see my late mother staring back. But it's just me, with her same small nose, full lips, and green eyes. The resemblance is uncanny, and for a heartbeat, I feel her presence again.

"The Edward Fleetwood I remember was no fool!" shouts a hoarse voice directed at my father. Hearing my father insulted in his own home causes me to become angry. I restrain myself against confronting the man, trusting that my father can handle the situation. But I know if it continues, my willpower will not be enough to overcome my anger.

"Since when is it foolish to doubt the words of craven bureaucrats, Stur? Perhaps you have spent too much time in the Apex, and not back home at Anveil," my father replies.

"I apologize for Stur, and I am confident he too is remorseful for the insult, Edward. However—we would not be here if the situation was not dire. All that is being asked, is that you and your daughter come with us until we can be assured that any uprising within Fairfield can be—resolved," says a man that I take for a diplomat.

There's going to be an uprising here in Fairfield? I ask myself. My thoughts are interrupted by the sound of the front door swinging open loudly. "Good morning, Governor, and you as well, Margret," greets my father to my best friend Kristoff's parents. Joseph, his father, is the Governor of the Realm of Fairfield. Such a position is considered prestigious in most every other realm, but within the small farming country of Fairfield, it is hardly valued, at least by the common folk.

"Kristoff wasn't in his bed this morning. Is he here with Aries by chance? I have sent my personal guards to search the town square for him," says Joseph in an urgent tone. I hear footsteps approaching the stairway, on which I am standing. I know that I should retreat into my room, to appear as if I wasn't eavesdropping, but I remind myself I am no longer a child at twenty-two years of age.

"He isn't here," I say when I see my father peak his head into the stairwell. He doesn't reply out loud but mouths the words, "Go find him. Now," he says with an urgent expression. I try and control my thoughts, to prevent my mind from flooding with various scenarios of what danger Kristoff may face. I walk back into my room and look at my sheathed sword; a finely crafted rapier I brought with me from the Apex when I moved to Fairfield over ten years ago. Swords are banned in the outer realms, but my father taught me that some laws are meant to be broken. I decide against taking it and instead grab a small dagger which will be easier to conceal in my shoulder bag.

I walk down the stairs and make my way to the door. "Where does she think she's going?" asks the man called Stur in a rude tone. I turn my head slightly, shocked that he feels entitled to question my actions.

"Wherever I wish," I reply in a direct tone, causing him to laugh.

"I forgot she is her mother's child," he says, raising his hands in the air, palms facing me to show that he means no offense. He is a short but stocky man, with a thick red beard. I cannot help but stare at his armor, which is perhaps the finest quality I have ever seen in person. The memory of lessons I was taught about Anveil reminds me that they are known for being expert craftsmen.

"While I am sure she is more than formidable, just as her mother was, it would be—far safer for her to remain here with us," protests a rather fancy looking man sitting beside Stur. I notice his silver hair, thin lips, smooth skin. He is wearing an elegant robe that would sow jealousy in even the most affluent member of the Apexian Elite.

"It is not your place, Beltrum," my father interjects.

"I will not go far," I lie, before exiting through the door, heading directly for the town square. My father and I both know something Joseph doesn't about Kristoff; his hatred for the Apex and their treatment of the common people. If there were to be a mob forming, I suspect he would be in the middle of it, doing what he thought was right to help those less fortunate. While he means well, I know that such a thing is quite foolish given his status as the Governor's son. It causes me great anxiety to know that he may have already been taken, to be used as leverage against Joesph.

I walk quickly along the long dirt road that will take me to the center of town. I am approached by a horse and simple carriage that seems to be moving much quicker than one would expect. I hear the sound of leather reins being pulled as the horse comes to a stop directly behind me.

"Off to the town, Aries? At a time like this?" Magistrate Kirby asks with a raised brow.

"I have my reasons," I reply, trying to sound nonchalant. "Is there something I should know?"

Kirby rubs his temples, looking more tired than I've ever seen him. "The Governor's in a frenzy. He believes the unrest from Carthage will spill into our streets."

I smirk, attempting to divert him. "Joseph always did have a flair for the dramatic. You'd think every gust of wind was a storm on the horizon."

Kirby chuckles, but there's a serious undertone. "Perhaps. But sometimes, the wind is a sign of a storm, Aries. Come, let me take you. But I warn you, the town's mood is—unsettled."

The ride to town seems to drag on due to my anxiety. I visualize seeing Kristoff in town before quickly leading him back to my house. Whenever I think about what happens next, I feel a sense of complicated grief. Part of me has wanted to leave Fairfield and return to the Apex since I first arrived. But now that it may be happening, I feel sorrow. Magistrate Kirby seems to sense my anxiety and keeps the talk about Carthage and their political unrest to a minimum. Still, I learn much about some of the hostilities they have shown the Apex and the High Church, both currently and in the past. The response toward Carthage has been without mercy, which seems to only increase the support behind their rebellion. I hope that the people of Fairfield are not seduced by Carthage, knowing that they too suffer similar oppression at the hands of the Apex.

"I cannot recall the last time I saw so many people within the town square," says Kirby in disbelief. "Thank you for the ride," I say before jumping off and making my way toward the town. "Aries, be safe!" he yells in a concerned tone. I do not respond, knowing that he will surely try and talk me into returning home. I remove my simple green cloak from my bag and quickly pull it over my head, making sure that the hood covers my hair. I am careful to keep my head down to avoid being recognized by anyone. My father may not be the Governor of a realm, but he is the treasurer, which may cause people to associate me with the Apex.

I hear murmurs of outrage amongst the gathering of people, who seem to be relatively peaceful—at least for the moment. I find someone

I trust along the edge of the square, a kindly woman who sells various fabrics. I lean in, lowering my voice. "Have you seen Kristoff?"

The fabric seller hesitates, her eyes filled with concern. "He went into the sanctuary—with some strangers. I'm afraid for him—and for my goods. I don't recognize most of the men, I don't know what to do."

"Head to the safety of the countryside. My father will make sure the treasury repays whatever goods you lose, but hopefully it doesn't come to that," I command, before making my way to the sanctuary.

I hope that Kristoff isn't being held against his will as I remove the dagger from my bag and conceal it within the sleeve of my left arm. The front door of the simple sanctuary is being guarded by two young men that I do not recognize. Most of the people who frequently visit the town square are known to me and my father, since he is responsible for collecting their taxes. I make my way to the back of the sanctuary, hoping that the secondary entrance isn't guarded.

After I turn into the pathway leading to the back of the building, I notice there is nobody at the door, so I quickly open it. There is a stone stairwell that leads up into the main room of the holy building of the Apexian Church. I walk quietly as I make my way into the nave, entering from behind the altar. The large stained-glass window illuminates the room, and I can see Kristoff kneeling before a man who has a sword sheathed on his hip. The captor stands with his back facing me, preventing me from seeing if I recognize the man. The confirmation that Kirstoff is in danger replaces my anxiety with an intense feeling of purpose that I need to protect him.

I remove my dagger from its sheath and carefully check the nave for any sign of additional enemies. He's alone. I walk as quietly as I can toward him. I have never killed before, but my love for Kristoff heavily outweighs any moral resistance I have. I am nearly within range to leap toward the man and drive my dagger through his throat before Kristoff sees me. He is unable to contain his reaction, causing the man to turn around and see me. He pulls his sword from its sheath as I rush to close the distance. I curse myself as a fool for not expecting Kristoff to give away my presence, before I refocus my mind on trying to survive the encounter, which is now far more hopeless.

"Stop! Don't hurt her!" yells Kristoff as he stands to his feet and pushes the man in the back, knocking him forward. He stumbles toward me and raises his sword just as he regains his balance. His strike is without skill, revealing that he is no true swordsman. I easily dodge the attack and grab his sword hand by the wrist with my free hand. I then drive my dagger through the man's forearm and twist it, causing him to drop the sword. He grabs the wound and steps back, yelling for his companions to help. I switch hands with my dagger and pick up his sword with my right. With sword in hand, I am confident I will be able to cut down the man and his companions if they are as unskilled as him.

"Kristoff!" I snap, motioning behind me. He complies immediately. Together, we slowly walk backward out of the sanctuary, the men stalking us closely.

With narrowed eyes and clutching his wound, the man speaks. "Leave him here, and we will let you live. We have many friends outside."

I reply defiantly, "No matter what happens, you will be the first to die."

We are nearly toward the staircase that leads toward the exit. I debate whether we should take our chances fleeing from them outside, or if I should try cutting the three of them down now. Kristoff would be of little help in a fight, probably serving to be more of a liability than anything. More for his safety than my own, I decide it is best to retreat.

"Last chance, girl. Hand over the redhead, and you're free to go. There is no need for you to die. No harm will come to the boy, he will only be used for ransom. Ask him, I haven't hurt him one bit," the man says, steadily walking toward us. I know that he is simply trying to buy his time and say whatever he thinks will get me to linger.

"You should be more concerned with your wrist—boy. If you don't stop the bleeding, you won't make it out of the sanctuary," I say, giving a nod for Kristoff to make his way down the stairs.

"Get them!" yells the man, causing his two companions to run after us.

I follow Kristoff out the door. I throw the sword on the ground, knowing that it would make us stand out. "This way," I say before rushing down the alley. He is much faster than I am, and able to run long distances without getting tired. Knowing this, he is careful to keep a pace that I can keep up with. We travel down the alleyways in an obscure fashion, hoping to have our pathway difficult to predict. I feel uneasy, given that at any moment one of our pursuers could emerge in front of us.

"I can't believe this is happening," murmurs Kristoff, his voice thick with disbelief and eyes wide with shock as we slow our pace to a brisk walk. The crowd has grown much larger, and they have begun to set buildings ablaze. The airship docking tower appears to be nearing collapse. "They're more strategic than I expected," I whisper to Kristoff. "Come, you need to cover your distinct red hair," I continue, giving him my cloak. I then take him by the hand and slowly walk toward the exit of the town square. He is shaking heavily, clearly afraid. Fortunately for us, I am too focused on our survival to let fear crowd my mind.

We nearly get to the exit before we hear several people from the crowd yell. "Hang him, hang him now!" I try to not look back, knowing that I will not be happy with whatever I see. But I am unable to restrain myself. A feeling of intense horror fills my heart as I see Magistrate Kirby standing atop the gallows with a noose around his neck. "Please, no! I beg!" he pleads, but to no avail. A member of the mob pulls the trapdoor lever, causing him to fall through. His neck snaps instantly. It takes a moment for me to register that I just witnessed one of the kindest people I know murdered.

Rage fills my body and I want to go and avenge him. Kristoff grabs me by the hand and pulls me away from the scene. "We have to run," he commands, causing me to break my gaze and head for my house.

I hear people in the crowd yell out at the sight of an airship, no doubt sent to squash the rebellion. Part of me hopes they rain fire upon them for what they have done, but I know deep down that will end in the loss of innocent lives as well. The Apex dominates the skies with their airships, which are advanced weapons nobody else has ever possessed.

I haven't felt this helpless since my mother died, and I want nothing more than to disappear until it's all over. Kristoff and I lock our eyes, and in unison, without saying a word, we begin to run full speed towards my house.

We arrive at the stone farmhouse in what feels like a couple of minutes. We burst through the door and struggled to catch our breath. The room full of adults pelts us with questions that we cannot answer with complete sentences.

"Aries, what's wrong? Is everything okay?" my father asks, concerned.

"He's dead, they killed him," I say before I am forced to catch my breath.

Kristoff's father Joseph's gasps loudly. "Killed who?"

"Magistrate Kirby," answers Kristoff, causing everyone to adopt pain-stricken expressions.

"An airship arrived, but the dock has been destroyed by the mob," I explain.

"Let them catch their breath. Here, have a seat," says Kristoff's mother Margret, as she motions for us to sit at the table, signaling for room to be made on the bench.

After Kristoff and I catch our breath, we start recounting the story of what happened in town. Hearing it said aloud makes me question if it actually happened, given how shocking it was.

Once we answer all the questions we can, Margret provides us with some warm tea; my favorite drink. I sip mine slowly so as not to appear rude, though the truth is, I don't feel much like drinking.

"Where are my manners? Edward, here you are," she says, while pouring some more tea into his empty mug.

"We better get to the ship. We don't have time for tea," Stur says bluntly. He's sitting at the table with his arms crossed over his chest.

"How do you expect to board an airship without a dock?" my father asks rhetorically, causing Stur to cross his arms.

"We need to get to another village, one far away from the turmoil," says Joseph.

"They shouldn't be hearing this; they have already witnessed enough. Aries, please take Kristoff upstairs," commands Margret.

Kristoff and I comply without objection, mainly because I know we will be able to eavesdrop from the stairwell. As we enter my room, I look at my surroundings much longer than normal. This has been my home for ten years. Now it seems so small, so different than it was just this morning.

When my father and I had first arrived here, I initially didn't like Fairfield. But now that I'm faced with the possibility of leaving, I find I don't wish to go. My cozy bed has a comfortable quilt gifted to me by a local woman, who was thankful that my father helped her avoid having to pay the Apexian Government exorbitant taxes. My white vanity may not be painted as nicely as one from the Apex, but my father made it for me himself so that I would feel more at home.

My shelves are filled with books upon books. In the Apex, there are countless libraries where I could access all manner of books. But those will never be as valuable to me as those I've collected over the years in a land with little to no reading material. The first book I received after moving was a historical account of ancient magic. Even though I don't believe ancient magic exists, I still read the book more times than I can count. I used to fantasize about how useful it would be to call upon the various elements and bend them to my will, just like the ancient people of Felicity supposedly did hundreds of years ago. This line of thinking suddenly stops as I remember that I want to listen in on the conversation. Luckily for me, Kristoff can focus much better than I can. He has grown accustomed to updating me on what details I miss when I am distracted.

"What did they say?" I whisper.

"Everyone but your father and mine think we need to make our way to the airship, but apparently, they haven't received direct orders. Our fathers are worried about trying to get through the mob, but the others think the mob must be gone since the airship arrived. Stur is outside of the house keeping an eye out to make sure that the mob isn't coming this way, and Beltrum went outside to go talk to someone," whispers Kristoff as he brushes his bright red curls out of his eyes. In all of the commotion, I forgot what Kristoff must have endured before I arrived. Part of me wishes I would have killed his captor when I had the chance. I tell myself the opportunity didn't present itself, but I know deep down I wanted to avoid killing if I didn't have to. I focus my attention on being thankful that he and I were able to get out of the situation safely.

"Why don't you clean up while we have the chance? I know how you cannot stand to have your hair a mess," I say, hoping to lighten the mood by poking fun at him. "While you do that, I will go and see who Beltrum is talking to. I don't trust him; he speaks too carefully for my liking."

"And how do you plan on sneaking up on him?" he asks, with a hint of doubt in his voice.

"Carefully, very carefully," I answer.

"You are the clumsiest person I know. Just yesterday you fell down as you were just standing still," he says, laughing.

"Wow, okay. I mean—I just saved your life, but you're already making jokes," I jest, prompting a smile from him.

I make my way to my window and carefully move the curtains so that I can slip out unseen. Overall, I'm not too worried. If I get caught, I'll probably just tell him how I don't trust him. Secretly, part of me hopes for the opportunity to confront him.

I climb out of the window and onto the wooden roof, being careful to walk as quietly as I can. I know that the surface is only held together by wood and clay. I've helped my father fix it over the years, which concerns me given the fact we are not skilled at labor. I know I can fall through it at any moment. As I get closer and closer to the back of the house, I notice a light blue aura illuminating the entire backyard. I can hear Beltrum's voice, but it sounds like a whisper. If I'm going to make out what he's saying, I need to get closer. There's something strange about him, but I'm not sure exactly what it is.

It's difficult to approach him because the roof is angled to prevent rainwater from building up. This means that I have to cling to it and slowly let myself slide down enough to get closer. I finally get within range to make out a voice. It either isn't his voice, or he's talking more directly and let go of his overly-proper speaking style. As I try to position myself to stop moving, I accidentally knock loose some debris which rolls down the roof.

"I beg your pardon, one moment," Beltrum says. I become anxious, thinking I've given away my position. I don't care to get caught, but I don't feel that my current stance on the roof allows for the most dignified position to explain what I was up to.

I focus on being as still as possible, trying to breathe quietly. Eventually, my patience pays off because Beltrum starts speaking again. "My sincerest apologies; I was merely ensuring that I am alone. As I was saying, the Apexian vessel has arrived and presumably, it is to transport Edward Fleetwood and Joseph Jamison, along with their families, back to the Apexian Capital."

I feel that even when he speaks during a secret conversation, he's annoying and insincere. "Originally, that was the plan. However, the vessel is at risk of being compromised and is being rerouted to the nearby lumbering village of Redwood, located on the edge of Fairfield. Edward is familiar with the terrain and can guide you to the location," says an authoritative voice which seems to have little interest in the group's circumstances.

"I humbly ask, may it not be easier to simply board the vessel here? We have it under good authority that the villagers pose no real threat to the original directive. Any resistance could be easily subdued with minimal collateral damage," Beltrum says. I can't help thinking he sounds weak and desperate, as if he's afraid to even ask the man a question.

"No, you have your orders. There are reports of insurgents in the smaller realms from Carthage. The worshiping of dark magic has been linked to the rebellion leaders and it does not appear that diplomacy is an option at this time. The ship has been instructed to use whatever means necessary to suppress the mob and will then head to meet you at the point. There is nothing further to discuss. Do not contact me again," replies the voice as the light blue glow suddenly disappears.

"So be it," Beltrum says aloud to himself.

My thoughts immediately go to the safety of the townsfolk. I've heard stories from Kristoff about how the Apex used lethal force to deal with the outer realms and ensure their obedience, but I never thought it could happen in Fairfield. As I make my way back through the window, my father greets me, giving a grim expression. I rarely see him panicked, but he's clearly worried.

"Take some clothes. Grab your sword, and that's all. We are leaving now."

"What's going on?" I ask, with terror in my voice.

"Just do it, honey. I will explain everything on the way, okay? We will replace whatever we leave behind, but we must go now. Kristoff, your parents have your things ready. Aries, please hurry. I will be waiting downstairs," he replies before making his way back to the others.

I quickly grab my satchel and fill it with a few comfortable outfits. I'm not sure why, but I suddenly feel a strong urge to grab my book about the history of ancient magic. Contemplating whether or not I should, I eventually shrug and put the book in my bag. I'll need to conceal it once we arrive in the Apex, given that it is banned by the High Church. People who subscribe to ancient magic are considered enemies of the Apexian Church and, by extension, the Apexian Government.

I place the satchel over my shoulder and make my way out of my room before turning to stare back into the small space. I know that I will most likely never see it again and want to take in its beauty and comfort one last time. Swallowing the lump in my throat, I close the door and start for the stairs. I get halfway down before my father yells, "Your sword!"

I quickly run back into my room and grab my sword from within my closet. I attach the sheath to my belt and leave the room, thankful that my forgetfulness gives me one more opportunity to say goodbye. Being forced to leave shows that Fairfield was actually my one true home all along. As I walk down the stairs, the front door swings open quickly. It's Stur.

"They're here."

With trepidation, I enter the living room. My father stands by the window, looking intently outside. Before I can ask, he voices the question. "How many?"

Stur, stroking his beard contemplatively, replies, "At least a few dozen, all appearing to be armed."

Kristoff's father's brow furrows in confusion. "Mistaken, surely. With the Apex here, those crowds should be scattering."

"We must leave at once. I was ordered to lead the group to Redwood," explains Beltrum, who surprisingly seems calm despite the danger.

"Impossible," Kristoff's father mutters, eyes narrowing on the mob now visible down the road. "I will simply go and order them to disperse at once. I am still in charge of Fairfield, and they will respect that," he continues in a tone that radiates hollow confidence.

"Everyone to the back room and stay quiet. If they continue on their way, we can head to the woods behind the house," commands my father.

"And if they don't?" asks Stur, with conviction.

My father pauses for several moments before replying, as he continues to look out the window. "Then we will do as we must. But until then, everyone remains quiet."

I follow the others to the back room, the air thick with tension. With every passing second, the sense of danger looms larger. I hope, pray even, that the mob will pass us by. Yet, a nagging voice within my mind whispers they won't. We stand in silence, minutes stretching like hours. Anxiety marks every face, except for Stur. He seems to be unbothered by the danger, maybe even welcoming it. My fingers trace the hilt of my sword, as I contemplate a silent question. Could I use it? Would I kill to protect us?

I hear the sound of the fireplace vent close. Smoke begins to slowly make its way to where we are standing. My father walks into the back room with a serious look on his face. "Cover your mouths. They are about to enter," he says calmly. I comply, my breath coming in short, ragged bursts. I can't tell if it's the thickening smoke or my mounting anxiety that's causing it.

"Once they see the smoke they will go back outside. That will give us a chance to run for the woods. When I say to run, Stur will lead the way. Aries, you and Kristoff stay right behind him and do not look back," my father commands in a serious tone.

My hands shake from the anxiety I feel. A surge of rebellion bubbles within me—I want to stay by my father's side. But deep down, I know that arguing now will only worsen our situation. I swallow hard, forcing trust. My father knows best. "Okay, I promise I will," I say, hoping to reassure him that I will listen.

"I will defend them with my life," says Stur, holding his axe at the ready.

"The rest of us will follow after, buying you time if needed. Do not hesitate to use lethal force," my father explains.

My heart sinks as I hear the front door slam open, followed by the sound of someone coughing violently. A sense of violation rushes over me, as I contemplate the safety of my home being desecrated. "It's on fire!" They shout loud enough for someone to hear several yards away.

"Go now. Be fast but quiet," my father commands before giving me a kiss atop my head. Stur opens the back door quietly and begins to run for the woods. Kristoff and I follow behind him. My lungs welcome the fresh air as we outpace the smoke plumes that follow us out the door. The tree line of the forest is within a few dozen yards when I hear the sound of fighting behind me. I resist the urge to look back, reminding myself of the promise I gave my father.

Stur crashes through the overgrown tree line, providing us a pathway. We hasten several feet into the woods before Stur stops and faces the way we came. I am pleased to see Kristoff's parents and Beltrum make their way into the pathway a few moments after us. I grip the hilt of my sword and prepare to rush back toward my house, since there is no sign of my father. A few moments pass and I see him entering the trees, his hands and face covered in blood.

"Are you okay?" I ask in a panicked tone.

He gives me a reassuring nod. "It's not mine."

The group waits as my father assumes the lead, guiding us through the dense trees. A feeling of relief washes over me as I acknowledge the gravity of the situation we just faced. My feeling of momentary relief is replaced by grief as the image of Magistrate Kirby's lifeless body enters my mind. I take a deep breath trying to push the thought away.

My father raises a hand, causing the group to stop. He tilts his head for a few moments, as if he is listening for something, before continuing to walk. We eventually come to a familiar dirt path that leads through the forest. I think back to the times that Kristoff and I spent playing in these woods, never considering that they would be used as our salvation. My father turns right on the path, which I know will lead us toward Redwood. With each step, we are getting closer to safety, I tell myself.

My words are immediately disproven as I look beyond my father, who has stopped at the sight of six men. They slowly approach, with their swords drawn. I recognize the face of the man who held Kristoff captive. I look behind us to make sure nobody is approaching from the rear. Stur comes and stands by my side, his axe ready for anything. Kristoff, who is now holding my hand, grips it even tighter. The man stops about ten feet from my father, his companions a few feet behind him. He seems to be surveying the group before finally resting his eyes upon Kristoff and me.

"I don't want any violence," he says, in what he probably thinks is a convincing tone.

"And yet you block our path with swords drawn," my father retorts.

"I will be clear. We want the Governor and his family. They will not be harmed; I give you my word," claims the man.

"What intentions do you have with them?" my father asks. I know he would never oblige such a dishonorable request. I believe he's simply trying to gather more information.

"A man could secure a ransom that would last a lifetime for such a high-profile member of the Apex."

My father's voice softens, and he asks, "Is the prospect of gold worth your life, young man?"

The man smirks. "Afraid so."

My father sighs, "So be it."

He draws his sword and approaches the man, who begins to retreat slowly. My father's pace quickens into a sprint, and he delivers an overhead strike that I recognize as a feint he taught me. The man raises his sword to defend, but my father pulls back his blade, lowers it until it's level with the man's torso, and drives it upward through his throat. Blood gushes from the wound as the man falls to his knees. The men accompanying him drop their weapons and flee at the sight of their fallen leader.

"Hurry, there might be others," my father commands before sheathing his sword.

The rest of our journey through the woods feels more like a run than walk, as we try to put as much distance as possible between us and the men who fled. I spot an opening in the woods just before my father signals for us to halt. He carefully steps out into the field to ensure it's safe for us to follow. He gestures, and the rest of us emerge from the woods. I gaze at the rolling hills of the countryside, noticing no one else in sight. My attention is drawn by the expressions of shock on the others' faces. Following their gazes, I turn to see dozens upon dozens of black smoke plumes rising high, emanating from the massive fires that have consumed the landscape.

Despite walking the better part of a day, I can still see the clouds of dark smoke in the distance. I have felt more fear today than any other in my life, but it has been surpassed with a feeling of intense anger. I am furious at both sides of this pointless conflict, and I cannot stop thinking about all the innocent lives that have been lost as a result. Those lucky enough to be alive may have nothing left. I try and remind myself to be grateful, seeing as how we at least have the luxury of returning to the Apex.

"We should rest here" says Kristoff's mother, before walking toward a tree line. Everyone in the group complies with the exception of Beltrum. I study his face, noticing a brief expression of frustration before he replaces it with a more empathetic one. "I really must insist that we continue on to Redwood. My last communication with the Spire indicated that we need to arrive within the next few hours."

"That's not going to happen," my father responds, before taking a drink from a water bladder provided to him by Kristoff's mom. He gives it a curious look, before shrugging and placing it to his lips once more.

"It must. Commander Bonafed has ordered it," he replies with a tremble in his voice.

"Then you need to scry with them and let them know the reality of the situation. These things happen in the field. Perhaps Ivar never had the opportunity to learn that from within the Spire," my father commands.

I know little about the Spire, except that it is where the highest-ranking officials of the Apex reside, and that it is essentially only accessible by airship. Why is the Spire so interested in us? I ask myself.

"I am sorry, but that isn't possible. Please, be reasonable. You of all people know how these things work," Beltrum pleads.

"Scry with them now and provide an update. That is an order!" my father shouts, visibly angry and walking towards Beltrum, stopping only when the two are standing eye-to-eye.

My father is much larger than Beltrum and appears far more menacing than usual because of how angry he is. I'm frightened to see my father this mad, but I know that his frustration is justified. Now is not the time to pander to some Apexian Commander. Especially if they haven't been in the real world for what could be decades.

"With all due respect, Edward, nobody here takes orders from ya. It's best to remember your place, lad," Stur replies, moving to stand beside Beltrum. I notice that Stur's body language has switched from relaxed to vigilant. Every muscle in my father's body seems to be tensed. I rise to my feet and place my hand on the hilt of my rapier. I don't wish to fight with Stur or Beltrum, but I will be damned if I let anyone threaten my father—under any circumstances.

"When my daughter's life is in danger, you better goddamn believe that I am giving the orders, Stur," my father says, giving the short man a threatening glance. "If anyone has a problem with that, then we are going to have a very different conversation. I promise you, lad, it will not end well for you, mythical axe or not," he threatens, holding the hilt of his sword.

"Please, let's just—" interjects Kristoff's father.

"No. He is going to scry right now and explain the situation. There will be no discussion. There will be no compromise. Do it. I will not ask again."

My father's appearance intimidates even me, despite not being the focus of his threat. I can sense Stur's blood boiling, but I can also see that he is feeling uneasy. It makes me wonder what my father meant when he said that Stur was aware of what he was capable of. Whatever was implied, the message has clearly been received by Stur, who gives no further protest.

Beltrum, sighing, pulls a crystal ball from his bag. I'd heard tales of their magical uses but seeing it firsthand is different.

"Some privacy?" Beltrum asks, a hint of desperation in his voice.

Without a word, my father denies the request with a firm shake of his head.

Resigned, Beltrum sits, cradling the ball. He murmurs an incantation, his eyes glowing that same eerie blue I saw from the roof. The ball mirrors him, swirling with blue smoke, which then clears to reveal the face of a man.

He is middle-aged and bald with a plain face, except for a scar running down the right side of his face. His eyes appear to be a light grey color, but that may be due to the nature of the crystal ball. When the face in the ball speaks, his voice is cold and unwelcoming, making me uneasy.

"What is it?" asks the voice I recognize from earlier, clearly irritated by the contact.

"It appears that we may be delayed and will not be able to arrive at Redwood by the expected time. Edward insisted I contact you to request certain alterations to the plan." Beltrum is clearly nervous speaking to this individual. I don't understand why, especially given the situation.

"Let me speak to him," the man says bluntly.

My father approaches Beltrum and kneels down to get a better view of the crystal ball.

"A few hours is not enough time to get to Redwood while traveling off-road," says my father, directly.

The man sighs. After some time, the man in the crystal ball motions someone over to him.

"When will it be convenient for you to arrive?" he asks in a sarcastic tone.

"Give us eight hours. If we arrive early, we will wait within the woods until the ship is ready," replies my father.

"So be it." The man turns to someone out of view. "Let the crew know to arrive in exactly eight hours. Give them orders to leave if the party is not there at the designated time," he commands. I officially cannot stand this so-called commander. His demeanor is arrogant, and his tone is nothing short of disrespectful. It is clear he has added the last instruction to show my father how little he cares about our well-being.

"You should be able to use the smoke from Fairfield as a point of reference. The ship was forced to firebomb much of the Realm—to disburse the rebellion, of course."

"I'd expect nothing less from your subordinates," replies my father, coldly.

"You'd do well to remember your place, Edward," the man replies, clearly enjoying the rise he got out of my father.

"I will, and you would do well to remember how you got that scar," says my father before walking away.

Suddenly, the blue light vanishes, and the glass goes back to looking like nothing more than a clear crystal ball. Beltrum quickly covers it back up and places it in his bag before rising to his feet. He tries to wipe the dirt from his robe, clearly bothered by putting it in such close contact with the ground.

"We should count ourselves lucky that the airship is being afforded to us in the first place, and now you insist on disrespecting the commander. I pray to the One True God that he still sends aid, and I shudder to think what his temperament will be once we return to the Capital," says Beltrum, obviously worried by the circumstances.

"If he doesn't, it will cost him his life. I promise you that." Such a threat is nothing short of treason, and I am shocked to hear my father say it aloud.

My father gives Beltrum a look that signifies it's best to let the conversation end. While Beltrum fears the commander, he must know that my father is the more frightening presence at the moment, given his proximity and current emotional state. Stur pats my father on the back. It's clear he holds no hard feelings about the interaction.

I wonder how the man got his scar and why my father knows about it. After everything that has happened in the last several hours, I'm beginning to question just how much I know about my father. One thing is for sure: the new information I have learned about him only makes me admire him more. I'm always viewed as a particularly defiant individual, and now I know where my rebellious streak comes from.

We gather our belongings and make our way to the edge of the woods, which become harder to navigate on account of nightfall. Once we reach the clearing, we can see the fires still burning in the distance. Despite being miles away, the blaze illuminates the night sky. I wonder if there will be anything left of Fairfield by morning. I can't stand the Apex for their decision, and what makes matters worse is how Ivar jested about the destruction as if it's nothing more than a game to him. I wonder how little a person must value human life to joke about such violence.

My father and Stur take turns scouting the way, or hanging in the rear to ensure we aren't being followed. I feel that the group is in capable hands between the two of them, and I pity anyone who tries to threaten us. After we walk for several hours, we arrive at a thicket of woods located just outside of Redwood. The early morning appears to be upon us, as chirps from birds sound in the still air. We stop just before we reach the edge of the woods, which happens to be atop a large hill overlooking the small woodworking village. The smoke from the chimneys gives a sense of normalcy. Perhaps the rebels haven't made it this far, I think to myself.

"We have about an hour before the airship should arrive," Kristoff's father states. "But where is their landing dock? They have to have one. All of the major villages have at least one."

"We better find it and be ready when the ship arrives," replies my father as he scans the village for the tower.

"Stur and Beltrum, you two are with me. We are going to go and find the tower. Joseph and Margret, you stay with Aries and Kristoff. Wait here quietly until we come back," says my father.

"I want to go with you," I plead. Not only am I worried about my father, but I feel safer with him near; even if it means we are closer to danger.

"It'll be okay, honey," he replies as he walks over to me and gives me a hug. "It won't take but a few minutes."

I hug him back. It's the first time I've hugged him since all this happened. I'm so thankful for him, and I feel guilty for not letting him know.

As my father leaves with Stur and Beltrum to find the tower, I watch until they drift out of sight. Several quiet minutes go by, and with each moment, I become progressively more anxious. "Where are they? The sun will be up any minute, and there is no sign of them or the airship," I ask aloud, wiping my sweaty palms on my pants.

"It would take an army to stop those three. If something was happening, we would see flashes of blue from Beltrum's arcane magic," replies Kristoff's mother.

Kristoff sits on a log beside his father, the two leaning against one another. Meanwhile, I feel ready to jump out of my skin. I simply can't sit still. I want to run around the village until I find them. I'm not cut out for this type of thing; for waiting, for inaction. I can't help but obsess over all the awful things that could be happening to them. I try to slow my breathing and calm myself as I look from the edge of the woods for any sign of my father. I'm startled from my vigil when I hear Kristoff's mother ask, "Can we help you with something?"

My heart sinks. Someone is here with us, which means that we've been discovered. This can't be good. I turn to look at who has found us and see a hooded figure standing about ten yards behind where we are gathered. The stranger doesn't respond to Kristoff's mom. They simply continue to stare. I can sense something dark and odd about them. Their body language is stiff, and they stand so still it looks as if they are frozen. Their face is hidden beneath their hood, which doesn't help put my anxiety at ease. I shake the fear from my mind and try to think positively. Perhaps this is a lumberjack who was equally startled to see us.

Kristoff's father clears his throat, gathering the stranger's attention. "I'm Joseph, Governor of Fairfield. We're on Apex business. Where's the airship tower?"

Kristoff and I stand together behind his mother, my hand resting on the hilt of my sword as I notice Margret do the same. Despite all attention focused on him now, the figure remains silent and motionless. I know something is off about the situation.

Kristoff's father studies the individual, taking small, tentative steps forward but stopping before he has even moved a few feet toward the figure.

Kristoff leans as he whispers to his mother, "Should we get help?" She gives a quick, worried shake of her head.

Joseph's voice trembles a bit, displaying his nerves. "Look, I don't know what you want, but if you have any respect for the Apex, you'll answer."

Still not speaking, the figure starts to move closer to Kristoff's father. The sun is beginning to rise, and the rays of light begin to illuminate the woods. In the growing light, I can see that the figure is dressed in leather. Their boots are worn and look like they are a decade old. The rest of their attire appears equally worn and dirty as if they are accustomed to roughing it. Though I try to peek at it discreetly, the figure's face is difficult to make out because of the hood they wear over their head. I wonder if perhaps they have been displaced by the uprisings and have been wandering the woods in shock. I've heard stories of individuals exposed to traumatic events and how they sometimes lose the ability to speak altogether.

Kristoff's father does not take kindly to the figure's behavior, and he removes his sword from its sheath. Even an amateur swordsman could tell that he is not skilled with the weapon, simply by how he struggles to draw the sword.

"N-n-now you have come far enough. Stay where you are," demands Joseph. The figure doesn't listen. They simply continue to press forward at a slow but steady pace. Kristoff's father begins to walk backward like a fearful animal putting himself into a corner. Seeming to realize he is bringing the danger closer to us; he ceases backing up. To my surprise, he raises his sword and holds it in an attack position. Knowing that Kristoff's father absolutely despises physical violence, his actions signify to me that the situation is dire.

In mere seconds, the hooded figure removes a weapon from his own belt, closes the distance, blocks Joseph's attack, and uses his blade to stab him through the throat. It's faster than anything I have ever seen. Joseph's lifeless body crumples to the ground. Margret screams loudly before turning to Kristoff and me, her voice chilling as she commands us to run. Kristoff and I are stunned, and neither of us move.

"Go! Now! Get the others," she pleads while pulling her sword from its sheath. I begin to pull on Kristoff, but he resists. "Please, Kristoff, we have to go now! Please!" I plead.

Kristoff eventually complies, and we run faster than we ever have before. I can hear the sound of blades clashing as we make our way down the steep hill. I want to yell for help, but I can't. My voice simply won't work. It's as if I'm watching myself react, as though I can't consciously make decisions, and I'm merely moving based on instinct. Finally, we make it to the bottom of the hill and come to a stop as we try to discern which way my father and the others had gone. I can't get my bearings. All of the cabins in the village look precisely the same.

I hear rustling from the trees atop the hill. Looking back, I can see Kristoff's mother running after us. She's limping but still making a good pace. I scan the trees behind her expecting to see the hooded figure that had murdered my best friend's father, but no one comes.

We wait for Margret to arrive. When she does, she's gasping for air and clutching her side, where she appears to have been stabbed. I notice a great deal of blood that's now soaking through her blouse and vest.

"I got him. I got him, Kristoff," she says as tears pour from her eyes.

Kristoff nods silently at his mother. "Help! HELP! She's bleeding!" Kristoff screams, aiding his mother to the ground. I press my hands against the wound as hard as I can. My father taught me that pressure can stop bleeding long enough for it to be cauterized, which could mean the difference between life and death. I'm in no position to move, and I'm not going to leave Kristoff alone, so we will have to wait for support.

We yell for help, hoping that someone will hear us and come to our aid. I feel utterly hopeless and am worried that the others may have already succumbed to a similar fate. My anxiety rises when I notice that the blood continues to pour from Margret's wound despite my best efforts to stop it.

"Kristoff, your father loved you, and so do I. Kristoff—please, if I don't make it—you have to be okay for us, Kristoff. We love you; we love you so much. Your dad loved you, Kristoff. You are our son no matter what." I've never seen Kristoff's mother so nervous, but it's clear she's panicking. Kristoff struggles to calm her down, telling her it will be okay and that he knows she loves him and that he loves her too.

To my horror, I notice that the trees are moving, from where they exited the thicket. I know what's coming and something inside of me changes. The fear and worry vanish and are replaced by a furious, overwhelming rage that I can't control. It feels as if my entire body will soon catch fire. I calmly show Kristoff how to hold the wound to try and stop the bleeding, then, with a single-minded focus, I stand up and drop my satchel to the ground. I find my hunting knife and place it in my left hand, and I unsheathe my rapier with my right. I move forward until I stand directly between the beast and Kristoff. They will have to go through me if they want to get to him and his mother, and I am prepared to die defending them. As the figure makes its way down the hill, I hear Kristoff's mother yell, "No! it's not possible, un-unless— REV-REV-REVENANT!"

I hear the word echo in my head. Revenant...what is a revenant? I search my mind for any speck of knowledge I may have about a revenant. I then remember the conversation I overheard Beltrum having and how there had been reports of dark magic, and then I am reminded about my nightmare. My mind switches gears and lands on the book I had felt compelled to take from my room. It speaks of a dark magic called necromancy. I know necromancy is typically associated with death, either control over the dead or creating it.

Given that Kristoff's mother thought she had killed their hooded attacker, I can't help thinking I'm dealing with some sort of undead abomination that obviously can't be killed by conventional means. It doesn't matter much to me. All I have to do is hold them off long enough for help to arrive. I hope that between my father, Stur, and Beltrum, one of them will know how to dispatch a revenant—if that's even what this is.

The figure continues to walk slowly toward me. I know that I will be at a disadvantage if I fight at the bottom of the hill, but I don't have a choice for now. My plan is to circle and get the high ground where it will be easier to dodge and parry any attacks.

"Well, don't keep me waiting," I taunt.

The figure doesn't respond. I notice its hands are empty, which means it isn't armed. But that doesn't mean much. I have seen how fast they are. As I watch, the figure continues to march slowly towards me. They are now little more than ten yards away, and their pace is slowing.

I walk towards them. If they aren't going to approach me, I will instigate contact. After all, sometimes the best defense is a good offense. I am hyper-aware of my foe and its potential movements. I am absolutely focused on the task before me. I can still hear Kristoff screaming, but it barely registers to me. I am fixated on this abomination and want to make him pay for what he has done. My blood continues to boil, and I feel an intense heat coursing through my veins. I get within five yards of the so-called revenant, just outside of the range I witnessed it cover before dispatching Kristoff's father. I then begin to circle, hoping the thing will remain still while I take the high ground.

As my father had taught me, I circle away from what I assume is their dominant hand to avoid opening myself up to a powerful attack. This means I'm moving to the right, leading with my right foot and arm, contrary to the traditional style of leading with the parrying hand and foot. I notice that the figure follows my movement with its head, keeping me fixed within its sights. Its behavior reminds me of a viper; watching, waiting, and striking unexpectedly. Unfortunately, they had been able to catch Kristoff's father unaware, but I won't make that mistake. My circling puts me parallel with the figure, but without warning, it turns its body and runs at me before I can fully take the high ground.

It's faster than I expected, but my reflexes are practiced, and I make a quick lunging strike aiming for the heart. The creature moves just enough that I miss the mark and instead land a solid blow to the middle of its chest, my blade piercing their dirty leather vest. But as the rapier continues to push deeper into its body, I notice no sign of pain from the monster. To my dismay, it continues to move forward even though it will be run through entirely.

I quickly adjust and cease lunging with the sword, trying to pull back to create space, but the Revenant grabs the blade with its hand. My strength is no match for the hooded figure before me, and I'm forced to let go of my weapon. Armed with only my hunting knife, I continue to circle away from it, finally finding myself on the high ground but unable to make use of the advantage without a sword. The creature continues its slow, terrifying walk towards me, unbothered by my rapier sticking out of its chest. Fear washes over me, chilling me to the bone. I know that I'm out of my depth, and there's no way I'll be able to defeat such a monster.

I debate my options; should I run, or get help in attacking it? Maybe me and Kristoff together would be a better match for it. Eventually, I decide it would be best to give them the chance to flee, and so, I continue to back away in the opposite direction, drawing the creature further away from where Kristoff stands with his wounded mother. I hope he can survive, even if I can't.

"What do you want? Why are you doing this?" I ask, hoping for some sort of explanation, but the Revenant does not respond.

From my vantage point, I'm able to get a better look at the Revenant's weapon. It's similar in shape and size to a throwing axe, but there's a sharp point of about six inches opposite the axe blade. The weapon appears to be a crude tool created to kill at a close range and pierce armor.

I try to summon my rage to quash my fear. If the fear takes over, I won't be able to defend myself. I need to stop focusing on what might go wrong and identify a strategy, something, anything that may help me defeat this abomination.

As the monster continues to walk towards me, I contemplate my next move. Off in the distance, I hear yelling. I look out of the corner of my eye, careful to keep my gaze fixated on the Revenant. To my surprise, I see my father running towards us with Stur trailing not far behind.

The Revenant also notices the yelling and turns towards them. Seeing the newcomers, it turns and moves in the direction of my father and Stur. Suddenly and without thinking, I run as fast as I can, charging into the creature with my shoulder, careful to avoid my own sword that is still sticking out of its body. The momentum from my charge sends the Revenant toppling down the hill, end over end.

I make a break for it, running down the hill as fast as I can, careful to avoid losing my balance. My father is in a full sprint coming to meet me while Stur makes his way to Kristoff and his mother. I can hear Kristoff screaming at the top of his lungs, and I know that his mother is gone. She must have lost too much blood. My heart aches at the thought. I can't fathom what is transpiring. When I reach my father, I collapse in his arms.

"Are you okay? What's going on?" my father asks, a mixture of relief and concern in his voice. "Impossible! How is he still alive?"

I follow my father's gaze and see that the Revenant has risen to his feet and is walking towards them once more. This time the Revenant is walking faster and with more purpose, as though he has finally found what he was looking for. I suddenly realize what is happening: the Revenant must have been sent to kill the Apexian Officials.

"It's a revenant. Kristoff's mom told us after she fought it. I ran him through, and he didn't even feel it. He just kept coming."

"Hurry, we have to get to the others," my father says calmly. Despite the circumstances, he is still as calm as ever. We quickly make our way over to find Stur who is comforting a blood-covered Kristoff as he weeps over the corpse of his mother. I feel guilty that I haven't handled the situation better. Perhaps if I did, I would have been able to save her.

"Stur, get them to Beltrum. He should be ready with the carriage," my father directs.

Stur nods and quickly rises to his feet. "C'mon lad, we have to go," he says in his best impression of a comforting tone.

"No, I can't leave her. I can't," replies Kristoff, overcome with sorrow.

"Kristoff, we have to go. She wanted you to be safe. She died to protect you. Come on, I am not about to lose you too," I plead, struggling to pull him up. "I need you, Kristoff. Come on!"

Kristoff remains unresponsive and unmoving, so Stur steps in and lifts him to his feet and says, "We both need ya, lad. Don't let her sacrifice be for naught. She died protecting you. You dishonor her otherwise."

Kristoff nods silently at Stur's words and looks up in the direction of the Revenant. While the group had been trying to get Kristoff to his feet, the Revenant had kept moving and was only one hundred yards from them and was getting closer. I notice that he's holding my now-broken sword as his own. The thought of my own sword being used to hurt my father makes me sick. I give my father one last hug and tell him I love him.

"I will not be far behind. Beltrum should have the carriage ready, hurry!" says my father, removing both his sword and parrying knife from his belt, readying himself.

I start to walk away towards Kristoff and Stur but stop. I'm worried for my father's safety and I'm not going to leave him. I want him to flee instead of fight.

"What of the airship? Can't they handle this?" I plead.

"They aren't coming. Go, Aries. I love you." Without another word he walks towards the Revenant.

I know I should go, but I'm rooted to the spot. My father expected the Revenant to come for him, but he was wrong. I am horrified when it runs full speed after the three of us instead, at a pace faster than any human should be able to run.

"Quick, get behind me!" says Stur. My father is rushing to intercept the monster but is not going to be able to in time. Forty yards become thirty, then twenty, fifteen. Soon the beast would be upon us, with only Stur standing between us and certain death, and I'm unarmed except for my hunting knife.

Stur grips his brilliant battle axe tightly as he stands firm, prepared to hold his ground. When it's within five yards, Stur, in an overhead motion, throws his axe directly at the beast. It has no time to react before the axe finds its place in the creature's abdomen, knocking it to the ground.

My father arrives, and with a downward strike, he attempts to slice off its head. To prevent its beheading, the creature sacrifices a hand, blocking the blow. The creature then uses his remaining hand to remove the axe from his stomach. He then begins to swing it at my father while making his way back to his feet. My father is by far the better technical fighter, and the Revenant's blows are easily dodged.

While the Revenant is focused on him, Stur grabs the beast from behind and slams it to the ground with a loud thud. Stur wrestles the beast and gets hold of its arms.

"Grab my axe and chop its fucking head off!" yells Stur.

With great haste, my father pries the axe from the Revenant's grip and swings it with the precision. I let out a sigh of relief as I see its head topple to the ground.

"Quickly, to the carriage," says my father as he and Stur gather their weapons. The group then runs in the direction where Beltrum is to be waiting with our means of escape.

We move so quickly that I barely notice the details of Redwood. It's a blur of log cabins, thick green grass, and sporadic pine trees that had been spared from the axes of the lumberjacks. I make sure to keep an eye fixed on Kristoff, ready to pull him up should he collapse from grief again. I wonder what he is going through. I know the pain of losing a parent, but for it to happen so suddenly and violently must be unbearable.

The group eventually slows to a walk and travels for another mile. There's an eerie vibe in the air and I realize we haven't seen any villagers during all of the commotion.

"Where is everyone at?" I ask.

"Many of them must have fled—," answers my father, struggling to find words.

"And many of them weren't so lucky," says Stur, finishing the statement.

"All this bloodshed, and for what? How can life be so meaningless to these people?" I ask rhetorically, frustrated by the devastation I can't make sense of.

"Any sign of where Beltrum is with the carriage?" asks my father.

"I reckon that large barn houses the stables," replies Stur as he leans against a nearby cabin wall trying to catch his breath.

I scan our surroundings, looking for a sign of Beltrum, horses, or anything that could get us out of here.

"There!" shouts Stur, referencing the blue ball of light shooting into the sky from behind the building he had mentioned. The ball continues to rise into the air before eventually erupting into a giant flash so bright it hurts my eyes.

"Hurry, if we can see it, so can anyone," commands my father.

I curse whoever created this village for making the roads so circuitous. It's as if the town was designed to be a maze, and no path seems to go in a straight direction for more than twenty-five yards.

Eventually, our group makes it to the back of the large wooden structure where the light of arcane magic is emanating. There are no people to be seen, but there are signs that many had recently fled, judging by the trampled ground and countless empty stables. I had forgotten that, after lumber, one of the most significant exports from Redwood was horses. Carthage must be trying to secure food, lumber, and horses for their rebellion. This is far more organized than I thought.

We arrive at a large stable with a sliding door, which Beltrum is struggling to open.

"Inside, I have found us a carriage and did my best to secure two rather scrawny horses to it," he says, looking profoundly exhausted.

"Beltrum, get Aries and Kristoff settled, Stur, you man the reins, and I will open the door," says my father, moving to push the large door open.

The two black horses Beltrum had attached to the carriage don't look full-grown. I suppose they're all that's left from whatever chaos had ravaged the village. Kristoff and I quickly board the open wooden carriage and sit on the bench seat facing opposite the horses. As soon as my father opens the door large enough for the carriage to get through, Stur snaps the reins, and the carriage jerks as the horses take off faster than seasoned horses would.

"Woah, woah!" commands Stur, prompting them to stop about twenty-five yards later than they should have, for my father to board.

"Edward, behind you!" yells Beltrum, who begins desperately searching his bag. Kristoff and I quickly turn to see the Revenant closing in on my father from thirty yards away, his crude weapon in his right hand. My father runs for the carriage, making it to the rear and jumping to climb on. Kristoff and I do our best to pull him inside.

While we struggle to get him inside, the Revenant throws his weapon.

"No!" I scream.

All I can do is watch as the crude, hatchet-like weapon flies through the air before landing in my father's back. We frantically pull him over the ledge, and he falls face-first onto the floor of the carriage.

"I am alright. My armor stopped it. Please—pull it out," says my father in a pained voice. I yank as hard as I can and release the weapon from my father's back. He was right. It barely pierced his armor, only a small bit of blood shows on the blade of the weapon.

"Stur! Let's go!" yells my father, eyes trained on the Revenant that is getting dangerously close.

"I am trying. Bloody things won't go!" Stur yells as he frantically snaps the reins.

We were so close, I think hopelessly. I want to do something to turn the tides in our favor, but I'm all out of fight, exhausted emotionally and physically. The relentlessness of the Revenant and its ability to escape death has defeated me entirely. For the first time since this all began, I accept that I'm about to die. It's just too much for us to overcome. There's a sad irony knowing my life is coming to an end while we're so close to getting away.

"Everyone, back!" yells Beltrum as he stands up in the middle of the carriage holding a glass vial filled with slowly circling blue smoke. We quickly get out of his way and stand behind him as he removes the cork from atop the vial. The smoke slowly creeps out, and as it does, he inhales it with a deep breath. His body shakes from the newly acquired power. He puts his hands in front of his mouth and begins to mumble under his breath. A blue ball of what looks like lightning starts to form in his hands, continuing to grow with the passing seconds. The monster halts at the sight of the ball and turns, beginning to flee, as if he knows he's in danger.

Beltrum lets the ball loose, and it flies at a blazing speed, much faster than anything I've seen, save for an actual lightning strike across the sky. The ball of energy travels about twenty yards before meeting the ground, sending dirt flying where it lands. I worry he missed, but then there's a flash of light and a loud explosion, which destroys everything in its vicinity. The sight and sound of wood shattering overwhelms my senses. Fortunately, it startles the horses, and they take off. The carriage barely creates enough distance between us and the town hall before the entire structure collapses, burying the Revenant in what I hope will serve as its grave.

An entire day slipped away since we fled the village of Redwood on this uncomfortable wooden carriage. Remarkably, the horses we borrowed carried us swiftly away from Redwood.

My father has altered our course to the coastal city of Mackinaw, sharing its name with the realm it resides in. Beltrum, has been mainly silent, yet I can tell he blames my father for the Apex abandoning us. This infuriates me.

I drift in and out of sleep during our journey, often waking to my father's persistent cough. When I am awake, my attention turns to Kristoff. He is consumed by grief and shows a complete disinterest in basic needs like sleep, food, or water. What he must endure is beyond imagining.

My anger kindles, as it often does, and I fume over how much I despise the politicians who are playing with lives as if they were mere chess pieces. I feel helpless. All I can do is sit with Kristoff, hoping my presence offers some solace, perhaps a reminder that he isn't alone.

Occasionally relief washes over me, as I realize my father emerged from the fight unharmed. Thankfully his armor protected him. I couldn't imagine what I would do if he was killed, like—Kristoff's parents. I want the thoughts inside my head to cease, because they only serve to increase my grief.

As the journey continues, my father confers with Stur and Beltrum on our plan, sparking heated debates. Beltrum demands contacting the

Apex again, but my father disagrees, saying we must obtain more distance from Redwood before exposing our location. Suspicion gnaws at me. Did the Revenant know our location? Where was the airship?

Eventually Beltrum's persistent questioning causes my father to explain his plan, which is to contact a person he believes can aid us, someone informed yet unaligned with the Apex or Carthage. Beltrum protests persist, which is unsurprising given his blind adherence to the Apex.

"We are getting close. Do you see it? Just there," my father's voice pierces through my troubled thoughts, pointing to the expansive body of water ahead. The waves crash and retreat, a display of the ocean's beauty and might. Its vastness, seemingly endless and shrouded in mysteries, captivates me. Yet, my heart yearns for different circumstances as I am confronted with the enormity of our loss. However, a glimmer of surprise interrupts the tide of sorrow—Kristoff sits up, alert, trying to catch a better glimpse of the water.

"It sure is beautiful. How long does it go on for?" I ask.

"Nobody knows, lass. Some say forever. The Southlands is about as far as anybody has been. Although you'd have no trouble finding someone there telling ya they been further," Stur answers, sparks flying as he sharpens his axe blades.

I know little about the Southlands, just that it's comprised of twin islands and is directly below Felecity. It is supposedly notorious for housing thieves and heretics. At least that is what the Apexian scholars taught me as a child. The Southlands is the only land the Apex couldn't force its rule upon. Oakland and Anveil became colonies, and Distle is rumored to be more of a puppet kingdom than a sovereign nation.

"You've been to the Southlands?" I inquire.

"Aye, count yourself lucky you haven't. It's a godless land full of all manner of crime. They don't worship the One True God there. Hell, they don't worship anything except coin, drink, and other people's property."

"So, it's like Anveil, except they steal?" I jest.

"Aye, but that's no small thing. Stealing is most despicable. And nowadays, most of us from Anveil have faith in the One True God."

"How were they able to withstand the Apex military?" I continue, steering the conversation away from religion.

"Believe you me, they couldn't. It was more about how they aren't worth the Apex's time. If the Apex wanted, they could firebomb the entire wretched continent in a few days."

"You have to admire a place so independent," I reply.

"Trust me, the Southlanders would give them trouble, and the Apex knows it. That's why they steer clear of the area," says my father before coughing, which is becoming more frequent by the hour.

"Bullocks! They would be too busy fighting amongst themselves. The clans there are constantly quarreling. In fact, I don't think they ever had a leader, let alone a king," says Stur, his grudge against the island nation clear as day.

"If only one of the clans got their hands on some airships, then they could force peace like the Apex," my father adds sarcastically.

Stur shrugs, then waves his hand at the air to signify he's done with the conversation and begins smoking his pipe. The smell of his tobacco lingers despite the ocean breeze. I wonder how he can smoke so frequently and still run for as long as he has.

I recall when Kristoff and I had stolen his father's pipe and smoked it out of curiosity. We both choked on the smoke and decided it wasn't for us. When his father caught us, he scolded us in his way, but he didn't tell Kristoff's mother or my father, for which I am forever grateful.

Kristoff's parents were very kind to me and my father. They were the only family we had after my mother passed. Nobody else knew how difficult it was to adjust to Fairfield. I miss them so much already and curse fate for taking them away too soon—and in such a violent way. I can't help but admire Kristoff's mother's bravery and how she died to protect us. If not for her, Kristoff and I would be dead.

Before I know it, we're told that we'll be arriving soon. I don't mind the ride as much now, the cool sea breeze finally wafting away the smell of Stur's tobacco and providing a sense of calm. The ships on the water tell me that life here is still normal. I wonder how much time will pass before the chaos finds its way this far.

Eventually, the carriage comes to a halt at a relatively small, yet well-guarded wooden gate. The structure is equipped with two large scout towers where bowmen are positioned. Additionally, fifteen soldiers stand sentry outside the gate. They mainly wear plate armor, save for their leather pants and boots. Their plate helmets have a metal piece that comes down from the top and covers their nose, but the rest of their face is visible. I imagine the mixture of plate and leather is to increase mobility. A set of full plate armor is valuable on the battlefield but has little use when you need to move quickly.

"State your name and business," commands a guard in a severe tone.

"My name is Edward Fleetwood. We are on official Apex business," my father says, struggling to control his coughing.

"What proof have you?" The guard responds.

Beltrum reaches into his bag, pulls out a piece of parchment, and hands it to the guard. He looks over the paper before waving another soldier over. I worry about what will happen if we're not allowed to pass. This level of security isn't typical for a busy coastal city like Mackinaw.

"Take a look, sir. Says they are on official Apex business," he says, before handing the parchment to the captain. He carefully looks it over and then thoroughly examines the group. We probably look worse for wear, and not how official Apexian operatives should. Our poor-quality carriage and adolescent horses don't help matters either.

"Typically, when the Capital has business here, they send word beforehand," says the captain.

"Our business does not pertain to the Realm of Mackinaw. We are simply seeking food and rest," my father replies.

"And where is it you said you came from?" The captain asks.

"My good sir, I understand that you have a duty to uphold, and I must say you are doing a rather thorough job. However, we are in a hurry and have already been delayed thanks to the uprisings in the North. Nevertheless, I would be happy to open a scrying channel so that you could ask your questions to Commander Ivar Bonafed, although I must warn, he hasn't been in the most pleasant of spirits—with everything going on," Beltrum interjects.

The captain grows visibly nervous at the mention of speaking to Commander Ivar Bonafed, which makes me hate the scarred man even more. I don't like how he commands such fear, even when he isn't around. Well, everyone besides my father.

"That isn't necessary. Let them through!" yells the captain. "Sorry for the inconvenience. With everything going on, we can't be too safe," he adds.

"I would expect nothing less. I shall include how well your unit has secured this area in my report. I wish you good fortune, fine sir," Beltrum replies.

"Where to?" asks Stur as the carriage slowly makes its way through the gates. "The tavern. They will either be there, or someone there will know where to find them. We will get rooms at the inn first and stable the horses, then I'll make contact," my father replies, looking exhausted, and rightfully so, since he did most of the steering since we left.

The city of Mackinaw is breathtaking. The roads are made of cobblestone and are filled with slowly paced carriages. The small seaside homes are handsomely decorated and remind me of the Apex Capital and its surrounding cities. I can tell the villagers value the way they look, a quality lacking in the people of Fairfield. I wonder what it's like to live in a town surrounded by so much beauty, yet away from Apexian oversight.

We could easily get lost in the city, but thankfully, the streets are fitted with wooden signs directing us where to go. It isn't long before we find ourselves pulling up to a large two-story stone building. It has an expertly crafted wooden roof of a rather unique design. I marvel at the building, assuming its stone construction is to weather the intense storms known to hit the coast.

A stable worker assists us in gathering our belongings from the carriage before taking over the reins so they can board the horses. We walk into the inn, which looks even better on the inside. It is decorated with paintings and flowers and has comfortable seats. Kristoff and I sit while my dad secures rooms from the innkeeper. I'm excited about getting a good night's sleep, or at least increasing my chances, since I'll have an actual bed.

I wonder if Kristoff will be able to get any sleep. He still isn't speaking, and I doubt he has slept once since we left Fairfield. He occasionally looks around, but for the most part, he seems lost in thought. I hope that he will open up soon so that I can speak with him and find a way to comfort him. I wish I could ease his pain, but I know that's impossible. The only cure for grief is time. When I lost my mother, I was devastated for months, and in many ways, I've never been the same again.

"It's sort of like the Apex, isn't it?" I ask within earshot of Kristoff, hoping to get a response. Instead, he continues to sit quietly, his head resting on the arm of the chair.

"Alright, we have two rooms. I will stay with Kristoff and Aries, and you two can stay together," my father says as he hands Stur a room key. I notice that he is looking pale and that sweat beads are forming along his hairline. Given that it's nice and cool inside the inn, thanks to the sea breeze blowing through the open windows, my father's sweaty face is troubling.

"Are you feeling alright, dad? You look pale," I say.

"Yes, I am fine. I think we could all use some rest," he answers with a smile.

We climb the spiral stone staircase that leads to the second floor. My legs burn by the time we reach the top of the stairs, and I feel like I could sleep for weeks. My father opens our bedroom door, revealing a large room artistically decorated with seashells, fishing nets, and flowers. There are two large beds, each stationed near a window. The fragrance from the flowers reminds me of the gardens outside of Apexian shops. My mother and I would often stop and smell them when we walked around town.

"You guys can have the beds. I will take the floor," says my father as he drops his bag to the ground. I do the same and immediately lay down, longing for sleep. "I am going to head to the tavern. I won't be gone more than an hour. Stur will be keeping watch until I come back. Do not open the door for anyone until I return."

"Wait, why do you have to go now? You need to rest too," I insist.

"Aries, it will be fine. There will be plenty of time for rest," he says as he walks over to me and gently kisses the top of my head. "Do not speak to Stur or Beltrum until I return," he whispers in my ear. I feel uneasy at his comment, but I nod and will follow his request without question. I know that if my father doesn't wish for me to speak to them, he must have a good reason. I have my reservations about Beltrum but feel as if I can trust Stur. He has demonstrated that he is willing to put himself in danger to protect me and Kristoff. If they meant us harm, wouldn't they have simply left us to die?

"Kristoff, I am going to get some sleep. Please try and do the same," I say, hoping he may respond, but there is only silence.

My mind races, jumping from one theory to another as I try to make sense of what is going on. I have so many questions for which I don't have answers, such as why our families received an escort from such highly skilled operatives. And why a necromancer would send a revenant after us. Not too much later, I drift to sleep. It's only a few hours into my slumber before I'm woken up by my father gently shaking my leg.

"As quietly as you can, get up and gather your things. There is no time to explain. You have to trust me," he whispers quietly to me. Assuming the worst, and sure we're in danger again, I quickly gather my bag and put my leather boots back on.

Kristoff is already awake and standing beside my father, his bag over his shoulder. His facial expression tells me that he is aware of everything going on, but his thoughts are somewhere else. My father leads us through the hallway, back down the spiral staircase, and out of the door. I can tell he was scanning the area for the others, and we are fortunate they were nowhere to be seen.

"We go on foot to the docks. We need to be long gone before they find out," my father says in a whisper.

"Okay, but why? What is going on?" I ask, trying my best to keep my voice down.

"I promise I will explain everything in due time. But for now, we need to go," he says, before carefully leading us away from the inn.

Eventually, we create enough distance between ourselves and the inn, so my father informs us we are heading for the docks to board a ship. After about a ten-minute walk, with frequent looks over our shoulders to ensure we aren't being followed, we arrive. The wooden docks seem to go on forever and are filled with various types of fishing and sailing vessels. Finally, we come to a relatively large and old-looking, but well-maintained wooden ship that is painted black. It carries three white sails, one large in the middle with a smaller sail on either side. It resembles an Apex airship, minus the large balloon structure in the middle.

"Edward! Well, don't wait, mate! The wind is good, and the moon is giving plenty light," says a portly man waiting on the deck of the ship. It's difficult to make out the man's appearance in the dark, but he speaks to my father in a way that tells me they are old friends. We hurry and use the outstretched plank to board the boat. Several crew members quickly begin to prepare the ship to depart.

"You have no idea how much we appreciate this, Benjamin. Thanks again," says my father, reaching out to shake the man's hand.

"Would ya keep it down? The lads would never let me hear the end of it if they knew my name was Benjamin. They call me Captain Rockwell," says the man looking around to see if any of the crew had overheard. He is a rather tall middle-aged man who looks in shape despite his ample belly. He has long dark hair that is starting to grey. His brown skin is covered in scars from what I assume is a result of a long life at sea. His demeanor is warm and welcoming, despite having a very hoarse and loud voice along with his intimidating stature.

My father laughs, "Well, sorry, but the secret is out. I went around town asking everyone if they knew Benjamin Rockwell." Both my father and the captain laugh, and I think about how refreshing it is to see my father laugh again.

"When my man at the tavern told me Edward Fleetwood and his family needed transporting to safety, I knew it must be mighty serious, and by no means would I ever forsake my friend."

"I am afraid it is. I am sure you are aware of what is happening in the North."

"Aye, it's a pity. You know my views on the Apex. Can't say I'm surprised—but still tragic, nonetheless."

"Is there somewhere we can rest? It has been days since we slept."

"Of course. You there! Show Edward and his kids where they can board, and make sure it's nice! No rats!"

We follow the crew member to our sleeping quarters beneath the ship's deck. It's a far cry from the comfortable room at the inn, but it does come with the promise of safety. The walls are lined with two sets of bunks, which are stacked three high. Kristoff quickly climbs to a top bunk while I and my father sit on wooden stools nailed to the floor. I can feel that the ship is moving; they must have lifted anchor and departed.

"I know you're exhausted, Dad, but I could really use some answers right about now."

"I'm sorry, I don't know where to begin."

"How about the beginning? Why did we have an escort in the first place?"

"Stur and Beltrum work for the Apex, that much is true. But they are part of a secret order called the Watchers. Apexian soldiers must obey orders without question, but their loyalty is nothing compared to the Watchers. For that reason—and even though I like Stur—and Beltrum for the most part—I'm not sure we can trust them, or rather the person they get their orders from. Their directive was to bring us back to the Apex, but judging by Redwood, we cannot rule out the possibility those orders have changed."

"Wait, are you saying they may have been ordered to hurt us?"

"Anything is possible, but I am sure Ivar wouldn't use them on account of our history. He would have sent someone else. But, then again, maybe he wouldn't just to be particularly sadistic."

"He sent the Revenant, you think?"

"Doubtful, but maybe he chose not to act. That way, it would look like he wasn't responsible for our deaths."

"So then where are we going, if not back to the Apexian Capital?"

"The Southlands."

"The Southlands? Why?"

"To be with your mother's family. That's where she's from, Aries. It's the only place I can ensure that you and Kristoff are safe," he explains, before a coughing spell stalls the conversation. "Can you please fetch me some water?" he asks, continuing to cough.

I rush to gather one of the bladders of water within my bag and quickly hand it to my father, whose hand is now shaking. "You need to rest, Dad. We can talk more in the morning. I know whatever you are doing is for our protection."

"You need to know, the Watchers recruit at birth, Aries. Your mom and I were Watchers at one time, as were Kristoff's parents. I guess I still am because you don't stop being a Watcher. They may not use you for a while, but when they need you for something, you have to do it without question, or you risk death. So, a few years after we had you, we were ordered to Fairfield to keep you all safe until the Watchers could commission you into service, that is if you possessed abilities, they feel are useful."

I can't help but feel frustrated at my parents for keeping this from me.

"So, the training my whole life, was that to make me ready for service?" I ask, unable to hide my irritation.

"Not exactly. Because of who your mother was, I was sure they were certainly going to try and commission you at some point. I wanted you to be prepared to decide for yourself, and to do that, to refuse them, you'd need to be able to survive, Aries."

I feel my frustration ease. I should have known better than to doubt him.

"What about Kristoff? Why wasn't he trained?"

"His father trained him in another way. He wished for him to become a diplomat, similar to himself, so that the Apex could utilize him in a way that would be much safer. You need to remember that the Apexian Church is made up of politicians. If he could navigate that world effectively, then he would be safe from field duty, not to mention if he lacks proficiency in combat, they would have little interest. No offense to Kristoff. I know just how strong and courageous he is, but there was a reason his father wanted to keep him from learning to fight." My father begins to cough again, this time to the point that he spews up mucus.

"Okay, seriously, you need rest. We can talk more tomorrow," I say assertively. I know that he rarely takes care of himself until I force him to. I help him to his bed where he begrudgingly lays down.

After laying down myself and trying to sleep, I toss and turn, unable to succeed. Initially, I'm so exhausted I thought it would be easy to sleep for a week, and now that I can finally lay down, I can't. My mind is racing all over the place. I feel like my entire life is a lie, and so is Kristoff's. I curse the Apex. I know something is terribly wrong with their so-called rule, and I vow that I will do anything in my power to fight against it. I long for the Southlands but am nervous about what it will be like. I cannot wait to settle in a land outside the reach of the Apex and their Watchers. My attention swiftly turns to my father. I worry about him and hope that rest will make him feel better. I think about how much I love him and how lucky I am to have him. Thanks to these comforting thoughts of him, I'm finally able to sleep.

I am awoken early in the morning by my father's coughing, and I quickly make my way over to him. He is covered in sweat from head to toe and appears to be extremely pale. "Are you okay?" I ask.

"Afraid not, Aires—there isn't much time."

"What do you mean?" I ask, panicked.

"Please, just listen, my dear. The Revenant's blades must have been coated with poison."

"I will get the captain. He can get help or take us somewhere."

"I'm sorry, but he can't. You need to listen because I don't know how much longer I can speak. My body already feels too weak to move. But you need to understand something. The One True God that the Apex speaks of is real, and the Apexian Church's High Lord does speak to him. Your mother said she heard his voice. He is the one who directs the Apex."

"Dad, I am sorry, but this isn't the time to talk about religion, is it?" I look over my shoulder. "Kristoff! Kristoff! Please get the captain. Tell him my dad is really sick." Kristoff, though startled awake, immediately hops out of bed and rushes above deck to find help.

"Aries, listen, your mother was told that a great war was coming. A war that would end with light vanquishing dark—once and for all, whatever that means. And—the masters of the elements will once again be called to take sides in the battle. While your mother held these things as truths, I always had my doubts, but the rise of the necromancer and his revenant is a sign. It could truly be happening. No ordinary magic user could create such a powerful revenant. Your mom's clan from the Southlands are some of the only living people that know how to evade the Apex, and more importantly, the Watchers. They are going to come looking for you, Aries. For you and Kristoff both. Please don't go with them, no matter what, even if it means killing. You have to seek out your mom's clan. Find the one your mother called the Crone. You have to find her. Find the Romani."

"You will go with us. Why are you talking like this? You can't give up, Dad, please. I don't want to be alone, please," I plead with tears in my eyes as I grip his hand tightly. It feels foreign to me; it has become so cold and fragile. He is shaking uncontrollably and appears to be in extreme pain. I can't believe that this is happening. Why didn't I consider the monster would coat its blades?

Captain Rockwell and a crew member burst into the room. "What's the matter? Edward is sick?" The captain asks, rushing to the side of the bed. I nod and proceed to fill him in on all that's happened with the Revenant.

"Quick, give me the tonic," he directs. They help my father drink from a jar of unknown medicine. It makes me uneasy not knowing what my father is being given, but I swallow my anxiety and tell myself to trust them.

"Lass, you may want to give us a minute while we try and figure out what's going on," says the captain.

"Absolutely not. I will not leave him," I reply quickly. My tone is filled with fear and desperation, which is enough to dissuade the captain from pressing the issue. I watch as they poke and prod my father, attempting to find the root of his condition. Looking exhausted, he eventually tells them they have done enough and that he needs time alone with me. The captain complies without resistance, deflating what little hope I have left for my father's recovery.

"Aries, I couldn't have asked for a better daughter. I know it wasn't easy for you at times, but I did the best that I could on my own. Lucky for me, you had enough of your mom in you that I didn't need to do much."

"Dad, you were always perfect. I couldn't ask for a better father." Despite my devastation, I try to put on a brave face so as not to cause him more pain.

"Your mom and I always argued about who you took after the most. She loved you so very much, Aries. Remember the scar on Ivar's face? Well, she gave it to him when he once vaguely threatened to commission you as a child," he says, laughing. "It's safe to say you get your fighting spirit and temper from her. He would have thrown her in prison or had her hanged, but luckily for us, the High Priest valued your mother immensely, and we were able to be positioned in Fairfield alongside Kristoff's parents. I know it wasn't the best place to live, but I hope it helped teach you to care about those who may have less than you—something hard to learn in the Apex Capital."

"Dad, it was all perfect, I promise. I have no complaints about how things were. I promise, okay? I need you to understand that," I say with tears streaming down my cheeks.

"Be careful in the Southlands. They don't take kindly to outsiders. You will be fine once you find your mother's clan, but trust nobody and protect yourself and your belongings until then. Life is different there. Law enforcement doesn't exist the same way you are used to. If someone wrongs you, it's your responsibility to hold them accountable or you risk becoming a target. Survival of the fittest and strength in numbers is the way of life there."

"I will be fine. Thanks to you, I can handle myself. I will keep Kristoff and me safe."

"I was proud to see you defend Kristoff and his mom. I have no doubt you will find your way. And I know you'll like it there because you are just like your mother. Sure, it has its dangers, but people get to live free there. It may be the only place in Felicity where people are still free."

"Do you know how I can find mom's family? I don't know where to begin."

"They are not just her family. They are your family too. Captain Rockwell is taking you to a port they are known to frequent. Of all the people I know, I trust him the most, but you can never be too careful, so don't share this information with him. Your mom's clan's name is Romani. In my bag, I have a bracelet given to your mom by the Crone. It will grant you an audience with them."

"Okay, got it," I say, smiling, and gently wiping tears from my father's eyes.

"Also, I have a letter for you from your mother, but you have to promise me that you will not open it until you meet the Crone. That was your mom's request." He examines my face for a moment before continuing. "Your mom's gift is the reason why the High Priest valued her so much. She was a seer. She used to have dreams that predicted things to come. She knew bits and pieces about all of this, about your life, so trust what guidance she has left you."

"I promise, Dad, I will keep the letter safe and not open it until I's supposed to."

"One more thing, Aries. Your mother told me to tell you this, nothing exists that is beyond the power of your own fire, never extinguish it—no matter what they tell you."

I am confused by what she meant but nod in agreement, nonetheless.

"Can you lay with me, please?" my father asks. His pain seems to be growing worse by the second.

I nod and lay with him. I hold him tight but am careful not to hurt him. I cry heavily as I bury my head into his chest. I can't believe I am about to lose the one person I feel safe with, the one person I could always count on to guide and protect me. I am terrified, angry, distraught, and every other negative emotion a person could experience. I do my best to hold on to the moment forever, but time seems to slip away rapidly. As we lay quietly, my father periodically tells me how much he loves me, but each time he speaks, he suffers another coughing fit, causing him intense pain. Eventually, his eyes close, and he says nothing more. He simply lays there, his taxed breathing the only indication that he is still alive. I try to speak with him, but he doesn't respond. Panicked, I scream for the captain, who is waiting outside the door.

He has the difficult task of telling me that my father has entered into a coma. He is alive but unable to speak. But, according to the captain, I can talk to him, and he will hear me. I am told that my father, the strongest man I have ever known, may be holding on for me and that if I say it's okay to pass, he can let go and be free of his pain and be reunited with my mother again.

I don't know the captain, but I am thankful I'm not alone for this. I fight back my tears as he comforts me. I am certain he must have been around his fair share of death. He simply listens and allows me to exist in my sorrow, which is all I want in that moment. I can't help but think his bedside manner is born of the unlucky experience of losing a loved one. Eventually, I gather the courage, and lay down beside him. Through tears, I thank him for everything he has done for me throughout my life. I share some of my favorite memories that I had with him, tell him to kiss and hug my mom for me, and that no matter what, I will be okay. I know this to be true because he has prepared me for whatever I may face. With one last kiss to his forehead, I hug my father and feel him take his last breath before passing on to the next life.

Captain Rockwell and his crew honor my father with a beautiful burial at sea. They make him look as he did in life, something for which I am immensely grateful. They lay him upon a wooden raft, his sword across his chest with the hilt in hand, a custom reserved for great warriors. I do my best to show my gratitude, but my intense grief overwhelms me. I wish I could take his sword, but as the crew tells me, it is custom for warriors to be buried with their weapons for protection in the next life.

Days upon days pass without me leaving the cabin room. The crew brings us food, even though neither of us feels like eating. I appreciate that we are left alone and not pressured into interacting. Despite Kristoff dealing with his own grief, the sight of me suffering inspires him to be there for me. Without him at my side, I am certain I would lose my mind. I envision myself as a leaf torn from a tree, slowly wilting on the ground until I fade into nothingness. I fantasize about tearing the Revenant apart, limb by limb, or bringing the Apex down—brick by brick.

As the days become weeks, occasionally, I make my way to the deck. At first, it's just to get fresh air and see the sun, but as time passes, I find myself in need of social interaction, and eventually, I feel good enough to help maintain the ship. Cooking and cleaning allow me to take my mind off my grief and help ease the guilt I feel for being a burden to the crew. I am thankful that Captain Rockwell and his crew cared so much for my father that they are willing to ferry Kristoff and I to safety. Without them, I have no idea how I could make it to the Southlands.

As time progresses, I am able to summon the strength to verbalize my gratefulness to the captain, to which he tells me it's a small gesture and the least he could do for the daughter of a man that meant so much to him.

As I come to find out, Benjamin is full of stories about my dad and had even been present at my parents' wedding. He tells me about when he met my mother and how beautiful, kind, and brilliant she was. He tells stories that seem more like tall tales than reality, making my father seem like a supernatural hero. I don't mind the stories, even if I know they are exaggerated. In fact, I welcome them because talking about the good memories of my father helps me avoid my grief and despair. I also use this tactic with Kristoff, which proves to help him replace his own negative thoughts with happier ones. I know neither of us will be the same, but our support for one another and the isolation that comes with being stuck at sea forces us to progress through our grief. Before we know it, we have some days where everything feels normal again. Of course, there are still episodes of intense grief and nightmares about what happened, but those moments have become less common.

The time it takes to travel to the Southlands seems to fly by, even though it's four weeks before we finally find ourselves dropping anchor and making port. Before leaving the ship and saying goodbye to the captain and crew, we are asked to meet with him in his quarters. When we arrive, we are surprised to see the captain waiting for us at a large table filled with all types of food. I can't believe the crew planned such a fantastic feast for us. Their generous act brings tears to my eyes, prompting the captain to come to my side, his own eyes welling up with tears.

"Now, don't cry, lass! You'll go and make me tear up, and then what? You think the crew will follow a captain known for crying?" he says, hugging me and Kristoff.

"Please sit, eat, and drink. The lads and I wanted to send ya off proper, and they wanted me to make sure that you know just how much you'd be missed."

"Really, this is perfect. You didn't need to do this," I reply, feeling thankful but guilty for the trouble they must have gone through.

"Every man on this ship is free because Edward brokered a deal with the Apex. Ya see, we weren't always known for being an upstanding merchant ship. Finest there is, I might add. Thankfully, your dad saw the good in us and was able to keep us out of trouble. So please, accept these offerings, and be happy!"

"Thank you, we will," I reply, knowing that further protests would ruin the captain's intentions.

Kristoff immediately begins to eat one of his favorite dishes; mashed potatoes with extra butter, which he adds himself by the spoonful. In fact, I have never seen a person who could eat as much butter as him.

"Wow, this is so good. They really outdid themselves," he says, speaking between bites.

"I am sure your father told you a lot about the Southlands, and I have been no stranger to these parts—in my younger days, that is. But you need to know, this is no Apexian Realm. A person's word here is their bond, and if they break it, well, let's just say the punishment is much worse than what the Apex could dish out."

I nod. "I have heard as much, but what exactly makes it so unsafe?"

"It isn't really unsafe per se, that is if ya don't go looking for trouble, but ya can't be someone that is an easy target neither if ya catch my drift. Your dad told me you had your own business to handle, and I respect your privacy, but just be safe," the captain says, looking at me pointedly with these words before standing up. "I wanted you to have a few things before you depart," he adds before he begins rummaging under his desk. After a moment, he offers a satchel.

"Really, you don't need to. "We'll be fine," Kristoff says, equally uncomfortable as I am when it comes to accepting generosity from others.

"It's no skin off my back, so don't ya worry. Just, please accept it. You wouldn't deny a man his right to honor his deceased friend by helping his kids, would ya?"

A smile creeps across my face. It reminds me of how my father had always seen Kristoff as his own, bringing back memories of younger days when times were happier. The captain's words hit their mark, and I am reminded that resisting his generosity is denying him closure for losing someone dear to him.

"My father would have been extremely grateful for all that you and your crew have done for us. Again, thank you so much, and we will gladly accept these gifts on both his and our behalf," I say appreciatively.

I take the satchel, then Kristoff and I open it to find several silver and gold coins, a map of the Southlands, and a compass. I can't believe they gave us so much. This is more wealth than I have ever possessed, and I know it's more than some people from Fairfield would ever see in a lifetime. This small fortune puts my mind at ease, knowing we have money to survive while settling in the Southlands. After all, I'm not sure how long we would have to be there before I would be able to find my family.

"Thank you so much, seriously. I can't even begin to tell you how much this means to us," I say in awe of his generosity.

"Don't mention it, lass. Just be sure to keep that safe. As me mum always said, don't put all your eggs in one basket. Make sure to hide it about, yea?"

"Sure thing. Thanks so much, and thanks for the advice," Kristoff replies, equally shocked by the amount of money we had just been given. "Say, do you have any advice about how to carry ourselves in a way that doesn't make us a, umm—target? I didn't have the best luck with that in Fairfield," he says nervously.

"Well, the key is to not go looking for trouble, and if trouble finds ya, don't be afraid to answer it with force. Much better to lose a fight than to run from it. I will say, the people down here aren't as judgmental as up North, so I don't think ya would find the same kind of trouble if you get my drift. See to them, a bully is considered dishonorable, and many of the Southlanders take issue with that kind of behavior," the captain carefully chooses his words so as not to offend Kristoff. I smile to myself, knowing what they both mean. Kristoff is worried that the way he carries himself would cause issues in the Southlands like it had in Fairfield, something I had been concerned about myself.

The feast with the captain is the most fun I've had in months, more fun even than some of the times when life was normal. After hours of revelry with the captain and Kristoff, the feast begins to wind down, and we decide it's time to say our long, hard goodbyes to the crew. As we do, I am surprised to see the crew members having to wipe tears from their eyes.

I am sad to say goodbye to the ship. It was a place where I experienced darkness the likes of which I could never have imagined, but it also forced Kristoff and me to find a strength we didn't know we had.

We walk down the outstretched plank onto a wooden dock that seems old and unsteady. Before us lies a village situated along the ocean. I see several buildings, many of which are surrounded by trees and heavy vegetation. Dirt roads lead to the various buildings, and I can see dozens of people walking about or standing outside of structures, speaking casually to one another. The groups milling about outside remind me of citizens from the Apex. People there would often loiter, speaking to one another, showing off their newest accessories and clothing.

Many people before us are dressed in clothing equipped with pieces of armor, such as vests, wrist guards, and shin guards. The atmosphere is lively, but with the way these people carry themselves, it's clear they are prepared for combat at a moment's notice. I can't help but draw a comparison between the town and the Apex Capital. In the Capital, people worry about fashion to show that they have money, as opposed to the Southlands, where protection and self-defense are interwoven into their own version of style. From what I can see, nearly every person, women included, carries a sword or large dagger on their belt. I don't see a single woman wearing a dress, which pleases me. I like wearing dresses occasionally, but I prefer pants. I also know that Kristoff has to be happy seeing other men who take the time to look good, judging by both their outfits and their hair.

"This is like no place I've ever seen," says Kristoff, looking around, clearly mesmerized.

"Looks like for once you aren't the only man in town with great hair," I say, pretending to fix my dark brunette hair like he would, if he thought his was messy.

"Now, if only we could find a place where women don't care about their hair, then you could finally fit in. Perhaps you were supposed to be born in Anveil," he replies laughing.

"Hey!" I shout, gently hitting him for his well-timed, yet true insult.

"We need to find a tavern and ask the barkeep if he knows anyone from the Romani," I say as I scan the area for some sort of sign that could direct us. Sadly, the buildings don't have signs indicating what they are, and I am not about to ask anyone for directions and give away that we are new here. Judging from the looks we received, I figure the people can already tell we are fish out of water, and I am worried someone may try and test us.

After a short walk, we come to a building where lively fiddle music plays and we can see patrons within drinking and carrying on. I figure this must be a tavern, presumably one of many, if Stur's assessment of the Southlands is to be trusted.

"Okay, let's stay calm. Grab a table, and then we can ask about the clan," I say.

"Then you better wait out here if we need to appear calm."

"Very funny," I reply sarcastically before taking a deep breath and saying, "Let's go," prompting a nod from Kristoff.

Once inside, we sit at an open table and patiently wait for a barmaid to make her way to us. Kristoff and I have never been in a tavern before. Fairfield didn't have any, and we were much too young when we were in the Apex. However, I have read many stories about people in taverns, which gives me some insight into how I should carry myself.

The atmosphere is something I find almost overwhelming, but I love hearing the music. Three people are playing instruments that resemble various-sized fiddles. They play in a harmony that rivals that of the most prestigious Apexian orchestra, but unlike the Apex, these people seem to genuinely enjoy it. The Southlands remind me of my mom since everyone seems so full of life and carefree. Now that I see it firsthand, I can understand where my mother got some of her tendencies.

A barmaid approaches us and asks us what we want to drink. She is dressed in tight leather pants and a scarcely buttoned blouse. I take in the woman's ensemble and raise an eyebrow. Probably trying to show as much cleavage as possible for better tips.

"Two pints of ale, please," responds Kristoff, who I can tell is enjoying the music and seeing people dancing. After a few minutes, the barmaid returns with our pints. While Kristoff pays for the ale, I can tell that the barmaid expects to receive a better tip from a young man such as him, who, unbeknownst to her, is immune to her womanly charms.

Keeping my laughter to myself, I slide the barmaid a piece of silver. "Say, you wouldn't happen to know anyone who could put me in touch with a member of the Romani, would you?"

"Who's asking?" responds the barmaid coldly.

"Name is Aries, and this is my brother Kristoff."

"And what business is it you have with the Romani?"

"Our business is our own. We mean no harm," I reply, trying to be diplomatic, but the barmaid is beginning to test my patience. She nods and walks over to the barkeep, who then motions to a table where a group of rough-looking young men sit. One of the men rushes over to the barkeep, who then begins to whisper to the man. The man appears stunned by the news and waves the table again. I wonder what is going on. Perhaps they are just excited to see that someone is asking about them?

As we wait to sort out our conversation, I wonder if they are possibly some of my distant family. The largest of the men responds to the call. He makes his way to our table. The man looks as if he lifts heavy weights regularly on account of how large his muscles are. He has pale skin, a bald head that looks to be intentionally shaved, and a rather off-putting face, with his sizeable, crooked nose, pierced with a big gold hoop. He carries a very uninviting expression as he makes his way to our table, which makes me think whatever he wishes to say isn't going to be pleasant. I can see the people of the bar begin to take notice and start to stare, so much so that the band ceases playing, and several people run outside.

"Are you the one asking about the Romani?" The man demands aggressively, placing his hands on the table in an attempt to appear intimidating. He's large, much taller than an average man, and stronger-looking. I wish I had my father's sword right now. Size wouldn't matter if I put a hole in his chest. My hunting knife is in my bag, which is currently on my back, making it impossible to get without him noticing. Kristoff doesn't carry a weapon of any kind. The only way to navigate this conflict is with words.

"Yes. Is that a problem?" I respond.

"We aren't from around here. We're sorry. We didn't mean to offend," Kristoff interjects before receiving a glaring look from me, letting him know to stop talking. We can't appear weak, and nothing makes a bully sense weakness like apologizing.

"Well, ya see, it is a problem, because those filth aren't welcome here, and neither is anyone who associates with them, who has ever associated with them, or who plans to associate with them. Am I making myself clear?"

Perhaps under different circumstances, Kristoff and I could politely walk away from the situation. But I'm frustrated, which happens whenever someone is unnecessarily rude. As angry as I am, though, I have no intention of starting a fight in an unfamiliar land, surrounded by strangers and unknown social customs.

Kristoff, who apparently has been changed by his grief, decides he's no longer going to be talked to like that by people who wish to prey on those weaker than them. In one swift move, he smashes his metal cup of ale atop the man's head as hard as he can. I'm shocked.

Unfortunately, while Kristoff meant to subdue the man, his blow only serves to further infuriate him. The man quickly flips the table over and lunges toward Kristoff, grabbing him in a bear hug. I grab a wooden chair and break it over the man's back, prompting him to throw Kristoff to the ground and come after me.

"Oh, I will hit a girl, especially one with manners like yours," the man sneers, spitting disgustingly as he speaks.

Backing up, I'm met by a group of his friends. They're yelling and joking, apparently pleasantly surprised that two strangers decided to start a fight with the biggest among them. The man grabs me by my throat with one hand, which is more than big enough to actually choke me. I attempt to fight off his hand with mine, but his grip is too strong. Kristoff jumps on the man's back, trying to return the favor by choking him as well. He's using a technique my father had once tried to teach him, but he's doing it wrong. Letting go of me, the man uses both hands to grab Kristoff and throw him onto the floor. Kristoff quickly gets up and faces the man once again. I've never seen Kristoff with this kind of fight in him. I would be proud if I wasn't worried it might mean the death of us both.

"Do you feel tough? Picking fights with strangers who are half your size?" he asks, squaring up in front of the man, doing his best to strike a fighting stance.

He doesn't respond. Instead, he starts swinging haymaker punches. Luckily, Kristoff dodges them with relative ease. The man's muscles must significantly diminish his speed, I think. Kristoff eventually runs out of room, and the man grabs hold of him by the throat, this time using two hands, which I know is more than capable of choking him to death. I'm on my way to attack the man again, but before I can get there, Kristoff sticks a finger into the man's nose ring and rips it out. Blood begins gushing as the big man stumbles back, screaming in pain.

He feels his nose trying to assess the damage. He makes his way to the bar and looks at a mirror to see what Kristoff has done to him. Everyone in the bar stands in shocked silence. The man turns towards Kristoff, blood dripping down his face. As he walks, he slowly removes a dagger from its sheath.

"You're going to die for that," he threatens.

"Oy! Take it outside, Wolfe. I ain't cleaning your mess up!" The barkeep hollers.

Kristoff and I are forcefully ushered out of the bar by the crowd, and we hit the dirt road with a thud. I look up to see three men, all with smirks on their faces, looking down at us. The man in the middle has short brown hair, a strong jaw, and large lips. His eyes are green, and they are looking directly into my own. He's tall and has an athletic build, but he's not the tallest of the group. The man beside him stands about three inches taller than he does, and he has light brown skin and dark curly hair, that's pulled back. The man on the right is short, but very large and appears to be strong. Of the three, he has the kindest face. He has dark brown eyes that match his messy brown hair.

The rest of the crowd exits the bar, forming a half-circle behind us. Kristoff and I get to our feet, brushing the dirt off our clothing. I debate whether we should run for it, thinking perhaps Captain Rockwell and his crew are still docked at the pier. The three men standing outside might block our way. The large man referred to as Wolfe exits the bar, tossing his dagger from hand to hand.

"Well, you fancy a straight-up fight, ginger, or should I let you get the first shot again?" he taunts.

"Did he say your name was Wolfe? What sort of name is that? Please tell me you didn't name yourself?" asks Kristoff, causing the three men behind us to laugh.

"Don't mean to be rude, but you got a bit of blood, mate," says the man with the green eyes, making his two companions laugh.

"Wolfe's face done sprung a leak, eh? Tricky business, them nose rings," replies the shorter friend, who is clearly enjoying seeing Wolfe in this state.

"This doesn't concern you, Lee. This is Guul business."

"That's where you're wrong, isn't it? See, I have it on good authority these two outsiders requested parley with me and my lads, but you denied them. Is that straight?"

Wolfe's face contorts with anger. He doesn't speak to Lee like he did to Kristoff and me. Despite there being only three of them, I get the feeling Wolfe is afraid. The man with green eyes, who is called Lee, gives Kristoff and me a wink, followed by jerking his head backward to indicate that we should get behind them.

"This isn't happening. We have to finish this," says Wolfe angrily.

"Looks like it's finished mate, judging by the state of your face. Best to quit while you still have one nostril left," says Lee's tall friend, causing even some of the people from the bar to laugh.

"If you want to press the issue, that's your call, and if I'm honest, I'd much rather you did. But, seeing as how they called a parley, and I'm the acting Romani Enforcer at this pitiful excuse for a pub, I must protect them until they can meet the head," says Lee.

"Wolfe, it's not worth it. Save it for the games, mate," says one of Wolfe's men, trying to nudge him away from the fight.

Wolfe studies the situation, gripping his dagger so tightly that its leather hilt screeches. Lee slowly removes his jacket, displaying a blade of his own fastened to his belt on his right hip. "Just say when."

Wolfe breathes heavily, blood and snot running down his face. Then, just when it looks like he's about to make a lunge, he turns and stabs his dagger into the wooden door frame of the bar. "I will see you at the games. You can count on that," he growls before walking into the bar followed by his crew.

"Good lad," says Lee, using his jacket to conceal his dagger once again, smirk still on his face.

"Sorry 'bout them, they don't care for our lot. But I figure you gathered that much by now. Name's Lee. This tall young fellow here is Jaseen, and this strong and sturdy man is Andrew. Who might you be?" says Lee, reaching out his hand to shake.

I'm thankful they arrived when they did. I shudder to think about Kristoff in a duel with that giant of a man. I know I wouldn't have let anything happen to him because I would have interfered, but that probably would have meant our deaths.

After introducing ourselves, I explain that I'm trying to contact the Romani. I also tell them that my mother was a member who gave me a bracelet to show that my story is legitimate. For his part, Lee is cautious before he says too much by way of detail. After looking over the bracelet for a few moments, he hands it back to me and states he will share the information with the Head, and lead us to them.

"Good thing we arrived when we did, aye. I don't think Wolfe would have survived another round with this one," says Lee, patting Kristoff on the back. It's probably the first time in Kristoff's life that he's had a fight he could say he won, even if the victory is controversial. Despite the danger it placed us in, I find his actions inspiring.

"Well, don't leave us hanging. Spill the details!" Andrew says, laughing.

Kristoff enthusiastically tells the story of what happened, and I find myself thinking that if I hadn't seen it with my own eyes, I wouldn't have believed the tale. The trio laughs heavily at the story, thanking Kristoff for putting Wolfe in his place. I have not seen him this happy in a long time.

As we walk, they explain the seaside town to us, giving pointers about safe areas and places to avoid. They tell us about the Faire that's going on, explaining why clans from all over the Southlands happen to be here now. It sounds like a celebration full of tests of skill, dancing, drinking, and food.

We've only been in the Southlands for a few hours and have already gotten into a fight that could have easily turned deadly. But I still don't feel like it was nearly as bad as Stur said. Thus far, it seems like an exciting place that's strangely dangerous—yet accepting and lively. It's as if there's no formal law enforcement, but many strict rules that guide things, making such a role unnecessary. After getting a tour of the town, we come to another tavern. This one is two stories and overlooks the sea, and just like the first tavern, I can hear live music coming from within. Several people outside of the pub welcome Lee and his friends by name as they arrive.

"Sorry, but I have to run in and get the go-ahead before you lot can come in. Don't worry, nobody will trouble you here. Not like you two would care though, eh," says Lee as he pretends to box with Kristoff. I feel that his dialogue is exhausting. He has so much energy, and he carries himself like he's larger than life. I know that in due time, I'll find his personality annoying. But perhaps in a humorous way, at least, I hope. While we wait for Lee and his crew to return, we catch sight of the full moon, which appears to rest directly above the sea.

"It's beautiful, isn't it?" says Kristoff.

"Yeah, it is. Sure beats staring at farmland every day. But hey, instead of the view, can we talk about how you fought a giant and won?"

"I don't know what got into me. It's like I'm just not afraid anymore. I can't really explain it."

"I know what you mean. If you get angry enough, then nothing seems scary, not even death," I say as I throw a rock into the sea, making a barely noticeable splash in the choppy waves.

"Yeah, exactly. I'd have gladly died back there. I hate what happened, obviously, but one good thing is I feel free. Life is no longer scary, and we have nothing left to lose," he says.

"Well, besides each other. But that won't happen," I say, realizing I'm frowning. I quickly dawn a fake smile.

"What if the clan doesn't accept me because I'm not related?" says Kristoff, changing the subject before the conversation turns to one of sorrow.

"If they don't accept you, then they don't accept me. We're a package deal. I debated lying to them, but I doubt they'd buy it on account of your fire hair and big ears."

"Do you think it can find us here?" says Kristoff, not fazed by my attempt at a joke.

I know he's talking about the Revenant, and I had considered it, but I doubt that it would be able to. "I don't think it can swim this far," I say, throwing another rock into the ocean.

"Who's to say someone won't just unleash him here like they did in Redwood?"

"That's why we are going to train every day. But honestly, I hope I get the chance to face it again, don't you?" I ask.

"More than anything. I am going to rip its head off and throw it out to sea. Let's see it put it back on then. Maybe it can spend eternity stuck on the seafloor. It deserves no less," he replies with conviction.

"Oy! the Head is ready for ya," yells one of Lee's friends, whose name I've already forgotten. I'm terrible with names, and judging by the clan's size, I worry there's no way I'll ever remember everyone.

We walk up the dirt path to the two-story tavern. It isn't exactly the nicest quality, but I like how welcoming it feels. The music is even better than at the other pub we had been to, although I know I may be a little biased with how things ended there. Once we step inside, the music comes to a halt, and everyone is staring at us, making our arrival awkward. Oh great, the two outsiders who have been causing trouble in town and almost caused a clan war just entered the pub and ruined the dance music. I had hoped we would be welcomed warmly, but after all that had happened in just a few short hours, I'm not so sure a warm welcome is possible.

"You look just like your mother, thank Gaia. I have been waiting for this moment for ages, Aries," says a plump woman wearing a casual dress and no shoes. Her hair is mainly white, with slight traces of brown. She is short, jolly, and extremely welcoming. Her dark brown skin is smooth and without blemishes. She gives me a big hug, lifting me off the ground, despite her short stature. "And who is this?" she says before also giving Kristoff a big hug. "Oh, blessed be! This is cause for celebration! It is destiny fulfilled, but I am sure you knew that."

I begin to cry, but I don't know why. Maybe it's because of how warm and friendly the woman's voice is. Or because she has welcomed us without question. Or maybe it's simply because this is the first nurturing voice I've heard from a woman since my mother passed. I finally feel safe for the first time since we left Fairfield, and I'm surrounded by people who are happy to see us, though I don't know a single person in the room. I try to hide my tears, and the woman takes notice and signals to the musicians that they should begin to play again. As the music fills the room once more, the woman walks us to a table on the second floor. I notice Lee seated there, along with several other people dressed similarly to him. They wear coats and have scarfs tied around their necks. Many of them wear clothing that's forest green, which I presume is a clan color.

"You two must be exhausted, bless your hearts. Food and drink for our friends, please," I hear the woman say to a barmaid.

Kristoff and I provide a limited description of the past few months to the woman, who listens intently, hanging on every detail. She is small and kind beyond measure, and she seems to possess a strange glow that I can't quite understand. It's difficult to describe, but I know there's something extraordinary about her, and that she is most likely the Crone my father told me I needed to find.

"There will be plenty of time to talk about everything in the morning," says the woman, smiling kindly. "Tonight is a celebration, a wonderful festivity. Our beautiful family has arrived. Everyone, welcome Kristoff and Aries, treat them both like blood, for in the eyes of Gaia we are all brothers and sisters, and for it is through the love of her that we are all beautiful!" she yells to the crowd below, prompting them to cheer and drink from their mugs.

"So, I understand you've met Lee and his friends. No finer blade in all the land than our Lee. He is going to bring our clan another tournament championship title at this year's Faire. That's why we are here, after all. This is the fall equinox, and every fall equinox, each clan from the Southlands meets to compete, share in brotherhood, and celebrate. Our Lee here will show you the ropes and keep you safe. I understand some Guul have already picked a fight with you. It's a shame because the Faire is supposed to help keep the peace, and yet they want to start a war."

I nod, drinking from the mug that has been handed to me by the barmaid. It tastes like tea with honey or sugar.

"Yes, all we did was ask if there was anyone that could put us in touch with your clan," says Kristoff as he slathers his dinner roll with butter.

"Your clan too," says the woman smiling.

His face lights up at her comment. "Sorry. Our clan. But then this large man they called Wolfe aggressively introduced himself. He started threatening Aries, so I smashed him in the face with a metal mug. There was a scuffle, and then I pulled out his nose ring."

"Oh, my dear!" says the woman laughing and slapping her leg. Her laughter extends for several moments and seems to be contagious to everyone at the table.

"And then he pulled out a dagger and wanted to fight to the death," Kristoff continues, "and that's when Lee showed up, and Wolfe backed down."

"He knew he'd have been dead in seconds if he challenged our Lee to a duel. Besides, they know the rule of parley. I have half a mind to go and speak to them myself. But all's well that ends well, and I don't want to ruin this blessed moment with further conflict."

The party continues for some time before I remember the letter my father had given me. "I was told by my father that I needed to give this to you, I believe. It's from my mother, and I am not supposed to open it until you get it. Also, I need to show you this," I hold out my hand displaying the bracelet. "I was told it belonged to you."

The woman takes the sealed letter and the bracelet from me and slowly studies it before smiling warmly. "Of course, dear. But it is not the time to open this just yet. I will let you know when. Thank you so much for the bracelet. I gave it to your mother years ago when she left for the north."

Before I could express my frustration about waiting to open the letter, the woman stands up quickly, clapping her hands. "I almost forgot. I have something for you!" I wonder how she could possibly have something for me, since there was no way she could have known I would be here on this day. The woman returns after a few moments with a wooden box that is a little over a foot long.

"Well, don't just stand there, open it. Actually, wait! Everyone! Gather around. Aries is going to open the box," says the woman.

"Bout time! Mum's been carrying that bloody thing around for years, not telling any of us what it was for and swearing us to an oath that we wouldn't look inside," jokes Lee, who makes his way over to our table, curiosity in his eyes.

I sit at the table studying the box while everyone in the pub watches me. They look on intently, and, once again, the music stops. I'm not typically bothered by awkward situations, but I feel my face reddening from everyone's eyes on me.

"Well, what are you waiting for? Open the damn thing! We've been waiting longer than you," jokes Lee, prompting a round of laughter.

I study the wooden box resting on my lap, trying to guess what's inside, based on the weight. After coming to terms with the fact I'll never be able to guess its contents, I take a deep breath and slowly open the lid—revealing a beautiful dagger.

The blade is flawlessly crafted but doesn't seem to have a sharp edge. On the metal, there's an etched symbol that I've never seen before, made up of three separate spirals which meet one another in the middle. Moving my eyes further along the dagger, I see that it possesses a small but formidable-looking crossbar that would protect its wielder's hand during a clash. Its hilt is wrapped in dark black leather that looks brand new. Most breathtaking of all is the bottom of the hilt, encrusted with a marvelous stone that sparkles in various colors of red. I'm at a loss for words. I can't believe this is mine and don't feel worthy of owning it.

"Your mother wanted you to have it, Aries. It was hers, although she never wielded it to my knowledge," says Mum.

"It's breathtaking. I don't know what to say. Thank you so much," I reply, eyes wide and mouth agape.

"That symbol is the triskelia. It means harmony. Between the mind, body, and spirit, the symbol promotes balance in those who wield it. And the stone, yay the stone. I love the stone. It is a blood-red amethyst, very scarce indeed. I don't think I have ever seen one so large." Mum smiles before continuing. "And this is the best part: amethysts are said to protect against negative emotions, such as grief and sadness, and they are believed to increase psychic awareness and disrupt psychic attacks."

"Does it actually work?" I ask.

"Depends on how much you believe, my dear. But that's with anything, I suppose."

"Aries, I think that is even better than Stur's axe if I'm honest," says Kristoff, equally mesmerized by the dagger.

"Thank you so much for carrying this for so long. You are the nicest person I've ever met. Seriously, thank you for everything."

I can feel my eyes welling up again, overcome by their generosity, and the connection I feel to my mother, who possessed this very same dagger. I don't know why my mother left it with the Romani. How could she have known that I would find my way to them one day? The last several weeks had challenged my entire belief system regarding magic, the world, and my parents, and it seemed that the more I learned, the less I knew.

Sensing that I'm becoming emotional, Mum signals for the celebration to begin once more. "There will be plenty of time to catch up in the morning. Tonight, we dance and celebrate. Come, Kristoff, show me how they move in your lands."

"Umm, they don't dance there," replies Kristoff blushing, clearly nervous about the prospect of dancing in front of everyone.

"Even better! Now I get to teach you, and I can't dance either, so we will both look a fool!" she says, smiling big as she pulls Kristoff to the dance floor.

"So, what ya think then?" asks Lee, nodding at the dagger. I notice that he's the only other person at the table.

"It's perfect. I have never seen such a remarkable weapon, save for an axe that was made in Anveil," I reply, still staring at the dagger, holding it up to the light.

"True, but it ain't all about the weapon. It's what you do with it, right?"

I sense that he's trying to feel out how skilled I am with a blade. "I think I will be okay," I say, smirking.

"Well, maybe you enter the games then? We could use another representative."

"Oh yea, and what event would you have me register for?"

"Whatever you like, love. As for me, the only event I care to win is the tournament championship. One-on-one duels, fighter's choice of weapon, so long as it's melee range, and made of wood as to prevent death, of course," he says as he kicks his feet on the table, one foot laying over the other, his hands resting on the back of his head.

"I'm confused. How can you be so calm now that you'll have to explain to everyone that you are going to be getting second place since I'm entering the duels as well? Seeing as you are supposed to be the favorite in all."

Lee laughs. "I have seen stranger things happen. Plus, no way your dad would let ya come all the way to the Southlands without knowing your way around a weapon. I wager you are a fierce competitor beneath all that beauty. Let's just say, no matter what happens, no hard feelings, eh?"

Lee spits in his hand before reaching it out so that we can shake on his proposal. I reluctantly spit in my own hand before shaking his, in what I think could quite possibly be the most awkward handshake of all time. To make it even more uncomfortable, I find myself staring into his light green eyes for far too long. I eventually pull my gaze away, hoping he hasn't noticed my lingering eyes. I find myself drawn to his charm and confidence, but, confusingly, I'm also annoyed by it. On the one hand, I want him to do well in the tournament because I know it would make him and everyone happy, yet I also want to see him fall flat on his face so he wouldn't be so cocky.

"Tell me—the big man from earlier, will he be in any of the events?" I ask, hoping to redirect the conversation before he has a chance to make a comment about me staring.

"Course he will. Every year he goes for tourney champion. Last year he came in second, despite being a twat."

"Really? Who'd he lose to?"

"Oy, mate! Who won the last tourney champion? I can't seem to remember," asks Lee to a nearby table of clan members.

"Why, of course, it was our very own, amazing, overly-talented, and equally false modest, Lee! Best dressed in all the land. Pity he has the personality of a wet sack of potatoes," says Andrew, causing those around him to laugh.

"Funny, never heard of him," I reply, prompting both of them to laugh.

I join Kristoff and the others on the dance floor, even though I'm not particularly fond of dancing. Then again, I've never been to a dance where the people enjoyed themselves. In the Apex, the dances were formal and served as a venue for citizens to show off their status and discuss business propositions. The Southlanders, on the other hand, were dancing and singing along to the music with not a care in the world about how they look, simply enjoying themselves and one another.

After many hours, the night comes to an end, and the clan retires to their sleeping quarters, which I discover are at a campground near the tavern.

There are dozens upon dozens of horse-drawn "caravans" as they call them, scattered throughout the camp. Each caravan has a fully enclosed carriage with two rows of open seats at the front of the structure and a cabin area that is much shorter than a typical Apexian carriage. I presume the cabin is shorter because it's made for sleeping, not sitting, and thanks to the Romani leaving their carriage doors open, my presumption is confirmed. Each of the carriages appears to have been built with comfort in mind. They are filled with thick blankets or quilts, and many comfortable pillows. The sight alone makes me instantly tired.

"Jaseen and Andrew, would you two please be so kind and bunk together so we can let Kristoff and Aries have one of your caravans for the night?"

"Not a problem, so long as nobody wets the bed, eh," says Jaseen as he slaps Kristoff on the back.

"No promises, mate," replies Kristoff, who does his best impression of a Southlander accent.

"To be fair, Andrew's caravan is like a luxury suite compared to mine, so it would be worth a little pee," says Jaseen.

I notice Kristoff's behavior has changed drastically since arriving in the Southlands. He's laughing a lot more and being far more social than I've seen him in months. I wonder what it must be like for him to finally feel accepted by everyone. While the Southlanders like to poke fun, it's clear that their words carry no harmful intentions.

Kristoff and I settle into the caravan that was lent to us for the night, both of us ready to get some sleep. When I lay my head down on the pillow, I think I'll drift off right away, but I find myself wide awake. There's so much that I want to talk about, so many questions, and so much I want to share with the one they called Mum. Not to mention, I want to learn more about this tournament I somehow talked myself into participating in. I'm not afraid of the danger the event may pose, but I'm nervous about being embarrassed in front of the entire clan, especially Lee. I wonder why I worry what he thinks. He is just an arrogant Southlander and I'd never hear the end of it, I tell myself, even though I know that isn't the only reason I don't want to be embarrassed in front of him.

"Do you think my parents would have liked it here?" asks Kristoff, sounding like he has already given the question a lot of thought.

"It would have been different than what they were used to, but they would enjoy it, I think. Don't you?"

"Yea, except for my dad. I don't think he would have liked all the fighting and loud music," replies Kristoff with a laugh.

"True, but you could teach him your nose ring removal trick, and he'd be set."

Kristoff and I share a laugh before finally drifting to sleep. I have many vivid dreams. Some of them are about the Southlands, while others are about what's happening to the North. I see two giant armies engaged in a pitched battle on an open field. They march toward one another. One group is dawning the Apex symbol of the One True God, and their opponents wield a banner with what appears to be a raven.

Men in armor meet head-to-head while large groups of archers fire volleys, trying to keep cavalries at bay. With force, the Apex cavalry breaks through one of the flanks, and it seems as if the enemy will be routed at any moment. Just before that can happen, airships begin to rain fire from above. These aren't Apexian vessels, though; these ships fly a coat of arms with a raven, matching the opposing army's banner from below. The casualties on both sides are catastrophic, and yet the battle rages on. When one man falls, another quickly replaces him. This cycle continues repeating until the Apexian army tries to flee, but it's no use. The opposing airships pursue and rain fire once again, blocking their retreat. The soldiers are forced to walk through the flames or turn and face the approaching army.

I awake to a cool breeze spilling into the caravan as Kristoff opens the door on his way outside. My dream lingers in my mind, and I can't help but wonder why it was so vivid. Perhaps Mum is right, and the dagger's amethyst possesses extraordinary abilities. Or maybe my hatred for the Apex causes me to imagine a made-up army giving them a taste of their own medicine. I smirk at the thought as I lay on my pillow.

I always struggle waking up in the morning, but with so much to look forward to, it doesn't take long to get up and prepare for the day. I even take the extra time to brush my hair and style it in a bun. It's difficult to change in the caravan since the ceiling of the enclosed carriage is so low, but I eventually succeed, very much without grace, and then step outside. I can see that most of the Romani members are already awake and sitting around small campfires directly outside their caravans. The aroma and sizzle of breakfast cooking on cast-iron pans fill the campground, instantly making me hungry.

"Wow, you actually did your hair for once," Kristoff says when he notices me emerging from the caravan.

"Har har har," I reply, still much too tired to concoct a witty comeback.

"Oy! Guys, come grab some breakfast. You need your strength. Today is registration day for the Faire, and you don't want to have to pay to eat there, highway robbery it is," says Lee, who is sitting at a campfire with Jaseen and Andrew, who seem to go with him nearly everywhere.

I sigh. "I just woke up, and he is already at it."

"At what?" asks Kristoff, laughing.

"At being himself."

"Oh well, since you put it that way. Yeah, he can be a bit much. But you must admit, he is very likable," he says, giving me a wink.

"Yeah, if you like overly confident people who try too hard to be funny."

"Weird, you didn't mention his good looks and dreamy green eyes."

We make our way over to Lee's campfire and sit on a pair of wooden, three-legged stools. We are given metal forks with two long prongs meant for piercing a piece of meat directly out of the pan and eating it without the need for a plate.

"See, this is proper eating. No napkins, no plates, just a fork, meat, and a bladder of sweetened cold tea," Andrew says before taking a big swig from his drinking bladder.

"So, tell me about this registration. What do we have to do?" I ask.

"It's more of a formality really. You just let them know your event, and then they make sure you are of age, not drunk, and all that good stuff. Simple," Jaseen says, using a large knife to remove the outer bark from a piece of wood.

"What events are there?" asks Kristoff.

"For the main ones, you got the tourney champion duels, of course. Then bow, the gauntlet, a horseback race, and lots of smaller events you can do throughout the day. You fancy any of those?" asks Jaseen.

"Well, I am pretty good with a bow, but what is the gauntlet?"

"It's brutal. It's a long run through an obstacle course, full of climbing and such. Then you got to solve a puzzle at the end. As with any race, whoever finishes first is the winner. The Swindletor Clan almost always wins it, sadly," answers Andrew.

"Probably because they are used to running from trouble," Lee comments. "They are known for thieving. They give the islands a bad rep if you ask me."

"Have to admit, they are a clever lot when it comes to making money without earning it," replies Andrew.

"How many clans are there in total on the islands?" asks Kristoff.

"Five in total of the major clans. It's a lot like your realms, except clans act more like a family than just being citizens of the same country. Well, the Romani at least," says Jaseen.

"So, each clan occupies a region?" I ask.

"Yep, exactly. Don't you worry, though, you lot will get the hang of it soon enough. Kristoff, can we put you down for the gauntlet, mate? I saw that look in your eye when he explained it, yeah, like a tiger this one! Even has the orange fur," says Lee before rubbing the top of Kristoff's head, messing up his hair. Kristoff doesn't seem to mind, but as soon as Lee is done, he quickly fixes his disheveled hair.

"I don't know, I think—" Kristoff begins before being cut off by Lee.

"Tell you what, how about we let the fates decide, eh? I'll spin you for it," says Lee.

"Sorry, what does that mean?" asks Kristoff, who sounds like he has a frog in his throat.

"Each coin has two sides, right? You toss it, and I call which side it will land on. If I am right, then you do the gauntlet," answers Lee before removing a silver coin from his pocket.

"And if I win?" Kristoff replies, clearly nervous about the proposition of losing.

"Well, name your terms, mate," says Lee, grinning.

"If I win, then Aries does the bow event."

The mention of my name draws me into the conversation. "Wait, I never agreed to that."

"Come on, it will be fun," Lee replies.

"Oy, everyone! Lee and Kristoff are about to spin a coin!" yells Andrew, prompting a crowd to gather around the campfire.

"Okay, toss it in the air to make it spin. Then, while it's in the air, I call out what I pick before it hits the ground. This side with the scratch will be top, and the smooth side will be bottom."

Kristoff nods in agreement, taking the coin in his hand so he can examine both sides, presumably to make sure it's marked correctly. I hope Lee wins. I know that I would completely embarrass myself in a bow competition. I don't have the patience to master the bow. In fact, it was one of the only weapons my father let me give up on because of how bad I was.

Kristoff flips the coin. It's in the air for what feels like an eternity before Lee yells out, "Top!" The coin falls to the ground, and everyone circles around it so I can't see the result.

"Make way, make way, not all at once," says Lee as he ushers his way to the coin, holding his hands in the air to demonstrate he hasn't touched it.

"Well, good news, bad news, mate," says Jaseen.

"Oh yeah, what's the bad news?" asks Kristoff.

"Bad news is you lost the spin. The good news is we finally have a proper contender for the gauntlet!" says Jaseen, prompting the crowd to cheer loudly, while Kristoff stands quietly looking petrified.

We spend the rest of the morning eating, drinking, and telling stories with the others. I'm still getting used to the behavior of the Romani, or maybe it's the behavior of all Southlanders in general. I gather that they often tell stories of one another in a highly complementary yet insulting way, but no one seems to mind. It reminds me of how Kristoff and I interact. We diffuse intense moments by poking fun at one another, which some find to be in poor taste.

"Now, remember lovelies, this is registration day, and any behavior violating the rules could get you, or the entire clan, barred from competition. We all know the Guul would love if that happened. So, let's behave appropriately, and remember: the Faire is meant to bring the clans together. And let us not forget, we are honoring the fall equinox and Gaia for her bountiful blessings, which come from the harvest. Winning is fun, but doing so without dignity is worse than losing," says Mum, standing atop a three-legged stool so that she can look out over the crowd of Romani, all of whom are much taller than her.

I notice she's wearing a gorgeous dress. It's yellow and green and reminds me of sunflowers. I can't help but smile, because even though it's still early in the day, there are fresh dirt spots along the hem of the dress.

"Also, we have two guests joining us today, and after the Faire, if they so choose, we may be lucky enough to make it official. Blessed be! Until then, please keep an eye out as they continue to learn the ways of our beautiful islands," she continues, drawing a round of applause from the crowd.

I hadn't really considered whether we would become official clan members. The plan was to meet up with my mother's family, but I'm not sure what we should do next. I'd love to train, learn, and improve as much as possible. That way, I will be able to destroy the Revenant, and whoever controls it, once and for all.

"Also, let's not go and blow your hard-earned coin on games of chance," says Lee, which prompts some of the clan members to push him around. Judging by their response and the coin flip from earlier, I assume Lee is the type of person to enjoy the thrill of gambling, perhaps too much even. Overconfident people often find themselves prone to gambling since they believe they can win, despite the odds.

After the crowd is addressed by Mum, we make our walk to the Faire grounds. As we draw closer, I can see smoke rising from atop the trees, followed by the sound of music, voices, and people cheering. I wonder how many people will be there, hoping it isn't too many, just in case I perform horribly in the event tomorrow. I am anxious because I don't know the rules. I wonder if the dueling event will be like fencing in the Apex Capital, where a person needs to touch the opponent with the tip of their dull blade to score a point, or if it is full contact, where people hit one another with full power.

"Here, I got you lot something," says Lee, handing each of us a green scarf. "Wear these, and I doubt anyone tries to mess with ya. Especially if they take Kristoff for the ginger who ripped out Wolfe's nose ring," he chuckles. "Still probably best to steer clear of the Guul, until they have time to gather their pride back."

"Thanks, Lee!" says Kristoff, who quickly fashions the scarf around his neck, tying his knot the same as many of the Romani members.

"Don't mention it. Should have known ole Kristoff here wouldn't have any trouble making his scarf look proper. I still have to help show our lads how to do it most times," says Lee, impressed.

Kristoff smiles shyly; he is still getting used to being complimented on his fashion. In Fairfield, he was bullied for it. In the Apexian Cities, being fashionable is expected. Still, it is rare for anyone to sincerely praise one another.

"Thanks, Lee, but isn't it a little hot in the Southlands for scarves to be a staple of the Romani?" I ask.

"Don't worry, it gets plenty cold in our lands. Plus, it's a small price to pay for looking good, yeah? Oh, and one more thing, make sure to keep your coin purses tied with a strong knot, as to stop thieving."

"Nobody will take my coins, I can assure you of that. Thievery isn't exclusive to the Southlands," I reply, becoming annoyed by Lee's advice. I typically welcome guidance, but there's something about how he gives it.

"Then what's this?" says Lee grinning widely, followed by tossing my coin purse back to me, before jogging off to catch up to Andrew and Jaseen. I let out a sigh before tying the coin purse back to my belt, this time with a much more secure knot. "He's never going to let me live that down. Now I am going to have to steal something of his," I say, annoyed.

Kristoff ties a more secure knot to his own coin purse. "You have to admit, he's charming. Maybe the most charming person I've ever met."

"Really? Hi, I am Aries. We must not have met," I reply, my voice full of sass.

The closer we get to the Faire grounds, the more I can smell the savory aromas coming from the food vendors. It wasn't long since we ate, but the delicious smells drifting about make me hungry again.

The Faire is much larger than I could have imagined. Countless tents and wooden structures fill a vast field. I notice a small man juggling torches that are literally on fire as he walks through the crowd. He's shouting to encourage people to shop from a vendor selling meats on a stick. There are dancers, musicians, people reading fortunes, and countless other shops selling all manner of clothing, armor, and weapons. I've never seen anything like it, especially the massive wooden coliseum structure in the center of the grounds. It's gigantic and looks to have enough seating to accommodate everyone at the Faire, and if by chance it couldn't, the others could conveniently watch from the several makeshift pubs that sit atop a large hill overlooking it.

"Please tell me that is not where the duels are going to be held?" I ask Kristoff nervously.

"You are done for. I mean, what else would that behemoth be used for?"

"Oy, Aries! Aries!" shouts Lee, trying to get my attention before giving up and walking over to speak to me. I ignore him as I stare at the stage, thinking about all the different ways I could look like a fool in front of what seems to be every single person in the entire Southlands.

"That's where it will be tomorrow! Exciting, isn't it?" says Lee, oblivious to my anxiety.

"Look, I don't know about this—it's a lot. Like, a lot of people watching. I have never fought in front of a crowd that big before."

"Trust me, after your first wallop, you will forget anyone is watching. Plus, our clan will be cheering you on, no matter how you do."

"Still, I don't know. Thinking about it makes me feel like I could puke."

"There ain't no rules about throwing puke at your opponent. Looks like you got a secret weapon, eh?" replies Lee trying to make me laugh. "In all seriousness, your mom was one of the greatest warriors in our clan, not just recently, but of all time. There's no way you can't hold your own in there. Plus, it ain't just about winning, is it? Failure teaches you to get better, so if you remember that, no matter what happens, you win."

I appreciate his support, and I have to admit it does help a little. I'm still worried about looking foolish in front of everyone. "I just don't want to look stupid," I reply.

"Look stupid to who? These people? You don't even know them."

"Yeah, but still."

"Still what? They aren't better than you. Hell, of all these people, only a few enter the tourney anyway. So, who are they to talk?"

"Yeah, I guess you're right." I sigh. "I hope I get paired against you first. That way, I have at least one guaranteed win," I say jokingly.

"Just look at me with those eyes, love—and I will be powerless," he replies, before walking away.

I wonder why he would say that so casually and then leave. How cliché is it for a man to say that to a woman? But, of course, I know I would be lying if I said no part of me liked it. And the part of me that did—wishes we could have finished the conversation.

Kristoff and I continue to explore the Faire, eating and drinking from the various vendors and spending way too much coin. It's safe to say we both love the food of the Southlands. It has a variety that Fairfield couldn't come close to. And there's a simple yet tasteful quality that Apexian food lacks. In the Apex, food is more about looking good, or being expensive or exotic. Most of the time, this does not equate to tasting good. I remember the time I had been so excited to eat octopus legs because they were so rare and popular. I threw up inside a fancy restaurant after I finally got the chance to try them. Most people's parents would have died from shock, but my mother and father thought it was hilarious. They never really fit in at the Apex. Sure, they could play the part when needed, but they didn't care about their social status.

Compared to the Apex, the Southlands is a dream, and the more I learn, the more I fall in love with it. Despite what Stur said about Southlanders, there were plenty of friendly people who were more than happy to explain things to us. Although, I did see more than a few questionable characters that I could tell were looking for easy targets. I wonder if the scarfs from Lee dissuaded them from trying something or if it was because I grabbed the hilt of my dagger and stared at them harshly, frequently embarrassing Kristoff and causing him to call me paranoid.

While wandering through the grounds, we come to an area with several large tents, each one labeled for their respective event.

"Are we sure we want to do this?" I ask Kristoff, partly hoping he's as nervous as I am and would talk me out of it.

"Yeah, definitely. I think I have a real shot in the gauntlet. If nothing else, it will be cool to say that we did it, right? Think of how many people in the Apex are terrified at the thought of coming to the Southlands. Not only did we do that, but we get to compete against them also."

"You're right. Let's do it. But let's make a pact not to laugh if one of us loses miserably. Deal?" I reply.

"Deal. But seriously, you fought a revenant. Stop being nervous. It's a bit ridiculous, really," says Kristoff, before walking away.

I now find myself inside a large tent full of hard-looking people, many of whom I notice are much bigger than me. I walk up to an old man sitting at a table with several papers in front of him.

"Can I help you?" he asks.

"Yes, I would like to register for the event."

"You realize this is the duel event? The one to decide tourney champion, miss?"

I am annoyed. Does he not think I am cut out for this type of event because I am a woman? "Is that a problem?" I ask coldly.

"No, lass. I must ask everyone before they register. Don't know if you can tell, but many people are drunker than usual—which is saying something for this lot. Being too drunk leads to them signing up for things that they didn't mean to. So, a simple yes or no, and we can get ya set up, miss."

"Oh, I'm sorry. "Yes, I would like to register," I reply, embarrassed at myself for assuming he was being offensive.

"And you give your word to fight with respect and dignity, with no outside influences, no cheating of any kind, only using wooden weapons, following the judge's orders, and promising to engage in no quarrel outside of the event because of what may have happened to you inside the event?"

"Yes, I do."

"Okay, and how much have you had to drink today?"

"Just water and tea."

He looks at me closely as if to suggest my report of no drinking at all is unbelievable. "No whiskey, no ale, no rum, no malts, no drinks of any kind that may have caused you to think you're tougher than you are? And mind you, once the pairings are made, you are required by the agreed-upon clan peace to fight, and nobody can fight in your place. Failure to do so could result in spending the rest of the tourney in the stockade, subject to ridicule and various food throwing."

"Yes, no drinks of any kind. And yes, I will be there tomorrow."

"Okay, cheers and good luck tomorrow."

"Don't you need my name?"

"Aye, and what's your name?"

"It's Aries Fleetwood, from the Romani."

"Thanks, sorry. Let's just say I can't answer no to the question about drinks. It's been a long day," replies the man, laughing. "Next, talk to that old geezer over there, and he will get your weapon selection down. Be quick as they need to handcraft them all by tonight."

I go and stand in a line of people waiting to speak with the other man who looks even older than the last. I notice Wolfe, is standing a few spots ahead of me. I hope he didn't see me, mainly because I don't want to let Mum down by losing my temper and getting the entire clan kicked out of the Faire. While I wait, I listen as people select their weapons, most of which choose swords, but some choose battle-axes or clubs. I wonder how most of these weapons would translate to being in the form of wood. As I consider the weapon choices of those in front of me, I suddenly realize that I don't know which weapon would be best for me. I had assumed I'd use a rapier, but if it's made from wood, it wouldn't be very effective. The rapier's strength comes from being quick and flexible, a quality unlikely to be captured in a wooden version.

While I contemplate what I would use, I hear Wolfe select a battle-axe, with a particular emphasis on it not just being big but the very biggest one in the event. After a long time of debating with the man about how big he needs his axe, and being told there is only so much they could do with woodworking weapons, he turns around and notices me. His face is just as unwelcoming as the first time I had seen him, only now it sports a gaping hole where his nose ring used to be.

"Well, look who it is," says Wolfe in an arrogant tone.

"How's it going, Wolfe? Attack any random strangers today?"

"Not yet, but it looks like I might get the chance tomorrow. Hopefully, I get to make Lee watch me crush you before I crush him."

"Wow, that's a lot of crushing, but I guess you did get second place last year, right? So close, but remind me, who beat you?" I say, prompting Wolfe to walk away, clearly angered by my comment. He must also be worried about getting kicked out of the Faire because that was too easy.

"Next! What weapon?" says the old man who only briefly looks up at me from the piece of parchment before him.

"What are my options?" I ask.

"We can make you nearly anything you want. So, you tell me."

"Do you know how to make a rapier?"

"Aye, but it would be snapped in half like a twig. If you fancy using a sword, you will have to go with a bastard sword. We can make it lighter for you if you prefer."

"Okay, I will take that. The name's Aries, from the Romani."

"Gotcha down. Good luck, lass."

I walk outside of the registration tent, more nervous than when I walked in. This is real now, and according to clan law, I can't back out. I wonder why a land of no laws cared so much about tournament event participation.

"Did you register?" asks Kristoff, clearly excited for his event that didn't involve the entire Southlands watching him potentially get beaten with a wooden axe.

"Yeah, I did. I had to go with a bastard sword because a rapier would break, they said."

"Damn, I didn't think about that. You will still do fine. I know you will."

We then continue to walk around the grounds going to the areas we had not explored yet. I take my mind off being nervous by watching several people fail miserably while trying to climb to the top of a rope to ring a bell. I notice most of the people trying the event are muscular, similar to Wolfe, and that those muscles do not help them climb. Pretty soon, these muscular giants are going to be swinging wooden axes at me in front of the entire Faire. I just need to make them swing until they get tired.

After a few more hours of exploring all the sites we could find at the Faire, we meet up with our clan members before making the walk back to camp as a unit. Each one shares their adventures from the day's events, ranging from great deals they made trading items all the way to laughing about how they made a fool of themselves. I enjoy the Faire, but I am excited to get back to the camp. Part of me wants to relax, and the other part wants to train. As much as I don't want to ask his advice, I know I should talk with Lee about what the events are like and what pointers he had. When we arrive at the camp, we see that several people are once again preparing food outside of their caravans.

"They sure do like to eat down here, don't they?" asks Kristoff.

"Yeah, I guess that's what happens when most of your food isn't taken by the Apex," I reply.

Seeing how happy people were in the Southlands often made me think about just how poor the conditions were for many of the people under the Apex's rule. I wonder what it would be like in Fairfield if they weren't forced to give away their crops and coin to the Apex. To make matters worse, the only direct interaction the people of Fairfield had had with the Apex in decades resulted in them becoming victims of a firebombing. Whenever I have these thoughts, my mind would eventually lead to one place: the Revenant. At first, I was afraid, certain the creature was lurking somewhere nearby, but then I thought about what it had done, what it had cost us, and my fear was replaced with rage that fueled my desire to face it again. Kristoff is right. If I survived an encounter with the Revenant, then I will survive a duel with wooden weapons.

"Aries and Kristoff, didn't you just love the Faire, my dears? Oh, wasn't it so lovely? I just adore all of the different shops and crafts. There is nothing more beautiful than people coming together to celebrate one another," says Mum, who although she is speaking to us, looks as though her mind is drifting somewhere else. I know this feeling all too well, but typically I am the one who would drift away while people spoke, not while I am the one speaking. "You both have a big day tomorrow, and I know you will make us all proud. I just know it. Please rest up. I asked Andrew and Jaseen to fill you in on what the events are like. Let me know if you need anything," she says before wandering off into the woods.

Kristoff and I receive a briefing about the rules of the contests at the Faire. Learning about the rules helps to put my mind at ease. I had been nervous because of the unknown, and despite hearing just how brutal the games could be, I feel better. I learn that duels were an ancient tradition which evolved from stick fighting. It reminds me of Apexian fencing, but unlike fencing, it requires you to finish your opponent or for them to submit. An opponent is considered finished if they are unable to stand within ten seconds from the time they were knocked down, or if they fail to defend themselves, either from exhaustion or injury. A person does have the option of quitting, but I am told this doesn't happen often. Quitting is a shameful way to end a duel. It would be much better to fake being knocked out if need be, which is something most people do.

Kristoff is told that the gauntlet is a maze that runs through the woods, and there is lots of climbing, various obstacles, and a puzzle he would have to solve. And there is running. Lots of running.

Each clan often favors certain events, and the Romani apparently don't care much for the gauntlet. In fact, Kristoff is their only representative in the last few years. I know that he will do well because he excels at all the tasks they mentioned.

I wonder about how rampant cheating is in the gauntlet, since refereeing such a large space would be challenging. I bring this point up several times, prompting Jaseen and Andrew to give Kristoff the go-ahead to cut someone if they cheat.

While Kristoff and I are mentally preparing for our events, I can't help but notice Lee's lack of nerves—and it irritates me. Instead of preparing for the games, he is doing what he always does: socializing and cracking jokes with the clan members. After getting a few laughs from one group, I watch him make his way to another campfire and start again. I do have to admit he is funny, even if he isn't nearly as funny as me or Kristoff. I know it's just a matter of time before he comes to speak to us, and I rehearse what I would ask him about the event, hoping that being prepared with my questions would make them sound like casual inquiries.

"How is the future first gauntlet champion of the Romani?" Lee cheerily asks.

"Not bad, but I wouldn't go that far," says Kristoff as he pokes at the fire with a stick.

"Bullocks. Jaseen and Andrew told me you are going to win, and they are never wrong. Plus, they said you may get to cut a Swindletor if they try anything, which will make you a proper champion in my book."

"Are you not nervous?" I ask, changing the subject.

"Between you and me, love, I am very nervous. But I always get that way before the games."

"You don't seem nervous at all," says Kristoff.

"It's the face, isn't it? My face is basically always stuck like this. Here how's this? Better?" he asks, trying to make an exaggerated nervous face. I laugh. I can't help it. I curse myself for laughing at one of his jokes and immediately try to stop laughing, but he keeps making silly faces.

"Okay, new plan: you show them that face tomorrow, and you are a lock to win," says Kristoff laughing as well.

"There will be a few members from other clans, but the main clans in our event will be Wolfe's clan, ours, and Clan Harald. Wolfe's clan is full of brutes. They pride themselves on being big and don't really have much in the way of smarts. On the other hand, Clan Harald mainly uses swords and fights more technically, the way you'd see in the North," says Lee.

"What weapon did you choose?" I ask.

"A dagger, of course."

"A dagger? How do you manage that?" asks Kristoff, who isn't well-versed in combat but knows range matters.

"It ain't the weapon, mate. It's how you use it. We don't fight here like they do up north," replies Lee.

"What do you mean?" asks Kristoff.

"Well, you won't find a group of bloody Southlanders standing shoulder to shoulder covered in metal, unable to hardly walk, waiting to get mowed down by knights on horseback, or worse, an airship. It's bloody mental how they go at it up north, and for what? To make some bloke they are forced to serve even more money," he replies.

"Yeah, but since it's wooden weapons, a dagger must make it harder, right?" I ask.

"A lot like your rapier, the dagger lets me stay mobile, and I can work the angles. Besides, you're allowed to kick and punch, just no grappling, really," he replies.

"Makes sense. I guess I never considered that most weapons were made for large-scale battles," replies Kristoff.

We speak around the campfire for what seems like hours before I decide to get some sleep. I know I will need to be rested for tomorrow, especially if I make a deep run in the tourney.

As I lay myself down, I can't get over how comfortable the caravan is to sleep in. The quilts and pillows are soft and cozy, and being able to feel the cool breeze and smell the aroma of the campfire makes it all the more relaxing. I also love knowing that I am surrounded by an entire clan of people trained to fight if something terrible were to happen. I wonder what my mother and father would say to me about fighting in the tourney. I know they would be proud regardless but winning will prove that I can defend myself and Kristoff. Perhaps they can see it from wherever they are. Thinking of them watching and cheering me on eases my nerves, replacing them with excitement. I am ready to take on the day and whatever may come from it.

The morning leading up to the event is a blur. I awake just after the sun rises—far earlier than I ever thought I was capable of. The early rise is so the clan could make it on time for Kristoff's event, but it doesn't stop me from complaining.

Mum gathers all the event participants in a circle, and one by one, she uses paint made from berries she had foraged the night before to draw green lines beneath their eyes. She says the paint is a symbol for luck and protection but also that it isn't entirely necessary; Gaia will be watching over us all anyway.

I've never heard anyone speak about Gaia or spirituality like Mum. It would be considered heresy within the Apex, a crime carrying a severe penalty, which often means a public execution. The longstanding history of public executions carried out by the High Church is one of the things I hate most about the Apex. Even as a young child, I knew it was horrific and wrong. Some people in the Apex feel as if the harsh laws of the Church are necessary for public safety.

After walking for what feels like hours, our group of Romani finally finds ourselves standing in a field on the edge of a large forest. Judging by the gathering of people, I know this must be where the gauntlet will take place. I notice that Kristoff is restless, but it seems to be from excitement rather than fear. I know he will do well. I've never met anyone who could run as long as him without getting tired. My main concern is whether the event will be managed fairly, and I worry he is too kind-hearted to prevent being cheated. Lee and Mum share my anxiety, and they make it a point to let those participating in the event know that they will take it upon themselves to rectify any foul play, which seems to irritate the people from other clans.

"Okay, wish me luck!" says Kristoff excitedly as he stretches his limbs in preparation for the challenge.

"Nah, mate. You don't need luck. Look at them. They're shaking in their boots," replies Lee, whose interest in Kristoff doing well pleasantly surprises me. He may be arrogant and think he's much funnier than he is, but he genuinely cares for his clan members, including Kristoff.

"Show these Southlanders what people from the North can do," I say, giving a smirk to Lee.

"Gauntlet competitors, to your places!" yells one of the referees, speaking into a wooden cone that amplifies his voice.

Kristoff and the others stand in their respective positions at the starting line. They await the beginning of the race, signaled by the banging of a gong.

"You have been over the rules. Remember: absolutely no foul play, stay within the barriers at all times, and may the best clansman win."

"So long as it's someone from Swindletor!" yells someone from the audience.

"Impossible! He said no foul play, didn't he!" yells Andrew, prompting a shouting match between the two clans. Even I join in, clapping and yelling at the top of my lungs, "KRISTOFF, KRISTOFF!" Then a large man wielding a great staff with a cloth-covered tip, slams it as hard as he can against the gong, resulting in the dozen or so runners taking off from their starting marks. Kristoff is in an early lead as the runners make their way into the woods before he quickly vanishes from sight.

"How will we know who wins?" I ask as the cheers settle down.

"They will come out of that trail there once they have completed the puzzle at the end, see there? That is the finish line," says Jaseen, pointing to the spot he mentioned.

"How long does it take?" I ask.

"Hour, give or take," says Lee, pulling an hourglass out of his bag and flipping it over to keep track.

We pass the time by talking about what the rest of the day will bring. I am far less nervous now, but I wonder if that's because I'm too busy worrying about how Kristoff. I hope he will win, even more so than I aspire to win myself. I know it would be great for his self-esteem. I close my eyes and try to visualize him coming out of the woods first, hoping that it will somehow help his chances of winning. It's nerve-racking rooting for him and not being able to see what's happening. When the sand at the top of the hourglass is almost completely gone, the clan members and I make our way to the finish line in the clearing.

I rub my palms against my pants, trying to wipe off the sweat that has formed. "God, I hope he wins."

"He will, trust me," says Lee.

"How can you be so sure? You haven't even seen him run," I say, irritated once again by his overconfidence.

"It's his eyes. That kid wouldn't know how to quit if you paid him. He'll either win or be carried out by the referees, passed out from exhaustion. With that kind of performance, he wins either way."

"Yeah, that is true. He is stubborn as hell when it comes to giving up."

"Someone's coming!" yells one of the members from another clan, causing the crowd to circle around the clearing.

"Who is it!?" I yell, shoving my way through the crowd, not caring if I make anyone angry. It's too far to tell who it is at first, and the fact that the person is covered in mud doesn't help matters. But as the winner draws closer, I see the way they run. Their posture is upright, with their hands moving slowly but steadily. I know it's Kristoff. He did it. He actually did it. But in a flash, my excitement dissipates. Two figures are closing in on his lead, moving at a much faster pace than he seems able to go.

The finish line is only fifty yards from him when the two contestants from the Swindletor clan get on either side of him. The trail leading to the finish line is narrow, providing little room for passing. Kristoff is going to have to try and cut them off to keep the lead.

The racer on the right tries to grab at Kristoff's shoulder, hoping to pull him off balance so they can pass him. As he does, the racer on his left makes a move to pass, and before he can, Kristoff throws a nasty elbow that lands square to his face, causing him to stumble and fall. They attempt to grab on to whatever they can to keep their balance, and unfortunately for their clansmen, it happens to be their leg, leaving both Swindletor members falling to the ground. His win secured, Kristoff stops running and triumphantly walks across the finish line, looking back at the two Swindletors struggling to get to their feet.

I try to run towards Kristoff, but Lee grabs me by the arm. "Careful, love, we don't want to ruin his moment." Letting go of my arm, he claps and cheers as loud as he can. The rest of the clan starts to cheer, too. I can't believe how happy they all are for him. Their support is infectious and in short order, I am clapping and cheering loudly with the rest of them.

Once he finds me in the crowd, Kristoff enters into a full sprint. We hug each other for a short moment before he collapses to the ground, exhausted but still smiling.

"Oh my god, you did it! I'm of course going to have to kill them, but I'm so proud of you!" I beam at him. "How come the judges didn't do anything? You are bleeding. Why are you bleeding? Lee, why is he bleeding?" I say, rambling.

"Relax, it's from falling down a ladder. And that was nothing. Trust me, it was way more violent in the woods," says Kristoff laughing, still trying to catch his breath.

A referee comes and takes down his name and clan information, instructs him on when and where the award ceremony will be, and comments on how amazed he is that someone besides a Swindletor had won. With a wink and in a hushed tone, the referee also thanks Kristoff for throwing the elbow, which he claims he didn't actually see.

The clan members carry Kristoff away atop their shoulders as they continue to celebrate. I am so happy that I nearly forget the duels will begin in a little less than two hours.

"We better head that way, yeah?" says Lee, slapping me on the back to get my attention.

"Ready or not, I don't have much of a choice. It's either fight or face the stocks," I say, causing Lee to laugh.

"Don't worry, we'd break you out in no time. Can't promise I won't throw any mud first, though."

After the celebrations calm, the group makes our way to the center of the Faire where the arena, I recently learned, is called the proving grounds is located. As we near the arena, I notice just how beautiful the day is. It reminds me of autumn in Fairfield when it's warm, but there's a cool breeze in the air, and the leaves are beginning to change into shades of bright red and yellow.

I am annoyed with my emotions regarding the event and how they continue to change. The night before, I was nervous. This morning, I was excited, and now I just want to get it over with so that I no longer must think about it. As we travel, the others talk about how excited they are, and Kristoff tells them stories of my fighting history, which makes their hopes increase, but only places more pressure on me.

Upon sight of the large crowd already gathered at the proving grounds, I begin to feel nervous again. I wonder why I agreed to such a thing. I could have easily enjoyed the event from the stands, cheering on Lee and the other Romani members. Soon, Lee, Jaseen, and Andrew say their goodbyes to the rest of the clan members, and we go to the tents that are set up for the fighters, located on the sidelines of The proving grounds.

"How do you feel?" asks Lee, whose tone is far more serious than usual.

"Ready to get it over with. How about you?" I reply.

"Reckon I am the same," says Lee. "Oh, a warning: the other contestants are going to try and get in your head. Pay them no mind."

I nod. I know I can't show weakness, or it would make me look like an easy target.

As we approach the tents, we are met by referees who ask us for our names so they can tell us whom we will face in the first round. There are thirty-two fighters in total, and the tourney will go five rounds. I receive the unsettling news that I am to fight last against a man named Acosta. So much for getting it over with quickly. Lee tells me that Acosta is a member of Wolfe's clan—a brute as he puts it—but someone notably more dangerous than many of the people here. The fighters are given their wooden weapons to inspect and make sure they are serviceable. If they are not to our liking, we can choose one of the alternates instead.

I debate whether I should refrain from using the sword in place of a club or something with more range. I fear I lack the strength to subdue people much larger than me with a wooden sword. Lee tells me that many of the female fighters use swords and that they will do more damage than I may think, even with a strength disadvantage—especially if I target the back and side of the head.

Next, I am fitted with the protective gear we are given to wear during the tournament. The helmet is much like a fencing mask. It has a cage covering for the face and lightweight metal protecting the rest of the head. We are also equipped with leather shin guards that are long enough to cover our knees, as well as leather gloves and wrist guards so long that they go up to the elbow, making it hard to move. The last piece of armor is a leather vest which seems too thin to absorb a blow effectively. Once I am equipped with my armor, I go about finding the weak points so I can exploit them on my opponent during the fight while simultaneously protecting them on myself. I know I am at a disadvantage in size, strength, and experience, but I am confident that my father's lessons on strategy and combat will give me an edge.

"This is it? You going to watch the first match?" asks Andrew, who is holding his helmet in one hand and his sizeable wooden club in another.

"No, it will just make me nervous. Maybe when it's closer to my time," I reply, fidgeting with my wooden sword, trying to get used to the weight.

"You sure? Lee fights second against some bloke from Harald I never heard of."

"I wouldn't miss Lee's fight. I need to see it firsthand so I can prepare my insults," I say, trying to fake a smile.

Andrew laughs, but it sounds forced. It seems it isn't just my nerves getting the best of me.

I can hear the referee yelling to the crowd to prepare for the first fight while going over the instructions. The loud cheers from the crowd quickly drown out any noise from the referee as both clans scream for their fighter. The banging of the gong sounds, and the fight begins. It only seems to last a minute before the crowd erupts in a loud cheer, which indicates that the battle is over.

"Please, a big round of applause for both contestants! They fought with bravery and brought honor to themselves and their clan! Next, we have the Romani Lee versus Devon from Clan Harald!" says the announcer.

Andrew and I make our way outside to watch Lee's fight. He stands within the white circle that is drawn on the dirt of the arena floor, his small dagger outstretched in his hand, ready to strike. His fighting stance is unique. His knees are bent, and he is slowly moving back and forth, prepared to pounce or dodge. His opponent is about his height and size but using a two-handed wooden sword that seems too big for him. His stance is very still, and he holds the sword directly in front. It reminds me of how the knights in the Apex hold their swords at attention. It's a defensive stance that the Harald clan member is probably hoping would counter Lee's attacks. I find myself feeling uneasy again. I hope he does well.

With a bang of the gong, the fight commences. Unlike with the first fight, there is far less cheering, and I can sense the suspense in the air. Lee slowly moves towards his opponent, who hardly moves at all. He is simply waiting for Lee to strike so he can mount a counterattack. It's an intelligent tactic most of the time, but given that he has the range advantage, I wonder why he would give that up by letting Lee close the distance. Lee is patient, causing the crowd, most likely full of drunk people, to yell for the action to begin. This prompts the Romani and Clan Harald members to yell for them to shut up. I can't help myself and laugh at how invested the crowd is in the event.

Lee gets within range of his opponent and feints a quick attack while circling towards the man's left hand, which I know is an effort to avoid his power. The man reacts to the feint and begins to swing at Lee, utilizing overhead and side thrust strikes. Lee's ability to dodge attacks is unlike anything I've ever seen. Each strike fails to land, and Lee responds with several fast but low-powered attacks to the unarmored thighs of the fighter's body, the wooden dagger held tip down in his hand. He begins to focus on his opponent's right thigh, hitting him repeatedly in the same spot with the tip of his weapon. Eventually, the damage starts to wear on the man, and his movement is impaired. Becoming frustrated, his swings become less and less tactful and look more like wild haymakers, which are even more effortless for Lee to dodge.

Finally, the man swings a wild side-swiping strike at Lee who ducks under it, causing him to be turned around. The fighter swings his sword wildly, trying once again to face his opponent. Lee parries the attack with his dagger and gives a hard side kick to the same leg he had been targeting all fight. The power from the kick causes the man to fall to the ground and drop his weapon. The crowd erupts in a mixture of cheers and boos as the fighter lies on the ground crawling towards his weapon. Lee backs up and readies himself while the referee begins counting to ten. I doubt I would have the insight to stop striking the opponent after they hit the ground and assume Lee must have developed this ability through loads of experience.

The fighter rises to his feet within a few seconds, using his sword as support. However, as he attempts to walk forward, he falls once again, this time gripping his leg. It's clear he can no longer continue to fight because of his injury, and the referee declares Lee the winner, prompting the crowd to cheer loudly, shouting Lee's name over and over.

I'm happy to see Lee win and I let out a breath I didn't realize I was holding the entire time. The announcer informs the crowd of the official decision and asks them to thank both fighters before announcing the next fight.

"Oy! Oy! That's my mate! Did you even break a sweat?" asks Jaseen as Lee makes his way toward him.

"To be honest, I was glad he went down when he did. It was a matter of time before the bloke got me with that broadsword," he replies.

"Nah, mate. He didn't even come close," says Jaseen.

I can see Lee is still focused on the event and doesn't want to celebrate too much. That's exactly how I would feel in his situation, especially if I was one of the favorites to win the entire tourney.

"Hey, good job. Seriously, that was impressive. He knew how to use his sword, and you made him look like an amateur," I say, wondering how Lee would take the compliment.

"Thanks," he says, smiling. Before he can say more, they are approached by Wolfe and two of his muscle-bound clansmen. The trio of Guul looks silly in the armor that seems much too small for their size.

"Hope you don't expect to win with a leg kick if you fight me," says Wolfe, causing his two lackeys to laugh in what I can tell is an attempt to appease their leader's lame joke. "Doubt you will be able to focus when I crush your girlfriend here," he continues.

"I'm not his girlfriend," I snap.

"I meant him," Wolfe says, pointing at Jaseen.

"Awe, is someone jealous, eh Wolfe? Won't be long till our match. Best save your endurance and move along," replies Jaseen.

I can't help but think Wolfe is what any local bully hopes to become, if given the chance. I can't stand him, and I hope that if we both get through the first round, I can fight him next. Win or lose, I just want to hurt him, but in the meantime, I want Jaseen to beat him.

The rest of the fights go by rather quickly. It's apparent that not everyone in the tourney is a skilled fighter. They fight bravely, but at the first sign of trouble, they become wild, eventually losing to superior technique and endurance.

As I ready to watch Jaseen fight Wolfe, I think about what I know about Jaseen. He's a couple of years younger than me and Kristoff, but despite that, he's exceptionally talented, according to Lee. I wonder how effective his large two-handed sword will be against a much bigger fighter with an even bigger weapon, not to mention he seems too skinny to wield his own weapon. I assume he's hoping the large sword will give him a reach advantage, but against Wolfe, he'll need speed more than reach.

With the sound of the gong, the fight begins, and unlike Lee's fight, they waste no time before engaging with one another. Wolfe's clan seems large, based on how loud their cheers are, and they seem to spur the man on. Wolfe is like an enraged giant, swinging his axe wildly. Jaseen is dodging his strikes, but his sword is slowing him down.

"Go for his legs!" I yell, hoping that he can hear my screams over the noise of the crowd.

Jaseen swings the sword at Wolfe's head as often as he can, in-between dodging attacks. Each time, Wolfe blocks it with his wrist guard as if it's a strike from a pillow. I'm nervous watching the fight because, despite my best wishes, I know it's a matter of time before Wolfe connects, and once he does, I'm sure the fight will be over. Lee stands in silence as he watches, following their movements like a hawk, gripping his wooden dagger.

To my surprise, Wolfe's swings become slower, and it looks as if Jaseen might take the upper hand. Instead of taking advantage of the opportunity, he toys with Wolfe, prompting the crowd to cheer and laugh. This worries me. Jaseen is a highly skilled fighter, but his young age leads him to think he's invincible and contributes to a lack of seriousness.

Wolfe swings with a downward strike that misses, and Jaseen follows up with his own overhead strike aiming for Wolfe's head. Before the strike can find its mark, Wolfe lets go of his weapon and catches the sword with both hands. Letting go with one hand, he quickly uses his free hand to throw a haymaker, hitting Jaseen in the head and knocking him off balance. Wolfe pries the sword from his hands, and while he's still dazed and off-balance, swings it directly for his head.

I feel a shock go through my body when the blow connects, making a loud noise, and resulting in Jaseen's knees buckling. He falls to the ground face first and unconscious. Lee quickly jumps the wooden fence that circles the dirt ring of the arena to check on him. I watch in suspense as Lee and the referee crouch beside him. He still isn't moving. Oh my god, I hope he isn't dead. Can a blow like that kill someone through their headgear? I kneel to the ground and imagine him coming round, visualizing him standing up and shaking it off. The crowd remains dead silent. After seeing the danger associated with the tourney firsthand, I can't believe what I got myself into.

More time passes with no sign of movement from Jaseen. I watch as Lee and the referee kneel over his motionless body, gently shaking him. There is movement in the stands, and I can see that several Romani are approaching the arena now. In the center of the group is Mum, moving as quickly as her short legs would take her. She kneels beside Jaseen and removes something that looks like a small vial from her bag. She uses her teeth to remove the cork, causing those nearby to move back. The action is too far away for me to hear what is happening, but I know whatever is in the vial must smell terrible based on the dramatic reactions. She directs Lee to lift Jaseen's head, which he does, but not before covering his nose with a scarf. Mum puts her finger over the vial and then tips it upside down. She then shoves her entire finger directly up his nose. Jaseen wakes up instantly. Instantly, he rolls to his side and begins violently throwing up. The crowd—except for Wolfe's clan—cheers at his recovery.

I'm relieved to see Jaseen awake. Given how long he was out, I had assumed the worst. I worry I can't survive a similar strike to the head since I'm much smaller than Jaseen. Unfortunately, my happiness about his recovery is short-lived after Wolfe and members of his clan laugh as the Romani members help Jaseen off the field. I cannot stand Wolfe or the Guul, and I gather that most of the other clans feel the same. They seem to be the least friendly, something they appear to revel in. However, even for a group of bullies, I find their behavior especially despicable.

The rest of the fights finish at a much faster pace, and despite my best wishes, the members of Wolfe's clan seem to run through the competition with ease. That is until it's Andrew's turn to fight. Unlike most of the other fighters, Andrew uses a massive wooden club, which allows him to utilize his strength. The Guul contestant is big like most of his clansmen, but I can tell that he isn't in great shape and it's only about a minute into the fight that he starts to tire.

When Andrew notices his opponent beginning to fade, he wastes no time in seizing the upper hand and knocking the man to the ground with a fierce strike to the back of the head. The man falls flat to the ground and struggles as he rises to his hands and knees, trying to gather himself as the referee begins to count. Despite the referee's instruction to back away from the Guul member, Andrew runs over and strikes him with a downward blow to the back of the head. This time, he collapses completely, throwing the crowd into an uproar.

After some deliberation between the referees, Andrew is disqualified from the event, and the other man is declared the winner. I wonder if he is even aware of what that means given how hard he was hit. I don't blame Andrew for what he did. It isn't like Wolfe's attack was illegal, but his behavior afterward was repulsive.

Despite breaking the rules and being disqualified, Andrew is welcomed into the stands as a hero. Many of them give him a standing ovation while glaring at the Guul.

"Serves him right," I say, watching Wolfe and the others help the man back to the fighter's tents.

"Yea, but a bit foolish. Now they are guaranteed to have four members in the next round," Lee says, spitting to the ground.

"I don't think he will be of much use in round two," I reply.

"Fair point but winning would have been even better revenge."

There is only one more fight before it's my turn. Lee and I stand silently inside the tent as the fight before mine commences. In preparation for my turn, I swing my sword and perform thrusts and techniques my father had taught me. I want to get the weight of the weapon down, but I'm also just trying to make use of my nervous energy. I wonder what my parents would think, watching me participate in such a violent contest. It makes me laugh, thinking about how my mom would have literally killed Wolfe if he boasted about knocking me out.

"How are you feeling?" asks Lee, pacing around nervously, appearing way more anxious than he was before his own fight.

"Nervous, to be honest, but looking forward to hurting Acosta after their little boasting session."

"If you can make him miss, he will tire. Please don't let him taunt you into being reckless."

"Please, you say? Why? Don't you want me to get hurt?" I say jokingly.

"Can you blame me? I mean, it would make the rest of us look bad," he says jokingly, looking at me with a smile.

Just then, the crowd breaks out in a cheer, and I know that means the end of the fight. I put my helmet and thick leather gloves on and make my way to the field. I'm far less nervous now. In fact, I don't feel much of anything. I'm focused on walking, as if I need to contemplate each step to avoid falling down.

"Please be careful, yea?" says Lee, running up to me and giving me a hug, then adjusting my helmet for me. I nod and continue my walk. The crowd grows louder as Acosta, and I make our way to the field. He is even bigger than I imagined and his wooden club, despite being rather large, seems too small for him. The man is slightly taller than Lee and has a muscular build like Wolfe, although he is noticeably smaller. He appears to be a few years older than most contestants, likely in his early thirties. He has an aggressive-looking face with dark green eyes and a large nose that looks as if it has been broken on multiple occasions.

The announcer goes over the rules, but my attention is fixated on my opponent. I think he's a large brute, an idiot, and an awful human. Someone who laughs at the pain of others and who is going to try and hurt me. I grip my sword tightly, not liking the way the sword feels beneath the thick protective gloves I wear. I contemplate the fight and run through strategies based on what he may do. I remember Lee's advice and figure it would indeed be best to refrain from engaging him until he grows tired. I need to keep my emotions in check, or else I'll lose my temper and become reckless. Unfortunately, my thoughts are cut short by the sound of the gong, which makes my ears ring.

As I suspected, Acosta charges at me like a wild boar. His attacks are feral and easy to dodge, partly because of how slow he is and partly because of how afraid I am of getting hit. I'm acutely aware of what he's doing, making it easier to dodge but harder to mount an offense. Swing after swing misses before Acosta realizes I'm trying to tire him out. He begins to walk slowly in an attempt to conserve his energy, trying to corner me before he strikes.

"Well, bitch, are we going to fight, or are you going to just run!" he yells, attempting to get a rise out of me.

He's unsuccessful. I couldn't care less about what he has to say at this moment. As he continues to stalk me, I slowly circle away from his primary hand. Then, just as he begins to throw more insults my way, I swing my sword quickly, landing an overhead strike to the top of his head. He swings back in response, but I'm far gone by the time the club makes its way to where I had been. I continue this for some time, landing quick strikes that don't seem to do much damage. His stance is far more restrained than most of the other fighters, which means that the weak spots in the protective armor aren't such easy targets.

"Who's not fighting now, bitch?" I say, frustrated about the brute's restraint. My comment causes him to lash out, swinging wildly at me before gathering his emotions and once again stopping. "Is Wolfe the only one from your clan that can actually fight?" I ask, resulting in him swinging more and more. "The rest of them seem bigger than you, too. How does it feel to be the runt of the litter?" I continue.

He yells in frustration, charging headfirst. I swing for his head once again, but he uses the club to block it, and then he lands a solid punch to my stomach. Even with the protective leather, it knocks me back, causing me to fall to one knee. The referee quickly slides between me and Acosta and begins to count. The punch takes away my breath, and I'm embarrassed by how weak I must appear, being knocked down by a stomach punch. As the referee continues to slowly count, I gather my breath and stand to my feet.

"Can you continue?" asks the referee, to which I nod. I decide I've had enough of playing it safe and that if I'm going to have a chance, I'll need to mount some sort of offense. The crowd cheers when the action continues.

Acosta runs towards me, hoping to capitalize on his knockdown. I sidestep his attack and quickly plant my feet in a stance that will allow me to move my body in a manner that will increase the strength of my strike. It lands flush on his primary arm, right above the leather. He turns to face me, attempting to lift his club for another strike. Before he can bring his arm all the way up, however, I swing my sword down. Again, the blow lands on his right arm, slightly above the armor.

Acosta backs up. He doesn't show any sign of pain, but I can sense that my strikes have done some damage. As he continues to back up, I throw as many vicious strikes as I can, over and over, each one aiming for the same spot as before. He gives up on holding his weapon with two hands and tries to swing it with just his left. The strikes are way too slow and easily parried by me. As he begins to fade, I can hear the crowd's cheers becoming louder and louder. Eventually, he stops attacking altogether and tries to use the club to block my attacks. It's no use. I start to attack him in different places and with a wide variety of strikes that my father had taught me. Acosta drops to his knees, hoping to use the referee's ten count as a break. The crowd lets out loud boos, knowing his intentions.

Once the referee gets to nine seconds, Acosta stands up and is told that he would be disqualified if he did that again. The action starts once more, but this time it's me who charges. I stare at his leg and lift my sword suggesting that's where I plan to strike, causing him to move his weapon to that area to block. But instead, I jump and come down with a diagonal slice to his neck, hitting him where there is no armor. He clutches his neck in pain, and I use the opportunity to strike at the arm that still holds his weapon. The club falls to the ground, which gives me all the opportunity I need to unleash a barrage of strikes. He does his best to try and block them with his wrist guards, but it's no use. His legs and arms are too battered to effectively defend himself, and I, with no remorse, continue to target his limbs instead of trying to finish the fight with head strikes.

After I land a particularly violent strike to his leg, he falls to the ground. The referee starts the ten count, and Acosta puts on a show of trying to stand before falling back down, similar to what Lee's first-round opponent had done—except they were actually unable to walk and Acosta was instead suffering a mental defeat.

The crowd cheers as my arm is raised in victory, and with a quick wave to the section of the stands where the Romani were sitting, I make my way back to the contestants' tent, still in disbelief that I managed to win a round. I feel a massive sense of relief wash over me. Now that I've won a match, I feel like I've proven myself competent. If I lose moving forward, I can do so without shame.

Lee is waiting for me at the fence that separates the tents from the field, grinning from ear to ear, sending a wave of excitement through me.

"Brilliant! Bloody brilliant! You are a proper swordsman. I knew it!" he says, slapping me on the back.

"That or Acosta is even dumber than he looks," I reply, trying to fix my hair that had gotten crimped from being under the helmet during the fight.

"Either way, you didn't just beat him. You destroyed his soul," he replies, handing me a bladder of water. "Come, let's get some rest. With the first round done, we move right into the next round of pairings. Best to regain your energy while you can, yeah?"

I nod and find a seat on the bench inside of the tent, the cool breeze and shade helping me to recover. I'm thankful that I'm only tired and not hurt from my fight.

I find out that my next fight will be against a woman named Pauli from Clan Harald. Lee tells me that Pauli is skilled with a sword but isn't close to my level. He also warns me that she is very experienced at hand-to-hand combat, which means I need to watch out for kicks and punches.

The rest of the fights go by quickly while Lee and I sit inside the tent talking. I'm not interested in watching any of the other matches. I'd much rather be with him, and until Lee is told that it's his turn to fight, I've almost forgotten about the event.

"Wish me luck, yeah," says Lee before quickly putting on his helmet and running out to the field, hurdling over the fence.

I walk as close to the fence as I can to get a good view of the fight. I notice that his opponent is already outside waiting while Lee is still running to the circle. His opponent is one of Wolfe's clansmen, who also wields a two-handed axe. I'm growing tired of seeing Wolfe's clan. They all look the same, and I can't help thinking that there must be some rule stating that everyone in his clan must be large, or else they're exiled.

Continuing to inspect his opponent, I grow anxious that Lee may face a similar fate as Jaseen. The announcer goes over the rules, and the fight begins with a banging of the gong. The large man slowly walks towards Lee, who is in his familiar fighting stance. He holds his dagger differently this time; it's pointing up, and his hand is gripped right below the crossbar, leaving much of the hilt exposed.

The Guul swings his axe at Lee's legs causing him to move backward quickly. Lee circles and, using the hilt of his dagger, he strikes the man in the center of his leather torso armor. I growl in frustration at his choice to use the hilt of the dagger instead of the tip, but I hope he must have a reason.

His opponent tries to hit him, but on each occasion, he quickly dodges the attack and strikes back with the hilt of his dagger, occasionally throwing light kicks to the thighs of the big man. The man adjusts from swinging his axe with sideswipes to overhead strikes, which follow through all the way to the ground. It doesn't help the Guul land, but it forces Lee to back up so far that he can't counterattack as easily.

I notice that Lee is patient and isn't adjusting his strategy to his opponent's new attack style. Instead, he waits for the right opportunity. Lee times the man's strike, and as the axe strikes the ground, he stomps on the weapon right below the wooden axe head, snapping it in half. The crowd cheers, seeing the former axe turned into a stick that will be far less effective. Not bothering with the ineffective weapon, the man attacks Lee with his hands. He succeeds in landing several blows, but each of them merely grazes Lee's armor. Unfortunately for Lee's opponent, each of his strikes results in a counterattack from the hilt of Lee's wooden dagger.

It's clear that the man is outmatched in hand-to-hand combat, and over time Lee lands enough strikes to the head to drop the man. He's able to get back to his feet on two occasions, but by the third time, he's so dizzy that upon standing up, he falls to the ground, face first. The fact he defeated the man with his dagger hilt had to send a message to the other members of the Guul.

I greet Lee at the fence and congratulate him, praising him for his patience and poise as I give him a water bladder. We then return to the tent to await my fight, which is only two matches away from happening.

"You must be Aries. I really enjoyed your first fight. Acosta is a bastard, and it was brilliant seeing him defeated like that. My name is Pauli," says a kind-looking woman extending her gloveless hand toward me. Pauli's brown hair is gorgeous and very silky. Her light blue eyes seem far too kind for this type of event. Then I remember I'll be facing this woman and begin to size her up properly. Pauli is slightly shorter and thinner than me, making me think I'll have a strength advantage.

"Pleased to meet you," I reply, shaking the woman's hand, confused as to why she introduced herself.

As we exchange greetings, I continue to size up my opponent, trying to determine how best to attack her in the fight. In almost all my fighting experience, I've fought people bigger and stronger than me, and I'm a little uncomfortable with the proposition of not having a speed advantage.

"I wish you luck and hope that we can put on a good show, yeah? Good fight Lee, nice seeing you again," Pauli says before leaving the tent.

"What was that about?" I ask, confused.

"What did you expect? That everyone would be rude like Wolfe and those morons from Guul?" says Lee laughing.

I realize I had focused so much on Wolfe's clan that I hadn't considered that some fighters were interested in honorable competition. It's refreshing to know that not everyone has ill intentions toward me, but I must admit it makes me far less motivated. My goal is to perform in the event and not be destroyed entirely, and I already achieved that. It's times like this my father would be able to help inspire me. He would find some way to encourage me to compete with passion, maybe by pretending to doubt me, which he knew would make me try harder, if only to prove him wrong.

Before I know it, it's time for me to enter the fighting arena once again. The crowd seems to cheer me on much louder than the last time, probably for beating someone from the Guul.

As I stand across from Pauli, I'm met with a bow that reminds me of how people greet one another formally in the Apex. I bow in return and following the quick run-through of the rules by the referee, the gong sounds, and the fight begins. Pauli's fighting stance reminds me of my own. She leads with her primary foot forward, holding her sword with one hand, waiting to lunge. Pauli's posture prompts me to switch to a two-handed stance where I stand sideways towards her, making myself less of a target for a lunging strike. Pauli adjusts and mimics my stance once again. I can't tell if it's an attempt to get under my skin or if she knows what she's doing. Either way, I don't care for it and decide to attack. I play it safe at first, throwing lightly powered strikes at half speed to see how Pauli would react. She easily parries most of the strikes with her sword, even landing a clean thrust of her own to my chest. It's absorbed by the armor and doesn't hurt, but it sends a message that my opponent is experienced.

I become more and more aggressive with my strikes, frustrated by how skilled she is at sword defense. I throw an overhead strike that I know will cause us to clash swords. During the clash, I throw a solid straight punch directly into the cage of Pauli's face mask, knocking her head back, and she responds with several punches of her own. The two of us continue to punch each other in the face until Pauli suddenly backs up. Not long after, my opponent starts closing the distance and goes on the offensive. Her strikes are quick and diverse, requiring me to employ a combination of blocks and dodges to avoid them. A few glancing blows hit me in the helmet, making an awful noise that hurts my ears.

I study my opponent, hoping to see an opening in her fighting style, but nothing stands out. Pauli is a fierce sword fighter despite her polite demeanor, and I can't help but wish I was fighting Acosta again. I decide that my best bet would be to make the fight more of a brawl, allowing me to utilize my slight size and strength advantage. Also, I feel confident that I am the more violent of the two. Whenever I succeed in forcing a clash, I land a hard punch or kick, causing Pauli to fall back momentarily. Once she realizes what I'm doing, she starts to avoid the clashes.

I throw a strike with misdirection that makes her think I'm aiming for her head again, but my strike lands hard on her thigh. She then attempts a strike of her own that I block with my left hand before quickly punching her in the side of the helmet, pushing her off balance. As she stumbles sideways, I bring my sword down, landing a crushing blow to the side of her helmet, knocking her to the ground.

Seven seconds go by before Pauli can get to her feet. I admire her toughness, knowing that many people her size would have been unable to recover from such a strike. Despite her resilience, Pauli begins to fade after the knockdown. Shortly after, I am able to land a solid blow to her head, knocking her back to the ground. When she falls, she removes her helmet and signals her submission. I can hear the Romani cheering for me, and I can see Lee pumping his fist from the sideline. This victory is nowhere near as satisfying as the one over Acosta. Pauli's polite mannerisms and fair fighting style make me feel a little bad for winning.

When Pauli is back on her feet, I shake her hand and bow to her.

"Great fight! You are excellent with your sword," says Pauli, who seems genuinely happy for my success. I wonder how someone as nice as her could have summoned such ferocity only moments before.

"You too! You had me real nervous. I am going to be sore tomorrow," I reply, unsure exactly what to say. Pauli raises my arm to show that she supports the victory, leading to loud cheers from the crowd. I can't help but look for my mother and father in the audience.

I know it's impossible, but I want more than anything for them to be able to see me right now, so I close my eyes for a moment and pretend I can see them cheering for me amongst the sea of people.

Only eight fighters remain, which means I have a one in seven chance of facing Lee, and I desperately hope it doesn't happen.

After a grueling day, both physically and mentally, we make our way to the camp. During the journey, many people congratulate me for my success and introduce themselves. I'm happy for the popularity but feel uncomfortable accepting so much praise. Lee, however, seems to thrive on the attention, which doesn't surprise me, but I still find it annoying. But, at least for today, I figure I'll give him a pass because of how kind he has been to me.

The arrival back to camp is very much welcomed. Everyone quickly disperses to their caravans and starts their fires so that we can have dinner before it's time to sleep.

I'm pleased to see that the clan members are especially happy about Kristoff's win, since it's the first time any of them can remember a Romani winning the gauntlet. Even Mum makes a special announcement about how proud and thankful she is for his victory.

We've only known the people of the clan for a few days, but we're already being treated like we're one of them. Lee told us that the Romani are known to be one of the more welcoming clans, and it isn't uncommon for them to accept those shunned by their former clans, depending on what law they broke.

"I know I should be tired, but I feel like I could stay up all night," says Kristoff, taking a break from being the clan hero to sit by the fire with me.

I'm enjoying looking into the flames and thinking about what tomorrow may bring. I'm proud of my performance and know that no matter what, I will survive with my dignity intact. And while I had originally not cared all that much about winning, now that I'm so close, I can't help but want to win it all.

"So, be honest, do you think I can win tomorrow?" I ask Kristoff seriously.

"I learned to stop doubting you years ago, but honestly, I'm terrified you'll face Wolfe. He destroys everyone he fights in one or two strikes. I seriously thought Jaseen was dead," replies Kristoff, concern evident in his voice.

"No thanks to you," I scoff playfully. "Apparently losing that nose ring inspired him."

"What, this thing?" he says, removing the golden ring from his pocket. "I have been holding it in case he starts to run his mouth. I figured showing it off like a trophy would put him in his place."

 "Do you mind if I use that tomorrow?"

"Uh yeah, sure. But why?" he asks, confused.

"If I'm going to have a chance of winning, I may need to make him lose control of his emotions."

"I don't know if that's such a good idea. It could end badly. Very badly."

"Who knows? It'll still be nice to have the option. It worked with Acosta. Up until I insulted him, he was sitting back and conserving his energy."

"Fair point. Just please be careful, okay? I like it here and don't want it tainted with you dying in some tourney," he says to defuse the tension. I know it's a joke but one laced with truth. Jaseen was knocked down with one strike. I figure it would be best not to focus on Wolfe too much since I don't know who I would be facing anyways. Even so, I would much rather face Wolfe and get knocked out than have to fight Lee. I frown at the thought and consider all the potential pairings that may happen in the tourney tomorrow. Once I get tired of going in circles with my thoughts, I decide it's time to get some sleep and see what tomorrow will bring.

The journey back to the proving grounds seems to go by rather quickly, and luckily for my nerves, many of the people are too tired to talk. It's also much colder today than the day before, which I hope will help make it more comfortable in my armor and helmet.

Lee tells me about the remaining fighters in the tourney and that many of them train for several months in preparation for the event. When I ask why it means so much to them, he goes on a big spill about honor but says that what it boils down to is the large prize of silver the winner will receive. I want to win so badly that I hadn't considered that there was a prize. I'm a fiercely competitive person but always view winning in general as prize enough.

The remaining eight fighters take our places on the dirt field of The proving grounds to be honored by the referees. Shortly after opening the second and final day of the tourney, the fighters are given their match assignments. I know that I lucked out when I was paired with Andrew's opponent—the one Andrew had been disqualified for hitting while he was still on the ground. Although, the more I think about it, the more worried I become since I'm unsure how he could have made it past the second round. Lee is given a much more challenging opponent named Julian, a member of Clan Harald. Julian is a middle-aged man that is well versed in dual-wielding swords. Lee had said Julian consistently makes it into the second day of the tourney and that he has won on three different occasions. It's plain that Lee looks up to him as a bit of a hero.

"Totally your choice, but you may want to consider using a spear or staff against Brutus. He's wearing a head wrap because of his injury. Just need to stay way outside and land some headshots. Trust me, he'd do the same to you if he could, so don't hesitate to exploit his injury," Lee whispers to me as we walk towards the tents.

"Good idea. I'm not as familiar with a spear or staff, but it would give me a lot of reach. Do you think he would be able to get ahold of it, though?"

"Eh, he's not exactly known for his hand-eye coordination, and his physique has become a bit soft as of late. He drinks," Lee clarifies at a look from Aries. "But do what you feel comfortable with, just telling you what I would do."

I contemplate what I will do in my fight against Brutus, playing several scenarios through my mind until the referee interrupts me to tell me I will be fighting soon.

"Can I switch my weapon for this fight? Is there a spear I could use?"

The referee looks at me puzzled but nods before he leaves to fetch me a spear.

"Good choice, love. Just hang back, and when he struggles to hold his arms up, finish what Andrew started, yeah?" says Lee as the two of us walk out of the tent.

I am given a spear from the referee. It's heavier than I had imagined, and I fear I've made the wrong decision. If I'm not able to wield the spear effectively, I place myself at significant risk. I put on my helmet as I wait for the fight to begin. Brutus is wielding a two-handed axe. I notice he seems a bit out of sorts, and I figure there must be some truth to what Lee said about his head injury. The referee bangs the gong, and we begin to circle one another.

The Guul typically charge their opponents, hoping to use their strength and rage to quickly end the fight. However, this time Brutus walks at a leisurely pace, clearly intent on defense. This plays into my and Lee's game plan. My spear allows me to attack with thrusts while staying far outside of his striking range. If he wants to mount any sort of offense, he will have to close the distance, and doing so would leave him open for a heavy strike.

We circle each other for several moments, with me throwing fast but light attacks while he tries to dodge or block them. Eventually, I attempt to thrust at his helmet, hoping to take advantage of his injury. Unfortunately, my timing is off, and he parries my attack, causing the spear to drop out of my hands. I make a move for the weapon, but Brutus closes the distance quickly and follows up with a strong strike that I can barely dodge.

Without my spear, I'm essentially defenseless. My leather wrist guards probably won't be strong enough to absorb a strike from his weapon. I make several attempts to get my spear back, but he cuts off my path each time before following up with a strike. I grit my teeth, knowing I'm going to have to risk getting hit in order to get ahold of my weapon again. I suppose if I can't grab the spear and am knocked down, at least my weapon will be given back to me by the referee.

I circle Brutus for a few moments before making a dash for the spear, but he is ready and closes the distance quicker than I anticipated. He swings his axe with a side-swiping motion that I know I will have to leap over. I jump, just barely avoiding the axe strike, and am able to land a solid punch right to his face mask. He stumbles back, which buys me enough time to grab my spear. He attempts to hit me with a solid downward strike that I have to roll to the side to avoid. I quickly stand up and scurry backward, dodging his rapid attacks. He throws another overhead strike, but I turn to avoid it and use my momentum to land a spinning attack to the back of his helmet. Dizzy and off-balance, he stumbles, trying to regain his bearings. However, before he can, I land a strong downward strike right to the top of his head. Brutus falls to the ground, removes his helmet, and waves his hands to signify that he is no longer willing to continue. With my victory, I will move on to the event's semifinals—two fights away from being this year's champion. I feel terrible about having exploited Brutus' injury, but like Lee said, I know that he would have done the same, given the chance.

I make my way to the fighters' tents, where Lee congratulates me. "Not going to lie, when the spear dropped, I got a bit nervous. Bloody brilliant work, though. Wish me luck!" he says before quickly running out of the tent for his own fight.

"Good luck!" I yell, caught off guard by how quickly his fight is starting. I'm nervous because of how skilled I heard his opponent is. Lee said not to worry; because it's the second day, and he doesn't have to hold back anymore. I'm not sure if he is saying that to try and overcompensate for feeling nervous or if he really means it.

Both fighters are welcomed warmly by the admiring crowd. They shake hands before taking their places in a show of respect that reminds me of Pauli.

The dark-skinned Julian is tall, though still a few inches shorter than Lee. He appears to be older, based on the hints of grey throughout his dark brown hair, and he carries himself in a confident manner that makes me particularly nervous.

Lee takes his familiar fighting stance while his opponent twirls his dual swords in a way that I know only a highly skilled swordsman could do. As I watch Julian, I smile a little bit; his actions remind me of my father.

The gong sounds, and Lee wastes no time. He throws his dagger, hitting the man in the head, and follows it up with a kick to his chest, timed in a way that allows Lee to pry away the man's left-hand sword. Julian has been pushed back from the kick, and before he can fully regain his balance, Lee is already on the offensive, violently swinging his own sword at him. The man does his best to parry the attacks, but there are too many, and Lee is far too fast. I have not seen him fight with such aggression before. From what I have witnessed, he typically fights defensively and only strikes when necessary.

The crowd cheers loudly as Lee pummels the other man, who, despite fighting bravely, is unable to withstand the excessive number of strikes. He attempts to clash with Lee to get a temporary respite from the strikes, but Lee throws a push kick knocking him backward before following up with a vicious strike that lands flush on the top of the man's head. He collapses to the ground but is able to stand up by the eighth second of the referee's count.

The fighters are given their weapons back, and with a wave of the referee's hand, the fight begins once more. Julian mounts an offensive, swinging his dual swords furiously, causing Lee to dodge frequently as he backs up. I can't believe how Lee is able to avoid the strikes. His footwork is the best I've ever seen. The other man's last-ditch offensive ends with him opening himself up to a perfectly-timed strike from Lee, which lands on the side of his head, putting a large dent in his helmet.

The referee starts his ten count, but the man is unable to stand. In fact, he is not moving at all. Lee removes his own helmet and kneels beside him, helping the referee to carefully remove Julian's helmet as they tilt his head upwards. Finally, the man comes to, and Lee and the referee help him to his feet. Lee bows to the man to show his great respect for the warrior, and the other man raises Lee's hand to symbolize he supports the victory, then the two bow toward the stands. The crowd is instantly on its feet, cheering loudly. I get the sense that I am witnessing a changing of the guard in terms of the crowd's favorite warrior and that Lee has bested his hero.

"I have never seen anything like that," I blurt when Lee makes it back to the tent.

"Thanks, love. Don't make my head too big, though. It will be an easier target for Wolfe to hit."

"I think it's plenty big already, mate," I reply sarcastically, using the word mate with a poor attempt at a Southlander's accent.

Lee laughs in response. "So, me and you, Wolfe and a bloke who is a spear fighter?"

"Yep, they still haven't released the matchups. Would they pair us, you think?" I ask anxiously.

"It's all random now. They try and avoid clan on clan in the early rounds, but later into it, they just pick them out of a hat."

We sit in the fighters' tent to rest before the next round starts. The referees take some time to honor the fighters from the previous rounds and remind the crowd of the winner's ceremony scheduled for later this evening. Then the referee in charge of announcing the matchups walks into the tent. Please, not Lee. Please, not Lee, I repeat silently. And I get my wish; I'm not facing Lee. Instead, I will be facing Wolfe and we are next. My stomach drops, and I change my mind, suddenly wishing I was fighting Lee. That way, even if I lose, I know I will survive the fight without permanent injury.

When he hears the news of me and Wolfe being paired, Lee cringes and asks to speak to the referee privately. I can see him waving his arms a lot, and I know that he is trying to talk the referee into letting him fight

Wolfe. Lee becomes visibly frustrated by the referee's refusal to change the matchups and turns away from the man in a huff, walking over to me. I have mixed feelings about what he just attempted to do. On the one hand, I'm happy he cares enough about me to try and change the pairing, but on the other hand, it is irritating that he thinks I need his protection.

I take Lee's doubt as the motivation I need to ignite my fiery competitive spirit. "I can tell you one thing: win or lose, he is going to regret facing me," I say before putting on my helmet and walking out to the field.

"Aries, wait! Make sure that you're always moving backward, and never circle into his right hand. And please promise if he connects—you'll stay down."

I cut him off before he can say anything more. "Don't worry, I like it here and don't have any plans to have it cut short by an idiot who Kristoff already beat up," I reply, attempting to put Lee's mind at ease.

I inform the referee I will be using my sword again and ask if I could also use a small shield. The ref nods and provides me with both. I make my way to the field, and nearly the entire crowd greets me with booming applause while they chant my name.

Maybe since I have everyone in the Southlands behind me, I have a chance, I say to myself. As I stand in position, while the referee repeats the rules and specifically tells Wolfe to fight clean, I ask my mother and father to lend me the strength, agility, and wisdom I will need to defeat Wolfe.

The gong sounds, and while I expect to see Wolfe rushing at me, swinging his giant wooden axe with the cruelest of intentions, no such thing happens. Instead, Wolfe is sitting where he is, leaning on the top of his axe. I grip my shield tightly in my left hand and stand in the fencing stance my father taught me, sword foot forward, ready to lunge.

"Yield before you get hurt, little girl," Wolfe says calmly. I know I need to tune him out lest his words make me do something reckless, but I must admit his insult is much better than his clansman's was.

I continue to press forward slowly, but still he doesn't react. He looks unbothered and not threatened in the slightest. "You haven't had any problem hurting people up until now. Why the change of heart?"

"Be a shame to damage the face of my future wife before the wedding night."

"I'd rather slit my own throat."

"Careful what you wish for," he replies, picking up his axe and placing it on his shoulder before slowly walking towards me. I land a solid lunging strike to the middle of his chest that doesn't seem to impact him at all. He simply keeps walking forward and laughing. I begin to circle and swing strikes at the exposed parts of his legs, but again he doesn't seem fazed. I know that I will need to throw more power into my strikes if I want to hurt him, and to do so, I will have to put myself at risk of counterattack. Wolfe would gladly take a strike, even ten, just to land one, and unlike his clansmen, he is far more patient. So, I decide to feint a strike for his thigh and follow up with a strong blow right above his elbow. Wolfe catches the blade with his left hand; his grip is too tight for me to pull my sword away, but I continue to try, as long as there is no signal he is going to strike.

"This is your last chance to quit," he growls.

His words infuriate me. I feel defenseless, and it reminds me of when I was helpless to protect Kristoff's parents, and powerless to save my own father. I'm reminded of how being vulnerable has cost me everything. My blood boils, and I no longer fear Wolfe, his axe, or his superior strength. If he expected to face a timid girl, then he is in for a rude awakening.

"Well?" he asks, still holding onto my sword. "Fuck you," I reply coldly, violently ripping the sword from his grip.

Wolfe laughs at my remark and suddenly swings his axe at me. He isn't using his full strength or speed, which means he's playing with me. I capitalize on his lack of effort and land a solid strike to the side of his head. It isn't strong enough to knock him down, but it sends a message that I shouldn't be toyed with. He continues to swing, but now he's using more of his strength and even comes close to connecting with his sizable wooden axe on a few occasions. In one instance, I try to use my shield to deflect his strike with hopes that it would provide an opening for a counterattack, but he is far too strong, and even with my shield, he is able to knock me off balance.

Finding limited success with head strikes, I decide to change my strategy and go for the lower body. My father taught me that there are two types of fights. There are honorable ones in which fighters do not cross boundaries, and there are fights for survival, where one should do anything necessary to win.

Given how Wolfe hurt Jaseen without remorse, I figure it would be best to proceed as if my life is in danger—but I know I will tell myself anything to justify what I am about to do. Each time I attempt a strike at Wolfe's thighs, he turns his axe to block me. I repeat the move a few times, trying to trick him into a false sense of security. Once again, I move as though aiming for his thigh, then suddenly redirect the strike and hit him as hard as I can between his legs. I can hear the crowd let out a loud groan before they begin laughing at the sight of Wolfe falling to his knees, clutching the injury.

The referee is shocked by what happened, as if it is unheard of for a fighter to target the groin. They never mentioned it in the rules, so it must be fair game. I don't care either way. After staring wide-eyed for a few moments, the referee starts the count, and after a few seconds, Wolfe stands back to his feet, visibly furious. He pushes the referee out of the way and charges at me, swinging his axe with everything he has, knowing if he lands a blow, I will most likely go down and be unable to continue.

As Wolfe's hulking frame barrels toward me, any sense of accomplishment I had for knocking him down is replaced by an intense fear of being hit. I dodge as quickly as I can, attempting to circle so that I can find an opening for a counterattack, but his pressure is too much. Whenever I circle after a dodge, he follows up with an even faster strike. Unlike his clansmen, he knows the value of fighting at different speeds so that he can try to catch his enemy by surprise.

I am entirely on the defensive and struggle to think of a way to subdue the human ogre. Against my better judgment, I attempt an overhead strike after I think I see an opening. Wolfe sees the strike coming and moves his head, letting the blow hit his shoulder. He follows up with a haymaker punch that lands clean to the side of my head. Everything goes black for a split second as I tumble to the ground, dropping my sword and shield. I am confused. I had seen the punch coming, but it had been too fast for me to react. My vision is blurred, but I can see the referee standing over me, counting with his hands. I can make out that he has several fingers up already but can't understand what he is saying. I debate whether it's best to stay down and let the fight end. I had already humiliated him in front of the crowd and would be lucky to walk away from the fight without serious injury.

Once again, I go against my better judgment and stand to my feet as the referee looks at me in disbelief. My hearing returns and my vision clears and I can see many people in the crowd cheering. Unfortunately, the members of the Romani aren't among the revelers. They have concerned looks on their faces, telling me I should have stayed down after all. The referee asks me if I wish to continue, seemingly giving me one more opportunity to bring the fight to an end without me being completely devastated. I tell the referee that I intend to finish the fight. He reluctantly hands my weapon and shield back to me. I curse the wooden sword, knowing that if it was an actual blade, I could quickly nullify Wolfe's strength, but since it is wooden, it may as well be as useless as my shield.

That's when it hits me. This isn't a sword fight, no matter how much they want it to look like one. I decide to hold my sword in my left hand and my shield in my right. The referee asks me one last time if I wish to continue, to which I nod. Wolfe shakes his head in disbelief, clearly as shocked as everyone else about my choice to continue. The referee shakes his head and waves his hand, signaling for us to continue.

"You may think you are showing heart, but you're really showing how dumb you are. The next strike will not be a punch I—" he says before being interrupted by me throwing my sword at his head and charging him. He attempts to lift his axe and strike at me, but my quick pressure catches him off guard, and before he can swing his weapon, I land a solid blow to his head with the edge of my shield. The shield's weight works to increase the power of my punches without slowing me down too much. I land several strikes, and with each punch, I jar his head backward, making it hard for him to swing with his full power. Eventually, he is able to push me back with a kick to the stomach, allowing him the time he needs to regain his composure and stand at the ready with his axe.

I can hear the crowd cheering me on. It is my first real offense during the fight, save for the low blow that humiliated him. It's clear from the blood beginning to seep out of his helmet that my strikes are doing damage.

"You're leaking, mate," I say mockingly, hoping to remind him of the exchange outside of the pub when we first arrived on the island. Wolfe uses his glove to check and see if I am telling the truth, and at the sight of the blood, he chuckles.

"Now I won't feel bad for having to hurt you."

I charge, carefully ducking under his swing and landing a strike to his thigh with the edge of my shield. I follow up by raising my arm and throwing a sidewinding thrust at his helmet. I can see that it once again shakes him, and I know this is my chance to land a crushing blow. I throw the strongest strike I can muster directly at his head, knowing if it connects, I will at least knock him down, if not entirely out. But, before the blow can land, I feel the crushing force of his wooden axe connect with my side. I once again fall to the ground, this time clutching my painfully burning ribs.

I gasp for breath as the referee begins to count. Wolfe removes his helmet, lifting both it and his axe to the air in celebration. If it hadn't been for his boasting, I probably would have been content to let the fight end but seeing him arrogantly assume the fight is over makes me forget about my pain. I'm angry, not just with Wolfe but with the rules of the event. I know he isn't nearly as good as he thinks, and he's only winning because his fighting style isn't hindered by wooden weapons. I hate how I can't move freely with my thick leather armor, and my helmet makes it nearly impossible to see strikes coming from the side.

The mood of the arena tells me those watching the fight feel like it's hopeless for me to win. I originally wanted to put up a good fight, and, objectively speaking, I have done so. But it isn't enough. I must put Wolfe in his place. I must win—no matter the cost. For the first time during the fight, I feel like I could seriously beat him. He isn't anything special. Just a strong man with a large piece of wood who's protected by armor that makes my toy sword useless.

"Do you wish to continue?" asks the referee as I stand to my feet.

"Yes, I do," I say, clearly irritated. The referee sighs and leaves to take his position before signaling to start again. I know being angry is going to make me reckless and that it will be in my best interest for Wolfe to be reckless as well. I remove my gloves and take the nose ring Kristoff gave me out of my pocket, then throw it on the ground at Wolfe's feet.

"I believe this used to belong to you."

I've struck a nerve. The tight grip on his axe tells me as much. While I watch his anger grow at the sight of the nose ring on the ground, I consider my best course of action. If I'm going to have a chance of winning, I need to be able to strike effectively, and to do that, I need to be as mobile as possible. I remove my helmet, and the referee jogs over to me.

"Do you wish to concede?"

"No, I want to continue."

"Then please ready yourself."

"I am ready," I reply, holding my shield in my right hand, this time adopting a fist-fighting stance instead of a sword stance. I stand sideways, my left foot forward, and my knees bent so that I can quickly strike or dodge.

"I am going to need you to put your helmet and gloves on, Aries. You could get severely injured," pleads the referee.

"The rules never stated I needed to wear any protective gear, but I really do appreciate your concern. I assure you, I will be fine. You should worry more about his safety."

The referee reluctantly relents and makes his way to signal the fight. I can hear Lee screaming from the sideline. His words aren't clear, but I know he's telling me to put my helmet back on or to stop the fight. The referee waves his hand to signal the action.

Wolfe stands gripping his axe, clearly enraged by the memory of losing his nose ring. He's a bully, and I know all bullies are cowards at heart. They need others to think they are tough, so the reminder of his public humiliation sends him into a rage. I know doing this would increase my chances of being hurt, but it would also allow me the opportunity to find the openings I need to finish the fight. Not to be outdone, Wolfe removes his helmet and throws it at my feet.

The crowd is silent as we circle one another. A single blow to the head for either of us would likely end the fight—more so if he hits me, but that's a risk I must take to win. Despite being furious, I'm acutely focused and feel entirely in control of the situation. Wolfe begins to stalk me, but instead of walking backward, I continue to circle, refusing to give up an inch. I need the contest to be decided quickly, while my rage still empowers me to fight without fear, to fight to win. I am my father's daughter and fear no man, regardless how big. As the distance gradually closes, Wolfe unleashes a flurry of attacks at me, but I see them coming and am able to dodge them easily, sidestepping out of range.

When he switches the direction of his swing, I adjust and step the other way. Using my left hand, I'm able to land a solid punch directly to his nose, which connects right as his axe passes by me without landing. My punch only increases his aggravation, causing him to throw a wild backhand of his own that hits me right in the face. Thinking the strike will stun me, he quickly tries to capitalize with a furious swing of his axe, but he doesn't understand how tough I am.

I trained nearly every day with my father and am accustomed to being hit, so a backhand, even from someone as strong as Wolfe, isn't enough to throw me off balance. Sensing that Wolfe is preparing for a full two-handed strike that seeks to end the fight once and for all, I know now is my one and only chance. I close the distance, using my left hand to grab the back of his head, pulling it forward as I slam the edge of my shield into his face with my full power. The shield crashes against his face with an awful nose-shattering noise.

Wolfe stumbles backward in shock, dropping his axe and putting his hands to his face. He is completely bewildered. In that split second, I know I can severely maim him, just like he tried to do to so many people during the tournament.

I have no remorse for him or any bully for that matter, but I know emotional pain will last far longer than physical. He will be the man spared from injury by the girl from the North. The girl who should never have been able to beat him. I throw a backhanded shield strike to the side of his head with half of my usual power. It is more than enough to knock him to the ground, but it is clear to the crowd the hit is far more restrained than it could have been. The referee begins the count, and as he says each new number, the cheers from the crowd grow louder until finally, he reaches ten and signals that the fight is over.

The noise is so loud that it hurts my head. Either that, or it is my adrenaline running out, causing me to feel the pain from my injuries. I find it odd that despite disliking Wolfe, which I still very much do, I respect him in that moment for being such a formidable adversary. The pain from my injuries continues to grow, and the burning sensation in my ribs returns, becoming so painful that it makes me sweat heavily. I hate the thought of the crowd seeing me acknowledge my pain and instead try to make it to the tents as quickly as possible, hoping to get some sort of relief for my injuries. With each step, though, the pain grows more unbearable until everything turns black.

I wake up suddenly to a horrible smell. As my eyes flutter open, I see Lee, Mum, and the referee kneeling over me. It takes a moment for me to regain my senses and I tell Mum it's fine to remove her short stubby finger from my nostril. The odor is horrendous, worse than anything I've smelled before. Unlike Jaseen, I don't puke, thanks to my "rock gut" stomach, as my father used to call it. I also despise puking so much that I've grown accustomed to holding it back.

"What happened?" I ask, confused.

"What happened? 'What happened,' she says. For starters, you put on the best performance I have ever seen!" Lee replies.

His words trigger a flood of memories. I just defeated Wolfe. My body aches, especially my ribs, where he hit me with his large wooden axe.

"Please tell me he's still out and that I wasn't down longer than him," I murmur, standing up painfully with Lee and Mum's help.

"Honestly, haven't looked to see," Lee admits, turning to look.

"He woke up just a few seconds before you, dear," Mum says. I'm skeptical but Lee seems to believe her, not looking in Wolfe's direction. Mum is mysterious, projecting a power that contradicts her humble stature and warm demeanor.

"So, what happens now?" I inquire.

"Well, you made it to the finals, love. But do you think you can continue? No shame if you can't; you're a winner in my book anyhow. Brilliant, truly brilliant. I can't even begin to—" Lee starts, before Mum interrupts him.

"Lee, let's get her to the tents and let her recover. She'll have plenty of time to think about what happens next. After all, this is her story," Mum says warmly.

"Don't you have your own fight to worry about?" I ask, clutching my side in pain.

"Yes, but I had to make sure you were okay. The crowd can wait or go on without me," Lee answers, looking down at me with a smile. My passing out must have worried him. I can't believe he seems to care so much.

"They will wait. Could you imagine them being denied the chance to watch the next match?" Mum reassures.

"They'd bloody well riot, I reckon," I reply, attempting to mimic Lee's Southlander accent. I laugh at my own joke, wincing in pain as my ribs protest.

"Serves you right. Laughing at your own joke," Lee says, chuckling. "Poor taste, especially from someone who showed mercy to Wolfe."

"Mercy, or forcing him to live with the fact that he was saved from serious injury by a girl from the North?"

"Oh, I hadn't considered that. You are devious, Aries Fleetwood," Lee comments, making me blush uncontrollably.

"Well, I best be off. Wish me luck, ladies," Lee says as he and Mum finish escorting me to the fighter's tent.

"Good luck, Lee. Not that you'll need it," Mum replies warmly.

"Good luck, but don't finish him too quickly, yeah?" I tease.

"Okay, I won't," he answers with a smile, running out before I can clarify I wasn't serious.

"I hope he knew I was joking."

"Oh, sweetheart, he would have done that without your request. I think he fancies you," Mum whispers with a wink, making me blush again. I decide to change the subject.

"Do you like his chances in this round?" I ask.

"Yes, though it could be harder than he expects. Lee can be—overly confident. His opponent trains hard and has been champion before."

"Does Lee train all year too?"

"Not as much as the others. Most of his success comes from natural abilities and faith," Mum says.

"I didn't think Southlanders were religious."

"He's not religious in the way you think. He believes in the old ways, the ones before the Apex and their One True God," Mum clarifies with a smile. "We'll have plenty of time to discuss faith and religion, which are topics you should never shy away from. They help us grow."

Mum looks me over. "Have you decided whether or not you'll fight on? Though, I think I know your answer."

"And what do you think that is? I'm not even sure myself."

"I think you're not one to let injuries stop you. It would feel like quitting, wouldn't it?"

"That sums up my thoughts, but I don't want to fight Lee."

"That answer has much more depth than it seems."

"I don't want him to take it easy on me, just because I'm a girl or because I'm hurt."

"On the contrary," Mum replies, "you will be Lee's hardest opponent for various reasons. Not only are you skilled and wise in battle, but your relentless spirit, the inability to quit, makes it particularly challenging. Lee's most significant struggle will be within his own mind, torn between not wanting to harm you and honoring your wishes for him to fight at full strength. I'm eager to see how it unfolds and trust that both of you will follow fate's path. Good luck, beautiful Aries. Now, you must wage war within your own mind. Remember, no matter the outcome, you and Lee have my full support." Mum kisses me on the top of the head and travels towards the exit.

"Oh, and don't worry," she adds, turning around, "We'll heal your wounds after the fight. I'd do it now, but rules are rules. And you wouldn't want to win through special treatment, right? Bye now."

Her words, while valid, don't simplify things for me. I know I'm going to fight, but if Lee wins, how can I ensure he's giving it his all? I also ponder whether I can push myself, as I don't want to hurt him either. Though injured, luckily, none of it is severe.

The crowd's cheers suggest an exciting fight is underway. I contemplate watching but just thinking about Lee fighting sends nerves crawling through me. I certainly want him to win, even if it makes the finals mentally taxing, like Mum said. After some thought, I decide we should compete as if it's any other opponent. Win or lose, I don't want anything held back. But how do I convey this to him? Perhaps he already feels the same. Mum's intuition about Lee's feelings towards me might be off, but she hasn't been wrong yet.

My thoughts scatter as the crowd erupts, cheering Lee's name. The fight took longer than his previous ones, and I suspect he indeed prolonged it on purpose. Moments later, he enters the tent, with a cut above his eye bleeding slightly.

"Bloody mask, am I right?" I quip, trying to ease the tension now that we're sure to face each other.

"I see what you did there," he replies with a forced smile.

"We won't have long before it starts. I was thinking, maybe I should concede. You earned the title defeating Wolfe. I mean, he was the strongest competitor. It's not fair that I got some guy with a toy spear," he suggests hesitantly.

"Please don't," I plead. "Let's just compete and may the best fighter win. Mum even promised healing after the fight. Though, I dread it might be with that awful substance in her vial."

"I suspect it's some horrendous tonic," he admits. "But honestly, I don't know if I can fight you."

"Why? Because I'm a girl?"

"I've beaten many girls in tournaments," he answers quickly. "That didn't come out right, did it?"

"I'm competitive, like you. Winning matters to me, and fighting you isn't appealing. But if I win, I don't want whispers saying you went easy on me because I'm a girl or injured. I've fought all my life and know what it's like to have success questioned," I assert with a hint of anger, hoping he understands my seriousness.

"To be fair, fuck everyone," he declares.

"What do you mean?"

"Who cares what people think? The only opinion that matters is your own. People will always doubt and talk, trust me. Especially here, where words are wind."

"So, you don't care what people think?"

"Only those I care about."

"I don't buy it. You care, that's why you compete. You crave the recognition from winning, just like the rest of us," I respond, getting frustrated with his smugness. As I grow more frustrated, he observes me closely, and when he speaks again, his tone softens.

"Honestly, I've been competing against myself. My father wasn't here to see me win last year. May he rest in peace. I wanted to make him proud, to show it wasn't a fluke. Reaching the finals is enough for me. But I see how much this means to you, so I give you my word: I will fight as you wish."

Mentioning his father brings pain to Lee's eyes, making me feel guilty for arguing. We share the grief of absent fathers, and not knowing what to say, I simply reply, "Thanks, Lee. That means a lot."

The referee enters, signaling that it's time. We gear up and walk towards The proving grounds.

"Leave her shield, mate," Lee jokes to the ref, who stops, confused by his statement.

"No, I'll take my shield, thank you very much," I retort, grabbing it. I know Lee's footwork is too quick for me to land punches with a shield, so I decide to hold it in my left hand and focus on using my sword. Lee isn't as big as Wolfe, so I can do more damage with sword strikes. But that's as far as my strategy goes. Thinking further is hard with all the emotions swirling inside me. I hate that I have to fight Lee. I wish I could fight Wolfe again, even with my injuries.

"Okay, focus, Aries," I whisper to myself, trying to formulate a plan. The fight can go two ways: either Lee is offensive, and I need to land a heavy blow, or he's defensive, and I should throw diverse strikes to catch him off guard.

With the banging of the gong, the finals begin. Lee assumes his familiar sideways stance, knees bent, ready to strike or dodge. I grip my sword tightly, knowing I need perfect timing and precision to hit him effectively. It wasn't until the end of my fight with Wolfe that I realized the event tests more than weapon skills. Lee knows this, relying on footwork, kicks, and punches more than weapon strikes.

I prepare to block his attacks with my shield, closing the distance. He seems to be planning on fighting defensively, relying on counterstrikes. I've seen him make fools out of opponents who swing wildly, and I won't make the same mistake. When I'm in striking range, I feint, but he doesn't fall for it. Instead, he throws a few feints of his own. As he raises his dagger for a feint, I pretend to strike with my shield and follow with an overhead sword strike aimed at his shoulder. I hoped avoiding his head would limit his dodging, but he side-steps, making me miss completely.

I follow up with more strikes, watching his footwork to prevent counterstrikes. He continues to back up, dodging my attacks. I can't tell if he's holding back or if my strategy of applying consistent pressure is working. His footwork reminds me of my father's, so I decide to use one of his tactics. I keep swinging at Lee, loosening my grip on the shield so it slides down my wrist, freeing my hand. Switching my sword to my left hand, I swipe at his head. He sees it coming and dodges, but this is a diversion. I throw an uppercut where his head will be after dodging, landing the punch. Switching my sword back to my right hand, I hit him solidly on the side of his head.

Lee stumbles from my strikes, and I don't relent, attacking continuously. As he tries to recover, he can't dodge as effectively and resorts to blocking with his wrist guards. I swing, landing several strikes while he keeps retreating. Suddenly, I feel my pace slowing, as I'm close to exhaustion. The smart move would be to back off and catch my breath, but I feel I'm close to landing a finishing blow and continue the assault. The crowd's cheers fuel me.

I throw a solid left hook with my shield, pushing him off balance, then attempt a downward sword strike at his head. Lee turns, drops his dagger, and grabs my sword arm, using my momentum to flip me over his back. I hit the ground hard, frustrated and confused. As the referee begins the count, I stand, grabbing my sword and leaving my shield. The fight continues.

This time, I focus on landing kicks to Lee's thighs, hoping to limit his mobility. Each time I kick, he retaliates with a kick to my plant leg. It's a test of perseverance, and I refuse to back down. The crowd is ecstatic with each exchange, and their cheers strengthen my resolve. I sense my kicks taking a toll as Lee's retaliations lose strength and speed. I adjust, aiming for accuracy over power, hitting the same spot on his thigh repeatedly. Eventually, he lifts his leg to minimize the pain, revealing his discomfort. I win the battle of wills, but I'm far from victory, and the satisfaction doesn't ease my exhaustion.

My breathing is heavy, and lifting my arms becomes a struggle. I decide to play defensively, I hope my kicks have hindered his footwork enough for easy counters. Lee closes the distance, slower than usual but still fast. He swings his dagger; I parry and counter. Each time I try, he blocks my sword with incredible coordination. I do my best to keep up, but fatigue makes it difficult. Turning my tactic against me, Lee switches his dagger to his left hand and lands a solid hit on the side of my head. It doesn't hurt as much as I expected, making me wonder if the leg strikes have weakened him. Then I hear the sound of metal denting and realize it's my helmet.

My vision goes dark, and when it comes back, I see only dirt before me. I'm face down, and the referee is still counting. Lee has granted my wish of treating me like any other opponent and has landed a blow capable of ending the fight. Misunderstanding how strong his strike was infuriates me and makes me feel foolish. Driven by my ire, I quickly stand to my feet, adjusting my crooked helmet.

"Aries, please stay down," pleads Lee, clearly distraught at the thought of having to continue fighting me. I do not wish to do him harm, but the strike was so skillful and effective that it ignites my anger. The referee gives me a concerned look before handing back my sword. It's clear the referee wants to talk me out of continuing, but his advice would fall upon deaf ears. I breathe heavily as I await his signal that the fight can resume. Lee shakes his head. "Please, I don't want to hurt you."

The referee waves his hand, restarting the fight, stirring the crowd back into a frenzy. I stalk Lee, walking slowly towards him while I drag my sword gently across the dirt field. He seems confused, unsure of how to proceed. I continue to walk slowly towards him, using the lack of action as an opportunity to regain my breath. Once I'm within range, I startle him by letting out a battle cry before I begin swinging with all my strength, holding my wooden sword with both hands. Lee is caught off guard but still attempts to dodge. I focus on his shoulders, torso, and thighs, landing several strikes, but none strong enough to knock him down. He tries to land counterattacks of his own, some of which I'm able to dodge. Those that land lack the power to stop my onslaught, and I push on.

I use a misdirection tactic my father had taught me. I make it appear that my strike is targeting my opponent's head, but instead, I come down with a powerful thrust to his thigh, right where I had previously targeted with my leg kicks. Lee yells in pain and drops his left hand to clutch his injury. Wasting no time, I follow up with a two-handed, sidewinding strike to the side of his helmet, doing my best to dent it, as he had done to me. The strike is a success and knocks Lee down for the first time in the tournament.

He falls to the ground and shakes his head before making his way to his feet, laughing. "Well done, love," he says, still trying to shake off the ringing in his ears. I want to continue to fight, but I am utterly exhausted. I gave everything I had, and he simply complimented me and laughed it off. My anger vanishes as quickly as my breath, and I drop my sword at his feet and take off my helmet before collapsing to the ground so that I can finally catch my breath.

Lee extends his hand to me, and I stare at it for some time before deciding to use it to help me leave the surprisingly comfortable ground. I can tell by his expression that he isn't sure how to act, worried that I may be upset. But as competitive as I am, losing very rarely upsets me, so long as the contest is fair, and I've given it my all.

"I hope we put on a good show," I say, still struggling to catch my breath.

"It was brilliant, never heard them cheer like that, especially, when you knocked me about."

"Knocked you down, you mean," I correct, causing him to put his familiar smirk back on his face.

"Look, no hard feelings, yeah? It was a quality fight," he says.

"Of course, but you better not have held back."

"Believe me, if I give my word, I always keep it. If I seemed off, it was due to my bloody leg, special thanks to you. Come, let's find Mum and drink whatever concoction she has for us, yeah? We need to get rid of this pain and get ready for the champions' dinner."

"Sounds good to me. I'm ready for my ribs to stop hurting so I can breathe normally again." I rub my side and smile sheepishly at Lee. "No offense, but nothing you did compared to Wolfe's strikes."

"Oh really, and how did that work for him?"

Lee and I walk to the fighters' tents, where we are greeted by Mum, Andrew, Jaseen, and Kristoff. Their congratulations and excitement make my headache feel even worse.

"The Romani has earned not only first but second place as well, tourney champion and runner up. When was the last time that's happened? Has it ever even happened?" Andrew asks, his enthusiasm barely contained. "Mum, has it?"

"Quiet, darling. Remember, they just got done fighting one another and may appreciate some peace and quiet," she says patiently to Andrew. Then she turns to Lee and me. "Here, I've made a cup for each of you. It is best to drink it quickly and maybe plug your nose." She hands us each a small jar containing a dark green substance that is so thick it barely passes for liquid. "Oh, I am so very proud of you two! You were both brilliant!"

Lee quickly downs his drink and makes an awful face indicating his disgust. Despite seeing that the green goo is less than pleasant going down, my ribs hurt so badly I am willing to face whatever horrible taste awaits me. With a couple of quick gulps, I chug it completely, doing my best to appear as though it is a simple glass of water. I wipe my mouth and give a smug look to Lee, who is still battling the aftertaste.

"Nobody get into a drinking contest with this one," says Jaseen.

"Lee doesn't even drink, remember?" says Andrew.

"Yesterday you were worried about being humiliated in the first round, and today you finish as the runner up. Not too bad for a girl from the North," says Kristoff, patting me on the back.

"Thanks, that means a lot. Especially coming from the champion of the gauntlet. Oh, that reminds me, did you see me throw the nose ring at Wolfe?" I ask, triggering a rapid-fire conversation between me and Kristoff.

"Yes! What did he say? Did he go mad? I bet he did because right after that you started wailing on him."

"Yeah, he was furious. I wanted to laugh, but I was so angry I could have ripped his face off."

"So why did you barely hit him at the end? Was it because you knew it would shame him? That's what I told Andrew and Jaseen, but they didn't believe me. They said you were being honorable. I said, 'She is plenty honorable, trust me, but not towards people like that'. And since Wolfe was the one who was already being disrespectful, I knew you wouldn't hold back."

"Yes, that's exactly why! I had to tell Lee and Mum that too. He is going to remember that for far longer than any wound I could have given him."

"Where is the ring? Did he take it? If not, I think I would like to hold onto it. Maybe we can still use it to make him angry if needed."

"It should be on the field, unless one of the referees took it or something. I doubt he would want it anymore. It's tainted."

Kristoff and I continue to chatter about the fight and the gauntlet. Now that the events are over, I can finally go back to feeling normal since I don't have to worry about competing. After a while, I realize the others are staring at Kristoff and me, since we completely ignored them.

"So, what now?" I ask the group.

"Well, that is up to you, my lovelies. The champions' ceremony isn't until nightfall, so I would recommend exploring the Faire until then. I am sure these three can keep you company. Do you need any coin until you get your prize money?" Mum asks.

"I think we're good but thank you so much. I honestly didn't even know second place received any money," I say.

"Oh yes, and it's a large amount, too. Kristoff also receives a decent sum for winning, but not as much. To be fair, he was just running," says Jaseen.

"If it was just running, why couldn't anyone from the clan ever win before?" asks Kristoff.

"Oy, Kristoff, if Jaseen could run, do you think he would have gotten whacked by his own bloody sword?" says Lee, causing everyone to laugh.

"Let's just say if it was a proper sword, Wolfe would be ashes right now," Jaseen replies, seeming to have a good sense of humor about his loss.

The group begins to make their way for the Faire, save for Mum who wanders off on her own, which is to be expected. I'm already beginning to feel much better thanks to the tonic she gave me. My headache is gone entirely, and my ribs only barely hurt. Not to mention I finally have my breath back and don't feel as if I'm going to overheat. I'm in desperate need of a bath, and I doubt I'll have the chance before dinner, which makes me feel gross, but from what I can tell, the women in the Southlands aren't held to the same unreasonable expectations of appearance as the women in the Apex, so I don't think anyone will mind besides myself.

"Is there someplace where I can get some new clothes? Mine are drenched in sweat and other people's blood, and maybe a bit of my own," I ask, smelling my dirty shirt.

"Same," Kristoff replies, who is probably even more interested in a bath than I am.

"There are loads of shops that sell clothes. Best let us come with you to make sure nobody is treating you like a knobhead," Lee replies.

"What is a knobhead? Why do you guys all speak so differently?" I ask, laughing.

"It means like a fool, yeah. Although I doubt anyone would try and make Aries the tourney champion finalist out as a mark. If anything, they'd fancy giving her a discount to say they sold her the outfit," Andrew replies.

"I think Lee just wants to go clothes shopping with her to make sure she doesn't outdress him tonight," says Jaseen.

I laugh. I like seeing how they interact, insulting each other for fun. It reminds me of how Kristoff and I are to each other. The trio is incredibly close, even compared to how close clan members typically are with each other.

The group comes upon a section of the Faire known as Merchant Square. The walkways are lined with countless vendors selling all manner of items. Kristoff, Andrew, and Jaseen venture off to get some food while Lee volunteers to accompany me. As we walk along the dirt road, an older lady beckons me to come over. The woman is well into old age and sits on a wooden rocking chair located right beside the door of a shop that looks to be selling various mystical items.

"Well, don't wait," says the woman, sounding almost irritated.

I give a confused look to Lee, who responds with one of his own. "I'm sorry, ma'am. Do I know you?" I ask, unsure of why this stranger requested my presence in the first place.

"No, dear, but I have something to tell you."

"And what is that?" I ask politely, not moving any closer.

"Someone is attempting to reach you."

"Really, and who might that be?" I reply, playing along.

"I don't know what you're selling, miss, but we ain't interested," says Lee.

"Ain't nobody trying to sell nothing. Do I look like I have use of coin? I can barely bloody walk," she spats. She turns her attention back to me. "I am not sure who or—what they are but be careful. They are searching for you, trying to give you a message. Be careful, darling."

"And how do you know this?" asks Lee.

"Now that part will cost ya," says the old woman, extending her palm.

"And there it is," says Lee, rolling his eyes. "We best be on our way."

"Stay away from crystal balls. They could let someone find you, even from across the sea," she says quietly so only I can hear. I can't help but feel concerned. Perhaps, after discovering my father, Kristoff, and I had snuck away undetected, Stur and Beltrum deduced that we would be heading for the Southlands, and they are now trying to seek us out. Or even worse, maybe whoever controls the Revenant is looking for us. I feel foolish. Kristoff and I have come to the Southlands and instead of laying low we have made a spectacle of ourselves. Now nearly every person at the Faire knows of the two outsiders from the North.

"How much?" I whisper. Regardless of whether I'm being swindled, I want to know if there is any truth to what she said.

"I'm far too tired today. Maybe come back another day," says the old lady before giving me a wink.

Her extremely useless answer frustrates me. The woman has no idea how threatening the situation could be if the Apex, the Watchers, or Carthage were looking for me. I take a slow, deep breath. I don't want to overreact. Instead of pressing the woman for answers, I decide it would be best to talk to Mum about it when I get the chance. If Kristoff and I had been followed, it should take weeks for whoever is looking for us to arrive in the Southlands, and by that time, we will be deep into Romani territory. Still, I suddenly can't wait for the Faire to be over.

"Do you think she was lying?" I ask.

"'Course she is. She's been selling knock-off magic for years. Mum and most of the other elders don't associate with her."

Lee's response makes me feel somewhat better, but I still worry it's only a matter of time before the past catches up to us. Even though I have only been here a short time, I love the Southlands and the Romani, but the excitement of everything has distracted me, and I have almost forgotten why I came in the first place. I know there is still much to do and to learn if I'm going to avenge my father and Kristoff's parents. I shake my head. There is nothing I can do about it now. Until I can sit and talk with Mum and make a plan of action, I figure it would be best for Kristoff and me to enjoy the night. After all, we both earned the right given what we have just accomplished.

Lee and I finally come across a shop selling clothes, many of which are displayed on wooden dummies. It reminds me of an Apexian boutique but with its own Southland flare added to it. The shop is managed by a young woman who appears to be in her late teens. She's a few inches taller than me and has long blonde hair, big green eyes, and an attractive face.

"See anything you fancy?" Lee asks.

"What do you think about this?" I ask, pointing to an outfit with slim brown trousers and a matching leather vest.

"I mean, do as you wish, but if it was up to me, I'd say get this," he responds, showing me a dress with a corset on the outside that would undoubtedly show a lot of cleavage.

"Be quiet," I say, laughing and slapping him on his arm. "Actually, you know what, I love it. Excuse me, miss? My friend here would love to try on that dress. Do you think it would fit him?"

"I am sure we can make it work," replies the young shopkeeper who is busy sewing lace onto a dress she's working on. Lee's face goes red as he blushes, making me laugh even more.

"How much for the lot?" I ask, referring to the brown outfit I had first noticed.

"I can make you a deal on that if you like, but tell me, are you the girl from The proving grounds?"

"I guess you could say that," I reply, embarrassed by the recognition.

"If you are looking for something nice for the dinner tonight, you should let me make something custom for you."

"That won't be necessary. I'm just looking for something that isn't covered in sweat and other people's blood," I reply.

"Oh, and you must be Lee!" The woman says, seeming to have just noticed. "Curious you two are friendly. Judging by your fight, I would have expected some hard feelings," replies the shop owner as she stands up and walks towards us. "Name's Marybeth. I am one of the tailors here. This is my grandma's shop."

We each shake her hand. "It would be an honor to style you for the event," Marybeth says, repeating her offer. "And you too, Lee. I will give you a great deal, only a few pieces of silver." Marybeth looks excited about the opportunity and seems very eager. I don't want to squash her hopes, so I agree.

"Not me, I'll be just fine in what I'm wearing," replies Lee.

"Nonsense, he will also need an outfit," I reply, giving him a serious look resulting in his instant compliance.

"Fine, but my dress better not have a bloody corset," he jokes.

Marybeth takes measurements from both of us and asks us for preferences on our outfits. I'm impressed by how well the tailor can read me; she doesn't once suggest a dress. I enjoy wearing dresses on certain occasions, but I still feel like I'm in unfamiliar territory and until I'm more accustomed with the area, I want to be prepared to fight or flee if the situation arises.

After taking my measurements and trying out several colorful options, Marybeth brings out a pair of cotton pants that are dyed a light green, paired with a form-fitting white blouse and a light pink vest. I initially think the outfit is too bright, but after noticing Lee's reaction when I try it on, I decide to go with it. Marybeth is an exceptional tailor, and she's able to make the pants and blouse fit my form in a way that causes Lee to stare openly, though he tries, and fails, to stop himself from doing so.

Next up is Lee, who is clearly uncomfortable having his measurements taken. I wonder if he has ever received a tailored outfit before. I know that he cares about style based on how he dresses on a regular basis, but most of his clothing is loose fitting.

Marybeth pairs maroon cotton pants with a white button-up shirt, and to finish the ensemble, she adds a light brown vest. Now I'm the one staring. I haven't seen Lee's form before, and now that his clothing is tighter, his fit physique is far more obvious. He isn't overly muscular like Wolfe and his clansmen, but it's clear he exercises to keep his arms and legs well-defined. When Lee notices me staring, he blushes once again.

"I don't know about this, isn't it a bit ambitious?" he says as he looks at himself in the mirror.

"Really? Coming from the two-time tourney champion? Besides, I think Aries may like it a bit too much for you not to get it," says Marybeth, causing me to snap out of my trance.

"Wait, what? Oh—yeah. It's—fine. You should get it, that is if you like it," I say to downplay how much I want him to wear it.

"I don't know," he says.

"Look," I interrupt, "let's get it so we can be on our way. I am starving, and the least you can do is get me some food after beating me in front of literally everyone at the Faire."

"Fine," he sighs before giving Marybeth a generous handful of silver, which is more than enough to cover both outfits.

Lee and I thank Marybeth for her time and make our way back outside to find some food. He introduces me to a vendor that specializes in making different kinds of stews. I love it, especially since the stew is warm and there is a cold chill in the air. It reminds me of the harvest time in Fairfield and the small market that is set up in the town square for people to buy food from various farmers. Lee and I continue to explore the Faire to pass the time. He fills me in on many customs and practices that I'm likely to encounter in the Southlands, and how each clan has its own unique culture. I love how each clan is so diverse, mainly because it's different from the Apex. The High Church refers to any people of a culture other than their own as heathens and savages. This was the rallying cry used to conquer most of Felicity many years ago.

Eventually, Lee and I meet back up with Kristoff, Andrew, and Jaseen so we can all make our way to the ceremony together. I notice that Kristoff now has a short sword attached to his belt.

"Good to see you spent your money wisely," I say with a smirk.

"Don't worry, Andrew and Jaseen made sure I got a great deal, especially after they told the blacksmith that I was the champion of the gauntlet. The people around here really take the Faire seriously."

"That's cause people train year-round for the chance to win, mate. Not everyone can just walk off a boat and become champion," Andrew replies, making Kristoff smile. He's clearly thriving from the support he's receiving from the Romani.

"I am not really looking forward to this. I would much rather be given my prize with as little attention as possible," I mention, finding myself growing more nervous as I think about the champions' feast.

"Relax, love. It's more of a party than anything. It won't last long, and then we'll all head back to camp. Say, you guys are heading back home with us, right?" asks Lee.

I assumed we would be heading to the Romani homeland, but I realize I haven't thoroughly planned it out or discussed it with anyone yet. "Yea, I think we would like to if you guys would have us," I reply.

"'Course we would! In fact, if you said no, the lads and me had a plan to kidnap the two of you," replies Jaseen with a shrug.

"So, how does one officially join the Romani?" asks Kristoff.

"Well, the first rule is no gingers, so we'd have to cut that mop off your head," replies Lee, who playfully messes up Kristoff's hair.

"Someone's jealous," replies Kristoff, frantically adjusting his hair, making Andrew and Jaseen laugh.

"But seriously, what all does joining entail?" I ask.

"Mum can explain it better, but it's more of a formality. Most of us were born into the clan, so we don't remember our ceremony, but as we came of age, we all swore fealty to the clan and gave our word to defend and honor it," says Andrew.

"What's fealty?" asks Kristoff.

"It's giving your word to do right by the clan and its people. Ain't like what you'd see in the Apex though. Each member is free, and it won't be like you belong to a lord or king," says Lee.

"Where we come from, fealty has an entirely different meaning," I say.

"I think the meaning is the same. But with our clan, nobody desires to control the lives of others—and that goes for most of the Southlands. Save for the Guul, of course. They revere their chieftain, and his word is law, so they won't hesitate to do whatever he says. Luckily, their current chieftain is relatively stable, at least for a Guul."

"What happens if someone disobeys the laws of the Romani?" asks Kristoff.

"Doesn't really happen much, mate. Mum is the head, and everyone knows she cares about us. If she wants something, she doesn't really have to make anyone do anything. They'd just do it 'cause they respect her."

I know what he means. I have only known Mum for a short while, but it's obvious what a kind soul she is. She's someone who only wants the best for her people. She also doesn't carry herself anything like leaders I've seen before, mainly because she doesn't take herself too seriously.

"If my mother believed enough in the Romani to pledge her fealty to them, and my dad told me we would be safe here, then I won't hesitate to do so as well," I say, prompting a nod of agreement from Kristoff.

"That's what we like to hear," says Lee, grinning from ear to ear and looking relieved, as though he worried we would go our separate ways after the Faire.

Kristoff, Lee, and I make our way to the Great Hall, which is a large wooden structure located in the northernmost part of the Faire. We're told no weapons are permitted inside and are required to check our blades at the door. Everyone does as requested, but I seriously doubt that Lee, Andrew, and Jaseen are completely unarmed after handing over their daggers.

Despite the Great Hall being so large, there is only one room inside, which is filled with several wooden tables and benches, with a magnificent, large table directly in the center. Chandeliers holding candles so bright and numerous they light up the entire hall are hanging from the ceiling by metal chains. Five banners hang from the hall's rafters, which I assume represent the respective clans of the Southlands. While the hall looks spectacular, this is a room that focuses on function rather than appearance. There are already several people sitting at the various tables, socializing, and drinking from their wooden mugs.

"Us simple folk must retire to the smaller tables while you lot get to sit amongst the elders at the table of champions," says Jaseen, smiling wide.

I find myself becoming increasingly nervous as we make our way to the table.

"Excuse me, where should we sit?" Lee asks a barmaid, who promptly points to our seats. The winners are seated in sections, which means that Kristoff is to sit with the other gauntlet competitors. I'm already nervous, but the thought of being so far from him makes it even worse. I know if things get awkward, he will defuse it with his humor.

Lee and I take our seats near the head of the table. Based on our location, it's clear the clans value the Proving Ground competitors above all. The seating order indicates that the empty seats next to me must be reserved for Wolfe and the other semifinalist.

"Please just kill me now," I say.

"Sorry, what now?" Lee asks, confused.

"I'd rather die than sit next to Wolfe."

"I'm sure it will be more awkward for him, and that should bring you joy, yeah?"

He has a point. Maybe he won't show up, I think hopefully.

Other people in the hall find their seats, some of whom look like competitors, and others who I figure are elders, both because of their age and how they dress. That's when I notice Mum making her way to the table. She's wearing a simple green and white dress that looks absolutely beautiful on her. I notice she isn't wearing any shoes, and now that I think about it, I don't recall ever seeing her in a pair. I smile to myself. Mum is a small plump woman who always seems to have a smile on her face, and yet she never fails to command a tremendous amount of respect from those around her.

"Hello, my lovelies. Are you excited for the feast? I have been trying not to eat all day, so I would have the room to put away the delicious food that will be served. I can't say I succeeded, but I don't think it will stop me," she says before wandering off to her seat towards the middle of the table.

I admire Mum. She doesn't seem to care about formalities at all, which makes me feel more comfortable.

"I always love seeing her at things like this. It's pure comedy. She doesn't care what people think," says Lee, who has leaned over so that only I can hear him. I can't help but notice he's wearing cologne. It smells so good that I don't want him to lean away. I wonder when he put it on. We have been together most of the day and I don't remember smelling it earlier.

I lean towards Lee, hoping to come up with a question to ask him that will allow me to linger long enough to get a better whiff. Struggling to come up with something clever to say, and without meaning to, I say, "Are you wearing cologne?"

I immediately feel my face grow warm as it turns red from embarrassment. I lean back into my seat and try to avoid his eyes as much as possible.

"Yeah, do you like it? Kristoff gave it to me. I typically don't wear it but figured I'd give it a go, it being the feast and all."

That explains it. Kristoff gave Lee the cologne on purpose. He knows I love fragrances and that if I get a whiff of a good smelling cologne, especially the one Lee is wearing, I will make a fool of myself. He's lucky he's seated away from me, or else I'd have half a mind to wring his neck.

"Do you like it?" he asks.

"Um, yes—you, you should definitely wear it—a lot," I reply, stumbling over my words. I would have never thought I would be glad to see Wolfe, but thankfully his arrival provides a distraction.

I notice he has a black eye, and his nose appears to be crooked and swollen. I wonder if his clan has access to the same kind of healing concoctions as the Romani do.

"Evening," he says unenthusiastically.

I feel sorry for Wolfe, though I don't know why. I wonder if he's such a miserable bully because of how he was raised. Perhaps all of his clan are that way. But, of course, the small burst of empathy for him vanishes shortly after he opens his mouth. He seems incapable of speaking without bragging or insulting someone.

"So, Wolfe, any exciting plans for this winter?" I ask bitingly. I notice Lee turns to stare at Wolfe, waiting to hear his response and see how much hostility he can pack into his answer.

He lets out a snort. "Same as every winter. Hunt and sleep."

"Sounds exhilarating. How about you, Lee? Anything exciting?" I ask.

"Hate to agree, but what else can you do in the winter?" he replies.

"Well, this is a riveting conversation," I say unenthusiastically.

"I'm surprised you're even talking to me," says Wolfe smugly.

"And why is that?" I ask, preparing myself for an argument.

"Isn't it obvious? The pub, the trash-talking, the fight we had."

I wonder if Wolfe, or perhaps anyone from the Southlands, understands sarcasm. "Yeah, I guess when you put it that way, there isn't much reason to speak," I reply, making Lee chuckle.

"Oh, leave ole Wolfe alone. He just takes some getting used to before he warms up. But after you get to know him, he's basically a big teddy bear," says Lee.

"Speaking of warming up, how's Jaseen?" asks Wolfe before taking a big drink from his mug.

Lee gives him a serious look. "Didn't you see? He made a full recovery. Sad we can't say the same for your nose. Looks like Aries finished what Kristoff started. Who knows? Maybe it's an improvement."

"I hate this so-called peace. I long for when the clans fought for land and reputation," replies Wolfe.

"Remind me, how did that end for the Guul?"

Lee's words strike a nerve, and Wolfe simply grits his teeth instead of responding. I don't know what his question implies, but I assume the Guul were defeated before whatever peace was made. I'm also willing to wager, Wolfe is either afraid of Lee—as demonstrated by his behavior on our first night at the pub—or that he's worried about disrupting the peace out of fear of how it would make his clan look.

Most people at the table are in great spirits, laughing and drinking, but most of the attendees refrain from associating with Wolfe. Even his other clansmen keep to themselves and don't interact much with anyone from other clans. Whatever peace resulted at the end of the conflict between the clans seems to be loosely held together, and while it's an attempt to improve the situation, I get the feeling the Faire fails to ease tensions between the clans.

Once all the seats are filled, a large man makes his way to the head of the table, looking out at those gathered in the hall before he takes his seat. He has a great white and grey beard, and despite his old age, possesses an athletic build. His eyes are light brown and hidden beneath bushy grey eyebrows. He wears a dark leather breastplate and wrist guards, indicating his readiness for battle. While the man gives off a foreboding look, his words are warm and welcoming.

"As many of you know, I'm the fool tasked with being the master of ceremonies for the feast, but some of you know me as Robert Highlander. A choice I imagine could only be a joke at my expense, seeing as how I am drunk nearly half the time and make a complete arse of myself the other half. So tonight, we feast and drink and honor our clansmen who competed to bring honor to themselves, their ancestors, their clans, and all the Southlands. No place in Felicity is as fierce as the Southlands, and our warriors are the greatest alive—save for the two who hopped off the boat and managed to win the gauntlet and finish runner up at the proving grounds." The crowd laughs especially hard at the comment about me and Kristoff, and I join in.

"They are members of the Romani, my dear, by birthright and allegiance," says Mum, standing to her feet as she speaks before quickly taking her seat once more. The crowd once again laughs, and I can tell most of them are finding nearly anything to be funny on account of how much they've drunk.

"Pity, Clan Harald would love to have them. But enough of my jealousy, let's get down to business. It's time to honor our champions, without whom we would just be another slave realm to the Apex. Their ferocity keeps those zealots from our lands. Their strength and endurance make us too much of a match for them, even with their flying warships. With them on our side, the Southlands will never be conquered. To them!" says Robert, prompting the crowd to cheer and drink from their mugs. "Now, my brothers and sisters, we eat and drink as one, for although we come from different clans and have different ways of life, we will forever be bonded by the old ways and the honor of being a Southlander."

I find myself inspired by his words. To me, they embody what I love most about the Southlands, particularly how the people here are unique and free.

The servers bring out food consisting of slow-roasted meats, various types of potatoes, and fruits and vegetables. I pile a wide variety of food on my plate to taste as many Southland dishes as possible. While I eat, Robert formally introduces himself.

"Aries, is it? I knew your mother, and I know for a fact she would be proud of your performance, especially knocking this bloke down," he says, referring to Lee before patting him hard on the back.

"Thank you. I wish she could have been here to see it."

"Me too. Sorry for my intrusion, but is it true she has passed on?"

"Yes, sadly—been over ten years now."

"Sorry for your loss. To her!" he says, drinking from his mug. "Tell me, is it true what they say about the North?"

"What do you mean?"

"That the Apex has fallen. Rumor is Carthage mounted an uprising and completely scattered their armies."

I'm not sure where he got his information, but I find it hard to believe it's anything more than wishful thinking, or a tall tale at best.

"There were uprisings. But last I saw, the airships put an end to it. I highly doubt Carthage would be able to stand against the Apex, even if they were able to unite with other realms."

"Well, that's just it, lass. Rumor has it Carthage found their airships and burned them while anchored in marshes not far from the Apex. Of course, after they took at least five for themselves. They said their prince turned himself over to the High Church to stand trial at the Spire. And while that was going on he had his men use the airships to burn the city. But again, this is just what I've been told."

"It's a creative story, though one I doubt actually happened," I reply before drifting into deep thought about what I just heard. It reminds me of my dream in which the Apexian army was defeated by enemy airships, and I wonder if there may be some truth to it.

"I must say, regardless of whether it is the Apex or Carthage that seeks to rule Felicity, the people will suffer," I add, making sure to communicate my dislike for Carthage, who I blame for unleashing the Revenant on my father.

"She speaks the truth. Never trust someone who wishes to be king, especially after their father has met an untimely death. Those lands are known for their twisted obsession with dark magic," Robert says thoughtfully. "But these are things you need not concern yourself with. You are in the Southlands now. The last free lands in all of Felicity welcome you!" With those words, Robert raises his drink and finishes it off.

I'm lost in thought while conversations continue around me. I'm anxious to know what kind of chaos has befallen the people with the war against the Apex raging on, a war that they may possibly be losing. I wonder what this would mean for the people of Fairfield. Those lucky enough to be alive after the airship rained fire on them, that is.

"I wouldn't let it trouble you, love. Tall tales are common down here. Sounds like something out of legend. No way someone wages war against the Apex and then turns themselves over," says Lee, attempting to ease my anxiety. I appreciate the thought, but he hasn't seen the things I have, like how the Revenant was able to wipe out an entire village.

"I, for one, heard tales from the horse's mouth with my own ears. I could see it in their eyes. They were afraid to even speak of the darkness they heard about in the North. Make no mistake, lad, there are dark forces afoot, and it's best if they both wipe one another out," says an elder sitting across the table from Wolfe.

"Oh yeah, tell us of these tales, old man," replies Wolfe, who seems uncharacteristically interested in the conversation. The man leans in closer. His worn face gives a grim look that is easy to see, even behind his thick white braided beard and long hair. The tone of his voice is just as grave and gives me the impression that whatever he is about to say, he believes to be true.

"Many a sailor has reported widespread murder and death to the North. People of great status are being hunted down and killed like animals in their own beds. Their homes were riddled with the corpses of their guards and yet there were no signs of any enemy. Only the mutilated corpses. Those with arcane sensitivity are speculating the work of dark magic, perhaps a demonic presence being wielded as a weapon, unable to be stopped by ordinary means. The Apex recalled all their notable officials, leaving many of the realms in ruin." He shakes his head sadly before saying, "You can ask any elder here and they will tell you—Carthage is known for embracing the demonic."

"Bullocks. If they were worshipping demonic energies, the Apex would've known it. They don't even allow other religions, let alone the full-blown study of dark magic," replies Lee.

I know the man's story to be true. The Revenant must be responsible for the killings. I find myself relieved the beast is occupied with other tasks, a thought I immediately feel guilty for.

The reminder of the Revenant only fuels my desire to get revenge on whoever controls it when the time comes. I only hope that I will be the one to kill them and that the Apex won't beat me to it. Although, by the sound of things, I doubt they will be able to. The conversation increases my fear, but I know if I'm going to face the monster again, I'll need to be able to speak of it without anxiety.

"Good riddance, let the Apex fall. And if some coward must use dark magic to get it done, then so be it," replies Wolfe in a cold tone.

"Ha! Spoken like a true oaf. You spend too much time swinging axes and not enough training your mind," says the elder before taking a gulp from his mug. "I'd expect nothing less from your lot, though," the elder continues, prompting Lee to laugh.

"I've yet to meet anyone who couldn't be killed by an axe. I'm sure if war comes, you and your lot can defend us by making deals for trade goods," replies Wolfe boastfully.

"Do you not see how trade helps keep the peace, boy? Surely even you cannot be that dimwitted," says the elder before standing up and leaving the table, appearing offended. Or perhaps he's simply wise enough to know arguing with Wolfe is a waste of time. I think that I could learn from his example, but I know it will be impossible to let an argument go, even with someone as dumb and insignificant as Wolfe.

"Perhaps the Romani can fight off the invaders with their herbs and handmade clothing," continues Wolfe, clearly looking to pick a fight with Lee.

"Another word, and I'll slit your throat where you sit," Lee growls. I am surprised and, admittedly, a bit frightened by Lee's comment. But what is more surprising is that Wolfe doesn't respond.

He simply smirks and takes a drink from his mug.

"You want to get some fresh air?" I ask before Lee does something he regrets. To my surprise, he agrees and rises to his feet while continuing to glare at Wolfe. We leave the Great Hall and stroll around outside. "Thanks, I couldn't take much more of that miserable idiot," says Lee.

"Yeah, don't blame you. But who knows? Maybe he'll mature one day."

"Doubt it. He's no different than his power-hungry clan."

"Yeah, someone wise once told me, never trust anyone who seeks power for themselves," I reply.

"Sounds about right." Lee is silent for a moment then, in a softer tone says, "Sorry for all the tall tales about the North. I know that was your home, and it couldn't be easy hearing all that."

"Well, he isn't exactly wrong," I say.

His face grows concerned. "What do you mean, love?"

I debate whether I should tell him. If I do—I need to be absolutely sure I can trust him not to speak a word to anyone else. Not to mention, I fear he will be afraid to have us in the clan if he knows a revenant may be hunting us. I turn away from him to think about what to say. If I tell him the truth, it will forever alter our relationship, not to mention my and Kristoff's safety.

I stand silently as I contemplate the various outcomes that could occur if I tell him, whether it be the entire truth or only part. My back is to him, staring blankly at the nearly full moon. The gentle breeze pushes against my skin, slightly moving my hair. I find myself overcome with sorrow now that I'm faced with the possibility—or certainty—the clan won't have us once they know what may be hunting us. Nevertheless, I decide it's best to tell him. Both for his own sake and to make sure we'll have as much time as possible to come up with an alternative plan. I take a deep breath before turning around to face him, still not exactly sure what words to use.

I open my mouth and try to speak, but I'm unable to. "It's alright, love. You can tell me when you're ready," Lee replies, his voice soft and comforting. I shake my head. "You know Kristoff and I came from the North, right?"

Lee nods. His unbreaking gaze makes it hard for me to speak, and I can see the concern on his face. Unable to look him in the eye, I stare at the ground.

"We had to leave urgently. There was an uprising—and—The Apex, well, they firebombed Fairfield to stop a riot. Before that, a mob of people came for us while we were waiting in my house. We barely escaped. Our fathers worked for the Apex, and we were supposed to head back to the Capital on an airship because of the chaos. But the airship left us, and we had to flee on foot. When we—" I pause. My lips are quivering as I try to fight back tears. Lee approaches me and holds my hand, the warmth of his touch sooths me.

"There was a man, well more of a beast, and he—he—well, it, killed Kristoff's father in front of us. His mom fought to defend us so we could escape. When she caught up with us, she told us it was dead, but it wasn't." I say my next words in a near whisper. "She died of her wounds in Kristoff's arms while I fought the thing for as long as I could. It was so fast and didn't seem to feel any pain. Luckily, my father arrived, and he was able to fight it off. Well, him and this man named Stur who's an agent for the Apex. They were able to cut its head off and buy us some time. We then ran to meet up with another agent named Beltrum, who turned out to be an arcane mage. The Revenant showed up again before we got to board the carriage. Its head was attached as if nothing happened. We were only able to escape because Beltrum hit him with a powerful blast that brought an entire building down on top of it. We never saw it again, but I don't think that stopped it," I say before taking a deep breath.

"We went to Mackinaw as a group, but my dad, Kristoff, and I escaped without Stur or Beltrum knowing. We went to the docks and boarded a ship captained by an old friend of my dad's. He didn't think we could trust the Apex, especially after they abandoned us, despite promising to get us out of Fairfield safely."

I take a deep breath and meet Lee's eyes once more. "He died on the ship, poisoned from the Revenant's blade that struck him in the back as he was boarding the carriage. He was a great warrior—it couldn't best him in a straight fight—fucking coward," I mutter, pausing to gather myself before I completely break down.

I push the memory of my father's death from my mind and continue, "But it's true what the elder said, and I have no doubt it was the Revenant that committed those murders. A powerful necromancer must be controlling it, and I will kill them both if it is the last thing I do." I sigh loudly trying to resist my grief, "we don't know if it's going to keep coming after us, and you all may be in danger. We probably shouldn't—we can't—it will put the clan at risk," I finish, fighting hard to keep my composure.

My speech has been rapid and pressured, my mind is all over the place, and I have struggled to make my words flow together. Lee uses his hand to wipe tears from my eyes, causing me to look up at him. I do my best to disguise my sadness with a small smile, trying as hard as I can to focus on his green eyes, which always seem to mesmerize me. Lost in his eyes, I am taken entirely by surprise as he suddenly presses his lips against mine. His lips are soft and gentle, and he pulls me close, lightly placing his hand on the small of my back. I feel electricity rush through my body as I struggle to breathe. He steps back, and I notice he is struggling to catch his breath as well. The kiss only lasted a moment, but the intensity stays with me. We stare at each other, equally confused and excited about what we just felt.

"I have no words—I am so sorry, Aries. I—uh," he stumbles on his words. I shake my head, trying to regain my train of thought, but my mind is thinking about the kiss that I don't want to let end.

"It's okay. I just wanted you to know. I understand that the clan and Mum can't risk having us with you." Lee's face takes on a puzzled expression, as if he is shocked by what I am saying. I wonder if perhaps he is just now considering the gravity of the situation. I hate that I let myself and Kristoff get so excited to see the lands of the Romani, only to have our plans ruined.

"No, love, that won't matter. We will keep you safe. Trust me, nobody would ever feel that way. Nobody will ask you to leave. This isn't the Apex. Dark magic can be dealt with here."

"But you don't understand! It may not just be the Revenant; it may be the Apex as well. We—we still don't even know what is going on exactly and who all may be looking for us."

"You're right. I don't understand, but I don't need to. There isn't anything that would cause us to forsake our own. Your mother was Romani, so it's your birthright. I would go to war if anyone tried to harm you. We," he adds quickly. "We would go to war for you—and Kristoff. Rest assured, there isn't a man, woman, or child within the Roman that would ever let a foreign threat cause us to forsake one of our own. In fact, we all grow up hoping for a circumstance in which we can defend our clan in such a way. Things are different here; way different it seems."

I feel a great sense of relief at Lee's response to everything I have told him. I hope he's correct about us still being allowed, and even if he is wrong, it makes me feel good knowing that he is at least willing to accept us.

"Is there a way I can talk to Mum? I want to make sure she has the full story before she welcomes us in," I say, turning to look at the moon again, finding myself tempted to kiss his soft and full lips once more.

"'Course you can, but I'd wager she is privy to most of it by now anyway. She has a way of reading people. I don't know how she does it, but she just does," he responds, still speaking in a soft, empathetic tone.

"Thank you, but for tonight, let's try and enjoy the rest of the feast. After all, you earned the prize fair and square," I say, smiling, and turning to face him once again. "I mean, who cares if I had just fought the strongest man in the Southlands and you fought some bloke with a spear." Both Lee and I laugh, which is usually the case when I try to mimic his accent.

"To be fair, I don't think Wolfe is the strongest unless you're talking about odor," Lee replies.

We make our way back into the Great Hall where most of the people are in high spirits, drinking and laughing.

"Ah, just in time for the prize ceremony!" says Robert Highlander, who is walking back to his seat at the head of the large table. "It's with great honor and significant jealousy that I hand over the winnings to the respective champions. This is a small reward compared to the honor you have brought yourselves, your clans, and most importantly, your ancestors. Trust that honor will remain long after you've pissed away these coins."

After he finishes his speech, the different champions are given a small wooden chest containing silver coins. Despite being surrounded by many Romani, I find myself feeling as if I need to protect the silver. I notice that Kristoff has a similar thought because after receiving his winnings, he makes his way over to us, looking a little unsure of himself.

"I'd like to file a formal complaint that my winnings as champion are half that of the runner up from The proving grounds," says Kristoff jokingly.

"Well, if you like, I'll duel you for it. Let's say winner take all?" I reply.

"Okay, but we are going to duel in a foot race," he says, causing the three of us to laugh.

Eventually, the celebrations come to an end, and the three of us meet up with the rest of the Romani outside.

During my first few days among the Romani, I thought it was a coincidence they always seemed to travel together, but it appears to be an unspoken rule. Typically, I wouldn't mind traveling with so many people—I love the Romani—but it's killing me not to be able to speak privately with Kristoff. I need to let him know what I told Lee, and that we kissed. Just thinking about what Kristoff will say takes me back to that moment, sending butterflies fluttering in my stomach.

As the group moves back to their caravans, I notice that Lee is staying close to me, which is a change from his tendency to mingle with as many people as he can. Occasionally, Lee and I lock eyes and we both smile in a way that would tell an observant onlooker something is going on between us. If I can't talk to Kristoff in private, I at least wish I could hold Lee's hand, but I don't know how he would feel about it. This sends me into a spiral of doubt about the meaning of the kiss. I hope it isn't some sort of weird Southlander custom to kiss people when they are sad, but I know that couldn't be it. It was so much more than that, especially when I recall the intensity of the moment. It was as if I could read his mind during the kiss, as if I could feel both his excitement and fear.

The journey back to camp seems to go by much faster than usual, thanks in part to the thoughts racing through my head. We have only been in the Southlands for a few days, and yet so much has changed. We've formed strong bonds with the people of the Romani, bonds that typically take years to develop.

Despite Lee's reassurance, my mind continues to doubt his words, and I am certain we will be denied acceptance into the clan. I do my best to stop thinking about it altogether, knowing that if I don't, I will drive myself mad with worry.

Kristoff and I arrive at the caravan we have been borrowing and go straight inside, wasting no time with a fire. I am so exhausted and ready to sleep that it isn't until I am lying down that I realize I haven't said goodnight to Lee, which reminds me that I still haven't told Kristoff about what happened. As I speak and recount my conversation with Lee, Kristoff simply nods, indicating that he shares my belief that it is best to talk to Mum before we accompany the clan back to the Romani lands. When I get to the part about Lee kissing me, his jaw drops.

"Are you kidding me right now? How did this—why did this—what?" he asks, clearly just as shocked as I am about what happened.

"I know! I was completely caught off guard. I was fighting back tears, and then he just did it."

"That's the most romantic thing I've ever heard!" Kristoff exclaims. "Well," he suddenly says, looking at me with raised eyebrows, "how was it?"

"It was nice."

"Just nice? Surely you can do better than that. The rugged yet beautiful Lee, who is basically the closest thing to a prince the clan has, kisses you after you share troubling news, and you say it was nice?" scoffs Kristoff.

"Okay, okay! It was perfect and romantic and better than I could have ever imagined a first kiss being. It was exciting and gentle at the same time, not aggressive at all, and it made me feel completely safe. His lips were so soft, and he smelled so good after a certain someone gave him cologne."

"Look, I just wanted him to get your attention. I didn't think it would lead to you two kissing."

Moments like these with Kristoff remind me just how much I love him. He is so excited and happy to listen to my story, and I love having someone to share things like this with. However, the mood quickly changes.

"So, what happens if she says no?" he asks.

"I have no idea, but I guess we'd have to find somewhere to stay while we train." Saying it aloud is surreal to me, as if my life has suddenly become one of the adventure books I read so often when I was a child.

"Yeah, I suppose you are right. Still, it would be nice to do that surrounded by friends," he replies, sounding discouraged.

"Yeah, I know," I sigh. "If it makes you feel better, Lee promised me that nobody in the clan would let fear stop them from welcoming us. We can learn so much more from Mum and the rest of them than we would be able to on our own."

"That, and you want to marry Lee," says Kristoff, prompting me to hit him with my pillow. Soon after, we both drift off, our exhaustion finally overcoming our anxiety about what the future may hold.

I embark upon another vivid dream. It's as if I'm witnessing it firsthand. I see the prince from my previous dreams. He sits at a table in the center of a majestic room, surrounded by people draped in robes. Despite appearing to be on trial, the man's facial expression is calm and unbothered.

I focus on his face, which I must admit is attractive. His smooth skin is without blemish, and he possesses hypnotizing sky-blue eyes. His light brown hair is shaved bald on the sides but remains thick at the top. He wears a fine black fur coat, which gives off a rugged, yet noble look. By all accounts, he appears to be out of place.

"Do you have anything to say for yourself, Nathaniel, Prince of Carthage? Or am I to call you King? After all, is this not what your subjects call you?" asks a plump elderly man whose face is hidden beneath a large, bejeweled hat. He sits in the middle of the room on a large stone podium that rises far above his colleagues, who are seated in two separate galleries connected to either side of his bench. He's clearly the High Priest.

"Shall I address my comments to the court, or is it church? Forgive my confusion, I expected to meet with the governing officials, and not— priests," he replies in a coy tone. The High Priest doesn't respond, so the prince continues. "I ask you to provide me with this so-called evidence. Your allegations have caused my people to be blamed for the uprisings."

His words are calm and soft-spoken, but they radiate confidence, far removed from how I would expect someone to communicate when on trial.

The High Priest scoffs. "So, you do not deny being called King, even though the High Church has not ordained your claim? There is but one King who presides over the six realms, and you—are not him."

"I care not what your wicked church has ordained. Carthage no longer answers to the High Church," explains Nathaniel.

The High Priest's face flushes with anger. "Your guilt is not even a question! We have multiple eyewitness accounts confirming that you and your followers have committed violence against the Apex. Not to mention the blasphemy and ominous signs of dark magic tainting your wake. And as for your claim that the High Church has no legal authority over the realms, I remind you that it is the One True God himself who has appointed me High Priest, and the Apex has and always will, follow the word of God above any laws of man. Will you admit your guilt before this court?"

"Absolutely. I have committed many crimes for the sake of my people, and I will commit many more." Nathaniel replies coldly, leading the court of priests into an uproar.

The High Priest slams his fist on the podium in front of him, inciting immediate silence from his colleagues. "I hereby find you guilty—fallen Prince."

"Could I address this so-called God you speak with? Or is that impossible since their existence is a lie?" Nathaniel asks sarcastically, sending the court of priests into an uproar once more.

"Silence! I will not have you defile this church with your vile tongue. A twisted tongue that has caused the very provocation that seeks to destroy the loose fabric of Felicity. A fabric held together by faith and faith alone. You indeed traveled here by your own accord, and it was my hope you had done so because you had seen the error of your ways and came to throw yourself at the mercy of God. I hoped perhaps you even wished to admit guilt to spare the common folk you led astray. Maybe then we could put an end to this futile uprising without military intervention. But clearly, I was a fool to hope for such a thing, especially considering your—lineage."

I watch as Nathaniel scoffs before rising to his feet, causing the guard behind him to grip his sword's hilt. Nathaniel raises his hands to indicate he means no harm. "Since your God isn't here, I suppose you can beg me on his behalf, but to forewarn you, I am admittedly biased and notoriously unforgiving."

Laughter ripples through the court until the High Priest silences everyone with a wave of his hand. He accuses Nathaniel of madness and orders his execution. As he finishes issuing his judgment, the doors to the room burst open.

"Your Holiness, I apologize profusely, but we must get you to safety. At least one airship has been compromised," says a knight in a panicked tone. He is accompanied by four other knights, each dressed in magnificent plate armor.

"What chaos?" The High Priest asks, furious and confused.

Nathaniel's face radiates confidence as he looks upon the gallery of priests. "If you all weren't such fools you would know—there was no way you could stop me. Why else would I have come?"

The High Priest curses vulgarly at Nathaniel, causing him to smile. "Finally, you break the façade." He starts to walk towards the High Priest, stopping only when the guard behind him firmly places a hand on his shoulder. He grabs the soldier's hand, and the man screams out in agony. His skin begins to rapidly decay, and after mere seconds, he falls to the ground, looking like a corpse.

"Seize him! He is demonic!" yells the High Priest, stirring the already panicking counsel into a frenzy.

The knights try to engage Nathaniel, but their efforts are hindered by the priests attempting to flee the room. Nathaniel's eyes begin to glow a dark shade of purple as he raises his left hand into the air, followed by a flash of light and an alarming sound which resembles thunder.

Suddenly, his once empty hand is now grasping the brilliant yet ominous scepter, I witnessed him claim in my previous dream.

He uses dark magic to cause the recently deceased soldier to rise, ready to do his bidding. The resurrected guard removes his sword and gives it to Nathaniel, who walks slowly towards the podium where the High Priest is trapped because of his fleeing colleagues.

The soldiers finally push their way through the crowd and attempt to stop him, but his undead servant holds them at bay. As each of the knights fall, Nathaniel uses his dark magic to bring their corpses back to life. He then commands them to tear their way through the mob of people, dismembering them violently, as they make their way to the High Priest.

"Your entire fleet is destroyed—save for those we took for ourselves. Ironically, they will now be used to erase all memory of your false God. You thought yourself invincible, sitting atop the Spire, your wealth only surpassed by your greed. But you neglected the old ways, which provide a power granted to those bold enough to claim it. A power my ancestors wielded long before the Apex existed. A power I must use to redirect this world onto its original path."

As if on cue, two of Nathaniel's undead soldiers seize the terrified High Priest and throw him to the floor at his feet, while the others continue to slaughter everyone else. The High Priest tries to crawl away, begging and pleading for his life. Nathaniel slowly follows behind him, and as though they share one mind, the corpses surround the pair in an escort as they make their way outside.

"Please, I will do anything. Please!" pleads the High Priest as he struggles to speak while crawling out of the room.

"Please! It cannot be! God, please! Strike them down, I beg of you!"

"Your god does not exist."

He weeps when he sees the destruction. The newly acquired armada rains fire upon the Spire's magnificent structures, destroying hundreds of years' worth of buildings and history in one great blaze.

"P-p-please, Prince Nathaniel!"

"A prince no more," Nathaniel sneers before handing the man over to his undead soldiers.

The High Priest's screams and the sounds of his flesh being torn from his body jolt me awake. My heart is racing, and I'm covered in sweat.

"What's wrong? Are you okay?" Kristoff asks.

"I think the Apex has fallen. We need to talk to Mum—now!"

I find Mum sitting outside her caravan. I'm unsure if she's an early riser or if she has yet to go to bed. The clan's matriarch is wrapped in a thick quilt and drinking what I assume to be tea from a simple wooden mug. Sensing our urgent approach, she takes a quick gulp of her drink before setting it down and standing to her feet.

"What is it, my dears? Is everything okay?" she asks in her familiar welcoming tone.

I don't know where to begin, but I hope speaking with Mum will allow us to find answers. Answers to questions I'm not even sure how to ask.

"It's okay child, just have a seat and let's get you some tea," Mum says as she gathers two fresh mugs and hands them to Kristoff and me. She then pours tea into each of our mugs from a kettle hanging over the fire. The steaming liquid feels warm in my hands. It's a kind gesture, but I'm in no mood to drink.

Before I know it, I've told Mum everything about why we ended up in the Southlands and our plan to avenge our family. Kristoff remains silent, listening and sipping his tea.

"So much pain and suffering for anyone to have to go through. I curse those involved! I'm so sorry for what you had to witness, but you are safe now," Mum says, tears in her eyes, clearly upset after listening to the story.

"We understand—" Kristoff says, looking down at his mug. "It may not be safe for us to come with you."

"You believe if you were to come, the forces seeking to do you harm would use that as a reason to retaliate against us?" Mum asks.

"Yeah, I do. Neither side seems bothered about what atrocities they cause," I reply in a defeated tone.

"Of that, I have no doubt. It is often the case with men who seek power. But what would it say about us if we were to forsake two innocents to appease evil? I do love that you care so much for us that you chose to speak honestly of this beforehand, but I am sure Lee already told you, people from the Southlands, and especially our clan, would never bend to the will of a foreign power. I do hope this puts your mind at ease and pushes away any further worries you have about whether you are welcome," Mum says warmly, melting my anxiety. Just then, I remember my dream and decide it would be best to tell Mum while I have her attention.

"There is something else. I've been having very vivid dreams lately," I say.

"Oh, I love dreams!" Mum exclaims, clapping her hands in excitement. "Before we go into dreams, let us make preparations to head to our lands. You can ride with me, and we can throw cards to try and find meaning," she says excitedly.

"What do you mean throw cards?" Kristoff asks, puzzled.

"Why tarot cards, what else? That's right, in the North, such things are forbidden. I will explain it later. Until then, make haste. We have a far journey ahead of us, and I long for the beauty of our homelands. I miss my mountain," Mum replies before giving us both a hug.

As usual, when I've had a conversation with her, I leave Mum with more questions than I had come with. I wonder how tarot cards could help me interpret my dreams, but I welcome the opportunity to learn if it means I could get answers.

Kristoff and I gather our things and place them outside of the caravan we have been borrowing.

"Sleep well, did we?" Lee asks as he approaches us, Andrew and Jaseen following not far behind.

"I was worried, but thankfully exhaustion helped me sleep," Kristoff replies.

"Yeah, about that—seen you talking to Mum. Probably said much of what I said the night before, yeah?" Lee asks.

"More or less," I say, smiling.

"I'd wager on less," Kristoff says with a mischievous grin on his face, making Lee blush. Andrew and Jaseen look puzzled, telling me they know nothing about the kiss. I wonder if it's good or bad that he didn't tell them.

"Well, don't wait," Andrew says.

"Our fearless leader is afraid, isn't he?" Jaseen adds.

"Shut it! But, umm—Aries, would you want to ride back with me?" Lee asks, sounding uncharacteristically nervous. I don't know why, but I enjoy seeing him anxious about asking me.

"I'm supposed to ride with Mum. We're going to throw cards," I reply.

"Oh, that's fine. I was just—"

"But as soon as that's done, then yes, I will gladly ride back with you," I say before kissing him lightly on the lips, prompting cooing noises from Andrew, Jaseen, and Kristoff.

Lee stands speechless and red-faced. I feel good about being the one to kiss him this time since he had caught me by surprise last night.

"You can ride back with us, mate, but no kissing." Says Andrew, before helping us with our belongings.

Jaseen winked at Kristoff and chimed in, "Speak for yourself, mate," making him blush.

Everyone packed their camps and prepared for the journey. The caravans stood in preparation for our departure not long after. I found myself outside the entrance to Mum's caravan, waiting, when I heard a cacophony of loud noises that made me wonder what was going on inside the small yellow caravan.

Mum suddenly flung the door open, only having to barely hunch despite the low ceiling. She is clearly excited.

"Welcome, child. Come in, come in!"

"Thank you!" I reply as I bend over to crawl inside the small caravan, being extra careful not to knock anything over. There are several items, all of which seem very fragile, hanging from the shelves that appear loosely secured to the caravan's walls. In the center of the floor is a small wooden table, made especially for a room the size of the caravan. I notice the deck of cards already sitting atop the table, along with a burning white candle and what appears to be a bundle of smoldering sage, smoking gently. I love the smell of burning sage; it reminds me of the times my mother would burn it and walk throughout the house, letting its smoke waft into each corner of every room.

"Have you ever had your cards read before? I know your mother loved them,"

"No, I never have."

"Oh, how I love reading someone's cards for the first time! I'm so excited, yay!" Mum claps and smiles widely.

"Okay, I am going to shuffle the cards, and then you need to cut the deck three times with your non-dominant hand," Mum explains as she shuffles the deck of cards vigorously before placing it in front of her. I take a deep breath and cut the deck three times, making sure to use my left hand, as instructed.

"Okay, here we go!" Mum says before turning over the first card. The image shows a large stone tower that is on fire, with lightning all around it. There's a person falling as if they have been thrown from the top. The card is upside down, but I can make out the words, "The Tower." Mum's face becomes serious at sight of the card.

"I take it that isn't good," I say, growing nervous.

"Well, not necessarily, my dear. The tower reversed can mean personal transformation, but it can also mean sudden upheaval. It represents change, for better or worse," Mum replies in a comforting tone.

"Well, no real surprise there, considering everything that's happened," I say.

"Very true, but this is about your future, and that's why it is curious. Although, your past can be the reason for a transformation, can it not?" Mum says as she flips over another card and places it next to the first one.

This card is also upside down and much harder for me to make out. I lean forward on my stool and tilt my head to the side to get a better view. I immediately notice the words "The Devil" and see an ominous-looking figure, similar to a demon. It has the head of a giant horned goat, the upper body of a man, and fur covered legs with hooved feet. A naked man and woman are standing on either side of the creature, looking at him as if in a trance. Above the demon is a symbol that I recognize from my book on ancient magic. A symbol banned by the Apex; the pentagram.

"This definitely can't be good—"

"Oh no, this is good. The devil isn't nearly as ominous as you may think, my dear. The creature represents the balance between opposing energies. When the card is reversed, it means you're on the verge of growth, but that you must let go of whatever is holding you back."

"I wonder why it appears so scary."

"Well, bondage is scary, my dear."

Mum removes another card from the deck and places it next to the reversed devil. This time the card is facing me, and I immediately recognize the card's name, "Ten of Swords." The image on the card shows a man lying face down on the ground with ten swords sticking out of his back.

"Now, this is—most certainly not good," Mum says, sounding truly concerned for the first time.

"What does it mean?" I ask anxiously.

"Betrayal that results in a deep loss or crisis. But the question is, from what or from whom does this betrayal come?" Mum says, puzzled as she continues to stare at the cards. "Any thoughts?" she asks me.

"No, not really. I mean, my father felt that we may have been betrayed when everything happened, but there isn't anyone left who could betray me besides Kristoff, and I know he would never do that."

Her face strains as she stares at the cards. "Very curious indeed, my dear. I've never seen these cards appear together in all my years."

"Lucky me," I say sarcastically.

Mum takes another card from the deck. She seems nervous now. The card she places down now is once again facing me, and it shows two naked people, one male and one female, standing beneath a large, beautiful tree while the sun shines overhead. The words "The Lovers" are written at the bottom of the card. I look up to Mum and see that her concerned expression has been replaced with a giant grin that extends nearly ear to ear.

"Oh my, I knew it—I just knew it. This card is beautiful," Mum says, clapping happily.

"What does it mean exactly?"

"Love and harmony, to put it simply. And not necessarily romantic love—though I must admit that's my hope," Mum says, winking at me. She means me and Lee. My face begins to blush, so I quickly try to change the subject.

"Well, it sounds like whatever pain and upheaval I must endure, I will at least come to find harmony afterward. Is that correct?"

"Yes, it is. See? I knew you'd be a natural. Your mother was the best I've seen," Mum replies, laughing.

She removes another card from the deck. This time the card is upside down and shows a woman sitting on a simple stone throne with her hands outstretched. Her right hand holds a sword, and her left hand is open, prepared to grab something. She is surrounded by butterflies.

"This card doesn't look scary necessarily but since it is reversed, is that a bad sign?" I ask.

"The Queen of Swords represents a strong female figure. A woman who embraces her warrior spirit and her femininity. This card represents what you can become if you continue your journey, but when reversed, it means she has chosen to embrace her warrior side more than her nurturing side."

"Which is a bad thing, I take it?"

"Why would that be, dear? Are men who are great warriors not revered?"

"I suppose. I just got the feeling it meant I was not representing the balance the queen of swords is supposed to symbolize."

"Many believe a queen of swords in this state serves as a warning to keep your emotions in check and not allow them to overwhelm you, else you may become too rigid. Balance is something we should always work towards, but when faced with certain circumstances, you must embrace the warrior side. I hope you remember this card. I feel as if your story demands it."

I contemplate Mum's words and feel an odd importance surrounding the card and what it represents. So lost in my thoughts, I miss Mum turning over another card. Again, it faces away from me, but I can make out the title, "The King of Cups." In this card, a king sits atop a throne with a cup in his right hand and a majestic scepter in his left. While the throne floats atop a chaotic sea, the man's facial expression is calm and collected.

"Oh my," says Mum, her brow creasing in puzzlement.

"What does it mean?" I ask, regrettably finding myself growing impatient with how much time Mum is taking to explain the meaning of each card.

"Sorry, it's just that I've seen this card come up reversed in only one other reading; the last reading I did for your mother. In that reading, it was also the fifth card."

My curiosity and anxiety grow, making me squirm in my seat. "Is it a bad sign?" I ask.

"It certainly can be. Typically, it indicates the need to be aware of emotions that may cause you to feel unbalanced. See how he appears calm during a storm? People often think it means that you should work towards that balance."

"So, what's bad about it then? That seems to be a reoccurring theme with the cards I've gotten."

"Well, my dear, it represents a powerful male figure that uses a silver tongue and manipulation to control others. A very vindictive soul that cares not for people but only for gaining power and maintaining it. There are no lengths he won't go to win. It's odd your mother also received this card, and if I recall, it seemed out of place. She assured me there was a great deal of significance associated with it. She said it represented a man who would bring about great suffering to all of Felicity—if not dealt with."

"I wonder if it's the prince—or king now—of Carthage, Nathaniel Cunningham."

"Perhaps it is. The problem with the cards is that they only give us a small glimpse, and it's up to us to find meaning. So, one more card, are you ready?" asks Mum, who proceeds to flip another card before I can answer.

This card is facing me and is titled "The Star." It depicts a beautiful naked woman kneeling at a large pond. In each of her hands is a bowl overflowing with water. It's nighttime, and there are many stars in the sky, with one magnificent star that is much larger than the rest sitting in the center.

"This is so good, oh so good. I was worried because of the other cards," says Mum.

I'm relieved the last card is something Mum feels is a good sign.

"And this card means?"

"It means everything. It's the symbol for hope and faith, as if to say the journey you walk may face a great deal of destruction and chaos but when it ends, there will be reprieve and balance, not only for you but for those around you as well."

"I see," I reply, my mind still buzzing after all I have learned. I'm still unsure if I trust the cards can predict my future, but I want to believe, especially since my mother did.

"Now tell me about your dream, love," Mum says behind a grin.

I go on to tell her the dream, providing her with every detail I can remember. Mum listens intently before her eyes take on a faraway look as she ponders the meaning.

"Do you think the Apex has really fallen?" I ask.

"That I'm not sure of. A dream could be your mind playing tricks on you, or perhaps you are blessed with visions in the way your mother was. She usually dreamed during a daytime nap, almost as if she fell into a trance. But they were never that vivid from my understanding. It's almost as if you are being shown memories from someone else, but I've never heard of such a thing before."

"Is it possible?" I ask, puzzled.

"My dear, this world is full of magic that would take countless lifetimes to fully understand. So, who's to say what is or isn't possible." Mum smiles at me warmly. "I think I've taken enough of your time. I'm sure Lee is excited for you to join him."

"Thank you so much for taking the time to give me a reading. Also, thank you for everything you and the clan have done for Kristoff and me."

"Oh dear, no need to thank us, but I appreciate your kind words. You are with your family now. You are home, and you are welcome here," Mum says as she crawls around the table to give me a big hug. She then beats on the wooden wall near the front of the caravan, causing the driver to bring the horse to a stop, the sudden movement knocking the deck of cards to the floor. I help Mum pick up the cards and notice one card that is flipped face-up. Mum quickly collects them, and while I don't see the entirety of the card, I catch a glimpse of the title: "Death."

"Are you alright, hun?" Mum asks me as I stare off into the distance. I quickly snap out of my trance. I want to know what the card means, but I don't think I can handle any more bad news. I decide against bringing it up, at least for now. I thank Mum again for giving me a reading and explaining the meaning of the cards. We say our goodbyes, and I make haste towards Lee and his caravan. I find him standing beside a horse with a beautiful brown coat with hints of red. He's gently petting the side of its neck, the horse nudging Lee anytime he tries to stop.

It warms my heart to see him interacting with the horse in such an affectionate manner. I love animals and despise people who treat them poorly. I was initially worried that people from the Southlands may be cruel to their animals because of how savage they were portrayed by the High Church, but the more time I spend around them, the less I believe anything I've been taught.

"How'd it go?" Lee asks, smiling as he looks at me before quickly turning his attention back to the horse.

"It went good, I think. A lot to take in—and I don't really know how or what to think about it," I say, nervously.

"I suppose that's pretty standard. The cards are fickle, to say the least."

"Do you believe in them?"

"Yeah, I think so, but I believe we can always change our fate if we don't like what's in the cards," he replies before giving the horse a big hug. "Oh, I'm going to be right behind you, you big baby," he says to the horse, who is clearly upset Lee is leaving.

"Aww, they really like you, don't they?"

"Well, don't sound so surprised! But yes, I think it's safe to say he and I are mates," he replies, laughing.

"Can I pet him?"

Lee gives me a slightly anxious look. "He usually doesn't take to strangers, just to warn you. So, stay away from his hind legs, yeah?"

I try not to take offense to the fact that he doubts whether the horse will like me. I've yet to meet an animal that didn't. Even the guard dogs in Fairfield would come up to me to be petted, much to Magistrate Kirby's dismay. Nonetheless, I slowly approach the horse from the side, careful to let it know that I'm not trying to sneak up on it.

"Hey there, big guy. How are you? My name's Aries. Is it okay if I pet you?" I say in a nurturing tone. The horse is hesitant at first, tensing up when I get near him, but I pause and remain patient while I wait for him to relax. I make sure to stand where he can see me without having to turn his head. I then slowly reach my hand out towards him, careful not to invade his space but close enough to give him the option to reach out with his head to greet me. The horse watches for a while, and I simply wait. Eventually, my patience pays off, and the horse begins to sniff my hand. I can feel the air from his snort on my skin, which tickles me to a point that I almost jerk away, but I'm able to hold still long enough for the horse to begin licking my hand. Taking this as a sign of his comfort with me, I begin to pet him, and he gently leans his head into me. "Hi there, buddy. You're such a good boy!"

"I'm amazed. I've never seen him do that with anyone. If I am honest, I thought he was going to run off or kick about," says Lee, with a shocked expression on his face.

"What can I say? Animals love me," I reply, boasting. I know his warning was for my own safety, but my competitive side enjoys proving him wrong. "What's his name?" I ask, continuing to pet him.

"We call him Red."

"Fitting. A little on the nose, but it suits him."

"We like to keep it simple here in the Southlands, don't we, Red? Kristoff already loaded up your things while you were getting your reading, so we are good to take off as soon as Mum gives the go-ahead."

I'm excited and nervous about the journey to the Romani lands, but I'm most nervous about riding with Lee. There's no doubt I'm fond of him, but there's a great deal of pressure when traveling with someone for so long. I worry we won't be able to keep a conversation, and then there will be an awkward silence. The kind people try to fill with small talk, which I hate. I'd rather sit in silence than talk about the weather or how much the crops have grown.

"How long of a trip is it?" I ask as I climb upon the carriage.

"As a group, a week or so. If you make haste, you could probably do it in about four days. It's to the Southeast, in the mountains," he replies, pointing in the direction we're heading.

I'm excited to see the mountains. It's one thing I miss about living near the Apexian Capital. Unlike Fairfield, which is utterly flat except for the occasional hill, the Apex Capital is situated directly below a mountain called the Spire which overlooks the city. To the east are massive snow-covered mountains which are always visible in the distance. The mountains serve as a natural barrier between the Apex and the independent country of Distle.

I know little about Distle, but from what I've been told, their king and nobles are showered with gifts by the High Church, making it easy for them to be manipulated by the Apex. The realms share a religion and culture, making it difficult to distinguish the difference between the two.

Lee eventually climbs aboard the carriage. It has a thick wooden divider that separates the horse from the riders, and the back of the seat is the wall of the enclosed caravan. Lee lightly snaps the reins to let Red know it's time to leave, and the horse walks towards the dirt road heading southeast.

I can't wait until I settle into my new life because it means that I'll be able to train and develop whatever skills I need to avenge my father and Kristoff's parents. My thirst for vengeance is just as intense as ever, but I find I'm also feeling guilty about how happy I've been since arriving in the Southlands. Almost as if not being sad means I love my father less than before.

"As we get closer to the mountains, let me know if you get chilly, and I can get you a blanket," says Lee, already making small talk much to my dismay.

"Really?" I ask in a sassy tone.

"I'm not following, love," says Lee, smiling.

"You get me alone on your carriage, a girl from the North that has never been to the Southlands and is about to journey across the continent, seeing things she has probably never seen before. And your first comment is about a blanket if the weather changes? Have to say, I'm a bit disappointed in your conversational skills, Lee."

"Oh, my apologies, love. Wherever are my manners? You will see some trees to your left. And to your right, well—more trees. Sometimes the trees will be so thick that you can't make out much of anything. Here in the Southlands, we call that a forest. After the forests there's some tiny green blades, we like to call grass. There will be lots of that. Also, we have water that doesn't move much. That's called—a lake. But then we get to the real views, the mountains. They are covered in forests and reach so high they touch the clouds—which is just mist, but we say it's clouds, you know—for dramatic effect. My favorite part are the hot springs of Little Watch, which no matter the weather, will always have warm water because they're heated by rivers of lava deep beneath the surface of the rocks. Care to learn anything else?"

I begin laughing aloud at his attempt to speak properly and with a tone like a storyteller. "Just one question: what if I have seen all of these things before? How are the Southlands any different from the North? I feel like I deserve a refund for how I was misled to believe it was different here."

"Well, that's where it's different, love. There's no such thing as a refund in the Southlands. Besides, I never heard of hot springs in the North, except maybe in the land of the giants."

"Land of the giants? Are we sharing fairy tales now because you feel too much pressure to talk?"

"Two things. One, I am immune to pressure. You forget you are talking to the back-to-back tourney champion. And two, the land of the giants is real."

I roll my eyes so hard I worry I may go blind. "I just puked in my mouth. Wait till next year after I've actually been able to train," I say with a sly smirk. When his smile drops away, I say, "Be serious, though. You really don't believe in giants, do you?"

"I do, why don't you? Haven't you seen a short person before? It only makes sense if there are tiny humans, there could be giants."

"But who has ever seen a giant before?"

"Why is the northern gate of Distle so large, especially compared to their western and southern gates?"

I'm impressed by his knowledge of the North and its realms, something I assumed most of the people from the Southlands lacked, and I struggle to develop a solid argument. "I don't know, looks I suppose. People from the Apex and that area often make gaudy structures simply to show off their wealth."

"True, but the north gate predates the Apex or even the Great War that divided Frankia and Carthage. And that's because it was built by giants. Who, upon the rise of men and their airships, resettled into the mountains of the north. The mountains would serve as the perfect barrier if you were on the run from airships."

I find it attractive that he has such a passion for debating, especially something most people wouldn't care to know, let alone come up with their own theories. "Say you're right, why would the giants not try and reach out to trade or travel to the other realms?"

"Could be their culture, but also, if you look at the area around them, they wouldn't have much of a route to travel. They are surrounded by swamplands and marshes to the south, mountains to the west, and the supposedly haunted forests of Oakland to the east. Perhaps they went even further, but nobody knows what's to the north. The Frigid Sea is far too cold to travel without knowing a destination."

We continue to talk about all sorts of things, mainly focusing on theories about mythology and conspiracies. I find it comforting that he knows so much about the North and that I don't have to explain much to him. Although I do find it cute when he has a question about something very simple or an assumption about the North that is entirely off base. Most of all, I love that he is interested in learning about the people and places he has never been, an interest we share. Listening to and debating with Lee does leave me frustrated, however. I am upset that I have been denied the opportunity to learn about the Southlands, thanks to the Apex.

Several hours pass by quickly, thanks to both our conversations, which I find easy to carry on, and the breathtaking scenery. I see lush forests flowing with life, and so many different types of birds that I lose track of the number. The lakes are stunning because they are often surrounded by spectacular pine trees that stretch far into the sky, reminding me of the village of Redwood. Thinking about the village reminds me of the Revenant and what happened to us that night.

My train of thought is thankfully interrupted by Lee's question. "So, how do they work?"

"I'm sorry, what? I wasn't really listening. How does what work?" I reply.

"No, I wasn't talking," he chuckles. "But I was wondering, how do the airships work? It's like suddenly, the Apex obtained airships. Most things improve slowly over time, like boats. They get new sails, or some bloke comes up with a better way to navigate. But then out of nowhere, they suddenly get dozens of flying ships. A bit odd, don't you think?"

I find comfort in the realization that I'm not the only one who spontaneously blurts out thoughts during a conversation. I smile, finding his enthusiasm about the airships endearing. "Well, nobody really knows how they work, and they keep all information about them secret. Even when you ride—"

His head snaps quickly as he turns to look at me, interrupting me mid-sentence. "Wait a minute! Have you been on one?"

"Yes, I have, but they don't allow passengers to wander around. You are confined to the cabins or, in some cases, an observation deck. And I have only ridden on one of the smaller ones used primarily for passengers. I've seen the Armada before, which is their military fleet. They are much larger than the passenger ships. The largest, Vigilance, is twice the size of the others. Also, they say that the One True God blessed someone with the knowledge of how to construct them. Upon their death, the means to make them died as well."

"Seems about right. They often have a flair for divine intervention. Vigilance, though? I've never heard of it before, or the Armada. I figured most of the airships were the same for some reason."

"Yea, Vigilance is rarely seen and is used only when they need a real showing of force that involves destroying something. It's armored around the apparatus that makes it fly. It's covered in so much steel, it's a wonder it can take flight in the first place. They say that it alone could take on the entire fleet of airships and that it has dozens of ballistae, each of which can cut through stone with ease. But the Apex is known to embellish things to make themselves appear stronger than they are. Probably why a loan realm was able to overthrow them so easily."

"Right, your dream. Kristoff was telling the lads and me about it. You believe it's true?"

"Yea, though I can't explain why exactly. I just know it is."

"I am no fan of the Apex, but in my experience, a regime change is usually not for the better."

We both sit quietly while I ponder what a world without the Apex would be like. Maybe it will be even worse—with more radical people in power. I wonder if Lee is concerned about what the people of the Southlands would do if the Apex tried to invade with the full force of their airships. I notice his fixation on ensuring that his clan is safe from threats. I admire this about him, but it's something I know to be exhausting, from personal experience. What would I do if I was commanding an army faced with fighting the Apex?

"You'd have to spread out and attack the balloons, maybe even use ropes attached to weights to bring them down," says Lee.

I jump slightly. His response is almost a perfect answer to the questions I'm asking myself. "Wait, how did you know what I was thinking?"

"Sorry, what? I was just thinking aloud." He shakes his head, then a small smile forms. "Wait. You were thinking about how to take on the Armada, too?"

We're startled when we realize we've been thinking the exact same thing, but we laugh it off, chalking it up to nothing more than coincidence.

As we continue toward the Romani territory, we go back and forth debating the best strategies and poking holes in the theories that seem too farfetched. I give Lee insight into my knowledge about the airships from my experience and what I've gathered from others, and he provides his own insight into military tactics, especially those from the Southlands. I enjoy this topic a lot. Not only does it make the time pass quickly, but I love that we seem to be a great team when it comes to problem-solving.

When it comes to these conversations, I'm typically viewed as too direct or critical, especially for a young woman, but Lee seems unbothered by it. He simply argues his point but also listens to my opinion and alters his stance if my suggestions are sound. I'm not accustomed to men being willing to change their views, especially with the way I tend to debate.

Eventually, the sun begins to fall below the horizon, and the troop of caravans stops for the night. I figure I would look for Kristoff so that we could bunk together, but Lee surprises me.

"If you care to, you can share my cabin tonight," he says in an uncharacteristically nervous tone.

My heart sinks into my stomach. I half hoped I'd be able to share his cabin, but now that the opportunity arises, I'm unsure if I should take it. I want to but I'm worried that he may get the wrong idea. I clearly like him, but I want to make sure we take things slow. I contemplate it for a few moments while staring at him, making him blush with embarrassment. I can tell by his anxious demeanor that his intentions are pure. I allow him to squirm for a bit longer, mainly because it brings me joy to see someone as renowned as him embarrassed talking to a girl.

"I uh just—meant, sorry, I shouldn't have—" He says, stumbling on his words as he scratches at what I think is an imaginary itch on the back of his head.

"Aww, you're so cute when you're embarrassed. I'd love to stay, but I'm going to be honest with you, I expect much better conversation skills than whatever that was," I reply, making him smile and snapping him out of his awkwardness.

"Well, in that case, maybe I'll just bunk up with ole Red here. He appreciates my conversation skills," he replies, smiling.

Lee and the rest of the Romani situate their caravans in several small circles on a field directly to the side of the road. Each circle acts as a mini campsite, where before bed, people sit around, tell stories, and eat food that has been cooked over fires.

I enjoy a hearty stew with beef and vegetables. The smell is intoxicating. Why is food cooked over a campfire always better than food cooked in a house? I think as I eat.

There is singing and dancing in every one of the mini campsites, and many people take the opportunity to praise me, Lee, and Kristoff for our victories at the Faire. Eventually, the long journey gets the better of the clan members, and one by one, they retire to their sleeping quarters for the night. Our safety hasn't crossed my mind much as of late, but I'm pleased to see that there is an appointed overnight watch.

I love the simplicity of Lee's caravan, which is far less decorated than the other two I've seen the inside of. There is a bed, a comfortable blanket and pillows, and weaponry hanging on the walls.

"Wow, I can see you went a little overboard with the decor. Mum's caravan doesn't hold a candle to this," I say as I lay down on the comfortable bed, sitting with my back against the wall as Lee takes off his scarf and overshirt. His undershirt has a loose collar, and I can see that he has a tattoo on his chest. I've heard that tattoos, which are strictly forbidden by the Apexian Church, are prevalent amongst the Southlanders, but I haven't seen many growing up.

"You care if I sleep without my shirt, love? If it's a bother, I don't mind keeping it on," he says.

"It's your house and your rules, so yeah, that's fine," I reply. Now it's my turn to stumble over my words, distracted by the thought of him with his shirt off.

"This isn't a house, it's a caravan, and this coming from the woman who not long ago was going on about my speech issues," he replies jokingly before taking off his shirt and crawling onto the bed to sit beside me. His body is muscular, like a soldier who regularly trains to stay battle-ready, though he isn't bulky.

I let my eyes fall to the tattoo on his chest, noting it's of a tree that is encircled by what appears to be braided roots. In the trunk of the tree, there is a dark red jewel. It reminds me of the blood amethyst that rests in the hilt of my mother's dagger. I don't know how long I have been staring. I gather it has been a while because he's now chuckling.

"Any longer, and it'll cost you. This here is our clan symbol, the Tree of Life," he replies. He lets out a long sigh and turns his face toward mine. "You know, sometimes it's hard being me. Everyone always wants to talk to me and tell me how great I am for being the tourney champion back-to-back."

"Thanks for ruining the moment. Do you have a night bucket I can puke in, please?"

"A what now?" he asks, laughing.

"A night bucket, you know for—when you have to go—in the middle of the night."

"Bullocks. You piss in a bucket in the North, and you keep it in your room?" he asks, shocked by the information. I laugh at his disgust.

"Yes, it is customary for people of a certain standing to use them, and they are emptied by a servant the next day. There weren't any servants in Fairfield, luckily."

"But until it's emptied, where does it sit?"

"Usually in a corner, sometimes in a closet."

"And yet we're the savages! We just go in the woods, you know, away from where people eat, sleep, and associate. And if it's too bad, we dig a hole and then bury it."

"Well, it's only for night use. During the day, there is what's called a privy, where people do their business. And mind you, this is mainly in the Apexian cities. People from the Realm of Fairfield did the same as you described. Except they'd usually just go out a window, or they would have an outhouse which sat a few yards away from their house. Sadly, I don't think there are many shovels because they don't tend to bury it."

"The Apex is such an odd place," he replies, dumbfounded.

"Still hard to believe it actually fell to Carthage," I say.

"Nobody can rule forever, but I never thought I'd live to see the day when the Apex fell. Even though I've often thought about how we could defeat them, I didn't believe it would come to pass."

"What would've been your grand plan? It seemed an impossible task."

"Impossible is right, not because of them though, but because you'd have to unite the clans to fight under one banner. If you could do that, it would be simple enough. Sounds like the bloke from Carthage figured it out. It's just like in chess; when the king falls, the game is over. The High Priest has always been the true power within the Apex. His death would cause a power vacuum that would prevent any counterattack."

My excitement about the game completely distracts my attention away from the previous topic. "You play chess here?"

"Yes, it's really popular, seeing as how it was invented here. Also, not to let you down, but even the Guul can read, despite what you've been told."

I roll my eyes. Of course, he would somehow have to relate this to the Southlands being better. "Does that mean you know how to play?"

Lee laughs at my level of excitement, which is so strong that I can hardly contain myself. I'm now sitting up on my knees, staring intently as I wait for his response. "Would you like to play? I warn you, though, I'm very good. Also, I never let people win, not even children."

"Yes! When could we play? Do you think anyone here has a board?"

"Nearly everyone has a board. It's the Southlands."

"Can we ask someone tonight?"

"No need, I have one."

"You have one, and yet you let me do this little dance trying to figure out where we could get a board?"

"It's cute to see you squirm, and it's payback for earlier," he replies, causing us both to laugh.

Lee quickly goes to the end of the bed and lifts the mattress, under which several compartments used for storage are kept. He takes out a wooden box that, when opened, reveals the chess pieces, and when laid flat functions as the chessboard. The chess set is handcrafted from the wood of an oak tree. It is as fine as any I've seen. I quickly set up the board and get myself situated to face him, allowing him to control the white pieces, meaning he moves first. I hope he will take this as a courtesy, but really, I want to assess what strategy he will use to allow me to better set up counterstrikes and traps.

"Wow, wasting no time, are we?" he says, laughing before making his first move.

I haven't had the chance to play much chess once I moved to Fairfield, unless I played with my father or Kristoff, but I love the game, and I feel confident that I will be able to beat him.

Typically, I find it difficult to focus on one task for a long time, but chess is one of the activities that gets all my attention and, in some regards, too much of it. I become so fixated on the game that on my turn, I sometimes forget to breathe until my body reminds me of its need for air.

Moving my pieces takes a long time because I try to play several steps ahead and consider what may result from my choices. Lee, on the other hand, moves quickly and efficiently while using conversation to distract me. This is something I've not encountered before, since it would be considered rude in the Apex, but I feel confident that his tactic won't work on me. It's obvious from his quick actions and casual demeanor that he doesn't take the game as seriously as I do, and I know I can easily beat him in just a few turns. Move after move, I progress my strategy, and I feel as if the game is all but won. But on the turn before I guarantee my victory, I hear, "Checkmate."

I look up to see him smirking in a very irritating way. I at first think he must have been talking about my next turn and accepting that he is about to lose, but the smile on his face makes me realize he won.

"You can't be serious. How?" I ask, trying to hide my frustration at not seeing my defeat coming. But after I look at the board, I see that he used his bishop and knight to secure checkmate. Utilizing knights for a checkmate is a sign of an advanced player, and I assumed, which seems foolish now, that he wasn't good enough to do such a thing.

"Wow—okay," I say, nodding, impressed by his skill. "Well done. Okay, again. This time I'm white."

"You take chess seriously, don't you?" he asks with a raised eyebrow. "Okay, but the loser has to pick up the pieces, house rules and all that."

"House? More like carriage rules," I reply sarcastically.

Lee laughs at my insult. "There's that fiery spirit we all know and love."

The game is much more intense this time because I know what I am up against. Neither of us can gain an advantage as we continue to foil one another, and eventually we reach an inevitable stalemate.

"Well, a tie. Satisfied?" he asks in a tone that I classify as smug.

"One more game, and if I don't win, we can stop," I reply coldly, still hyper-focused on identifying the best way to beat him. "But this time, you go first."

"You sure, love? That's giving me the advantage."

"I'm sure," I reply flatly.

Once again, the game starts, and we play with more focus than either of the previous games. Lee remains silent. There is a flurry of moves in which we both trade off several pieces. Finally, I use one of my pawns to cross the board, and right after it becomes a queen, I place Lee's king in checkmate.

"Cheeky, very cheeky, but I love it! Good game," replies Lee happily.

"You didn't let me win, did you?" I ask, narrowing my eyes. "Because that would be really insulting of you."

"No, of course not! You have my word. I haven't lost a game of chess in years, though, so I am impressed, and a little scared to be honest. You got all intense and quiet, and for a split second, I thought you may physically harm me," he says, laughing.

"I thought you Romani were fearless," I retort, forcing a smile, struggling to snap out of the trance I entered during the game.

"Nah, we fear plenty, but nothing I've ever encountered is as terrifying as you wielding chess pieces. Even scarier than when you tried to knock my head off."

Lee and I continue to talk about the tourney and whatever else comes to mind. Before we know it, the light from the candle has shrunk, telling us how much time has passed.

"Wow, I didn't realize we had been talking for so long," I say, struggling to keep my eyes open in the dim light and feeling like I could sleep for an entire week.

"How about them conversational skills now, eh? Told you I have quality conversations."

I'm beginning to love how annoying he is when he's being arrogant. Without saying anything, I gently press my lips against his. I keep them there until it feels just right, then I turn over, make myself comfortable, and in a sarcastic tone, I say, "Night, mate." A devious smile spreads across my face.

XXII

The next few days pass quickly, which surprises me since long trips are usually full of monotony.

The beauty of the Southlands continues to astonish. After we leave the lush, grassy plains we've been traveling over, we find ourselves approaching the foothills of the Romani Mountains. Unlike most mountains I've seen. These are covered in pine trees, and it's common for a lingering fog to blanket them. How effective would the fog be in deterring an airship attack? Maybe that's why the Apex never attempted to colonize the South.

When I become bored, I imagine what life will be like here. Lee tells me the Romani have inhabited the mountains and the foothills beneath them since the beginning of time. Apparently, his ancestors used them to survive, and nobody has ever conquered them because the terrain is nearly impassable, unless you're familiar with it.

Reaching the safety of the mountains is something I long for, yet I worry the happiness I'm feeling will be ripped away from me. All I can do is hope that whatever forces are after me and Kristoff won't find us.

"Not much longer now. Maybe a day and a half before we arrive," says Lee, who seems to sense the stress I'm feeling.

I smile gently, grateful for his effort to distract me. "You said the mountains were safe against invaders, right?"

"No safer place in the world, save for the Soulmi lands, but the snow and wilderness there are more deadly than any living enemy," he replies, smiling at me.

"I hope you're right. I haven't heard much about the Soulmi. What's their story?"

"They tend to keep to themselves, but we trade often and have always helped one another. About the closest thing a clan could have to an ally. If we came under attack or needed food. They would gladly come to our aid, and vice versa. They value the old ways more than any clan. To them, survival and being in tune with the spirits of the land are valued above all else. Which makes sense given they tend to live in places exposed to harsh cold and all manner of fierce beasts."

"Sounds like it would be the safest place from the Apex or whatever new regime will be ruling the North."

"What's the matter? Don't you think I can keep you safe? Although, truth be told, I don't think you need much protection in the first place, judging by how hard you hit. I mean for a girl, that is," he says jokingly.

I punch him in the shoulder, and he rubs his arm. "See what I mean."

"What do you think will become of the North if the Apex has fallen?" I ask, still deep in thought.

"Same thing that happens when any regime falls: chaos. Eventually, someone will take power for themselves and start up a new rule that is more of the same. Hopefully. The North continues to fight amongst themselves and not pay us Southerners any mind."

"I feel bad for the people. The Apex was oppressive and needed to change, but without them. There will be widespread suffering. I doubt Carthage has a plan to govern such a vast network," I say pessimistically.

"Not much we can do about it either way. I hate it for the common folk. The good thing about the Southlands is that there are no monarchs or nobility. Everyone here is a free person and treated as an equal. If a member of our clan can't make it, we all help so they have what they need. And, if you want to make a name for yourself, you must earn it. You can't just be born into it. Honestly, having a famous parent makes life even harder because you are judged twice as hard."

It must be nice to have a community that supports one another. This is something I never witnessed in Fairfield, although I can't blame the people since they barely had enough for themselves. "What about you?" I ask cautiously. "We've never really spoken about your parents."

"Not much to be said really, my mum loved to partake and drank herself into an early grave. My father died in a duel with a member of the Guul. He was a great fighter whose best years were behind him, and the man who challenged him knew as much, and took it as an opportunity to make a name for himself."

"That is horrible—I'm so sorry," I reply, not sure how to respond.

"Why are you sorry? Did you help the bloke kill him?" he says lightly. I usually love his dark sense of humor, but I am afraid to laugh.

"So, what happened to the man who killed your father? Was he arrested?"

Lee laughs. "People don't really get arrested down here, even if it was a violation of clan law, which in this case, he was within his rights. Of course, good old dad could have refused the duel, and no harm would have come to him, but he was more prideful than smart."

"So, this man killed your father and got to live his life?"

"Well, yes and no. He got to live his life, or what was left of it, but let's just say it was cut short after my dad's son got word of what happened. He traveled all the way to the Guul lands and challenged Foy to a duel, which he tried to refuse until his chieftain stepped in and told him that refusing a son the right for vengeance would result in banishment."

"Do you have a brother?" I ask.

"Sure don't," he says.

I laugh. "Did you really just refer to yourself in the third person for that entire story?"

Lee smirks. "People usually like it when I tell the story that way. Makes for a more dramatic delivery than just saying me and some of my lads traveled for weeks just to goad an old man into fighting me."

"Now I see why you're so popular. It's your great storytelling, isn't it?"

"It sure isn't my cooking skills, that's for certain."

"I can vouch for that," I say with a short laugh. "Sorry for all of the questions, but were you and your father close?"

"It's fine. I don't mind talking to you. After all, you shared a lot about your past and what brought you here. But no—we weren't close, really. Truth be told, he was a bit of a tyrant. Well-liked by our clan but hated by the others. Not many people were as skilled as my father, and he knew that, so he would often pick fights and make enemies that didn't need to be made, especially if they were Guul. He was also awful to my mum, which didn't help with her drinking. Although once he died. The drinking got worse, and it didn't take long before she joined him in the next life. It never made sense to me."

"How old were you when she died?"

"I was fifteen."

"Wait, so you were only fifteen years old when you dueled your father's killer?"

"Not hard to do when you've been raised to fight your entire life. If you think I am good with a wooden dagger, you should see me with Romani steel," he says, sounding overly arrogant. The smile he's trying to force tells me he's attempting to lighten the mood. I know he tends to do this when things get too serious. It's something I recognize easily since I'm the same way.

"So, if you didn't like your father much, why try to avenge him? Especially when you could have easily died yourself?" I ask, curious about the customs of the Southlands. Admittedly, I'm a little jealous. I wish that I could simply challenge the person responsible for killing my father—not only the Revenant but whoever was controlling it.

"I never really gave it much thought, if I'm honest. It's just something you do. A duel to settle an argument is usually fought to first blood or fought like the tourney. Instead, Foy insisted that he and my father fight to the death. Foy had many opportunities to challenge him while my father was still in his prime, but instead he waited until my father's best years were behind him. Which is a nice way of saying he was an old drunk who was very out of shape. Foy did what he did, knowing I would have to retaliate or risk a clan war. So, I figured I would give him what he asked for."

"That makes sense, but didn't you worry giving him what he wanted only helped his cause? Imagine the clout he would've had if he killed not only your father but you as well. And I'm sure over time, in telling the story, his clan would neglect the part about you being fifteen years old. Or what about if Foy had a son? Wouldn't the cycle of revenge just continue?"

"Welcome to the Southlands," says Lee laughing. "That's the way it is here. Blood feuds and revenge are a way of life. Historically. The land was in constant war. Entire clans and families were wiped off the map on a whim. Sometimes a war could rage for years, all over a simple argument. So, imagine what it would be like if someone killed someone they shouldn't have. I don't know if it was because of the glory war brings, or if it was to avoid appearing weak," he shrugs. "Either way, that's how things were back then, well, before Clan Harald started to mediate clan interactions, which helped put an end to it. Oh, and he did have a son. You met him and crushed his soul harder than I ever did."

My eyes widen when I realize who Foy's son was. "Wolfe?! Why hasn't he tried to avenge his father?" I ask, still shocked by the revelation.

"He's probably just waiting for the right time. The Guul are even more barbaric than the rest of us when it comes to revenge. Meaning his lot doesn't respect him much since he hasn't made a move to avenge his father. I think that's why he works extra hard to show everyone how strong he is. Hate and vengeance are powerful motivators, but if a person is a coward at heart, it won't make them crazy enough to face certain death." Lee looks at me for a moment. "You probably think we're all barbarians like they told you, huh?"

"No, not at all. I wish the North was the same way. If it was, I would challenge everyone who played a part in my father's death."

"Their time will come, I give you my word," Lee replies, looking directly at me with a serious expression. I grab his hand and squeeze it, my breath catching in my throat. Anytime we touch, it makes it hard for me to breathe. I don't know why I find myself so into Lee, but my feelings are growing stronger by the day.

We ride on in silence for a little bit, and I think about what Lee had said, wondering if I would still seek revenge if I knew that it would kill me. Only a week ago, I would have said yes without question. But now that I feel some semblance of happiness, my answer isn't quite as clear.

"Would have been nice to have you to talk to back then. Maybe you could have talked some sense into me. If I'm honest, though, I'd have done it all the same, I bet. Nothing like winning when the odds are against you. I bet you can relate to that. Look how well you did in your first tourney, even having never been to the Southlands or seeing how we fight. All the others have seen each other compete for years and know each other's strengths and weaknesses. Not to mention being a girl from the North can have its own disadvantages."

I know he's complimenting me but it's hard to take it that way. "What do you mean 'a girl from the North'?" I ask.

"You have that scary look in your eyes again," he says with a giant smirk, staring at me in amusement. "Just saying, how many girls up North train to fight?"

I can't help but see his logic despite disliking being judged on account of my sex or where I come from. I know he's right though; even the girls in Fairfield weren't trained to fight. In fact. The High Apexian Church viewed self-defense as a male responsibility, and thus forbade women from learning any sort of defense since it was deemed acting in a manner reserved only for men.

I was lucky my father viewed the religious edicts as foolish. I remember what he said to me when I had stopped training so I could be more like the other girls: "If you are attacked, do you think one of those priests in their fancy robes or the One True God will come to your aid?"

I lose myself in thoughts about my father and mother and how much I miss them both. I'm grateful I've been taught to take care of myself. There isn't much I can be thankful for as of late, but I know things would be much worse for me and Kristoff if I let myself be like one of those Northern girls.

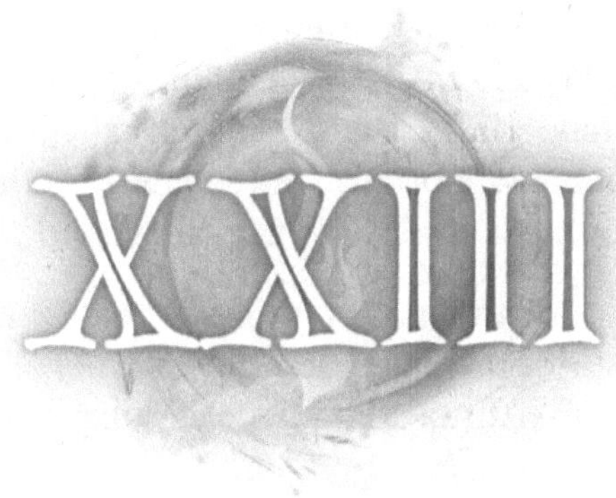

Before I know it, Lee is nudging me awake, informing me we're approaching one of the main camps. He explains they don't have cities, only encampments. Which doesn't seem much different from a small village, but it's a far cry from an Apexian City. The road cuts through the hills, with many forks and paths leading into dense forest. I wonder how anyone could possibly remember how to navigate these roads without getting lost.

"How much longer is it?" I ask, trying to look for evidence of a village in the distance, but my view is obstructed by the large pine trees and foothills of the mountain.

"Won't be but a couple of minutes at this rate. Soon we'll be in Little Watch," he replies, giving me a tired smile.

"If it's so little, how can it accommodate all of these Romani?" I ask.

"The majority of these people will return to different camps within the Highlands. Only a few of us will stay at Little Watch," he tells me.

"How did it come by its name?"

"The camp got its start as one of our original border outposts. The main path to the Highlands passes through Little Watch, and if someone wishes to invade, they will have to first overcome the forces stationed here. It hasn't been tried in over a hundred years, but historically the warriors would set up ambushes and traps to delay the invaders while runners were sent up the mountain to bring in reinforcements from the Highlands. The loss of life was always staggering for the enemy and minor for the Romani, so they started calling it Little Watch because defending it took little effort. Our borders now extend all the way North near the sea, wrapping around the Soulmi Mountains. Most Romani still prefer to live in the Highlands where it's safest. Only a few live in the valleys and plains these days."

"I love it. In the North, most of the cities, roads, and keeps are named after some priest or religious practice, which is confusing when you're trying to learn them. Although it was easier than trying to navigate these roads."

"Yeah, that is partly due to the mountain but mainly to confuse outsiders. That's also why we move camps from time to time, even though we don't have to worry about attacks these days. I suppose we still do it because we have grown accustomed to needing a change of scenery, plus there always seems to be a wedding or some sort of holiday to celebrate, so we travel a lot anyways."

"Anyone who would invade this terrain is not mentally well. It would be absolute madness," I say, looking over the side of a large steep hill.

"Many have tried, and all have failed. Some clans never recovered, and their names have been lost to time. The mountain has been our source of protection and our strength. It gives us everything we need to survive, and because of that, we cherish it as if it were our mother."

I rarely see Lee serious about anything, but when he speaks about the Romani lands, he does so in a way that shows the pride he has in his country.

I can't explain why, but it feels as if I have known him my entire life, despite it only being a few weeks. I know I'm falling deeply in love and doing so very quickly. This terrifies me. On the occasions that I worry about getting hurt, I try to protect myself by looking for things about him that annoy me, so I can have a reason to dislike him and distance myself. This, however, proves to be difficult because I have grown to find most of his faults attractive. Recently, I told myself he doesn't take anything seriously, but this argument has been invalidated after I see how he feels about his clan and country.

The winding road continues to pass through dense forest and dangerous hills before eventually giving way to a large grassy area overlooking a massive ridge. Without having to ask, I know we've arrived at Little Watch. The ridge faces the north and has several wooden watchtowers along it, providing an addition in height above the valley below. Areas of worn grass indicate where the caravans typically rest along a line of large pine trees.

I find it humorous that despite being in a nearly impassable spot at the base of the mountain, the Romani still place their caravans along the tree line for added protection. Although I must admit their vigilance and paranoia make me feel much safer, especially considering I'm still unsure of who or what could be after us.

I've barely been able to speak to Kristoff during the long journey and am not entirely sure where he is. After searching, I spot him riding with Andrew, his red curly hair moving in the wind. No matter what he's up to, Kristoff always makes sure his hair looks good. Fortunately, this is something the Southlanders seem to value. Their preoccupation with aesthetics still surprises me since they are referred to as savages in the Apex.

Kristoff leaps from the caravan before it stops moving and makes his way to me. He's smiling broadly as he looks around Little Watch. A sentiment I understand, a feeling of security and satisfaction. There was a profound amount of uncertainty when we fled Fairfield, but now, for the first time since that day, we have a stable place to live. Now that we are finally here, I have a nagging feeling saying I'm supposed to be sad. As if I must still be mourning the loss of my father, and being happy means I don't care about him.

"Hard to believe, isn't it?" asks Kristoff as we stand near the edge of the ridge overlooking the valley. "It's so much better than I could have imagined," I reply.

"Me too. Do you think—" Kristoff begins before hesitating, concerned about ruining the moment.

I frown at him, suspecting he's thinking about our parents and whether they would have been happy to come to Little Watch. Instead of saying anything, I grab his hand and stand quietly with him, savoring the moment. I wish our parents could've seen this with us. At the thought, my mind fills with anger. They could have—if not for that abomination. I will avenge them no matter the cost. I will work harder than I ever have, to learn whatever I need to, not only to end the Revenant but to bring justice to everyone involved.

"We will avenge them. You have my word," I say to Kristoff.

"I know we will, but for now, let's celebrate. We still need to get settled, and I was told we can swear our oaths to the clan under the next full moon, which will make us official. Are you nervous?" he continues.

"I'm not. It seems right, you know? My mother was a member, and that makes me feel better. How about you?" I reply, breaking my gaze from the valley to look at Kristoff, who has tears running down his face.

"I'm not worried. I can tell they are good people, and, not to be cliché, but it will be an honor to join. I have never felt so at home in my life. The people here don't judge me or put me down. I feel guilty about this, because I hate what led us here, but I'm glad everything happened the way it did. If it didn't—we wouldn't be here."

"Don't feel bad. I know what you mean, and I feel the same way. Besides, it's not like you wished it to happen. Us being here is a silver lining to a tragic situation. We deserve a silver lining for once, so let's celebrate, like you said. We will have plenty of time to hate ourselves for being happy later," I smile at him. "I think the full moon is in a day or two anyways. I bet Mum knows for sure. We should go and ask. I haven't spoken to her much this trip."

Kristoff nods in agreement and lets go of my hand to wipe the tears from his eyes, almost as if he just realized he was crying.

Eventually, we come to Mum's quaint yellow caravan and find the short, plump woman lying sprawled out on the dirt, staring up at the sky. She is moving her arms and legs in a motion that reminds me of when the children of Fairfield would make snow angels in the winter. Her dress must be getting filthy in the dirt, but I know Mum doesn't care. She is a strange woman and unlike anyone I've ever met, but she is also the warmest and most welcoming person. It is impossible to feel uncomfortable or sad around her, as if your troubles were ice melting away in the summer sun.

"Oh! Hi, my lovelies, what a beautiful day," Mum says before quickly jumping to her feet and hugging us both. I don't usually like hugging people, but I enjoy them from Mum.

"Kristoff and I were wondering when the next full moon is. We were told we can swear our oaths on that day."

"Oh yes—yes, of course, I nearly forgot. Thank you for reminding me. I must begin preparing at once," she says before rushing for the door of her caravan.

"When is the next full moon, Mum?" I ask urgently before she fully retreats inside her caravan.

"Why, it's tonight, of course!"

I suddenly feel anxious. I'm not sure what the oath ceremony will entail, and I have no idea if I need to prepare in some way. I recall Lee saying the ceremony is mainly symbolic and not a major ordeal, but I can't help but think that his definition of major might be skewed.

"Well, it looks like we better make ourselves presentable. I wonder where they bathe. I'm sure there must be a river or lake somewhere nearby," Kristoff says, focusing on how he will look, as usual, rather than on what will be expected of him.

We find Andrew and Jaseen, who show us where we can bathe. Just as Lee mentioned, there is a cave near the camp that houses a hot spring. I've never seen such a thing in person, but I've read they stay warm all year long. The cave also provides privacy, something I've been concerned about not having. When we reach the spring, I see that there are two different caves, allowing more than one person to bathe at a time. I take a large torch from Andrew and make my way a few hundred feet inside. I stand before a well-lit room with several torches perched along the cave walls. There is a table for my clothing and other belongings.

I quickly undress and slowly walk down the hand-carved stone steps into the water. It's the perfect temperature, not too cold and not too hot, though I discover the closer I move to the middle, the warmer the water is.

I sit quietly in the pool and feel as if my stress is melting off my body and slowly floating into the sky, just like the steam drifting up from the water. I lean my head back, and for the first time in a very long time, I feel at peace and completely relaxed. It doesn't take long before I find myself drifting off to sleep, which is an inevitability when I take warm baths.

Within a dream, I look upon a dimly lit room where several men are gathered around a magnificent wooden table, on top of which is a carved map of the Northern Realms. I notice there is a burn mark where the Apexian Capital should be. The man the High Priest referred to as the fallen Prince of Carthage is sitting at the head of the table, staring quietly at the map. He maintains the calm and collected facial expression that he had in my last dream, wearing the same black fur coat. I attempt to wake myself, knowing I need to get ready for the ceremony, but no matter how hard I try—I can't. A feeling of entrapment sweeps over me, causing me to grow more and more afraid. My emotions drown out the words of the people at the table. I can see their mouths moving but hear no noise. I focus on calming my mind in an effort to hear whatever they are saying.

Finally, after some time, my mind clears, and I hear the voice of a timid man. "The remainder of the Apexian forces are in full route. Any significant leadership remaining has fled to Distle. I advise launching a full invasion to stomp out any future resistance."

"There remains the matter of those within the six realms who are still loyal to the Apex. One can presume a counter strike will occur once the routed forces regroup with their leadership in Distle, but this will not occur for some time. Perhaps it would be more prudent to first secure your rule of the newly claimed realms. To that end, we need our forces centralized to stomp out resistance," another man responds with confidence.

"A counterstrike will be inconsequential, at best," says the fallen Prince, his eyes fixed on the map. "The Apex did not govern properly. This weakness will serve us well. Prepare messages to be delivered to each of the realms, which will include instructions about their future self-governance. We will allow each to establish their own leadership."

"But my lord—" the man who advocated invading Distle attempts, only to be silenced by the raising of the Prince's hand.

"They will swear fealty to Carthage. Paying tribute to secure their position—at a considerably more reasonable rate than the Apex required. All religious practices of the One True God will be banned immediately. Anyone caught following the religion will be exiled. If they lead religious practices or conspire to convert another, they will be sentenced to death. Save for this, people are free to practice whatever religion they wish. From this moment henceforth, the One True God will be referred to as the False God. Furthermore, each realm must pledge to never show hostility toward one another. Any and all disputes between realms will be overseen by Carthage. Let it be known that we shall be the first amongst equals."

"Very wise, my lord. The opportunity to rule presented to those with ambition will surely prevent any talks of rebellion. However, there is a concern that banning the religion of the One T—the False God, will not be taken well by those who reside in realms closer to the capital," the advisor notes.

"I imagine when they have money in their pockets and food on their tables. They will quickly forget about their old religion," the irritated Prince responds through pursed lips. "The Apex used religion as a way to distract hungry people from realizing they were poor. Instead, we will feed them and give them a quality of life that does not require seeking comfort in a lie. You bring up a good point, though; it may take some time for them to adjust to this change. Make sure you personally coordinate educational centers in each of the realms designed to teach the people about the fallacies of the False God, starting with the realms closest to the capital. I will leave you two tasked with creating the correspondence for the realms and designing how the new rulers will be selected. I trust my intentions are clear and that you will have no problem working out the details. Is there any news regarding the Apexian assets that went missing from Fairfield?"

"We have tracked—"

The dream ends abruptly as my lungs struggle for air. I open my eyes to see that I had slipped beneath the water. I quickly break the surface, fighting to catch my breath. My mind is flooded with thoughts, but before I can make sense of them, I hear Andrew yelling into the cave, asking if I'm okay. I quickly reply so that he knows I'm fine. I climb out of the hot spring and dress myself hastily, rushing to find Lee and Kristoff to tell them about my dream.

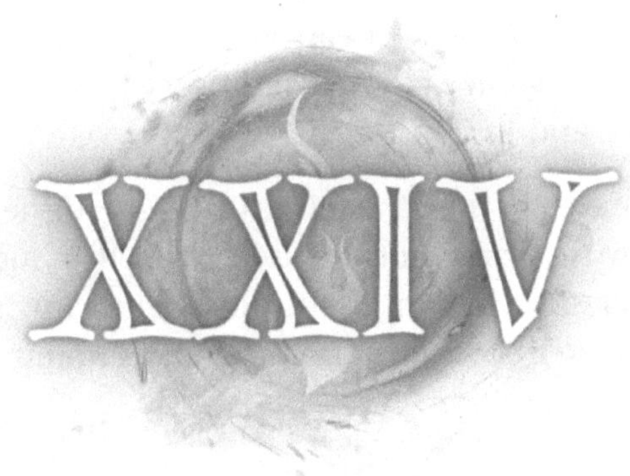

I run out of the cave, barely speaking to Andrew who is still waiting at the entrance. I can hear him following behind me, probably confused and concerned as to why I'm running.

Before I know it, I'm out of the thick forest and back on the ridge. Despite my urgency, I can't help but notice the breathtaking view as the sun begins to set, casting shadows on the valley below.

While I stop to appreciate the view, Andrew catches up to me. "What's the matter? See a ghost?"

"Sorry about that. I just really need to talk to Lee and Kristoff," I reply, feeling bad that I made him worry. I know Lee trusts Andrew, and they're as close as brothers, but I don't want him to think I've lost my mind. The last thing I want is a negative reputation, especially since I still technically haven't joined the Romani.

"Assuming Kristoff is done combing his mane, I'd imagine he is with Lee and the gang at the wagering tables," says Andrew.

"Oh, Lee has a gambling problem, does he?" I ask in an inquisitive tone.

"Shouldn't have said that," he says, smirking. "I'm sure he's just showing Kristoff the ropes, helping to prevent him from being swindled."

We walk until we come to a group of caravans with tables set up a few feet from their entrances. Many Romani are standing around, cheering or groaning, depending on how their wagers fare. I notice most of the people here are men. I bet women have too much sense to throw away their coin on games of chance. I eventually find Kristoff sitting at a table with Lee and Jaseen.

The game master is quickly sliding three overturned cups around on a table. I know the game and can see Kristoff trying to track the cup hiding whatever object he needs to find. The cups stop, and Kristoff guesses. The game master lifts the cup to show nothing hidden beneath.

"Double your wager, and I'll let you guess between these two," the game master says cheerfully, taking Kristoff for an easy mark. Kristoff reaches for his coin purse, but before he can, Lee throws a couple of coins onto the table. The game master takes them and places them in a wooden box. Kristoff contemplates for a bit, deciding carefully between the two, finally picking another cup, which the game master reveals is also empty. "There's no way," says Kristoff, irritated.

"Okay now, show us then," says Lee.

The man lifts the third cup, which also reveals nothing. The men around the table, including Lee, begin to laugh.

"See, Kristoff, the trick is to make them think they have a fighting chance, when in reality they never did. That's the Romani way. It's a wonder anyone plays these games. Say, how much did you make at the fair?" asks Jaseen.

The game master shakes his wooden box as he holds it to his ear. "Not nearly enough, Jaseen, my boy." The man opens the box and gives Kristoff and Lee back their coins. "Being Romani means no other Romani can swindle you. There are other games which are inherently harder to fix that you could gamble on, but these here are reserved for the other clans," says Lee before giving me a wink.

I love to see Lee and Kristoff interact. Since I care deeply for both of them, I'm thankful they like one another. Seeing them smiling and carrying on makes me hesitant to share my dream. Do I really want to ruin their fun by telling them? I can tell them tomorrow after the ceremony, so I push the images from my mind and tell myself it will be a problem to deal with then. Deciding to put it aside until tomorrow makes me begin thinking more logically, and the whole thing seems far less scary than when I first woke up. I need to learn why I'm having the dreams, but it can wait.

"I imagine it's time for you two to get over to Mum's tent so she can prepare you. Not too late to back out if you're having second thoughts," says Lee, smiling at me.

"What's the matter? You don't want to be the second-best Romani at next year's Faire?" I say, making light of the situation.

The closer we get to the ceremony, the more I begin to worry. It isn't that I don't want to join the clan; it's just that it's happening so fast. I know that it's the way things are done in the Southlands and that being in a clan is similar to pledging loyalty to a realm, but instead of one leader or a king, it's to the entire clan. This is a concept that I prefer over following a single person; however, I still have questions I need to ask Mum before I decide fully. I think it's best not to bother Lee with my concerns, so I can spare him from unnecessary worry.

"No place I'd rather be than the South, and if I had to pick a clan to join it would be the Guul, but since they wouldn't have me, I suppose the Romani will do," jokes Kristoff.

"I could see you as a Guul. But first I'd need to steal that comb of yours and get you on a diet of pig fat and push-ups," says Jaseen before messing up Kristoff's hair, causing him to quickly fix it.

We say our goodbyes to Lee, Andrew, and Jaseen before making our way to Mum's tent. We walk in silence while I contemplate the ceremony and what the future will hold for us as official members of the Romani. I realize not much will change, except perhaps becoming more active members of the clan and doing our part to keep the camp running smoothly, which is something I know both Kristoff and I will do without issue. I also wouldn't mind having to defend the clan if needed. The more I think about it, the less worried I am. The only request I wish to make is that they allow me to seek revenge when the time comes. This doesn't seem like it will be an issue given how Lee was able to avenge his father, but it's something I want to clarify before agreeing to join.

"Any reservations?" I ask Kristoff.

"Honestly, no," he says confidently, after a bit of a pause. I'm happy he's ready to join, but I worry what might happen if I change my mind and decide not to. I don't want my decision to alter the way he feels, but I want us to either join or not, together.

We reach the entrance to Mum's caravan, which is easy to spot thanks to all the torches she has around it. We find her standing to the side of the caravan, going through a large barrel. She looks frazzled. The prospect of Mum managing a ceremony makes me anxious.

"Why, hello lovelies! Please, come inside. We have much to discuss and not much time," says Mum, whose cheerful expression soothes my worry.

We accompany her inside, both sitting down on two small wooden stools. Mum's caravan is far more organized than the last time I saw it, but the familiar fragrance of flowers and the outdoors remains. I wonder how the inside of the caravan smells more like the outdoors than the actual outdoors.

"So, first things first, what questions do you have? I can only imagine how you must be feeling," says Mum, who is uncharacteristically focused.

"What's it like being a member of the clan? I guess I'm nervous because where we come from, an oath or swearing fealty is essentially the same as giving up your freedom. Both of our fathers were officials who had sworn fealty to the Apex. Because of this, they had to do whatever the Apex commanded," says Kristoff. I'm certain he asked more for my sake than his own. I'm notorious for hating being told what to do, and he knows it.

"That sounds dreadful," Mum says with an expression on the verge of disgust. "It's nothing like that here though, love. There is no dictator or High Priest issuing commands. There are systems within the Romani where that type of leadership may be present, but such is the nature of armies and their soldiers. Of all the clans, the Romani are most like a family, and while no family is perfect, we all must look out for one another," replies Mum compassionately.

"Lee mentioned that his prize winnings would go to the clan. What did he mean by that?" I ask, kicking myself internally for not asking such questions before now.

"In the North, they have taxes that each person pays to the Apex in the name of doing their part. It's similar here in a way, but there is no requirement that people pay if it puts them in a dire situation. I know it's different than what you're used to, and I could see why you would be confused. Romani always give back to the clan somehow, whether it be with coins, supplies, or their time. Lee is a clan enforcer. It's likely he's giving a portion of his winnings to make sure new recruits have the armor and weapons needed to defend the clan."

"That makes sense, and we have no problem doing our part. But, if I'm honest, there is one thing I am anxious about. You know the story of how we came here and how—" I pause, trying not to get emotional. I look at Kristoff, who gives me a forced smile. "So, umm, the person, or people, responsible for our parents' deaths, I want to bring them to justice, and I want to make sure being a member won't prevent that from happening."

Mum takes my hand and places it into her own. "My love, this isn't a prison. If you ever want to leave the clan, you can do so at any time, and while we would hate to see you go, we will never try and stop you from following your heart. We often partake in too much wine and too much song, and we are not typically the type to seek conflict, but nobody can harm our family without repercussion. I have no doubt you will honor your family and avenge them by bringing those responsible to justice—and we will be there with you when the time comes. We would never stand between you and your right."

Mum's voice is always so innocent and joyful, so it surprises me a great deal to hear her speak in such a violent manner. Violent or not, Mum's words expel my anxiety about what the oath will mean, especially the part about it not being a life sentence. I also appreciate not being made to feel crazy for wanting revenge. The Apexian Church taught that revenge was animalistic and evil. To faithfully follow the One True God, a person couldn't seek revenge and should have no violent or aggressive thoughts whatsoever.

"I'm in," says Kristof, looking at me for confirmation.

"Me too," I say, smiling.

"Great!" says Mum, clapping her hands and smiling wide. "All that is left is to swear your oath in front of the clan, or at least the clan members here at Little Watch. It's nearly impossible to get this many Romani into one place. Besides, we didn't want to wait for another moon, and who knows when the snow will come. It just wouldn't have worked."

I laugh at Mum's immediate return to her normal state of scattered thoughts. We enjoy her homebrewed tea and biscuits while we continue to chat and share in each other's company. Eventually Mum stands up and opens her door, motioning for us to follow her outside. I'm shocked at the sea of torches lighting up the night's sky, positioned all along the ridge of Little Watch.

We slowly walk behind Mum, who is in an almost trance-like state. We pass lines of Romani dressed as if they're preparing for war. They stand at attention, each holding a wooden shield fixed on their arm, and their weapons raised. As we pass, the line of soldiers begins to bang their varied arms—axes, swords, and spears—slowly against their shields. As we continue to walk, the sound of them banging on their shields grows to a thunderous height.

We end up in the middle of a circle, facing a line of Romani, looking at us. Mum signals for silence, and all at once, the noise stops. Mum stands facing me and Kristoff while the rest of the Romani wrap around us. I'm nervous, but in a good way. I can't believe others thought the Southlanders were a bunch of unorganized savages.

Mum moves close to us and asks how we're doing. Kristoff and I smile and nod in response.

"Should we kneel?" asks Kristoff.

"Goodness! What for? the Romani do not kneel," Mum replies sweetly.

The fact we don't have to kneel is greatly appreciated. I hated having to do that during religious functions within the Apex.

Mum instructs us to listen carefully and, when she asks us to, to repeat after her. She also assures us both that we look great. Her presence provides an aura of comfort that makes me feel calm despite knowing a couple of hundred people are staring at us.

"Welcome, everyone! Thank you oh so much for joining us for this exciting moment. Nothing warms my heart more than oath ceremonies because it means our family is growing larger and stronger. After all, we are strong because we are family. We are family through bond!" she shouts, and to my surprise, the crowd roars back. "We are strong because we are family! We are family through bond!"

"As the Romani Head, I've been given permission to speak for the clan, and we agree that these two should be granted official acceptance into the Romani if they so choose. We also have an enforcer paramount with us tonight. What say you?" says Mum before looking towards Lee.

"On behalf of the enforcers, I agree these two should be offered the opportunity," he replies in a formal manner that I find entirely uncharacteristic of him.

After Lee's statement, two men place a cauldron with a large flame directly in front of Kristoff and me. I can see a metal rod resting in the flame, its thick leather handle protruding outside of the cauldron, safe from the heat.

Mum walks in front of us and does her best to speak loud enough for everyone to hear though she still maintains her calm, peaceful demeanor. "What say you, Aries? Do you wish to take our sacred oath, thus becoming a part of our family?"

"I do," I say quickly, the words rushing from my lips.

"Repeat after me. I, Aries Fleetwood, will treat my fellow Romani and our lands as family. I will do them no harm, bear them no ill will, and help in times of need. I will defend them, I will fight for them, I will kill for them, and I will die for them. For I am Romani, and we are strong because we are family; we are family through bond," says Mum, and I repeat each word. They echo in my mind, and I find myself uneasy over the significance of what I'm saying, but I remind myself that my mother had sworn the same oath, and my anxiety dissipates.

Kristoff repeats the oath as well. I do my best to keep my eyes fixed on Mum, but I can't help glancing at Kristoff. It makes me happy to see him smiling so widely as he recites the oath. I know he's proud to be a part of the Romani. And while I'm glad he's happy, my heart aches knowing he had never really fit in anywhere before now.

After we both swear our oaths, Lee steps forward and whispers in my ear. "Apologies, love, but this part we couldn't mention. Each Romani is marked with our brand. It's a way for us to identify ourselves to one another. Where would you like yours?"

Anger and fear swell in my stomach. I don't want to be branded. I know it will hurt, but that isn't what bothers me. I don't want to be scarred for life.

"Mine's on my forearm, easy to hide, but one of the most painful places. The upper part of your arm may be the least sensitive spot. Best not to show pain, or else the gang won't ever let you live it down," he says before kissing my cheek and walking to the cauldron to remove the rod. Despite being angry at him for not telling me, I figure I've come this far and I'm not about to back out now.

"I want it on my forearm," I say coldly, showing no fear in my eyes despite being very much afraid.

"You sure?" he asks, concerned.

"Did I stutter?" I say, prompting the crowd to laugh.

"Okay, okay, have it your way, love."

I look at him the entire time, choosing to focus on his light green eyes instead of looking at the hot iron rod. He grabs my wrist tight and proceeds to press the brand against my skin. I do my best not to wince, but I instinctively try to move my arm away from the pain. Thankfully, Lee holds a firm grip, giving the illusion that I'm staying still. After a few seconds, it's over. I breathe a sigh of relief, proud that I didn't cry out in pain. But my arm is sore, and so is the inside of my cheek from where I was biting it.

"Umm, I will definitely be doing my upper arm," says Kristoff nervously.

"No shame in it at all, mate, Andrew and Jaseen both have theirs there as well. And if you just count down from five, we can get this taken care of in an instant," says Lee.

Kristoff begins to count, "Five—" but before he can even get to four, Lee quickly presses the brand against his arm holding him close with his free arm to prevent him from moving about.

When the hot metal is removed from his skin, Kristoff lets out a groan. "Make whatever jokes you want. That hurts!" he yells, causing the crowd to laugh and cheer.

After it's done, the group breaks their formal ranks and comes up to us, welcoming us to the Romani, now as official members. For the first time in a very long time, Kristoff and I feel like we have a family.

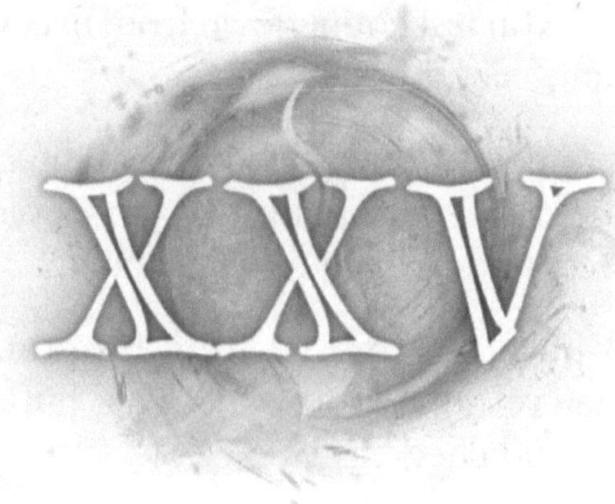

Six months have passed since we swore our oaths to become clan members. Fall has turned to winter and winter to spring, and I find I'm more in love with being a Romani than I could have imagined. My days are filled with great company keen on keeping one another laughing and fed. But my favorite part of the winter is when Kristoff and I join Lee, Andrew, and Jaseen as enforcers.

Being an enforcer is relatively quiet in terms of action, but we practice every day as if a threat is imminent. In addition to our training, the enforcer class of the clan is also tasked with ensuring that no outsiders, whether it be another clan or nomads, threaten the safety of the Romani, our territory, or our interests. The amount of organization and unity amongst the clan is awe-inspiring.

The Romani rarely travel during the winter months, replacing our caravans with large round tents, called lavvu, which sit atop a circular four-foot-deep trench. The structure is larger at the bottom, and the higher it goes, the narrower it becomes. At the top of the structure is a small circular opening, about the size of a dinner plate, which allows the smoke from fires to exit safely. Despite being fond of our winter home, I find myself longing to see more of the Southlands, growing more and more restless as each day passes.

When spring arrives, and the weather breaks, the enforcers are to travel to the edge of the Romani territory to ensure that traders can safely do business with the other clans. Lee informs me that assaults on merchants have been common in previous years. He suspects the

Swindletor clan is behind the attacks, despite their adamant denial and accusations it must be outlaws they expelled from their lands. The prospect of stopping bandits makes me long for combat, hoping to put my newly acquired skills to the test.

Each day, we train in some form of weapons combat, whether it be sword, dagger, axe, or bow. I excel with most of these, save for the bow, which I am still absolutely dreadful at. Kristoff, who does not fare well in hand-to-hand combat, is a natural with the bow, and after a few weeks of training, he became one of the best sharpshooters in all the Romani, second only to Jaseen.

Requiring little practice with the bow, Jaseen takes his other weapons training particularly seriously during the winter, stating that he is preparing to redeem himself after his humiliation in the tourney. His drive and work ethic impress me. I've never seen anyone who practices as much as he does, and in time his hard work pays off, finding himself able to best Lee during nearly half of their practice sessions.

I awake to the sound of Lee moving around inside our lavvu. It wasn't long after I joined the Romani that I took up quarters with him, which is bittersweet. On the one hand, I am able to spend more time with him and grow as close as lovers can, on the other, it means I spend less time with Kristoff. Lucky for me, however, Kristoff has his own lavvu, situated right beside ours. Even though we live close, I still miss our late-night conversations about nonsense. Lee and I also have late-night discussions, mainly about combat tactics and overcoming battle scenarios. I learn a lot from him, and he's happy to teach me everything he learned from former Romani enforcers, especially those who had fought when the clans were at war.

I discover the last real war in the Southlands happened a generation before he was born and ended with the Romani gaining significant territory from the Swindletors. Our ally in the war, Clan Harald, gained lands from the Guul. The Soulmi remained neutral but provided the Romani and Clan Harald with desperately needed food and supplies. Lee talks about his father becoming a hero, defeating the Swindletor chieftain in single combat, which was the turning point in the war. He tells me the outcome had been a blessing and a curse. This was the time his father seemed to have peaked, and it made the rest of his life unbearable by comparison, since he failed to recreate the glory he received from the duel.

What I love most about Lee is his mind and how he can remain unbiased, looking closely at problems to see what dynamics occurred to create them instead of responding emotionally. It reminds me a lot of my father who always remained calm in the face of intense chaos, keeping his emotions in check.

My thoughts are interrupted when Lee shakes my leg. "Morning, love. Best be getting ready. Today is a special day," he says in a hushed tone.

"Really? And why is that?"

"I have a surprise for you, that's why."

I feel a rush of energy. I love surprises, especially from Lee, who always seems to pair them with a puzzle or objective. "I don't deserve you. You are the best," I say in a grateful tone.

"Yea, yea, I know. Part of me is hoping you don't earn it this time. I made the clues much harder than usual, and I won't help no matter how much you beg."

"I have never once begged or even asked you for help," I say before giving him a big hug.

"Fair enough. But this time, it will be different," he replies, reaching inside of his jacket to remove a piece of parchment. I snatch it from his hands, quickly opening it and reading the words scrawled there: You must face your highest fear. I think for a moment before knowing that he must mean the highest watchtower on the ridge of Little Watch. It isn't a challenging clue to solve, but the task itself will be difficult since I'm afraid of heights.

"Gave up on trying to make hard clues, I see," I say, hoping to get a reaction out of him. But instead, he simply smirks at me and says nothing. "Fine, let's go to the watchtower. I hope it is worth risking my life for."

"So dramatic, love," he replies before attempting to give me a kiss which I pretend to rebuff, but only for a moment before placing my lips on his. I love how we are still playful with one another after being together for several months. I've heard most relationships lose their spark after the first couple of months but ours feels even stronger than before.

I get dressed, and Lee and I leave the lavvu, making our way to the highest watchtower in all Little Watch.

Looking up at the tower makes me shiver with anxiety. Why must it be so much taller than any watchtower should be, especially when I'm already atop a ridge?

"You're coming with me, right?"

"'Course I am, but ladies first."

I let out a sigh before climbing the wooden ladder that leads to the tower's cab. I'm terrified of heights but do my best to take it one peg at a time, focusing on my breathing. Whenever Lee tries to speak to me, I tell him to be quiet, thinking his silence will make me less anxious.

After a grueling climb, I reach the cab of the tower. I quickly pull myself onto the wooden floor and lean up against the wall, doing my best to pretend I'm sitting in a room on the ground.

"Wasn't so bad, was it," says Lee, who enters the cab and looks out the window. We stand in silence for a few moments before I gather the courage to look around. In the corner, I notice a bow with a quiver full of arrows. I instantly feel discouraged about what the next task might be, cursing Lee for exploiting my weakness with the bow.

"Pulling out all the cheap tactics for this, aren't we? Just imagine how bad you're going to feel when I still complete it."

Lee rings the large bell within the watchtower. I look out the window and see Kristoff, Jaseen, and Andrew carrying a straw practice dummy, placing it within thirty yards of the tower's base before running in the opposite direction, knowing my dreadful aim would put them all at risk.

"Do I really have to hit that?" I ask.

Lee nods with his sometimes lovable, mostly annoying smirk plastered on his face. His green eyes stare back at me, taking pleasure in my torment. I grab the bow and acquaint myself with its weight and pull strength. I nock an arrow, take a deep breath, and do my best to hit the target, missing wide right. I repeat this numerous times, each shot missing by several feet.

"Remember, love: let go of the draw, don't jerk back."

"I'm sorry, I don't remember asking your advice, Lee, enforcer paramount and master of bows," I say, mocking him.

I'm running out of arrows and only have a couple left. Lee always told me that if I failed to complete a task during one of his scavenger hunts, I wouldn't get the surprise, but I've never failed, so I don't know if that's the truth. Not wanting him to give me special treatment, my motivation to hit the target is renewed. I try to remember my father's lessons from when I was a little girl, before he allowed me to give up on the bow. I find myself opening both of my eyes and staring the target down. I take a deep breath and hold it, making sure to keep my eyes trained on the target while looking down the arrow. Then, I let loose. I watch the arrow fly and stick into the leg of the target dummy.

"Great shot, love. Honestly didn't think you'd make it."

"That's offensive but can't say I blame you."

Climbing down the ladder is far scarier than climbing up. However, it's quicker since I'm in a hurry to get down.

I walk over to the target dummy and see a piece of parchment attached to its chest with a dagger. I remove the dagger and look at the parchment. It's blank. I run my fingers across it, and it feels as though someone had written on it, but no ink can be seen. I remember reading about invisible ink in one of the adventure books I loved as a child. I think for a moment about the story to see if I can recall how the invisible ink was revealed. Then it hits me. I take the parchment to the nearest fire and place the document over the heat. In no time, I see the word "blacksmith" bleed through.

"Well, that's disappointing," says Lee, who clearly expected the clue to prove more of a challenge.

"Please tell me you didn't use your piss, mate," says Andrew, who I presume is the one tasked with placing it on the dummy.

"Course not. I used Jaseen's."

Everyone laughs and then stops, staring at Lee wondering whether he's serious.

We travel to the blacksmith located deep within the forest outside Little Watch. Upon arrival, the blacksmith gives us a shocked look.

"I thought you said it may be later on today, or even tomorrow before she solved it."

"Looks like I overestimated my cleverness," says Lee happily.

"Or foolishly underestimated hers," the blacksmith snorts. "Lucky for you, I didn't," he says, leaving the group to collect my surprise. Though I do my best to keep calm, I'm beyond excited. The blacksmith returns and hands me a lightweight sword resting inside of a black leather sheath.

I let out a sigh, knowing that Lee spent far more coin on it than I am comfortable accepting. I love gifts and surprises but told him not to spend a lot on them. Although he never listens and seems empowered by defying me. I remove the sword from its sheath, revealing a brilliantly crafted Romani steel rapier resembling the one I lost fighting the Revenant. Lee must've had the blade designed using information he obtained from questions he asked about my old sword.

The sword I hold now feels even lighter than my old one, at least from what I can remember. I don't like that he spent so much on it, but now that I'm holding it, I'm glad he did.

"I don't know what to say, it's—it's perfect," I say before passing it to Kristoff to inspect. I rush over to Lee and pull him close, kissing him deeply.

"That's pure Romani steel too. It can cut through armor and won't break," says Andrew.

"This is just like your old one. How did he know?" asks Kristoff as he twirls the sword around, unsure of what to do with it.

"C'mon mate, got a steel trap up here," answers Lee, tapping his temple.

"And the moment's gone," I say, smiling and rolling my eyes before hugging him. "Seriously, thank you so much. You're the best."

We are interrupted by a Romani who hands a letter to Andrew. He reads it and gives it to Lee. "We've been summoned for a parley with Olly from the Swindletors," says Lee before handing the note to Jaseen.

"He's a snake. What does he want?" asks Andrew, a confused look on his face.

"The weather only just broke, and already we have to travel and deal with those scum," says Jaseen, frustrated.

"Wait, why do we have to leave at his beck and call? I thought we didn't care what the other clans thought," I say, annoyed by the news.

"Believe me, we don't. Mum wrote the letter and said we best meet to find out what they want. Apparently, his letter didn't say much, just requested my presence specifically. I want to leave sooner rather than later so we can survey the meeting spot. We can't be too safe when it comes to them," Lee replies.

Knowing that Mum recommended we go and that we aren't going against our will makes me feel better. Not to mention, my defiant attitude has cooled, making me quite happy for the opportunity to travel. We quickly gather our provisions and set off on horseback toward the Cove, the location specified by the Swindletors.

"What is this cove anyway?" asks Kristoff, as he stretches his back from within his saddle.

"Each clan has a particular place where they meet for clan-to-clan business. The Cove is right at the border between our territory and the Swindletors'. In fact, the land that makes up the Cove has technically not been claimed by either clan. Doesn't change the fact we approach from the plain and they have to climb up a steep, hilly path from the beach, so it's safe to say that it's our land," says Andrew.

"Who wants the land that close to the beach anyway? They can keep the wind and the sand, give me the mountains any day," says Jaseen.

"So, does it sit on a cove?" I ask, still confused.

"I know what you're thinking, love, but whatever reason it has for its name has been lost to time. There isn't a cove within a mile of its location. You will find lots of names don't make sense down South," replies Lee, who never seems to grow tired of my frequent questions.

"What is a parley then?" asks Kristoff.

"I always seem to forget you two weren't born here. A parley means that we meet under oath and will not disrupt the peace nor brandish any weapons on neutral ground. Typically, one clan asks another to parley, and the receiving clan has the choice to say no if they don't wish to. If one clan denies the parley and they were to still meet, it wouldn't be under the agreement of peace. Too bad for us Mum already sent word that we accepted the parley. I never trusted a Swindletor, and I never will. If they weren't such cowards, they would no doubt attack us as soon as it supported their interests," says Jaseen, making no effort to hide his disdain for the Swindletor clan.

"Imagine what would happen to them if they did that. By oath, the other three clans would have to declare war as well. Sort of ironic that in a land of no laws we have plenty of them," says Andrew, his comment being followed by Lee's and Jaseen's laughter.

"Oh, we have plenty of laws, just no judge or court to enforce them. Our judge is Romani steel, and my hand is the executioner," says Lee attempting to sound poetic.

"Excuse me, I think I'm going to be sick," I reply, finding his words cringe-worthy.

After a few days of riding, the party draws closer to the meeting point. As we progress, Lee grows more vigilant, frequently scanning the horizon for any signs of an ambush. Having ridden through the night, we are now less than an hour from our destination.

"This is the closest Romani camp to the Cove. I need to make sure the enforcers here are aware of the parley and are on guard in case we need reinforcements," says Lee before leaping from his horse and walking into a dense thicket of trees.

I stretch, finding it difficult to remain comfortable in my saddle, which means I offered to stay awake to lead the horses more often than I should have during the night. I don't require much comfort, but sleep is one thing I can't do without.

"So hypothetically, if we needed them, how many enforcers could come to our aid from a camp this size?" asks Kristoff.

"Maybe one or two official enforcers here, but all Romani are trained to fight, so you would have a few dozen, I suppose. But more importantly, they would send word up the mountain and summon the full force of the Romani, which would be well over forty thousand strong," answers Andrew.

"True, but we would all be dead before that could happen," replies Kristoff, before taking a large breath and exhaling.

"Fair point, but if there is any clan you shouldn't fear, it's the Swindletors. They haven't done much combat training since the war. As I recall, you handled them quite well during the Faire. Perhaps we should announce we have Kristoff with us, just to strike fear in their little black hearts," says Andrew.

"I must admit they are proper scum after all," says Kristoff, giving his best impression of a Romani accent.

"Indeed, they are," says Andrew, laughing.

After a few minutes, Lee returns and mounts his horse. I frown upon seeing his expression. He's uncharacteristically quiet and holds a blank gaze. I don't like it when he isn't himself, but I understand it's necessary given the circumstances. We ride until we reach a wooded area with a small dirt trail that doesn't appear to have been used for a very long time, judging by how overgrown it is.

"This here is the barrier. The path leads us to the Cove, or rather the tower where the meeting will be. Be alert and no fooling about; for all we know they're already here, and these woods could be full of enemies," says Lee before securing his horse to a thick tree branch and placing his weapons in his saddlebags.

The rest of the group does the same. I hate leaving my new Romani steel sword unattended. I'm uncomfortable being completely unarmed—a first for me—choosing to leave my mother's dagger back at Little Watch, thinking it wouldn't be much use in a fight anyway. Not to mention it means way too much to me to risk losing or breaking it.

"Never understood why anyone would build a neutral meeting spot in the middle of a thicket," says Jaseen as he scans the woods for any sign of life.

"A more open setting would be ideal," agrees Lee from where he waits at the trailhead.

Once the group is close enough, Lee grabs Kristoff and says, "You're the fastest and can run for days. If I give the signal, you don't ask questions, you run straight to your horse and head for the camp we just left. You start yelling and waving your hands like a fool when you get near it. Then you lead them right back here, you understand?"

Kristoff looks concerned, as if what Lee is saying is a certainty instead of a possibility. He nods, and Lee turns and walks quietly down the path. The woods are thick, and in some spots, the trail is nearly impassable. We make sure to clear any limbs we find so we will face as few obstacles as possible if we need to make a hasty retreat. Nobody in the group speaks, and we walk quietly to sneak up on the tower.

Finally, we come across a large stone tower which sits atop a ridge overlooking the ocean. The breeze whips through the trees, and I can smell the salty sea in the air. To the Northwest of the tower is another overgrown path that I presume leads to the Swindletor lands. The prospect of being so close to their territory makes me uneasy. I tell myself not to be anxious, and that any feelings of anxiety are irrational.

We slowly approach the tower, stopping and surveying the area while Lee goes to the door. He raises his hand to knock, but before his fist reaches the door, it swings open.

"No need to knock, stranger! Why, how long has it been? You look like you survived the winter well. And who do we have here, eh?" replies a short, squirmy-looking man with a receding hairline, which he tries to disguise by shaving his head bald. He's rather skinny and stands a few inches shorter than Lee. His eyes are a cloudy green color, and his right one is lazy, unable to stay focused on where he is looking. His voice makes my skin crawl; with every word, it sounds as if he's trying to scam me out of my coin. I can't stand people who are fake and ply others with compliments. They must never be trusted.

"Morning, Olly. Isn't this a little early for you lot? Summons read like we wouldn't be meeting for another day," says Lee, in a tone that I have a hard time identifying. He seems to have his typical witty and charming demeanor about him again, which makes me curious.

"I could say the same for you, mate. But at least for us, it's much harder to plan an arrival, seeing as how you can't predict the wind," Olly answers in what I presume is a passive-aggressive manner.

"We happened to be in the area anyway, so we figured we would swing by and get this over with. Lucky for us, you're here. Where's the rest of your clan?" asks Lee.

"They're inside. Come on in. That's what I like about you Romani. Right to the point, no interest in the niceties," replies Olly, moving out of our way so we can file inside.

Lee enters the tower and looks around before telling the group to come in. Everyone comes inside but Andrew, who remains outside watching the door after a signal from Lee. He's by far the largest in the group and would be the most foreboding in a hand-to-hand fight.

We enter a small circular room with little to no decoration, apart from cobwebs and dust. The tower's roof has a single large window that allows sunlight to enter, preventing the need for candles or fire. I notice just two other clan members standing behind Olly, which makes me feel better. They're both just as small and squirmy-looking as him. Clearly, if this is some sort of trap, there would be more. Then again, maybe they want to catch us off guard. I do my best to stop trying to figure out the Swindletors' motives because I know I'd end up driving myself mad with worry.

The three of us stand behind Lee, who sits on a stone bench directly in front of Olly. "Well then, get to it," says Lee.

Olly takes a deep breath followed by a loud sigh as if whatever he's about to say is difficult for him. "Look, mate—you know I've always done right by you and the Romani—" attempts Olly before being interrupted by Lee.

"Before you butter me up, are you speaking on behalf of your clan or yourself?' replies Lee coldly, taking Olly by surprise.

"Well—I guess I would have to say I am speaking on behalf of me, but you as well. This has to do with all of us, really," he replies.

"So, to be clear, you aren't speaking for the head of your clan or the clan as a whole? When you answer speak direct and plain," Lee says with even more conviction than before. His demeanor makes me feel less anxious. He's far more confident and direct than Olly, placing control of the conversation in his hands.

"No, I'm not. Now can I get to the point?" Olly asks, looking at his clan members before shaking his head.

Lee stares at him and waits for him to go on.

"So, like I said, there is no easy way to say it, but your boy here is putting us all at risk."

"This is your last warning—speak plain. I'm not entertaining your Swindletor bullshit," Lee replies tersely.

"In the North, the ginger is wanted. The Apex is gone, mate. Carthage is the new power, and they have the airships, so the rest of the North is swearing allegiance to them."

I'm furious. He's talking about Kristoff. My mind is racing as I try to piece together what must have transpired.

"If you brought me all the way here to tell me one of my clan members is wanted by a foreigner, I may have to make the Romani the first clan to break parley and bash your fucking head against that stone wall until your eyes bleed," Lee replies, standing to his feet so he's towering over Olly.

I'm relieved to see how angry he is, and despite being furious myself, I hope he will show restraint. Olly is clearly afraid, and he raises his hands in surrender.

"They're going to pay a huge reward. They never said if he was wanted for a crime or what. It could have been for his own good for all I know," he says.

"Who's they? And how do you know they would make good on the promise?" Lee asks, sitting back down.

I'm starting to grow concerned since he is entertaining this line of conversation, and I find it increasingly more difficult to bite my tongue. Kristoff stands motionless, shocked at the prospect of being wanted.

"His weight in gold. And even offered to transport him back."

"How generous," Lee says sarcastically. "And you believed them? Surely even you aren't that stupid."

"Yeah mate, it's legit," Olly replies before throwing a sack at Lee's feet. "See?"

Lee lifts the bag and opens it, showing them what's inside. He gives a wink that only I, Kristoff, and Jaseen can see.

"Okay, and if we agree, then what?"

"They can transport him right now. Their ships are at anchor right off the coast," Olly says, becoming more enthusiastic the longer Lee entertains the conversation.

"Ships? Why bring more than one?" Lee asks.

"Would you travel these waters with just one ship if you were them?" Olly snickers.

"With people like you patrolling the shores, of course, I would. You lot," Lee says, speaking to Olly's clansmen, "does Olly speak for you as well?"

They look to Olly, then back to Lee, but say nothing.

"Yes, I speak for them and can broker whatever terms we all agree upon."

"What about the ginger? Does he get to agree on terms? Should we bring the foreigners here so he can broker a deal over his captivity?" Lee asks sarcastically.

"Obviously not, mate."

"So, you speak for the two clansmen here with you and the foreign army at our shores? Is my understanding correct—mate?"

"You're overcomplicating it, Lee. Look, we can all be rich, and you still get to keep the girl. Why do you care about the ginger anyways?"

"You hear that, love? I get to keep you. How nice! Olly and the foreign army are going to allow me—ME—a Romani enforcer, to keep you," says Lee, hitting his chest to accentuate the "me." His face turns stony again. "I will ask you two once more. Does he speak for you?"

Olly attempts to speak, but Lee raises his hand, silencing him. Olly sinks his head like a dog who knows it's in trouble. Both Swindletors shake their heads no and step away from Olly.

"My father always said there was honor amongst thieves. I guess the old man was wrong about that. So—we are going to decline your offer, but I appreciate the sack of gold you've given us. You know, for our troubles and all."

"It ain't that simple, mate," says Olly in a weak tone, his voice cracking.

"You got something more to say?" asks Lee.

"If I don't take him to them—they're going to storm the beach and come after him themselves."

"By which time we will be gone," Lee replies furiously. I've never heard his voice sound more terrifying. He's angry beyond measure, and I worry about what may transpire.

"If they don't find him, they're going to raid your territory. There's at least fifty of them, fully armored. Please—use your reason. Spare the lives of your clansmen."

For the first time since this began, I am wholly afraid. There's a small army ready to attack the Southlands, the one place I thought was safe, and it's all because of me and Kristoff. I don't know what to do or say. I'm at a loss and wish this were one of my dreams that I could wake from.

Lee's face falls to a grim expression, which is the first time I've ever seen him appear worried, and to my dismay, he stands up and spits in his left hand before outstretching it to Olly, whose face lights up with a smile. Olly stands to his feet and spits in his own hand. "Trust me, mate, it'll be worth the gold," says the small man.

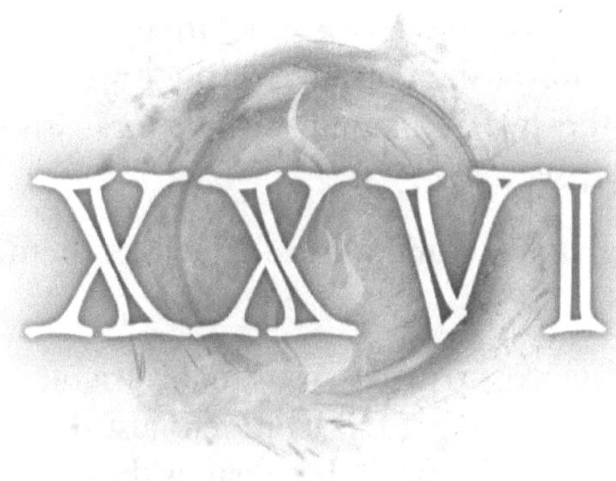

"I'm sure it will be," says Lee, before shaking Olly's hand. They stare at each other as they shake hands for a few seconds. Then, without warning, Lee grabs Olly by the throat with his free hand and shoves him violently against the stone wall, causing him to fall to the ground. He tries to climb to his feet using the wall as support, but before he can get up, Lee rains kicks down upon him.

"Please, stop! The parley! You can't!" Olly begs.

"I can't? I can't!? You bring a foreign army to our shores, threaten my brother, threaten my lands, and you have the nerve to yell parley and plead for mercy? the Romani don't show mercy to traitors!" Lee shouts before wrapping both of his hands around Olly's neck. He attempts to resist, but he's no match for Lee.

I can't believe what I'm seeing, and despite my fear of what's going to happen, I love Lee more than ever for the way he's defending Kristoff, his brother, no matter the consequence or the risk. After he's sure Olly is dead, Lee loots his pockets, removing a small knife that was hidden in his belt line.

"Imagine packing a blade for this exact scenario and being too weak to use it," Lee says before looking at Kristoff and giving him a sympathetic smile. "Oh, and Kristoff?"

"Y-yea?" Kristoff's voice trembles.

"Run."

Without hesitation, Kristoff bolts out the door and makes his way to the horses. I and Jaseen go outside to find Andrew still standing sentinel. Lee stands at the entrance of the tower with his back toward us, addressing the two remaining Swindletors, who are still standing beside Olly's corpse.

"Where is the attack coming from?" he asks them in a commanding tone.

One of them speaks up in a very justifiably frightened tone, "We don't know. Honestly, Olly didn't tell us much, just that it was easy money. He thought you would take the deal without question. He never considered it wouldn't work out."

"When did they think the parley would be?" Lee growls.

The two men put their heads down in shame.

"Don't make me ask again."

"Olly sent a signal that you arrived when you first got to the woods. They'll be storming the beach any minute now. We need to get out of here," says one of the Swindletor clansmen in a terrified tone.

"You, quiet one, you're going to go to the beachhead and stand where we can see you over the ridge. You tell them once they produce the gold, you will signal us, and we will send Kristoff down. Tell them you won't send the signal until you see the gold on the sand and that no more than six soldiers may be guarding it. If they land with more, tell them to get back in their boats and row at least one hundred yards away. You got that?" Lee instructs.

"Why me? Why don't we all just flee?" The Swindletor asks.

"If you wish to join Olly, you're more than welcome to stay. If you run off or signal to them that something is wrong, I give you my word— the Romani will wipe out your entire clan, starting with your mate here. We aren't giving them an inch of land. The Romani do not flee."

Lee's comment works to motivate the frightened man, who immediately sets off for the beachhead. Jaseen remains at the door, watching the other Swindletor while Lee and I look out over the ridge, waiting to spot the landing party. Andrew goes to the horses to gather the weapons and ensure that our group isn't being circled or flanked.

"How you feeling, love?" Lee asks me as he overlooks the ocean.

I grab his hand and hold it close before leaning up and kissing him deeply. The kiss takes us both to a place free of fear and anxiety, away from thoughts of what's to come before the moment is expectedly ruined by Lee's humor.

"Looks like I'm going to have to kill people in front of you more often, eh?" he says, smirking. "If that's what you're into, then I'll oblige."

I lightly slap him on the chest before smiling and looking back out over the ocean, still unable to see any enemy ships.

"I wager Kristoff can get the attention of the camp in about twenty minutes, judging by how fast he can run and ride. That means it'll take about forty minutes before we get a few dozen Romani with shields and weapons. If we fail, the entire clan will come down in full force to retake whatever lands may have been lost, and then, I imagine, they'll march on the Swindletors. Many people will die because of Olly unless we can fight off fifty or so northerners—assuming he wasn't exaggerating. I like our chances if it's just fifty," says Lee, thinking aloud.

"Please don't take them lightly. If what he said is true, this army has defeated the Apex. They could be more battle-hardened than you expect," I urge.

"True enough, but even battle-hardened soldiers won't do well at sea for long periods. And, no offense, but Romani train from the time they're able to hold a weapon."

"I'm just saying, if we're outnumbered, let's not underestimate them like the Apex did. I've seen the forces at his command," I say, snapping Lee out of his analytical mindset. He puts his arm around me and pulls me close. "Sorry, love. You're right, it would be foolish to underestimate them."

Just then, we see three large ships come into sight. They have golden sails sporting a large black raven with outstretched wings.

"That's Carthage's symbol," I say, suddenly feeling nervous at the prospect of coming face-to-face with the army of the man responsible for the death of my father. But my nervousness is rapidly replaced with a fiery vengeance. This is exactly what I want. I need to grow stronger and avenge my father by killing the Revenant and his master. What better place to start than by killing his soldiers?

Andrew returns with the weapons, somehow managing to carry them all. He's a large man, so strength is expected of him, but he often seems much stronger than his size alone indicates.

I quickly refasten my sword belt and remove it from its sheath. It hasn't been used in actual combat, but I know it won't fail me.

Jaseen, who apparently has better eyes than either of us, points out that a landing party is being lowered into the water from one of the three ships. After some time, the small boat reaches shore, carrying half a dozen men in full plate armor, shields and all. They exit the vessel and begin speaking with the Swindletor Lee had sent to the shore.

"I swear, if he tips them off—I'm going to kill his entire clan," says Lee, watching closely for any sign of deceit.

Eventually, one of the soldiers raises a banner dawning Carthage's raven symbol and waves it, at which point the ship on the far left lowers another boat. It takes longer to lower the craft this time and I assume it must be carrying the gold they had promised.

"We are running out of time. Once they realize we aren't going to deliver Kristoff, we'll have about fifteen minutes before they can storm the ridge," says Lee.

The second landing party—four men all in full plate armor and a wooden crate—makes it to shore. Two men lift the crate from the boat and carry it to the Swindletor for inspection.

"Check the gold. Check the gold," Lee mutters under his breath. If this is going to look like a real deal, the man will need to verify that the gold is legitimate. After what seems like an eternity, the Swindletor walks to the crate and waits for them to open it.

"Jaseen, run to the clearing and see if they're coming," commands Lee. He obliges and begins running as fast as he can.

"After he sees the gold, I hope he walks up here. But more than likely, he's going to signal us. Then it won't be long before they catch on," Lee tells me.

My anxiety starts to resurface. I'm all for fighting, but I had assumed we would have at least two dozen soldiers with us, and I know those three ships could easily carry fifty men, if not more.

The Swindletor continues to talk to the soldiers before eventually looking to the ridge and waving his hands.

"He was supposed to tell them no more than a half dozen. The other four need to leave," says Lee, frustrated.

"He didn't forget," I assert. "He was too scared. What are we going to do?"

"If we can draw them up the path, four against ten is about the same odds we would get full force against full force anyways," says Lee.

"Too bad Kristoff wasn't here," I say. "He could pick off a couple of them with his bow, and we could take the beach."

"Sadly, none of us can run or ride as fast as him or shoot as well. Except for Jaseen, who I sent away like a fool."

The soldiers are becoming frustrated with the Swindletor and the lack of response from his signal. "I'm going to try and buy us some time," says Lee calmly.

"Are you insane? You can't do that! Don't be stupid. We will use the terrain the best we can and make them fight us coming uphill," I reply, frustrated by his readiness to put himself at risk despite it clearly being a bad idea.

The aggressive hand motions from the soldiers turn to shoves. Eventually, one of them draws their sword, and the one with the banner begins waving it. My stomach drops. The invasion has begun. We only have a few minutes before the beach will be swarming with fully armored soldiers.

The Swindletor flees, barely dodging a sword strike as he makes his way to the trailhead. Four of the soldiers give chase while the others remain with the gold.

About that same time, Jaseen returns, panting and out of breath. "No sign of them yet. Just wanted to update you."

"Catch your breath, ready your weapons. We are going to head those four off while the odds are even," says Lee, pulling his Romani steel sword from its sheath.

The four of us ready our weapons and walk slowly towards the trailhead. As we make our way down the descent, I move close to Lee and whisper in his ear, "No matter what happens, I just want you to know I think I'm in love with you."

A wide smile breaks out on his face, and he whispers back, "I know I'm in love with you. And that's why I'm asking you to please stay in the back until the first push. After that, they will be no match for you, their only advantage is their momentum and weight."

I'm too focused on him saying he loves me to hear what he has asked of me. After a moment, my brain catches up, and I realize what he has said. Before I can say anything in protest, we hear the rustling of footsteps coming up the trail and see the Swindletor running for his life toward us.

"How far behind?" asks Lee calmly.

"No idea."

"Then look," replies Lee.

"No way."

Jaseen points his sword at the man while Andrew casually lifts his battle axe to his shoulder. Reluctantly, the Swindletor goes back. When he spots his pursuers, he gives the four of us a nod, signaling that the soldiers are close. Andrew takes the lead, followed closely by Jaseen and Lee. And though I don't like it, I do what Lee has asked of me and hang back.

We walk a few yards before the path begins to curve to the right, and we see the four Carthage soldiers slowly walking toward us. They look exhausted from running up the hill in full armor while carrying heavy metal shields. On sight of these men, my mind becomes hyper-focused, and I start to analyze my threats. The soldiers are fatigued and clearly lack discipline, having taken off without orders to chase down the Swindletor man. They are heavily armored, which gives them a significant advantage in a fight with battle lines. But this is no such battle. This is the Southlands.

Just as I expected, the soldiers approach our group two-by-two, with the two men in the back using their shields to push against the soldiers in the front, providing momentum. I'm worried their charge will be too much for Andrew, who's tasked with pushing against them alone. He's the strongest person I know, but I don't think he's powerful enough to withstand such a charge, especially without a shield of his own.

Before I can contemplate how best to approach the problem, Andrew charges the line, holding his large battle axe horizontally across his chest. His strength is unexpected and too much for them to withstand, and he quickly knocks the two soldiers in the front off-balance, causing them to stumble backward. Then, as if they had practiced it a hundred times, Jaseen and Lee quickly leap out from behind Andrew, attacking the stumbling soldiers before they can regain their footing or raise their shields. Lee swings his sword upwards at the perfect angle, slicing one man's throat, which begins spraying blood out of the wound. Jaseen comes down on his opponent with a heavy overhead strike that's absorbed by the man's helmet. The enemy is knocked to the ground, but I'm unsure whether he's dead or simply dazed.

I see Andrew scuffling with the remaining two soldiers, and I'm worried they will land a strike at any minute. Holding my sword at the ready, I sprint and stab one of the men through an open spot in his armor, through his armpit. His arm is immobilized immediately, giving Andrew the advantage he needs to push the soldier to the ground.

Jaseen is dueling with the man he knocked down, whose armor seems impenetrable. I quickly approach them and wait for an opening. When I see it, I lunge my sword directly into the soldier's eye, pushing it through the back of his head until I feel the tip meet his metal helmet. I look beside me and see Lee standing over the body of the last soldier, holding both his sword as well as the fallen man's weapon.

"Everyone okay?" asks Lee. "Wait, do you hear that?"

"Drums," says Andrew, picking up his axe.

"Let's fall back. They're probably forming up their line," says Jaseen.

We run to the ridge, hoping to survey the situation before the enemy has time to organize. Unfortunately, as soon as we arrive, any sense of success we had from our fight is replaced with a feeling of defeat, after we look down upon no less than fifty Carthage soldiers forming a battle line on the beach. They look to be infantry, and an officer is already shouting orders at them.

Their leader looks up at the ridge and sees us gazing back at him. The staring contest ends when Andrew raises the head of one of the fallen soldiers high in the air. He cups the head against his forearm and begins to spin in circles before he gathers enough momentum and lets the head fly. The head sails an unbelievable distance, landing just a few feet from the officer. Despite the impending threat, I'm impressed with how miraculous of a throw it was. But the officer isn't amused. With a wave of his hand, the soldiers form two single-file lines and begin to march towards the trailhead.

The real battle is coming now. And we're still without reinforcements.

"We should fall back to the horses!" I shout, feeling utterly terrified, though I'd rather not admit it. Everyone, except for Lee, moves as if we're about to retreat.

"You hear that?" Lee asks excitedly. Soon, we see Kristoff running out of the woods, accompanied by two dozen Romani.

"We made it as fast as we could," he says, panting.

"You're here now," Lee says with a quick smile. "Alright, here we go. Listen fast, yeah? Four dead foreigners are on the trail to the beach, one without their head thanks to Andrew here and his thirst for theatrics," Lee says, making everyone laugh. "They wear full plate armor, which makes them slow and easy to wear out. They have metal shields and quality steel swords. We counted around fifty or so infantry. How many bows do we have?" Lee asks.

A show of hands reveals we have a total of four bows, including Kristoff, who is already getting his arrows ready. The reinforcements brought desperately needed shields for us and the others. They are circular and made of wood, and although they won't be as strong as those we face, they'll provide support in preventing us from being entirely pushed back or shot with arrows.

"We let them approach the ridge and form our line right at the exit of the trail. Harass them with arrows as long as you have enough for when they make formation. Aim for the face and neck. They're also exposed on their armpits and thighs. We don't need to kill them all. If we give them enough losses, they will rout. Jaseen, you take a bow and help direct the harassing fire," Lee commands. "Be conservative with your arrows," he adds.

We quickly create a horseshoe formation where the enemy will exit the trail. While they have superior numbers, I know we have the tactical advantage thanks to the terrain. While we wait, I can hear arrow fire from our archers shooting into the woods.

"Got one, right in the face," Kristoff says calmly. I never imagined I'd see him in a battle, let alone be relaxed during one. In fact, despite his success in practicing with the bow, I often worried that he wouldn't be as good in an actual fight—clearly, I was mistaken.

"So, are we even. I have two kills, and you have two," I ask jokingly to Lee, attempting to calm my nerves by talking.

"Pretty sure I got two, and you have one. I couldn't see much, but I think the shield did him in, or rather Andrew crushing his face with it did."

"He was going to bleed out, and he wouldn't have been able to defend himself anyway. You can't let Andrew steal my kill."

"You're the best woman alive," he replies, chuckling at my competitive spirit.

"They are moving up the trail, not far now!" yells one of our archers.

"You four, fall back to the rear and fire at will, careful not to peg one of us. Romani! This is what we dream of! Defending our lands just like our mothers and fathers before us. Think of your children, your nieces, and nephews; think of your elders and what happens to them if we cannot hold this ridge! We know the price of failure and what it means for our loved ones. They'll be murdered, raped, or sold into slavery. That's the cost of failure! That's the cost of weakness. Will we be known as the Romani who failed to protect their families?" proclaims Lee as he walks amongst the defenders, careful to interact with as many as he can. The group replies with a resounding "No!"

"Didn't think so! We are strong because we are family. We are family through bond!" Lee yells, resulting in us repeating the clan slogan loudly.

Everyone begins hitting our weapons against our shields as loudly as possible. I'm behind Andrew, who I know is by far the best person with a shield on either side. We hear the footsteps of the enemy growing closer, and had I not seen their numbers with my own eyes, I would suspect there were far more than fifty, based on the noise they're making.

We've formed two lines in a horseshoe formation, about ten soldiers in each. I know our small numbers give little room for error, and I hope the line holds. If it doesn't, we will be quickly overrun, and our retreat will easily be blocked. Before I can worry too much about what could happen, I hear Lee yell, "Shield wall!"

At his command, both lines interlock their shields as tightly as we can, preparing to withstand the initial enemy rush. I've never seen a shield wall before coming to the Southlands, but I've learned it can help a group withstand a cavalry charge if done right. The Carthage army does their best to push through our line, but they fall right into the vulnerability created by the horseshoe formation.

While the soldiers are trying to push the Romani directly in front of them, they become easy targets on their flanks. The enemy is surrounded, and soldier after soldier is cut down. Their corpses litter the ground, making it even more difficult for their fellow soldiers to charge or retreat.

My rapier is highly effective at striking enemies from the flank, particularly due to its thin blade, that allows me to easily attack from the openings between shields. I've maimed two soldiers before their commander catches up to them.

"Cut through the forest, you idiots, you're being outflanked!" he yells.

Heeding their commander's words, the soldiers break ranks and change direction to force their way through the overgrown forest. They'll overrun our formation if they're able to come through at different points.

"Fall in line! And Ease! Ease!" shouts Lee, who is reorganizing our formation into two straight lines. "How many did we kill?" he asks.

"At least ten!" yells a clan member.

"We can't let them form up outside, they still have too many soldiers, we'll be overrun if they do. On my command, get ready to push forward!" Lee shouts.

I see several soldiers coming out of the trees. Before they can form a solid line, Lee gives the command to push forward, and we envelop the stragglers, dispatching them with haste. Arrows fly into the openings they created in the forest, and I hear Carthage soldiers falling.

In the first two waves of the fight, we kill fifteen soldiers without a single casualty on our side, but the Carthage soldiers have stopped coming through the spots in the forest. Instead, they form lines so they can rush all at once. Their commander must be competent, but his lack of battlefield vision is keeping him one step behind.

"Ease! Ease! Archers, fall in behind the wall and fire on my command!" Lee yells.

The Romani start to fall back until we are close to our own entrance to the ridge. I can't work out whether Lee has a plan of attack or if he is preparing to order a retreat through the woods. I don't know much about organized battles in practice, but I've read that many casualties occur during a retreat. I hope he isn't out of ideas, but if he is, I have no shortage of my own.

"Lee! Put our archers into the thick tree line and let them fire at will, then I'll lead five of us to the tower so we can flank them after they form up!" I yell, overriding my filter. I don't want to undermine Lee's authority, but I trust my idea will work.

Lee thinks for a minute about what I've suggested. "You heard her!" he yells. "But if anyone lets her die, I will kill you myself. Archers, inside the tree line for cover. Keep pressure on their back row, aim for their commander. This is where we kill them! This is where we defend our home! Our fellow Romani will drink to our victory for generations!"

Me and five other Romani enter the tower, hoping beyond hope that we will remain unseen by the enemy.

After a couple of minutes, the Carthage soldiers march one by one through the openings in the forest. Roughly thirty soldiers form their line about forty or so yards away from us. The tower is to the right of the Romani, and if it's timed correctly, I know that the flanking maneuver could end the battle. I can almost hear my heartbeat from within my chest as we await the signal from Lee. I try and control my breathing, knowing the risk becoming winded will pose.

Lee shouts, "Aries! Now! Front row, charge! Aries! Now!"

Me and the others quickly slip out of the tower entrance and hasten towards the enemy formation. We run quickly but quietly, as if being quiet will somehow make us invisible in broad daylight. I hear the clash of steel and the sound of the soldiers struggling to push one another back. The fighting is intense, and neither side is securing a significant advantage.

Just before we can reach the formation, we are spotted by the enemy commander, who is standing along the tree line, outside of the range of the Romani archers. My heart sinks. Not only will he interrupt the success of the flanking maneuver, but we will be highly vulnerable once the formation adjusts.

"Back row! Move to the—"

The commander's words are suddenly silenced as he falls to the ground, presumably dead. The sight of their dead commander sends the enemy soldiers into a panic, and their formation quickly breaks down.

From there, the flanking maneuver works to great success. Me and my unit devastate the backline of the enemy shield wall. The fighting breaks into a melee, greatly favoring our superior experience with person-to-person combat. Not to mention, the Carthage soldiers have become far too tired by this point to wield their weapons effectively.

As we fight on, I hear some of the enemy soldiers yelling for retreat, but the majority do not comply. Suddenly, I'm knocked to the ground by a heavy blow from the blunt side of an enemy sword.

As I fall, my grip slackens, and I drop my shield and sword. Panicking, I try to quickly get to my feet. The soldier who knocked me down presses his advantage and is now towering over me. I crawl on my hands and knees, quickly picking up my sword and spinning around. Just as the soldier is preparing to swing his weapon, I thrust my own sword upward as hard as I can. The tip of my blade finds its home through the soldier's groin, incapacitating him instantly.

I'm furious I came so close to being hurt—or worse. Fueled by my fury, I get to my feet. I don't bother with my shield; it slows me down and I'm not accustomed to using one, anyway.

I hate that these men are in the Southlands—in my family's lands—and I begin to fight in the way my father had trained me, striking down all enemies I can find. Their heavy armor and swords weigh them down and make them easy targets. I kill several and injure many others, removing them as threats.

I slit the throat of a soldier attempting to strike a Romani from behind. I look around for any additional enemies to challenge, but none are to be found.

All I see are Romani clansmen cheering at our success over the enemy. Relief floods my heart. We have survived. The odds were not in our favor leading up to the battle, but we did it.

I scan the battlefield to ensure the others are okay, and I realize I can't find Kristoff anywhere, his bright red hair notably absent from the celebrating Romani. The longer I look, the more panicked I become. I begin yelling, searching frantically for him, and asking the others where he is. Eventually, someone yells, "He's over here!"

I turn my head toward the call and see Kristoff laying on the ground, motionless. My heart sinks, just as it had when my father died.

"Kristoff!" I shout as I run over to him.

"I need to run more," he says jokingly, trying to catch his breath.

"Don't ever do that to me again!" I shout before helping him to his feet and hugging him. "You're brilliant. You are the literal best with the bow," I continue.

"Yeah, and how about that last shot? Pretty lucky, huh? Not going to lie, I only thought I could get close enough to distract him, but then their commander fell over."

"I wasn't sure who fired the arrow, but I'm not surprised it was you. And I'm not exaggerating, without your shot, we would've been done for. He was just about to alert the backline to our ambush when you got him. We wouldn't have won the battle without you, and all you're going to say is that it was a lucky shot?" I ask, laughing. "You may want to embellish a little more. You are a Romani, after all."

"I can't wait to hear how we repelled an army of thousands with just a couple dozen Romani," replies Kristoff, before being nearly knocked over by Andrew, who is unable to contain his excitement.

"What a day, huh? Can you believe it?" Andrew goes on. "We made them look like proper fools. They won't be coming back anytime soon; I can tell you that much. And you, mate!" he turns to Kristoff, "I always believed in you, but shooting in battle is a lot different than a target, and you didn't disappoint. And then there's Aries, fighting as if she was possessed by a demon. I've never seen bodies fall so quickly. Maybe I should get me one of those swords."

"It would look like a toothpick in your hand, mate," says Jaseen, a big smile on his face, as he approaches.

"True enough. Best to stick with my battle axe, I suppose."

"It's good to see everyone is okay," says Lee, who is notably much less excited about the victory.

He grabs me and pulls me close before gently kissing me. "If something would've happened to you, I would have gone mad. But, with that said, there is nothing better than loving a woman who can take care of herself and even protect her man."

"I, uh—I, umm," I try to reply but can't find the words, distracted by his kiss and the look he's giving me. I know I would go mad if something happened to him as well.

"We lost five Romani. Another four are significantly injured. Horrible—but it could have been much worse. We left a couple of their soldiers alive so that we can try and learn more about what brought them here," Lee says.

I don't like that any of our clansmen have died, but I know that their deaths were not in vain.

"They gave their lives to protect the clan," I reply, holding his hand while looking over the battlefield.

It's the first time I've really looked at the fighting grounds and seen it for what it is—a field of death. Corpses lay motionless all around us, some of which are being looted by the Romani. Several more of our clansmen come through the woods carrying the large wooden crate filled with gold.

"Splitting up the gold will definitely lift their spirits," Lee says quietly to me. Then, a bit more loudly he says, "I will make sure the families of the fallen get double shares."

Lee gathers the survivors and divvies out the gold equally to everyone, ensuring enough is left over for the families of those whose loved ones died during the fighting.

I've never seen a battle, let alone been present afterward to partake in the spoils. Kristoff and I still have some of the money from our prize winnings, along with the money we brought when we came to the Southlands, and part of me feels guilty for keeping even more gold for myself. I look to Lee and notice he hasn't taken any gold for his own coin purse, instead adding his share to the sum meant for the families of the fallen, inspiring me to do the same.

Several hours after the gold is separated, hordes of Romani begin making camp in the countryside next to the thick forest that separates the Cove. I notice that many come ready for war and seem disappointed that the battle has ended before they arrived. I can't blame them and would be lying if I said I didn't enjoy the thrill of battle. Especially fighting off an enemy that sought to take Kristoff from me and slaughter countless innocents.

"How many people are going to come?" I ask Jaseen, who is also watching the camp grow before our eyes.

"I can't say for sure. This hasn't happened in my time. I'd wager thousands of Romani by nightfall, even more in the coming days. I imagine a fair amount of Clan Harald and Clanless will show up as well," he replies.

"I must admit, it does feel much safer with this many Romani. The odds seemed bleak for a moment back there," I reply.

"We beat them easily, even outnumbered three to one. Can you imagine how it would go if the odds were even? I felt like we were doomed for a moment myself, but if we wanted to retreat, we would've had to drag Lee away kicking and screaming. He wouldn't retreat. It's as if he cannot visualize defeat," he tells me.

"If he would have tried to go to the beach, I was going to stab him myself," I say, sounding entirely serious. "Maybe just in the leg or something though," I add with a shrug, prompting Jaseen to laugh.

I know Jaseen is right, but I don't like the idea of speaking ill of Lee behind his back. Jaseen's comment makes me think about all the ways the battle could have gone wrong, which increases my appreciation of our victory.

"Reckless or not, there's no man I would rather fight beside than Lee, and no woman I would rather fight beside than you. What happened here will be talked about for years and years. It's a reminder to the other clans that the Romani are not to be trifled with," says Jaseen.

"What happens since Lee broke the parley?" I ask, having forgotten about it until now.

"The parley was broken when he threatened hostility from the Carthage army, anyway. Not to mention, he brought us here under false pretenses. Only a clan representative can request a formal parley, so there won't be much that comes from that, apart from other clan members being more cautious when they try and parley with us."

"The Swindletors are awful. I bet they're a major reason the Southlands get a bad name in the North," I reply.

"You don't even know the half of it," he replies, with a hint of sadness in his voice.

"You seem to really dislike them, I mean more than the rest of us," I say. "Do you have history with them?"

"Yeah, you could say that," he replies, not meeting my eyes. "A story for another time perhaps. Tonight, we celebrate, and no celebration is as epic as a Romani wake after a battle. It's going to be the stuff of legend," he says, giving me a quick smile and making his way to the camp.

I rejoin Kristoff, who suggests we explore the encampment. We haven't been around this many Romani since arriving in the Southlands.

As we wander through the camp, it's hard to envision what the empty field used to look like, because now it resembles a city made up of tents and caravans. One of my favorite things about the Romani is how quickly they can turn any location into a village—since their homes have wheels.

Continuing through the densely populated camp, we meet people eager to greet us and give praise. We hear whispers such as, "That's Aries, the one who led the ambush and killed a dozen men by herself!" or "There's Kristoff the Ginger, he killed their commander from two hundred yards away with just one arrow." The tall tales bring a smile to our faces, and we don't bother to correct them. Lee had once told me that reputation is a powerful weapon and can be used to dissuade people from challenging a clan member or the whole of the Romani. So, while I don't like the idea of taking credit for things I didn't do, I figure it's best to let the rumors spread.

In the center of the camp is a large tent, big enough to fit a hundred or so people inside, with armed Romani standing at the entrance. When the soldiers notice us, they signal for us to come over.

"Proper work you two did today. You more than earned your place as enforcers. First pint is on me tonight," says a big man, who is resting his hands on a large, broad sword sticking into the ground. "Lee is inside waiting for you, sent runners to find you, but I guess they got lost, probably at the gambling tables."

I can't help but cringe at the thought of him putting so much weight on his blade, worrying it may bend or break. I resist the urge to mention this, and instead I smile politely and walk into the tent with Kristoff. I see a group of people standing over a table located in the center of the enclosure. The table is covered with wooden figures, and as I get closer, I notice those gathered are looking over a map of the Southlands. They seem to be discussing how to defend our territory from an invasion or perhaps planning to attack the Swindletor territory. My stomach sinks at the thought of them going to war with another clan, hoping the harmony of the Southlands will not be disrupted on our account.

"Just who I wanted to see," says Lee, who smiles warmly and motions for us to come stand by him.

"Do you know much about the naval power of the North, Carthage specifically, and what warships they may have?" asks an older Romani man who has a long, white, neatly braided beard.

"Truthfully, there wasn't much of one in the outer realms, or in the Apex, for that matter. They banned most things that posed a threat to them. Any ships made were for fishing or transporting goods," replies Kristoff.

"True, but how long has Carthage been defying their rules? How long have they been in power? For all we know, they could have an entire fleet by now," replies a woman who speaks in a stern tone.

She is tall for her gender and has short grey and brown hair. Her eyes are a piercing dark blue and I get the sense she's staring right through me. She has an athletic build and tanned skin, giving the impression she is often in the sun. She has an attractive face and a voice that is intimidating and confident.

"It has been well over a year that they have been defying Apexian regulations, and that's just what I know, it could be much longer. I think the bigger threat will be the airships, though," I reply.

"Many airships were destroyed when the Apex fell, unless Carthage now knows how to make them. I doubt they have enough to ferry an invasion force. They could harass at best, and we wouldn't meet them in the open field. They would have to come to the mountains," replies the woman.

"That or terrorize the countryside and bargain for the other clans to join them," I add. I don't like this woman minimizing the devastation the airships could do, especially since I've seen firsthand what even a lone ship is capable of.

"Fair point, but we can't control what the other clans do. That is why I say we pull all Romani back to the mountain and only allow a small number to trade along the river here, with Clan Harald, or perhaps the Guul if necessary. Cutting off trade with the Swindletors would allow us not only to punish them for their actions, but also remove the need to have Romani so far North," continues the woman.

"People count on that money to survive. We can't just cut off trade because we are worried about an invasion that may never come. Did any of the northerners make it back to their ships?" asks the old, bearded man.

"They sunk two of their own ships, and whatever forces remained fled in the one they left afloat. We assume they went back North. I'm sure we will find out more from the two prisoners we took. But we must be ready. I don't think we should leave our lands in the North to the outlaws and fiends. We can patrol the waters and send a signal if a force is approaching. They aren't true fighters, and a gathered army of Romani would have no trouble repelling them. We lost a few soldiers in the fighting, but we were outnumbered nearly three to one. We fought in a shield wall, so it wasn't like we had a strategic advantage that gave us the victory," Lee explains.

"And what if Aries is right and they do come by air?" The woman asks.

"Then the Romani flee to the mountain. Hide in the forest during the day, travel by night. If they come and harass us, we can sail an army straight to Carthage and end the threat. It's what we should have done years ago," Lee replies, becoming increasingly irritated by the woman who is disagreeing with every suggestion.

"We need to wait for Mum before we can cast a vote, but I'm with Lee. I don't think we can afford to fall back to the mountain. It will make us look weak to the other clans and disrupt the economy," says the old man.

"What's worse, looking weak or stupid?" snaps the woman.

"Being weak is stupid," I reply, making Lee laugh.

"I guess I should have introduced you two. Aries, this here is my Aunt Trina."

In learning that the woman is related to Lee, I feel terrible for being rude to her, and I can't believe he hasn't mentioned his connection to Trina earlier. Then again, I know it wouldn't have really mattered. I find it nearly impossible to bite my tongue, regardless of the social setting.

"Pleased to meet you," I say, outstretching my hand. She shakes it with a firm grip.

"I like her. Reminds me of myself," says Trina, who seems to welcome my direct nature.

The old man with the braided beard clears his throat. "Thousands of people didn't come here to see us bicker over strategy. We should be celebrating and honoring our heroes. It's not every day you repel an invasion! Ginger, come with me. We're going to make some money at the wagering tables. How do you feel about missing the mark at just the right time, to make us both some coin?" he asks, keen on profiting off Kristoff's ability with the bow.

"I like it fine, so long as they aren't Romani," answers Kristoff as he joins the man to head out of the tent.

"Such a good lad," replies the old man.

"Aries, do you mind joining Lee and me?" asks Trina. "We are about to meet up with some members of Clan Harald."

"Of course."

We exit the tent, and as we do, we are joined by more and more enforcers. We walk to the edge of the camp where several horses are waiting for us. I notice that my horse is a young black stallion that doesn't like being behind the other horses. Whenever Trina tries to pass them, the black stallion picks up its pace and cuts them off, prompting Lee and the others to laugh. I do my best to try and keep the horse in line but can't help but admire its competitiveness.

It's only a few minutes of riding before our group comes to a stop at a small hill, overlooking a meadow that is already overgrown despite spring only recently arriving. I look behind us and can see the light from the camp in the distance. I feel a sense of security wash over me. There's no way another meeting with another clan could be dangerous, given the number of Romani behind us.

"So, what's this meeting about anyway?" I ask.

"Suppose it's a formality. Clan Harald wants to see what happened before they pretend to think long and hard about what to do— then decide to do nothing, as usual. They are an honorable lot, but they are too fixated on upholding balance and keeping the peace. The

Swindletors will easily weasel their way around any punishment, so there really isn't a point in evaluating their actions for a violation of clan law," says Lee.

"Well said. The only thing that keeps the Swindletors at bay is the fact they are bloody cowards. I don't know what will come of it, but whatever we decide will be based on the words of Romani Elders and not what Clan Harald thinks," replies Trina.

Soon our group is approached by a dozen horses. Two of the men are holding a banner that is black with a golden symbol on it. As they draw closer, I can see that the symbol is a circle with two smaller circles beneath it, both connected to the larger circle.

"What is that symbol supposed to be?" I ask, confused. I have seen many banners throughout my life, and this must be one of the most curious looking.

"Ah, that's the troll cross. It's supposedly a good luck charm for warding off evil," answers Lee.

"Not the most foreboding, but who am I to judge, I guess," I reply, causing Lee to laugh and Trina to smirk, which I assume is about as close to laughing as she can get.

"They try to act too much like northerners if you ask me. Sure, we have a symbol too, but you don't see our soldiers carrying it around everywhere. No Romani would want to carry a banner instead of a weapon," says Trina.

The members of Clan Harald slow their pace as they draw closer and come to a halt a few feet away. To my surprise, their leader is a young woman who wears very clean, polished armor, and a black cloak that reminds me of the knights of the Apex. She's an attractive woman who appears to be in her mid-twenties. She also possesses long, well-groomed brown hair, big dark green eyes, and a petite build. From her face, the woman appears kind, despite dawning a complete set of armor.

"Good day, Lee—Trina," says the young woman, giving them both a slight nod. "Glad to see you are doing okay. We got word of what happened and wanted to see if we could be of assistance."

"We have it covered, Rose. Fortunate timing that you were so close to our location," Trina replies coldly.

"I am sure you do," Rose replies behind a smile that hides her disdain for Trina better than her tone of voice does.

When I first met Trina less than an hour ago, her direct and argumentative demeanor was infuriating, but now that I see it put to good use with Rose, I can find an appreciation for it.

"Do you mind if we take a look at the battlefield, and speak to the prisoners you have taken? We have orders to gather a statement just in case there is a convergence of the clans, with your permission, of course. Naturally, many will find it hard to believe that the Swindlers were conspiring with a foreign enemy with the intent to harm another clan. But I, for one, cannot say I'm surprised."

"There won't be a need for one. Olly conveniently wasn't speaking for his clan, which means the Swindletors can easily deny involvement," Lee answers.

"At some point, they are going to have to face justice. How often do they claim their clan members go rogue after they escalate clan tensions?" Rose asks.

"Maybe we should draft more rules? That seems to be working," Trina says blandly, adjusting in her saddle. "You are all free to look over the battlefield, but be reminded that it is sacred ground, and weapons are not to be wielded at the Cove. As for the prisoners, you may not speak to them. We are still in the process of investigating. Until that process is complete, we are not ruling out any possible conspirators in this plot," Trina says in a tone that strongly suggests Clan Harald are suspects as well.

"Understood," Rose replies coldly, dropping her fake smile and the pretense of kindness.

Rose directs her attention back to Lee, and I don't like how she looks at him.

"Do you mind if we look over some of the weapons from the northerners? We have been investigating several deaths along the outskirts of our territory, and we are wondering if their weapons fit the description," she asks.

"What description is that?" I can't help but ask, even though I'm not in a position to speak.

"Not at liberty to say, that is, until the investigation is over," Rose answers in an unenthusiastic tone.

"If it was up to me, I would say we aren't at liberty to let you then," I reply, which makes Lee snicker.

"Rose, you should probably get acquainted with Aries. She killed a dozen northerners today, and I'm told she only stopped at twelve because there were none left to kill," Trina says.

"Yes, the tourney runner-up. Glad to see your skills in practice extend to real fights as well. What say you, Lee? Are you able to grant our request, or will it need to be an elder?" Rose asks.

"You can survey the battlefield and talk to Romani who fought if they wish to speak. All weapons and materials have already been looted, and, unfortunately, Aries is right: we're not at liberty to let you see the weapons. We would need to know exactly what you are looking for before considering your request. It seems more often than not, Clan Harald thinks of itself as law enforcement, but this isn't the Apex, nor will it ever be," Trina answers before Lee even has a chance.

"Fair enough," Rose says with a curt nod. "I will try to get permission to disclose the details. Thanks again for your time and for agreeing to meet. Lee, it was very good to see you, as always. I can see you're doing well," she says, giving Lee a genuine smile.

Rose is trying to flirt with him—and doing a poor job of it—and I wonder if she knows that he and I are together. I'm frustrated, regardless.

"Try not to get murdered on your investigation, although I hear your cross protects trolls. Or your troll cross will protect you from trolls. Sorry, I am not very familiar with the concept," I say.

"I appreciate that. May you stay safe as well, although a woman of your stature should be fine," Rose replies before turning her horse and heading for the Cove.

"I don't like her at all," I say coldly.

"Agreed. Rose is a dimwitted upstart who used her looks to climb the ranks. I doubt she has ever seen battle, yet she parades around like a knight from the North," Trina replies.

"Likewise, I could watch you talking to Rose all day," I reply, trying not to laugh.

"Between the two of you, there is enough fire to burn down any army," Lee says.

"And anyway, what sort of investigation would require her to look at weapons? I bet she was just using that as a way to be nosey," I add.

"There have been some killings, but we assumed it was outlaws or people from Swindletor. Rose is a lot of things, but in my experience, a liar is not one of them," Lee says.

I don't like him providing her a compliment, even though it's a minor one at best. So, what if she doesn't lie? I ask myself rhetorically.

On the ride back to camp, my frustration is replaced by anxiety. I have a couple of theories about what could explain complex to identify wounds, and neither of them brings me comfort.

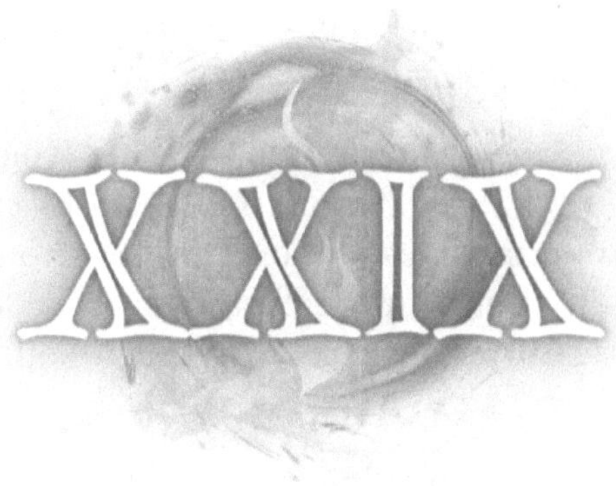

I return to camp shortly before nightfall. The moon is bright and so large that it fills most of the night's sky. The funeral ceremony for our fallen clan members begins, and I stand alongside the rest of the soldiers who fought in the battle. The bodies of the fallen rest atop large wooden pyres. They are wrapped in beautiful cloth from head to toe, and they wear elegant, handmade wooden crowns.

An elder says a few words regarding their bravery and sacrifice, which will allow them to be reincarnated as great warriors in the next life. The pyres are then put to the torch and soon after, erupt into a large blaze. As the bodies burn, the crowd chants the Romani slogan, "We are strong because we are family. We are family through bond." I can't help but be overcome with emotion. I think of my father and how badly I wish I could've given him a similar funeral. I feel like he of all people deserved it, but circumstances prevented it from happening.

I worry about the families of the fallen and wonder how they'll cope. Lee explains that their family will be taken care of and that nobody in the Romani ever goes without, especially the loved ones of those who pass while defending the clan.

I'm thankful for the Romani and everything they stand for. I feel a great sense of pride being one of them and want to continue doing my part to help, whether in battle or giving back to those in need.

Feasting and drinking follow the funeral, and not long after the celebration starts, I find myself longing for the quiet comfort of my lavvu. I've reached my limit for socializing and I'm ready for bed. Thankfully, Lee agrees, and the two of us retire to a caravan he has rented from another Romani.

My sleep during the night is restful—which is typically the case when I sleep next to Lee. Partly because he's fond of cuddling and partly because he's so warm it's as if I am lying next to a cozy fire. When morning comes, for once, I awake first. For a while, I just stare, holding him close, appreciating how lucky we are that both of us survived the battle.

I don't know what I'd do without him. It hurts to imagine such a thing; I know all too well the pain that comes with losing someone you love. My moment ends abruptly when Lee is awoken by a knock on our caravan door.

"What!?" I yell, irritated that someone has disturbed his sleep. Lee simply laughs.

"Oy, Rose is asking to meet with you!" replies a voice, sounding nervous, thanks to my response.

"Just a minute!" responds Lee, kissing my forehead before getting dressed.

"Wow, okay," I say.

"What?" he asks, confused.

"Rose wants to meet, and you rush out of bed to see her? Why can't she wait?"

"She can wait, but whatever she wants is probably about those attacks."

"You're no fun. You are supposed to argue back," I say, smiling.

"Didn't you get enough fighting yesterday?" asks Lee, also grinning.

"Never," I reply before tackling him back into the bed. I lay on top of him, holding down both of his arms. "You leave when I say you can," I continue before kissing him.

"I'm more than okay with that, love. Why don't you come with?"

"I think I'd rather eat an entire cauldron of Andrew's special stew than listen to her voice," I reply facetiously.

"Looks like somebody has a death wish. Are you sure you can't come along? Please? For me?" he says while making a pitiful face.

I stare at him for a moment before finally giving in with a heavy sigh. "Fine, I'll come. But only because I want to make sure you don't miss out on anything important, not because you have the most adorable face—when you beg."

We get ready and make our way out of the caravan. It's a cloudy day, with a strong gusting wind that brings about a chill. I see Rose standing beside two of her clansmen, one with the banner of Clan Harald in hand. I frown, pitying the man. It must be unbearable to have to carry the banner around everywhere, especially when it's already obvious which clan they're part of.

"Well, looks like you had a long night. Did you two just wake?" asks Rose.

"We don't share your clan's love for waking early," answers Lee.

"Especially when there wasn't much sleep the night before," I say before grabbing ahold of Lee's arm, prompting him to smile at me.

"So, what is it you have for us?" asks Lee.

"We thought you should know that from what we gathered, the foreign soldiers don't possess any weapons that could have been responsible for the killings," replies Rose, whose demeanor has changed because of my comments.

"Care to enlighten us about these killings?" asks Lee.

"I have been given authorization to do so," Rose nods. "We have been investigating several mysterious killings over the past few weeks. There doesn't seem to be a connection between the victims, and the distance between each crime is far-reaching. The first victim was at the edge of the Swindletor territory, and the last is all the way at our southern border."

"Sounds like the work of more than one person if they're that far apart. How do you know the killings are related?" asks Lee.

"The way the victims are killed is unique. The bodies are severed, with what looks like butcher's tools rather than an ordinary weapon. The cuts go clean through the bone."

I feel my heart sink into my stomach. I try not to think the worst but can't help but wonder if the killings are the work of the Revenant, or perhaps Stur, or even agents from the Watchers with similar weapons.

"You believe it could be a butcher gone mad?" I ask.

"Unlikely, but the killings are rather strange. Can you please send word if you encounter anything similar?" Rose asks.

Lee nods. "Thanks for the information. Good luck on trying to catch whoever is responsible. If they make their way into our territory, you won't have to worry about them. As you know, Romani justice is less forgiving than most."

"That it is. Say, not to cause concern, but we heard some Romani talking about Mum not arriving yet. With the state of things, you may want to confirm her whereabouts. Although, the Romani tend to speak in half-truths more than most," Rose replies, causing Lee to snicker.

I wait until Rose and the others are clear of earshot before speaking. "I have a terrible feeling about this."

"It's okay, love. Mum never arrives on time. She's probably off somewhere picking herbs. Besides, she always travels in a group. I can assure you that we don't have the same problems with bandits and killings as Clan Harald. They are too forgiving, being so committed to peace. It allows these things to happen."

"It's not that. It's just—the way she said those people were killed reminds me of—"

"I know, love. It's not that, I'm sure. Let's go check on Mum."

After asking several clan enforcers, Lee and I learn that Mum has not arrived, nor has there been any word about a delay. So, after some nagging from me, Andrew, Jaseen, and Kristoff join us to travel north to try and find Mum along the road.

Not long after departing the camp on horseback, we come across a group of Romani heading south. The group informs us that they last heard that Mum and her party stopped in a forest. Mum stated that the grove was sacred, and she wanted to commune with nature. I don't know what that means, but it sounds like something she would do. Lee thanks them for the information and confirms their questions about the battle and what happened. We then head for the woods, which is thankfully only a few hours' ride north of our position. The wind is starting to pick up, and the dark clouds forming in the sky tell us it could storm at any moment.

"I hope we can get there before the storm comes," says Jaseen.

"What's the matter? Scared of a little water? Oh, that's right! You can't swim," says Andrew.

"No need to swim when you live on a mountain," replies Jaseen.

"Isn't that Mum's caravan?" asks Kristoff, who is pointing at the small yellow caravan parked near a clearing at the edge of the dense forest. These woods don't seem nearly as vibrant as other forests I've seen in the Southlands. I don't know if it's the dark look of the forest, what Rose has said, or the looming storms in the distance, but I have an awful feeling. The feeling eases somewhat when we arrive at the caravan and notice that everything seems to be in order. We dismount our horses and secure them to the caravan before making our way to the trailhead. Shortly after we start walking, a Romani enforcer comes out of the tree line and greets us from a distance.

"Oy! What brings you lot here?" he asks.

Before we can reply, the enforcer falls to the ground face first, with a double-bladed axe sticking out of his back.

Shock washes over me, and it seems as though everything is happening far away. I can't hear what is being said to me, but I can see that the others are yelling. Then, a lone figure comes into view, walking slowly out of the woods. It's the Revenant. It's found us.

My worst nightmare has come true. No matter how hard my mind tells my body to move, it won't. I'm completely frozen until Lee stands face-to-face with me.

"Take Kristoff and run! Run!" he yells, shaking me and trying to get me to focus. "Find Mum!"

I take a deep breath and remember the fear I felt the night I first saw the Revenant. The night it brutally killed Kristoff's parents. The night it fatally wounded my father. My fear is replaced by anger. I promised myself I'd be ready when I saw it again, and I spent the entire winter preparing myself for just. Nearly every day I was thinking about how I would defeat it when the day finally came. Perhaps I'm not prepared, but I would rather die than run again.

"No, I'm going to end this," I reply coldly.

Lee looks at me in surprise, then turns to Kristoff. "It's probably you it wants. Once we attack, you run and find Mum."

"And—do what?" asks Kristoff, visibly afraid.

"Bring her here," replies Lee.

I want to argue, but before I can, the Revenant begins walking towards us. My anger boils up inside me, growing to such an intensity it feels as if heat is radiating from my skin. I remove my sword from its sheath and decide I'm not going to wait. I must take the fight to it. I'm not going to allow it to stalk us and kill us one by one. I plan to remove its head and take it as far away from its body as I can.

To the dismay of the others, I rush towards the Revenant alone. The closer I get, the faster I run until I'm finally upon it. It's wearing a black face mask, which has two wide slits for eye holes, and a small slit across where its mouth would be. It continues to walk towards me at the same slow pace. I lift my sword in the air and come down as fast and hard as I can with a strike intended to sever its head. Before my weapon reaches its mark, the Revenant raises its axe to meet my blade. The clash makes my sword vibrate so hard it hurts my hand.

I am thrown off balance, allowing the Revenant to capitalize, knocking me to the ground with a punch to my stomach. The force of the blow throws me several feet backward, and I struggle to catch my breath. I finally stand back to my feet and look on as I see Lee, Andrew, and Jaseen surround the Revenant. They move slowly and purposefully in complete unison. The Revenant approaches Lee, and panic grips my heart. I can't bear to see him struck down. But to my surprise, Lee is able to dodge the Revenant's blows. He's taking extra precautions, focusing on avoidance rather than attack.

Meanwhile, Jaseen swings for the Revenant's neck with his sword, but it blocks the attack. Thankfully, the clash doesn't knock him off balance, and he maintains a strong grip on his weapon. Lee also swings his sword for the Revenant's neck, but his attack is blocked too. Jaseen and Lee rain attacks down on the creature one after the other, but the Revenant is so quick it seems as if their strikes will never get through its guard. I worry such a flurry of blows will tire them and by extension make them vulnerable.

Andrew pulls a jagged-looking spear with a nasty hook for a blade from behind his back. There's a large silver chain attached to the end of it, which he begins to wrap around his hand. He then uses his great strength to throw the spear through the Revenant's back, slowing its movement. Andrew digs his feet into the ground, pulling the chain with all his might trying to subdue it, but despite his size and strength, the Revenant continues to move forward.

"Wrap the chain around it!" yells Jaseen.

He tries to get close to the Revenant but letting go of the tension causes him to be flung forward, falling hard onto the ground. The Revenant quickly turns and raises its axe in the air, prepared to strike a defenseless Andrew. With great speed, the Revenant's hand swings the legendary axe downward, but before it can reach its target, it is met by an upward strike from Lee, whose blade severs its hand, dropping it to the ground, along with the axe it held.

Jaseen swings for its neck, but it ducks beneath the blow, countering with a strong elbow which knocks him to the ground. By this time, Andrew has returned to his feet and wrapped the chain around the Revenant's neck, pulling it backward. But not before it is able to punch Lee with its remaining hand. He tries to regain his balance, but his legs wobble with each step. Jaseen charges the Revenant and tackles it to the ground, allowing Andrew to wrap the silver chain around its body. Lee regains his bearings and assists them with binding the creature. The Revenant lays flat on the ground, face-first and motionless. Jaseen grabs Stur's axe, careful to keep his weight on the good arm of the Revenant so it can't throw him off.

"No! Let Aries, it's her right," shouts Lee.

"Hurry, Aries!" yells Andrew, whose voice quivers with uncharacteristic fear.

It pains me to move, and I worry that at least one of my ribs may be broken. Regardless, I run as fast as I can, somewhat hoping I won't reach my destination. I can't believe I've found myself faced with the monster once more, and once again, it's trying to turn my entire world upside down. Part of me feels hopeless, thinking that whatever they try will fail. I hope the silver chain will make a difference this time, and, as far as I can tell, it does seem to be working to subdue the monster. As I stand over it and look down on the beast that has killed my father and Kristoff's parents, I am ashamed that I am still afraid and barely able to look at it. I know I should be angry or in a rage, but all I feel is fear.

Reluctantly, I grab the axe from Jaseen and look down at the Revenant. It stares back at me, sensing what is about to happen. Its black mask creates the illusion of an expressionless face, save for the two eye slits that hide a faint purple glow.

I grip the axe tightly, visualizing my swing. This strike will bring me one step closer to vengeance. I raise the axe slowly, preparing to sever the beast's head. I plan to bring the axe down at the base of its neck, right above the shoulders. Perhaps it won't kill him, but I hope removing its head from its body will at least neutralize it as a threat. Just before I follow through with my swing, I hear Mum's voice screaming, "Wait! Wait, my child!"

I look back to see Mum running towards the group, coming from the woods, followed closely by Kristoff, who is struggling to keep up with her. I grudgingly hold the swing back, trusting she must know something I don't. The fact we are waiting with the Revenant still alive right at our feet makes me extremely uneasy.

"We shouldn't wait," I state.

"She's right, Mum. This thing nearly took us all out," urges Jaseen.

"Killing a puppet without knowing its master is unwise, my loves. Now tell me, who has done this to you—you wretched, wretched thing?" asks Mum, who gently uses her hand to lower the axe I'm holding.

The Revenant doesn't appreciate her presence and begins to thrash its arms and legs against its binds. Mum slowly moves her hands towards the head of the Revenant, with her palms facing it.

"Yes—dark magic, unlike anything I've ever felt. Although—this wasn't done against your will, was it? It couldn't be—you—you agreed to this, but why would anyone? I guess the wind and the trees were right. A necromancer has arisen once again, and so the balance must rise to correct. Now, I command you, with the spirits of this land as my ally, who is your master?" Mum asks firmly, sounding as angry as I have ever heard her. "I said, who is your master?"

The Revenant begins to thrash even harder as if in pain. This confuses me because as far as I knew, it didn't feel anything. After a moment, something that I can only describe as dark purple smoke begins to drift out of the eye slits in the Revenant's mask. It reminds me of the time arcane energy had seeped from Beltrum's eyes when he used magic back in Redwood.

Almost too quickly for me to process, the beast jumps to its feet and uses its head to strike Mum, followed by her collapsing to the ground. Lee, Andrew, and Jaseen try to regain control but are unsuccessful. Now using the chain as a weapon, the Revenant defeats each of them before dropping the chain and turning its attention to me. My hands are shaking as I try to hold the axe steady. I watch as the Revenant bends down and grabs its severed hand. Then, with a discharge of purple energy, the hand reconnects to its arm.

It then charges, and I know I will be dead in a matter of moments if the beast wishes. But I decide I will not allow certain death to stop me from putting up a fight. I quickly analyze the situation and hold on to the hope that a perfectly-timed strike from the axe will sever its head and kill it.

The Revenant is almost upon me as I grip the axe in my right hand, standing with my left foot forward. I plan to do a spinning attack, rotating clockwise, and striking down at the Revenant's neck before it can touch me.

It comes into range, and I begin to spin, but the Revenant catches my axe hand right before I can connect. I can't believe how strong it is. I drop the axe from my right hand, hoping to catch it with my left, but before I can, the Revenant strikes me in the chest, and I fall to the ground. Then, it picks the axe up and walks slowly toward me until it's standing directly over me. The only act of defiance left is to die a good death, free of fear or pleading.

"Well, do it then," I say calmly, finding strength in the hope that I may see my mother and father in the next life.

Right before the beast could strike me down, Kristoff appears and attempts to tackle it. He's barely able to move it with his efforts, and the Revenant uses its elbow to strike the back of Kristoff's head, knocking him unconscious. I use the distraction as an opportunity to get to my feet. Unarmed and with my body badly injured, I know fighting is useless, but I'd rather die on my feet than on my back in the dirt. While the Revenant is still staring at Kristoff, I punch it in the back of the head as hard as I can, having little to no effect—outside of hurting my knuckles.

The Revenant turns to face me and I grab its head, digging both of my thumbnails into its eye sockets. I can feel its eyeballs move deep into its skull. Using my full force, I press hard, causing the beast to shake its head and backhand me to the ground. Purple energy flows from the eye slits again.

The ground begins to rumble, and I can feel it moving beneath me. The Revenant pauses and surveys the area before continuing forward, stalking me once more. Before it can reach me, roots burst from the ground and knock it backward. A terrifying voice fills the air, which sounds painful to my ears.

"Enough! I will undo you! For I am the Crone and protector of this land! You have threatened my children for the last time."

I look over to see Mum facing the monster, her palms lifted in the air. Her expression is far more serious than anything I have seen from her. The beast, realizing Mum poses a serious threat, switches his focus from me to her. Suddenly it throws the axe with deadly intent. It moves so fast through the air that I can barely follow it. Before the axe reaches its destination, dozens of roots burst forth from the earth, striking it and changing its trajectory.

The beast then rushes at Mum, trying to dodge and avoid the roots that continue bursting up from the ground. It avoids them for a moment, but eventually, the overwhelming number proves too much. The beast trips and falls to the ground and Mum uses some of the larger roots to pierce the Revenant's body, impaling it in several places. The roots lift the beast in the air about six feet from the ground. Then, more and more roots begin to wrap around its cursed body, strangling it.

"Back to the earth, where your kind places its dead," says Mum in the same terrifying tone.

Thick purple smoke fills the air, causing the roots impaling the Revenant to wither and fall to the ground. The Revenant lands hard on the ground and immediately gets to its feet. This time, instead of coming after Mum, it runs for its axe, grabs it, and flees. Mum does her best to bind the beast again, but the further it gets from her, the less effective the roots seem to be.

Mum drops her hands to her sides, and the ground stops shaking. She walks over to the group and, one by one, helps them to their feet. She places her hands on my rib, replacing the pain with a warm sensation.

"Once we get back to the mountain, I will heal this properly, but I must preserve my energy in case the Revenant returns. I am sorry I failed," says Mum, her voice full of remorse.

"If it wasn't for you, we would all be dead right now," I say before giving Mum a hug. "Did it cut anyone with its axe? Please tell me it didn't cut anyone. That's how my dad died—"

I look at Lee in time to see him lift his hand away from his stomach, revealing a blood-covered palm. The terror that rushes over me nearly knocks me off my feet.

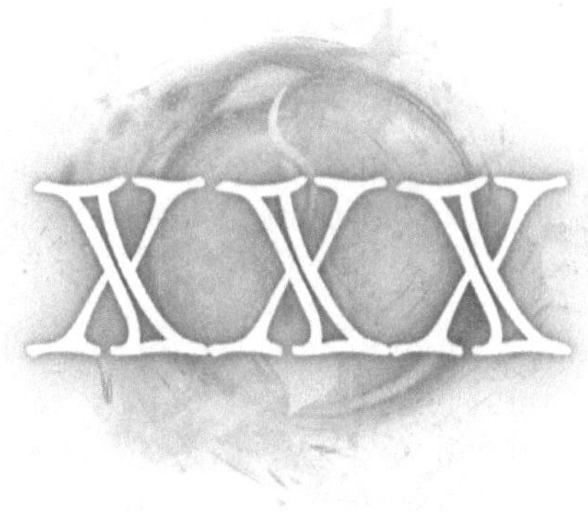

I watch as Mum places her hand over Lee's wound, green light protruding from her eyes. She keeps her hands there for several moments while my anxiety grows. I'm worried she won't be able to heal him, just like Captain Rockwell couldn't cure my father.

"I sense no poison, child," Mum says softly. "I will look closer when we return, but we need to hurry, before I am too weak to defend us."

"Would you be able to tell, though?" I ask.

"I assure you, he will be healed," Mum answers, giving Lee a reassuring smile.

"Everyone, ride as fast as we can to Little Watch, but stay together. Kristoff, you can ride with me. Jaseen and Andrew, please gather your fallen brother."

The group nods in agreement, but nobody speaks. I can sense the feeling of defeat and fear in the air. I doubt the three of them have ever experienced such failure, especially at the hands of something as terrifying as the Revenant. It isn't long before we are back on the road and begin making our way to Little Watch.

Shortly after we arrive at the safety of Little Watch, we are ushered into tents and assessed by Mum, who gives us horrible tasting concoctions. After drinking mine, I fall fast asleep. I awake lying beside Lee in the tent that was set up for us to recover. Despite the awful taste of Mum's concoction, the drink has done the trick, and I feel back to normal—physically at least.

Internally, I'm a mess. I can't help but feel terrified about what happened. The Revenant is in the Southlands, and even Mum couldn't kill it. Although, I do feel safer being around her. She's the only person I've seen who could make the beast flee.

My mind is a collection of negative emotions. I feel guilty for coming to the Southlands and placing them all in danger. I feel ashamed because of how utterly afraid I am of the thing. I hate feeling helpless, especially when I was facing the monster that took my father from me. I wish I would have been more courageous and fought the beast without fear like my father had. But no matter how hard I try to control my emotions, I am afraid. Terrified, in fact.

"Mum is sure you weren't poisoned? Do you feel okay? Any coughing, exhaustion, pain?" I ask Lee, still worried she may have missed something.

"I'm positive. Not sure why a beast that strong would use poison anyways. Doesn't seem to need the subtlety it brings. I'm really sorry, love."

"Why are you sorry? I'm the one that's sorry," I reply.

"I thought we had it. I had no idea anything could be that strong or fast," he continues, sounding depressed.

"It's okay. I knew exactly how strong and fast it was, and yet I still placed you all in danger by coming here."

Lee looks puzzled and puts his arm under my head. I shift so I am resting on his chest. "So, what then? You just wander around aimlessly until this thing kills you? How's it your fault a homicidal monster is trying to kill you? Surely you don't feel like you're to blame, love."

"Well, if we had never come here, it wouldn't have either," I reply, fighting to hold back my tears, trying to keep my bottom lip from quivering.

"And then it would have found you somewhere else, somewhere where you were without family. Look around, love, do the Romani seem mad at you or upset that this is happening? No, they don't, and you know why? Because we have a long history of protecting wayward souls who are running from all manner of danger. You didn't put us at risk. You're one of us by blood and oath. The beast is to blame—or the one pulling the strings, rather. Even now, hundreds, if not thousands of Romani are seeking it out. Each of them eager for a chance to slay the beast, both for glory and vengeance for their family. So please stop blaming yourself. Honestly, it's a touch offensive," he says, humor coloring his words and making me laugh a little as I let my tears flow.

I look up at him, and his green eyes stare back at me as he smiles. "You sure?" I ask.

"Never been more positive, love," he replies before kissing me deeply.

His kiss has a magical property that completely takes me away from reality, making me forget whatever strife I am facing. I savor the moment before reluctantly breaking the kiss. I don't want to stop, but I figure I should check on the others. Lee's validation on the situation is crucial, but I will feel better once I'm able to gauge how everyone else is feeling.

"Can we go check on Kristoff and the others?" I ask.

"Of course, love," says Lee before springing up from the bed and putting his shirt on.

We quickly make our way outside, and I notice there are far more Romani than typical at Little Watch. Many men and women are walking around with a demeanor that suggests they are eager for action. I appreciate their presence and the sense of safety it provides, but I can't help feeling as if they are being naïve. I hope that they don't get their wish, and none will find the Revenant because it will probably be the last thing they ever do.

As we continue to walk, I see Andrew running toward us, much faster than I've ever seen a man his size run. My heart sinks. Something must be wrong.

"What now?" I say in a defeated tone. Lee grabs my hand and holds it tightly, giving it a reassuring squeeze.

"It's—it's—Kristoff. He's missing," Andrew says between gasps.

"What do you mean he's missing!?" I scream. Anger fills my veins, and I feel as if my skin will burst into flames at any moment.

"Wasn't someone watching him? How could he be missing?" asks Lee, concerned but far calmer than I am.

Andrew hands me a piece of rolled-up parchment. "He snuck out, and when Mum went to check on him she found this inside of his caravan."

I quickly unroll the parchment and immediately recognize his handwriting, which is far neater than most.

"Dear Aries,

Thank you for always being my friend, even when nobody else wanted to be. I feel horrible for leaving like this, but I knew you would stop me if I spoke to you first. Ever since I found out it's me that Carthage is looking for, I have wanted to leave to protect you. Shortly after that, we were attacked by the Revenant, and people died, all because of me.

After what we've been through, I never thought we could be happy again, and the world seemed too bleak to handle, but we met the Romani, became part of their family, and despite all the grief and sadness, I felt truly happy. I know that you have been truly happy also, and I can tell you and Lee really love each other. I will do whatever it takes to make sure your happiness is no longer at risk. Please, if you care about me, you will honor my wishes and not come looking for me. Stay in the Southlands with Lee and the Romani. Please just be happy. Our paths will cross again after I make this right. Please trust me to do so.

Sincerely,

Kristoff"

Despite the thoughtful tone of the letter, I'm furious. I didn't ask him to flee, nor would I ever have done so, and yet he took it upon himself to make the decision for me.

"He's going to get himself killed. Look," I say, handing the letter to Lee, who quickly reads it.

"I'm assuming he's going to try and turn himself in or draw the Revenant away. I don't even know. I am at a complete loss," I say, rambling out loud, trying to make sense of the situation.

"We must go after him. He will get himself killed if we can't find him. How long ago did he leave?" asks Lee.

"Couldn't have been more than an hour, maybe two at most," Andrew replies.

Lee signals a group of Romani over and whispers to them. They sprint off in separate directions, spreading the word to more and more people, who then also run off.

"Aries, you know him better than anyone. Which way do you think he would head?" asks Lee.

"I really don't know. He knows I would come after him right away so he wouldn't make it easy to follow him. I wonder if he had a horse. If he didn't, he'd be going somewhere horses couldn't travel, which I bet he would do if he wanted to remain undetected. I'm also sure he figured you would scramble the Romani to help find him."

"If you're right, then he's heading north or east, but east wouldn't be where he would go if he was turning himself in," said Lee.

"Yeah, he would need to head north, probably toward the Swindletors. Surely, they would be the only ones capable of ferrying him north," said Andrew.

"What if he isn't trying to turn himself in? What if he is trying to fight the Revenant, or lead it away?" I ask.

"We really should ask Mum, shouldn't we?" suggests Andrew.

"I don't think we have time, and no offense, but it's difficult to find answers in what she says," I reply coldly. I love Mum, but I don't have time to try to sort out the meaning of her words right now.

"Perhaps—but it may be best, love. He could have said something to her that helps us. He couldn't take any main roads, or he would be easily discovered, so I think you're right, and he's heading to the east first and then making his way north," replies Lee.

I know that Lee's words are valid and that even if Mum couldn't use tarot cards to predict where he was heading, she may know something they don't.

Andrew, Lee, and I make our way to Mum's caravan, where we see Jaseen standing guard outside. He gives me a distraught glance. He must have heard about Kristoff. Without a word, I give him a hug.

"It's going to be okay. We'll find him. He's just trying to protect us," I say, trying to comfort Jaseen, who has grown very close to Kristoff.

I enter Mum's caravan to find her fidgeting with wooden tablets at her table. "I see you have heard about Kristoff. I'm so sorry, child."

"Do you have any idea where he may be going or what he was thinking?" I ask.

"I personally do not, but there is someone who might. These events were destined to happen," Mum replies, her voice full of sorrow.

I take a deep breath and do my best not to show my irritation, but this is precisely what I was hoping to avoid—a convoluted discussion about supernatural forces. While I clearly believe in magic, having witnessed it firsthand many times, I'm not sure if I believe in fate and prophecy, especially in the face of such an urgent situation. The Revenant is very much real, and it will absolutely hurt Kristoff. Or take him to the North where he'll be killed—or suffer a worse fate.

"Mum, I really need to focus on finding him, and I was hoping maybe he said something that would let us know where he planned to go," I reply, trying to ground the conversation in reality.

"I told you, love, I don't know where he planned to go. I do know he cares deeply about you and wants to protect you. He has kind eyes. He isn't cut out for war. I hate to see him wrapped up in this. I am not sure what fate is playing at, but as I said, there is someone who knows, child," Mum says in her calm and kind tone.

My heart is racing, and blood pounds loudly in my ears. "Trust?" I snap. "Trust who or what exactly? Fate?" I scoff. "Because, as far as I am concerned, fate can't be real. If it was, why would these terrible, horrific things continue to happen?" I'm breathing heavily and am unable to calm myself. "But please, by all means, present the person who knows what fate has in store so I can ask them." I glare at Mum who meets my gaze with soft eyes. I know I'm taking my anger out on the wrong person, and my shoulders slump. "I really don't mean to be angry with you, Mum, but I just can't take any more of this. It's always something, and I don't have the luxury of believing in a magical force that will make sure everything is all right. I must find Kristoff before he gets himself killed or kidnapped," I say.

"I know, child, and I don't blame you for being angry. It is your armor, and you are under attack. If you do not trust fate, then perhaps you would trust your mother. She is the one who knows where Kristoff is heading." Mum holds up a hand when I open my mouth. "And before you get even angrier, my love, it is her who foresaw these events; not every single detail, of course, but she did envision the future. The power to expel what cannot be killed lies hidden above the Cove. It is written in the letter your mother wanted me to have. These are her words that she asked me to tell you at this exact moment. If you do not trust me—or fate–right now, then please trust her."

My head is spinning. This is too much to process. I take the letter from Mum and read word for word what she has said. "But how could she know? I don't understand," I say, sounding more hopeless than encouraged. Mum simply smiles.

I take a deep breath and steady my mind, focusing on the task at hand. We must find Kristoff before he is harmed. There will be plenty of time to think about my mother being a prophet and what all that could mean.

"We were just at the Cove though, and Lee said there isn't an actual cove for miles and miles," I say.

"That isn't the original Cove, child. It was moved there after the Romani territory expanded. The real Cove is located to the northeast of here. I'm sure Lee can guide you. But you must hurry, child."

"Thank you, Mum," I say, giving her a small smile. "I'm sorry for snapping. Did Kristoff know any of this?" I ask, holding up my mother's letter.

"He did. He said it came to him in a dream. Your mother's words, that is. A rather curious proposition, even for me. But there will be more time for that later. Go now. Time is very important. You must arrive precisely when you need to. I will pray for you, and remember, Gaia watches over all Romani."

I give Mum a hug and exit the caravan to prepare to head towards the Cove and hopefully catch Kristoff. I explain what I learned to Lee, Jaseen, and Andrew as we rush to gather our weapons and supplies needed for the journey. Lee is shocked to learn that the Cove used to be at a different location.

On the outskirts of Little Watch, we come to a rugged and narrow path, far too rough for horses. "I'm not sure Kristoff knows how to get to the Cove. Mum said he had a vision in which my mom's words came to him, so he may know because of that, I guess," I say, shrugging.

"Maybe. Let's just hope we find him before he gets there. But I must say, it wouldn't be a bad idea to get this weapon if it can dispatch the Revenant. Imagine what else it could do if it's that powerful," says Lee.

"You sure you don't want us to come with you two?" asks Jaseen.

"I wish you could, mate. But we need you two leading the search north. Apart from Aries, you are the only other people who know how Kristoff thinks. Not to mention, all the Romani are in an uproar after what happened at the Cove. You would get wind of any increased conflict before us. You are both too valuable to our defenses, and the clan can't spare us all being gone," replies Lee, before giving Jaseen and Andrew a hug.

"Fair enough," Jaseen says. "But if you aren't back in two days, we'll come looking for you. So, try not to make a holiday out of it. Oh, and when you find Kristoff, please slap him upside his head for me, yeah?"

Lee and I say our goodbyes to Jaseen and Andrew before making our way into the thick forest. The further we get away from the safety of Little Watch, the more nervous I become, expecting the Revenant to leap out from behind a tree or be in the middle of the road waiting for us. I know Lee feels anxious too, and part of me wonders if it would be best to head back and ask more Romani to accompany us. Maybe a dozen or so would be enough to finally take out the Revenant.

Eventually, I'm able to steel my mind, remembering how ashamed I felt after feeling so terrified at seeing the Revenant again. It has taken everything from me and was now responsible for my best friend in the world fleeing in an attempt to sacrifice himself.

Just as I open my mouth to ask Lee how long the journey would be, I hear a rustling coming through the brush of the forest.

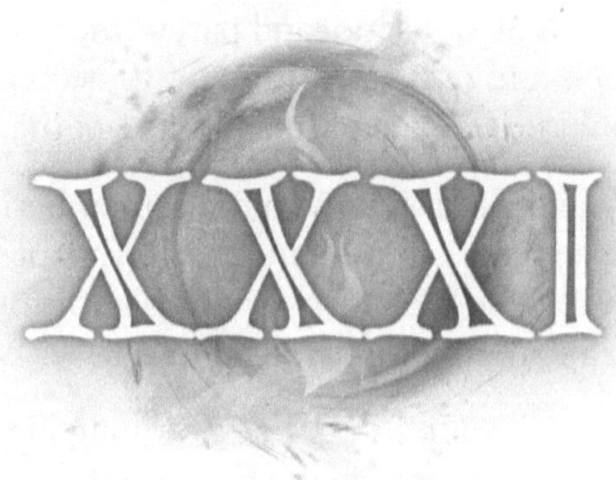

We both remove our swords from our sheaths and crouch, waiting to see what's coming through the brush. To our relief, it's a small white-tailed doe galloping away from something.

"Probably got spooked by all the Romani searching the mountain for the Revenant, who I'm sure is long gone by now," Lee says, seeing the need for reassurance in my eyes.

"The Cove isn't too far from Little Watch. If we make good time, we should be able to get there tomorrow before midday," he continues, now holding my hand as we walk. I'm thankful for him, and I can't help but feel less afraid in his presence. He appears calm, as usual, but then again, he often acts as he has a death wish, so I'm not sure if his calmness is something I should take into consideration.

"What if we walk through the night?" I ask.

"That would get us there by sunrise, I expect. But then we run the risk of getting there before Kristoff. I don't know much about visions and that sort, but I'm sure he'll still need the sun to guide him."

"Fair enough, but to be honest, I don't know how I feel about sleeping in the woods, especially with how cold it's been getting at night. And with that thing out there."

"I don't think it's coming for us, love. It seems to be fixated on Kristoff."

I know it's an attempt to make me feel better, but reminding me the Revenant is after Kristoff, who is out on his own, troubles me, and my face can't hide it.

"I shouldn't have said that," he says quickly. "I mean, we aren't the ones in danger, right? So, we need to get to him, then we will be—you know what? I'm going to shut up now. Actually, no, think of it this way: the soldiers want him alive, and the Revenant was definitely holding back until Mum almost killed it. So, I bet he wouldn't hurt Kristoff anyway," he continues, stumbling over his words like a child trying to explain themselves to an angry parent.

I usually love when Lee chokes on his own words because it's funny, but instead of being funny and confusing, this time his words make a lot of sense to me. The Revenant is merely a puppet that follows orders. Whoever is controlling it clearly wants Kristoff alive, or else they could've paid the Swindletors to assassinate him, something they very likely would have done.

Eventually, we find ourselves nearing the edge of the thick forest and approaching a large stretch of plains that leads to the Eastern Sea. The sun is already beginning to set, and it won't be long until nighttime, so we stop to make camp in the cover of the trees. Lee makes sure to clear a path to the plains, providing a quick retreat if necessary. He also sets up various noisemakers around us, hoping they will alert us if anyone gets within range of our camp. Once he's done, he sits down beside me, and we both rest against his backpack of supplies.

"Probably going to be another cold night, love, best if you snuggle up extra close," he says playfully.

"Wow, even with everything going on, you can't help but flirt and push your luck," I reply, smiling.

I love how he speaks to me as if he's still courting me, despite us already being together.

"You've got to be tired, love. Why don't you get some sleep? I'll take the first watch," he says softly before kissing my forehead.

"Are you sure? Aren't you tired?" I ask.

"Yeah, I'm sure, love. I'll be fine," he says, pulling me closer to his body to keep me warm.

We rest beneath a heavy wool blanket which does a great job at keeping us comfortable. It doesn't take long before I'm asleep and begin to dream. My dreams are incoherent and hard to follow. What I can manage to comprehend is an intense feeling of fear and anxiety mixed with anger and heartbreak. When I open my eyes, I'm nearly blinded by the sun shining directly at me. I quickly wipe the sleep from my eyes and blink rapidly, trying to adjust to the light.

"Why didn't you wake me up so I could keep watch?" I ask angrily.

"It's fine, love. I didn't sleep, and I wasn't about to wake you. It would be a crime against nature to ruin such a beautiful sight."

"Oh please, like you have an issue waking me up any other time. You probably fell asleep too and woke up just before I did."

"There may have been a fair bit of dozing off on my part, but I did leave the noise traps, to be fair," he says.

I shake my head at him and begin to gather our things. The two of us quickly pack up the camp, making sure to drink some water and eat some bread before setting off again.

I hope we'll see Kristoff out in the open. The plains stretch for miles, and there is hardly anything that obstructs our view. The edge of the plains gives way to large bluffs, which drop off into the Eastern Sea. We walk near the edge of the cliffs and look out at the ocean. Sometimes the waves strike the side of the bluffs so hard that the water nearly reaches us.

"I don't think I have ever seen waters that rough," I say.

"Aye, that's why these lands are largely uninhabited; hard to know which days you can fish. Not to mention it's difficult to launch a boat. They used to use ladders or wooden elevators, but they were accident-prone, to say the least."

We continue to walk for hours before coming upon a path that leads down to the water. "This is near the cave that leads to the old Cove. Down below is a beach that could have served as a meeting ground, for those rare instances when we met with other clans. Back in those days, there was next to no diplomacy. And landing a boat here is nearly impossible—I bet that's the reason the Romani chose it. It was a way of saying, 'don't bother trying to negotiate with us,' without actually saying it," Lee explains.

"So, where's the actual cave? We still haven't seen any sign of Kristoff. Do you think he could be in there?"

"Possibly. We'll know more once we get to the beach and see if there are footprints. It's possible he got lost in the woods and was found by a group of Romani, or even turned back around when it got dark out. We'll find him, love, one way or another."

"I hope you're right, but I say we at least check the cave and see if he turns up," I reply.

"Of course, love. If there is a weapon somewhere in there, I don't know where it could be hiding. I have been there a few times over the years, and it's about what you'd expect from a seaside cove: dark, damp, and a little bit creepy, full of nasty spiders the size of a fist."

Lee continues to talk while we make our way down to the beach, but I'm barely listening. It's hard to hear him over the strong wind, and the words "I hope Kristoff is here" keep running through my mind, blocking out nearly everything else. I picture him staring blankly at the cove, confused as to what he's looking at, perhaps even remorseful for leaving in the first place, and thankful he won't have to travel back alone.

I contemplate the conversation with Mum and the implications that fate and prophecy have on my life. I don't like the idea of not being in control of what happens to me, but given my desperation, if it means getting Kristoff back safely, I will gladly obey fate.

We eventually make our way to the bottom of the treacherous pass, staring at a damp, sandy beach. Lee kneels to the ground, looking closely at the sand.

"What is it?" I ask.

"Tracks. I don't know for sure, love, but they look to be close to his boot size."

I rush over and look, unsure if they're his, since the wind is shifting the sand about so much. But the longer I inspect the footprints, the surer I feel they are indeed his. Who else could it be? We don't know of anyone else that would be coming to this place, and we haven't seen a single person since we headed east from Little Watch.

Lee and I pick up our pace and begin jogging. We eventually come to a large beachhead, that's far wider than the rest of the beach. To our left is a massive rock formation that stretches from the coast all the way into the sky. The plains look to end abruptly at this spot, giving way to the large, ominous-looking mountain, with its jagged black rocks that rise as far as the eye can see.

As he tracks the windswept footprints, I follow Lee's path along the base of the rocks until we come across a large opening which I know must be the Cove.

Lee removes a torch from his bag and lights it before walking slowly into the cave, one hand holding the torch, one hand resting on the hilt of his sword. I follow as closely behind as I can, nervously hoping that we find Kristoff waiting inside.

The pathway of the cave is steep, leading us underground. I walk carefully so that I won't slip as I descend to the floor of the cave. The inside is precisely how Lee described it, cold, dark, and a little bit creepy. It isn't very large, so it doesn't take long before we know for sure that Kristoff isn't inside.

"How far back does it go?" I ask, hoping there may be a pathway that I can't see.

"This is it, love."

"So, if Kristoff was here, how would he have gotten out? We don't see any prints leading away from the cave or heading in the opposite direction of the way we came," I ask, confused.

"That's a very good question, love. Kristoff! Hello!" he yells, his voice echoing off the cave walls.

I struggle to make sense of where he could be. There must be an explanation. I look closely at the walls of the cave, running my hands along them, searching for clues of hidden passages. In the mystery books I read in my youth, it wasn't uncommon for the characters to find a hidden entrance inside a cave that opened when they pressed a spot on the wall. Though I search as thoroughly as I can inside the dimly lit cave, I have no luck, stopping only when I hear something.

"What was that sound?" I ask.

"Probably just the wind, love."

"Yeah, but it wouldn't whistle like that if it was coming through the entrance of the cave. That means there's a tunnel somewhere nearby!"

Lee nods. "Beauty and brains, eh? You must be right. But the question is, where? Do you feel it?" he asks as he tries to use the torch to find where the wind is coming through.

"Wait a minute. Over here," I say, now running my hands along the floor of the cave. "What are these?"

Lee crouches down beside me, using his torch to light up the area I'm indicating. The light reveals a symbol carved into the floor of the cave. "Do you recognize what that symbol is?" I ask, confused.

Upon closer inspection, we see there are three symbols. The first is a straight line, possessing a diagonal line, which starts from the top and runs down to the right of it. Shortly below that line is a matching diagonal line the same length as the first. Next to that symbol is a marking that resembles the letter S. The last symbol is another straight line, sporting a diagonal line coming from the top and going down to the right, except unlike the first, it has only one such line.

"Hmm. These look like Soulmi symbols. The type they use to cast ruins. They're like tarot cards; said to help tell the future," Lee says, sounding just as puzzled as me.

"Do you know what they mean?" I ask.

"I'm trying to think. Pretty sure the one that looks like an S is the symbol for the sun or for light. And that one, just the one line, I know for a fact is water. It is a pretty common symbol for the Soulmi. They believe water is a key to prophecy. I'm not sure what the other one means."

I consider what the combination of the symbol for light, the symbol for water, and a third unknown symbol could mean. My mind jumps from one possibility to another, but none of them feel right.

"Okay, let's break this down. What do we know? My mother knew this place was necessary to find a weapon that could defeat something that can't be killed by conventional means. That could be the sun symbol. The symbol for water may be suggesting that this place is significant for the prophecy. But how? And what about the other symbol?" I ask aloud.

I lose track of time trying to figure out what the symbols could mean, and before I know it, the waves start to seep into the entrance of the cave.

"The midday tide will be coming in soon, love, and the cave will be underwater."

I continue to stare blankly at the symbols, only partly listening to what Lee had said.

"Love, the water. It will fill the cave soon. We have to go before we freeze or drown," he says empathetically, knowing that I wouldn't want to leave without Kristoff. When I still don't move, he tries again, "We have to go. Now." This time he gently pulls my arm to move me toward the entrance.

"Water!" I burst out. "What if the water symbol isn't about the prophecy at all? What if it's saying to use the water?" I ask excitedly.

Lee stares at me with eyebrows raised, waiting for me to elaborate.

"How much water will fill the cave when the tide comes in?" I ask.

"I don't know. I imagine the entire cave will be submerged, love, but we can't afford to stay in here and find out. If we're wet when the sun goes down, we'll freeze. The wind rips through the plains like you wouldn't believe." He stares at me, so I go on. "To keep from freezing to death, we'd have to start a fire, and if the wind doesn't blow it out, the fire would be visible for a mile or more," he says, almost pleading with me to understand the seriousness of the situation.

"You've never seen this other symbol, with the two lines instead of just the one like the water symbol?" I ask, ignoring his words.

Lee shakes his head and looks nervously at the water that is seeping into the cave, growing higher by the second.

"And is it common for them to use symbols that look very similar?"

"As far as I know, they are all very different."

"How old do you think this cave is?"

"I mean, thousands of years old, maybe more. I'm not totally sure, love. But we can talk about this later. Can we please get out of the cave before the water comes all the way in?"

I ignore his question. I'm on the verge of figuring this out and can't tear my focus away from the symbols. A few more minutes pass, and the water is beginning to fill the floor of the cave.

"I think I've got it. Do you trust me?" I ask.

"'Course I trust you, but what do you mean, you got it?" he asks nervously.

"You were right about water being the symbol for vision, but over time, words and symbols of a language can be combined, and they begin to mean the same thing as the language becomes simplified. What if when these were written, the symbol for water and the symbol for prophecy were actually two different symbols? That would mean that one means prophecy or vision, the other means sun or light, and the last means water. If that's true, I bet the water is the way to the weapon," I say rapidly, excited about figuring it out.

Lee pauses for a long moment and, after giving my words some thought, he nods in agreement. "That—well—you're amazing. I think you're right. I feel like you're right. So that has to be it. Why else would they use a cave that's submerged in high tide? The issue now is what happens when it fills with water?"

I grab his torch and wave it as high as I can reach, trying to illuminate the ceiling of the cave. "There, do you see that? It looks like there's an opening. When the water completely fills the cave, we'd be able to swim up to it."

Lee grabs the torch and extends his arm as far as possible, trying to see the opening himself. His height helps him light up more of the ceiling, clearly revealing an opening. "You are brilliant, love. You're right. I can see it. But if we're going to do this, we need to get ready just in case it doesn't work. Let's hurry and put our stuff above where the tide will be. We won't be able to take our swords; they'll weigh us down."

I nod in excitement, and we quickly leave the cave and head for the beach. By the time we return, the tide has submerged most of it. The water is freezing, and I don't know how long we will be able to withstand the cold. To try and stay warm, we huddle against one another. Lee does his best to keep the torch free from the water, which is now approaching my head.

"It shouldn't be much longer now, love," says Lee before passionately kissing me.

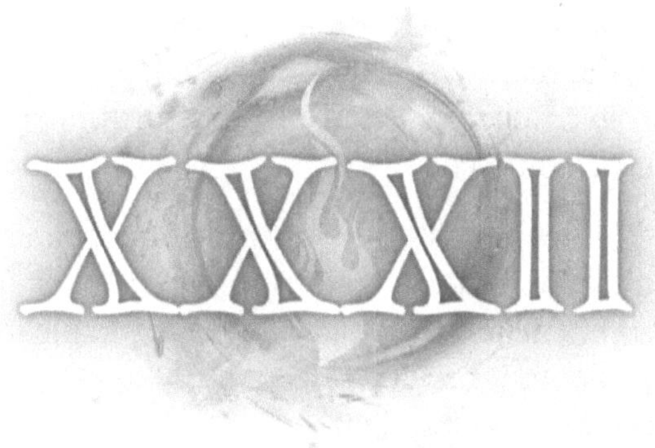

I struggle to float over the floor markings as I wade in the water that's now over my head. The waves push against me, knocking me against the wall of the cave. I don't say it, but I'm beginning to wonder if my idea will be the death of us. We're both tired and keeping ourselves afloat against the waves is becoming difficult. To make matters worse, neither Lee nor I are strong swimmers, something we hadn't even discussed before taking on this endeavor.

"You doing okay, love?" Lee asks, sounding out of breath.

I nod but don't speak, trying to save my breath and energy.

"It won't be much longer now," he says, trying to sound encouraging. But his tone tells a different tale.

As the water grows higher, we find ourselves pressed against the wall, unable to swim back down to where the markings are. I begin to panic and try to kick my feet as hard as I can to get back.

"Stop, love! You are going to wear yourself out. I think we have to stay against the wall and wait for the cave to completely fill, then we can swim for the hole."

I nod and try to rest against the wall, which becomes easy when we allow the force of the waves to keep us in place without struggling to stay afloat. However, this respite is short-lived because a few moments later, we're fighting to keep our mouths above the water. The cave ceiling slants downward from where the markings are, and we're pushed against the wall where the roof of the cave is at its lowest, making it nearly impossible to get a breath. The power of the waves prevents us from reaching the markings. The torchlight has also been extinguished by the high water, meaning the only light in the cave is the little bit coming from the entrance.

I take one last deep breath before going underwater, hoping that the waves will settle and allow us to swim to the opening. Yet, to my panic, they don't let up beneath the surface, and I'm unable to swim to a place where I can get another breath. The longer I toss about underwater, the more I feel as if I'm about to die.

Suddenly, I feel Lee's hand jerking me to the bottom of the cave. At first, I think he's drowning and pulling me down with him, but his grip isn't one of panic. He pulls me low to the ground where the waves don't seem to be as strong. Staying as close to the cave floor as we can, we swim back towards the markings before pressing our feet against the ground, using it to spring straight upward. We exit the water in the narrow path we had seen in the ceiling of the cave, and we use the crevices in the walls to steady ourselves so that we can catch our breath.

"This is it, love. We can climb up from here. You're a genius, but for a minute, I didn't think we were going to make it."

"Me neither. But it doesn't look like we're out of it yet. Now we must climb," I respond, still trying to catch my breath.

"True, but at least we can breathe."

I take the lead, beginning the process of climbing up the narrow cavern. I make my way steadily onward, stopping occasionally to make sure Lee is doing okay. He's moving at a slower pace, but I admire that he continues on without complaining.

The passageway is cold and damp, and I worry we will be climbing forever. And while it's hard to see, part of me is glad that it's dark so I won't see how high up we must be. Eventually, we reach a ledge with a smooth stone walkway that feels manmade.

"Do you think you can get the torch lit?" I ask Lee as I help him up over the ledge.

He lays down, trying to catch his breath. "We just survived drowning and climbed higher than anyone has ever climbed in the history of the world, and you're already onto the next task?" he asks. I stare blankly, until he complies.

"I have my flint rock in my boot, but I don't know if the torch will catch since it was submerged. Hopefully, all the climbing gave it some time to dry out," he says, removing the small flint rock from his boot.

"You climbed all that way with that in your boot, didn't that hurt?"

"It hurt like you wouldn't believe, but I didn't want to lose it. And I have yet to lose anything I put in my boot."

"Fair enough. Why don't you get some rest while I try and light it?" I ask, kissing his forehead while he puts his boot back on.

I bite off a piece of the wet cloth from the top layer of the torch and replace it with a piece from my own arm sleeve, which has already begun to dry. After just a few times of hitting the flint rock with the edge of Lee's dagger, an ember forms on the cloth. I gently blow until the ember grows into a flame. Soon, the tunnel around us is illuminated. It resembles the dungeon of a keep more than a cavern, and we're sitting on a stone floor that appears to be crafted by highly skilled masons.

"Wow, I wouldn't have guessed this is what it looked like," says Lee, awestruck.

"It reminds me of books I read as a child," I say, trying not to show that I'm on the verge of being overcome by emotion.

Despite my efforts, Lee knows something is wrong and he comes over and holds me. We stand quietly, holding one another and taking in the moment. As I stand wrapped in Lee's arms, I wonder when the last time anyone has been here. Then I wonder whether Kristoff had made it. He was very good with puzzles and far better than anyone I knew when it came to climbing and feats of endurance, but I doubt he would have been brave enough to try such a thing, which causes my grief to grow.

"Let's keep pressing on, shall we? If Kristoff is here, he may have already found the weapon or he may need our help. Although, if he made it this far, I don't think he needs us for much of anything anymore," says Lee.

I slowly walk through the corridor, occasionally stopping to observe some of the strange markings I find along the stone walls. Unfortunately, I can't make out their meaning. I wonder if the symbols have been made by an ancient civilization or if they are perhaps secret Soulmi symbols. The tunnel eventually leads to a grand stone staircase with a ray of light shining toward the top of the stairs. I quickly climb, eager to find daylight. The stairway gives way to a large opening that leads me outside.

I find myself in a majestic gorge, surrounded by the dark, jagged mountains I had seen from the beachhead. There is thick, luscious grass, pine trees, and a stream being fed from a waterfall. I stare in wonderment. I never would have guessed such a place could exist in the middle of a mountain.

The stone path I'm on extends further, and without saying anything, I continue along the way, looking at my surroundings in awe. After walking around the base of the gorge, I come to a stone bridge. It leads over the stream before winding into a thicket of trees.

"Do you think this was made by the gods?" Lee asks.

"I don't know if it was the gods, or the God, or just people, but this isn't like anything I've ever seen or read about. It's amazing," I reply.

As we move deeper into the trees, I feel the air growing warmer, as if I'm basking in the hot summer sun. "Kristoff!" I yell, hoping he will hear me, but I receive no response to my call.

Not long after we enter the thicket of trees, we exit and find a small stone staircase, which leads to what looks like a temple. We slowly climb the stairs, and I'm afraid of what we may find at the top, but I must admit I'm excited. As we reach the top of the stairs, I hold my breath, releasing it when we see a magnificent stone-carved base with a matching stone structure about eight feet above it, suspended in the air.

"What in the world—" Lee says, confused by how the stone is staying suspended in midair.

I look around for some sort of explanation but can't find any. "Look! There is that symbol from the cave! The one that looks like an S," I say.

Lee moves closer to the stone and touches it, looking for additional markings. I follow behind him, reaching my hand out to feel for myself. As my hand touches the stone base, the space between the two structures fills with a radiant light, causing us to shield our eyes and step hurriedly away.

"What did you do, love?" Lee asks, concerned.

"I'm not sure. I don't think I did anything," I reply.

"Look! Do you see that? Something is in the light. It's a weapon, I think! It's the weapon!" cheers Lee.

I stop shielding my eyes and see a magnificent spear suspended between the two stones. I stare at the spear for a while, half expecting myself to wake up from what is surely a dream. It's all so surreal.

"Do you think we should try and grab it?" asks Lee.

"We should, even if Kristoff isn't here. This is how it's supposed to happen," I say, eager to get the spear and find him. I hadn't given much thought to what the weapon would be, but now that I see it, I want to take it and get back to Little Watch.

"Which one of us should grab it? I'll try if you want me to, but the thing didn't react to me," says Lee.

"It needs to be me. I know it. This is why my mother wrote the letter," I answer. I take a deep breath and walk slowly towards the spear.

As I get closer, the better I can see the magnificent weapon, radiating within the brilliant light, floating in midair between the two stone structures. I give Lee a glance and see him smiling at me, watching intently. I smile back. I'm so proud of how far we have come. All our hard work and suffering have paid off, and now we will have the weapon necessary to destroy the Revenant and avenge my father.

I slowly stick my hand out towards the light, and right as my fingers make contact, I hear a booming sound, like thunder. I'm knocked off my feet and thrown backward, landing hard on the stone floor, hitting my head in the process. My vision goes black, and I'm unable to move.

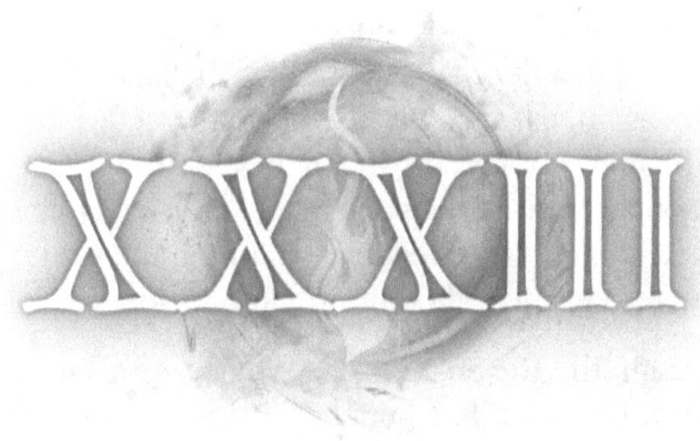

I finally manage to open my eyes, but my vision is blurry. I roll over to my stomach and use my hands to push myself up. I wonder why Lee isn't helping me up, thinking he must have been knocked back by the blast too and I worry whether he is okay. As I get to my feet, my anxiety is overtaken by pure terror when I see Lee at the base of the stairs fighting the Revenant. He's yelling something, but I can't quite make it out. All I can hear is a muffled ringing. I shake my head, trying to regain my hearing which must have been affected from the blow that I suffered when I fell. Suddenly, the cloud in my head clears and all of the sounds around me hit at once, overwhelming my senses.

"Run! Run! Go! Now! Please wake up and run!" yells Lee, who is clearly sobbing.

His voice tells me that he knows he is no match for the Revenant, especially without his sword. I watch as the monster grabs Lee by his wrists and holds him still while it looks up at me. The Revenant isn't concerned with him. It is after me and no one else.

I try to rush down to help Lee, but my body won't move. As much as I want to blame the blow I had suffered from touching the light, I know that has nothing to do with it. I can't move because I'm petrified. Each time I've encountered the Revenant, I lose, and there never seems a way to beat it, which leaves me feeling helpless. I hate the Revenant beyond belief. I want to move. I must move. If I don't, Lee will be killed, and it will be my fault. Over and over, I tell myself I must move, and yet my body does not respond.

Lee continues to put up a fight despite having his hands secured. He kicks and knees the monster, but not once does it react to the blows. Eventually, Lee, in a fit of anger, smashes the face of the Revenant with his head, but again, the creature seems unaffected. I look on in horror, struggling to catch my breath. In my desperation, I plead to the One True God, or the gods, or anyone who will listen. I beg my father and mother for help, and plead that they send me the strength to take back control of my body and fight, but nobody responds.

Soon enough, the Revenant tires of toying with Lee and throws him to the ground, landing a few punches to his face, which causes him to stop moving altogether. The monster then straddles him and, with one hand, begins to strangle the life out of him.

Lee is going to die if I don't act. Tears begin to flow from my eyes and burn down my cheeks. I let out a furious yell and the Revenant looks up at me. I try to move, but now it feels as though my hands are chained to something. I struggle and pull with all my strength, but I can't move.

I thought my fear had frozen me to the spot, but now I see it is something else entirely. I look down to see two strands of light linked to my wrists, pulling me towards the altar. The strands of light burn my wrists, but the pain isn't enough to stop me from resisting. The rage inside me continues to grow, and as it does, I start to yell and fight more aggressively against the light that is holding me back. Finally, the strength in my legs slowly comes back to me, and eventually, I can walk to the edge of the stairs. But the further I move, the harder it is, and the more pain I feel.

With its free hand, the Revenant begins to hit Lee in the face while it looks up at me. The monster doesn't seem to care that he's unconscious and would feel nothing. It continues to hit him, tormenting me with each blow. It's already taken everything from me, and now it's about to kill Lee, the love of my life, the one person I've felt safe with since my father died. In this moment, I decide I won't let the Revenant kill Lee, no matter the cost to me.

"I am going to kill you! I don't need a special weapon to do it! Come here and face me, you coward!" I yell furiously.

My skin begins to burn, and I feel like my heart is going to beat out of my chest. I've never been so full of rage in my life, and I know if I can get my hands on the Revenant, I will rip it limb from limb. I focus all of my energy on breaking my right arm free from its bond, but as I do, the pain in my body grows more intense. Defiantly, I continue to raise my arm in the air, using all of my strength to swing it forward, yelling in rage while I do so.

Suddenly, I feel the bonds break free as if they are shattering glass. I clench my fist tightly, preparing to finally end the Revenant that has followed me to the Southlands. As I do, I hear the sound of thunder and see an intense flash of light. The flash is so intense that it engulfs the Revenant and Lee, sending the Revenant flying backward. When I look to where the spear had been, to my surprise, it's no longer suspended within the light, but has materialized in my hand. The force from the spear sends an intense rush through my body, empowering me with an energy I've never felt before.

I quickly make my way down the stairs to check on Lee and notice that his face is unblemished despite the Revenant's attacks. He's breathing and his eyes flutter open when I touch him. "What happened?" he asks, staring up at me, confused. Even if I wanted to tell him, I couldn't because I don't know, nor do I care. What matters is that he's alive, and I have the spear. Now that I know Lee is okay, all I care about is ending the Revenant once and for all.

The beast stands to its feet and stares me down, Stur's axe held tightly in its right hand. Without warning, it charges towards me faster than I have ever seen it move. To close the distance between us, I run to meet it. I can't believe how fast I'm moving, and I struggle to maintain my balance, like a child just learning to walk.

The Revenant swings the axe viciously at me, but now I can easily follow its movements. And not only that, but I can keep up with its pace as well, and I realize it seems to move much slower than me. I effortlessly block its attacks with my spear, which despite its length, is lightweight and easy to maneuver. And it is strong, able to withstand blow after blow from Stur's Axe.

The Revenant's eyes begin to glow purple, as had happened when Mum had trapped it. It's summoning all of its strength to kill me. I smirk at the thought. It knows I'm a threat. Wasting no more time, I impale the spear through the monster's stomach and lift it in the air, shocked by my own strength.

The monster lets out a terrifying scream, shaking violently. It tries desperately to get away from the spear. I smell something strange; something akin to what I imagine is the smell of rotting flesh as it burns. I walk, still holding the monster in the air, until we come to a large tree. With a mighty thrust, I bury the tip of my spear deep into the trunk of the tree, trapping the beast. The Revenant drops the axe and tries to use its hands to break free, but when it touches the spear, its hands begin to burn as well, and it quickly pulls them away. After several more tries, the monster ceases resisting and trying to escape, finally conceding defeat.

"Who are you?" I ask.

The monster doesn't speak. Instead, it stares at me.

"I said, who are you? Speak, and I will make this fast."

The monster doesn't answer, increasing my frustration.

"I know how this works. You can hear what I'm saying and see what's happening. Just know when I'm done with your beast, your puppet, I'm coming for you. I know exactly who you are and what you have done," I say, attempting to sound unfazed by the silence.

I violently rip the Revenant's mask from its face, revealing a more disgusting and terrifying sight than I could've imagined. It's as if someone had peeled all the skin off a human face. It's missing a nose and has two ghastly black eyes. There are no lips, and its collection of teeth looks more like jagged arrow tips.

"I am going to ask you one more time, who are you?"

The Revenant puts its hand against its throat in what I assume is an attempt to speak. I raise an eyebrow at it and wait. Eventually, an extremely hoarse voice, barely audible, escapes the fiend's lips. "Kill me, please," the Revenant croaks.

"I asked you a question, who are you?"

But the Revenant only continues to beg for death. For the first time since it crossed my path, I feel sorry for the beast, imagining how much of a hell it must be to be trapped in eternal servitude, unable to pass on peacefully. In all the time I've spent thinking about what I would do during this exact moment, I never thought I'd feel remorse for the creature. I shake the feeling from my head. I always figured I would have no issue refusing mercy and separating its head from its body, burying it so that it must live out eternity completely immobile and in darkness.

I remember all that it has done to me and Kristoff. I consider how at this point it may have even killed him. I think about my father's death and how sick and weak he became because of the Revenant's poison. I wonder what kind of pain and torment it has caused countless others in its pursuit of me. I think back to nearly losing Lee because of it. And then my mind is no longer conflicted.

"I know you willingly gave your life to become a revenant, so you won't find any mercy from me. I'm going to cut off each of your limbs and bury them far apart. Your head, of course, will be tethered to a weight and dropped to the bottom of the ocean."

I grab Stur's axe from the ground. True to my promise, I use the axe to slice the Revenant's arm off at the shoulder, dropping it lifelessly to the ground. Lee is on his feet and has joined me. He grabs the arm and throws it far away from the Revenant's body in what I assume is an attempt to prevent it from reattaching. After giving him a nod, I turn back to the Revenant and chop off its other arm, then I begin to hack at its waist until its legs fall from its body.

All that remains when I'm done is a torso and a head. "I suppose it's fitting I'm the one to finish what my father started—with this very same axe," I say before I separate its head with a perfectly accurate strike to its neck. The head hits the ground with a dull thump, and I eye it as it rolls a few inches away.

I have Lee remove his shirt, and I wrap the head inside of it. Lee looks at me blankly, confused by my actions.

"Imagine being unable to die and having to spend eternity staring at the bottom of the ocean floor, while your body has been dismembered, and the pieces buried."

"Remind me never to piss you off, love."

"It was Kristoff's idea," I say coldly.

The two of us do our best to dig shallow graves, burying the various limbs and torso, before sitting down at the stairs of the altar.

"How you feeling, love?" Lee asks, as he puts his arm around me and holds me tightly.

"I know I should feel good," I sigh. "I honestly never thought I would be able to kill it and avenge my family, but I don't know—I just feel kind of empty and worried about Kristoff—and the future," I say.

"Yeah, it doesn't feel like what you think it would, does it? I think it's because no matter what you do, it won't bring them back. Just know they would be proud of you, and you brought them honor by avenging them."

"Do you think I was wrong not to show it mercy?" I ask.

"I don't. It's a monster and has done horrible things. I'd like to think I would have done it the same way if it was me, but it takes a lot of conviction to carry out such a punishment."

"Well, conviction is never something I've lacked, at least according to my parents. You would have loved them."

"Do you think they would have liked me?"

"They would've loved you because I do, and they would see just how much I mean to you."

We share a deep kiss and enjoy each other's company as we sit on the stairs silently. I'm glad I have Lee to share this moment with and help me process my thoughts. Talking with him helps me understand my feelings, which, given the circumstances, are as foreign to me as the events I just witnessed.

"So, what do you plan to do now?" he asks, sensing my mind is beginning to focus on what will come next.

"The first step will be to find Kristoff. Hopefully, he's still in the Southlands. Maybe he is back at Little Watch waiting for us. But I also need to learn more about this spear and the power it possesses. Maybe I can find books about it, or maybe Mum knows something."

"I think we should talk to the Soulmi. They seem to know the most about ancient magic, and their symbols were in the cave."

"Yeah, true. Then, and I hate the thought of leaving the Southlands, but I will have to head North and deal with the person responsible for all this. It's going to be hard to get close to Prince Nathaniel, but when I do, I'm going to kill him, even if I'm alone."

"Not alone, you will have me, love," he says as he squeezes me tight.

"You would come with me?"

"Of course, I would. You and me taking on Carthage and airships and dark magic? I wouldn't miss it for the world."

"Do you think we can do it, just the two of us?" I ask.

"Well, us and give or take fifty thousand Romani compelled to avenge what happened."

"I could never ask them to do that."

"You won't have to. Kristoff is family, and you know that means—"

I interrupt him with a passionate kiss. There has been enough talk about fighting and the future for one day. I want to enjoy the peacefulness of the moment and focus on his lips. Maybe even celebrate the accomplishment of eliminating the Revenant as a threat. I know the future will be full of strife, but for now, I need to take my mind away from all of it. I hope that somewhere my father and mother are looking down on me, proud of the woman I've become.

My peaceful thoughts are interrupted by a voice. I look around for a moment before I realize it's coming from the Revenant's severed head.

The voice sounds clearer now, and much more normal than when it had spoken earlier.

"Good luck," it says coldly.

The End